YESTERDAY THE RAIN

Irene E. Bratek

VANTAGE PRESS
New York

My heartfelt thanks to
Ms. Amy J. Scanlan
Boom Boom Graphics & Productions
Dearborn, Michigan 46124
For her creative talent and efforts in designing the beautiful cover of this novel.

FIRST EDITION

All rights reserved, including the right of
reproduction in whole or in part in any form.

Copyright © 1998 by Irene E. Bratek

Published by Vantage Press, Inc.
516 West 34th Street, New York, New York 10001

Manufactured in the United States of America
ISBN: 0-533-12625-8

Library of Congress Catalog Card No.: 97-91330

0 9 8 7 6 5 4 3 2 1

Dedication

This novel is dedicated to those special people in my life who have made the most impact, given the most support, and loved me no matter the circumstance.

Especially to my loving son, Tony, my beautiful daughter-in-law, Aloma, and my three enchanting and sweet grandchildren, Ryan, Jenni, and Emily. They have been the focal point in my life since the first day each of their respective lives entered mine.

Certainly, to my loving sister, Maria, who has been my best friend, confidante, and God's special blessing since the day I was born.

To my loving parents, Frances and Michele, who loved me unconditionally. They exemplified the meaning of trust, respect, dignity, love of God, and especially love of family, which taught me the humility to handle success and the strength to cope with adversity. They inspired me to believe in myself and to enjoy and share my God-given talents.

To Matt for his friendship, love, and support over the years and for making the publishing of this novel a reality.

To those wonderful gentlemen in my life who befriended me during times of doubt and confusion, who offered me kindness and tenderness and taught me the meaning of love without expectation.

And last, but not least, to David for the absolute joy of knowing you!

Thanks for your love, the memories, and the inspiration to write this novel!

Acknowledgments of thanks
to
Donna Cecil, JoAnne Ellerbrake, Sarah Gardella, Sally Janz,
Kathy Masterson, Julie Stoddard, and Dave Richardson for their love,
support, encouragement and personal contribution of time during
the creation of this book.

And to

Michaela Hector
for her love, exuberance, and much-appreciated support and assistance
during the final days of preparation prior to submitting the manuscript for
publication.

One

Exhausted, Rachel rolled over on her back and lay quietly, looking at the familiar ceiling.

With her eyes closed, she breathed deeply and recounted the past couple of hours of lovemaking with Corey Davidson, the man whom she loved dearly but was not in love with. And little did she suspect that this would be the last time she'd make love to anyone for a very long time.

As she left the bed, Corey stirred, and his long, strong arms reached for her.

"Where are you, you ravishing beauty? Where are you, little kitten?" he uttered softly. He sat up quickly when he realized that she was gone.

The water in the shower was usually invigorating and therapeutic, but realistically, Rachel knew it could never wash away all the disappointments and frustrations of unfulfilled nights and the endless search for her one and only love. The one love who would set her free from this consuming torment. Again, the pounding of the spray on the shower door somehow lulled her into a world of fantasy where her dreams, secrets, and wishes lived so vividly. Once a haven, that too was becoming out of her reach, out of her realm, and out of her world. One turn of the cold water tap, and the sudden return to reality was enough to prepare her for the conversation with Corey that she knew was inevitable.

Unhappy endings and Rachel Radcliffe had become synonymous over time. The constant mixing and mesmerizing thoughts of the past, present, and future circled in her mind. At this moment, how could she, calmly, with a deep sense of sincerity and compassion, tell Corey that it was over? Tell him that this on-again, off-again friendship-romance relationship was just too much for her to endure every day?

"You'll see," echoed a voice from the past, "someday, my sweet Rachel, you'll be faced with the same kinds of decisions I've had to make, and it won't be easy. Believe me," said her mother, "you can't intertwine your life with someone's and expect to extricate yourself when you've grown tired and weary of the connection without hurting and maybe alienating that someone very deeply."

Why do children have to come to learn that their parents' counsel is most times so accurate? In this case, it was right on. Of course, Mama was rarely wrong in anything. Rachel's every living moment was filled with some snippet or other tidbits and pieces of advice that her very loving and caring mother had instilled in her.

Rachel stepped out of the shower and wrapped herself in a lavish terry-cloth towel. She peered into the mirror and gazed at the reflection that had been changing so dramatically in the last year or two. Though her skin was flawless and her features almost chiseled, upon closer scrutiny, she could see the little crow's-feet appearing under and at the sides of her eyes. The three-way mirror into which she peered perhaps overdefined these inevitable harbingers of old age. She couldn't stop that process, and she'd heard that the more one worried about it, the greater the problem. She patted herself under the chin and turned sideways to observe her profile. "This is not the time to critique wrinkles. Corey is waiting, and you've got to get this situation settled—once and for all!" And with the resolve that was so characteristically Rachel's, she took a deep breath and opened the bathroom door.

Corey was still lounging on her king-sized bed when she entered the bedroom all wrapped up in one of her oversized, luxurious towels. When he looked at her, his eyes spoke volumes. With his arms outstretched, he beckoned her back to bed.

"Your sweet essence precedes you, my beauty, and I'm ready and anticipating an encore of this morning's breakfast treat."

With the slightest bit of hesitation, she bent her head and walked toward him.

"Corey, you know I'll be late for my appointment if we proceed with this idea of yours." His expression changed, and with almost a smirk on his face, he responded.

"Well, now," with the tone of his voice deepening a couple of decibels, "for some strange reason, I had hoped it would be 'our' idea. But something tells me, from the tone of your voice, that there's more afoot here than just a declination of my offer."

Rachel continued to dry herself off and, with as much control as she could muster, sat down on the edge of the bed directly opposite of where he was now sitting and picked up Corey's hand and sandwiched it between hers.

"Corey, you've known me now for what seems like ages, and you know how unsettling it is for me to deal with the relationships I've had in my life. You and I have been 'an item' for over fifteen years now, and I've tried to match your fervor for its commitment and continuance. It's just not working for me."

His reaction was one of shock, and he interjected.

"Let's stop this right now," and he leaped off the bed and began to scurry about, looking for the items of clothing he had so anxiously removed the night before. "I love you, Rachel—no, I adore you, kitten. And you can't tell me that what we've shared over the years in friendship and then romance in more bedrooms than I'd care to recount didn't have some impact on you, as well! I realize that acting has always been an aspiration of yours, but I wouldn't like to believe that this is what's it been all these years. Hell, that's not even acting—that's downright deception." She could feel the tears welling up in her eyes, as much as she longed to display the strength and courage it would take to do this, her voice broke.

"You don't understand, Corey, I love you, too, but that's not what this is all about. I feel like I'm two people; one here with you and the other standing outside myself, looking at us and not recognizing who I am. I know that must sound crazy, but it's very real to me." Her heart was pounding.

He came to her and embraced her gently, stroking her hair and uttering comforting sounds.

"Kitten, kitten," a name he had long ago coined for her, "don't you think I can sense your uneasiness? Two people can't intertwine their minds and their bodies the way we have and not be aware and sensitive to the other's needs and misgivings. Let's talk about this. Tell me what I've done to bring this about. My God, kitten, there are other options here other than breaking up." He continued, "If you wish, we can back away from the amount of time we've been spending together. Maybe you could go to New York and see Amber and Tony for a spell. It's been a while since you've seen them, and I know Amber would be ecstatic to see you."

There was a long pause before Rachel responded.

"Corey, I've been thinking about this for a very long time. It's not you—it's us! No, it's me. And while visiting Amber sounds like a magnificent idea, and I'd do it in a heartbeat, but I just don't want you to think that it will change what's happening here right now. It's taken a great deal out of me to even broach this subject, and I won't be dissuaded from what I see ultimately happening between us."

"Hmmmm," he sighed. "that's much too final for me to accept, kitten." Rachel responded quickly.

"Please don't call me 'kitten,' Corey, you know how I dislike the condescending tone of diminutive and cutesy names."

"All right, Ray-chel!! I *still* won't believe that you and I can just go our merry ways and pretend that this relationship was nothing more than a passing fancy!"

"No one . . . " she hesitated as she moved toward him, "I didn't say, nor did I mean to imply that it was totally over between us, Corey. I just can't stay in this relationship that lacks direction, and for whatever reason, my focus *is* on my life's direction. If you care for me as much as you've indicated, then I need your support and guidance—that will never change, Corey! I'm not going to pitch fifteen years or so out the window just like that!! Try to understand . . . be a little patient with me." By now, it sounded as though she were pleading. "I had hoped you'd be more consoling and understanding, but given the manner in which I've approached this entire situation, I can certainly understand why you'd be upset with me."

Rachel always had the ability to disarm him with her innate inclination to blame herself for whatever was going wrong in any particular situation. Corey sighed, and with his hand on his chin, looking so forlorn and rejected, he spoke more softly.

"I will be supportive. I will be conciliatory, and I will be understanding as long as you realize that I'm just not willing to give you up because you're going through a time of uncertainty in your life for which I may not be the total cause. Let's get on with this day and agree to have dinner tonight to continue this discussion."

"Okay. Dinner it is! But Corey, please don't try to change my mind. Don't make this any more difficult than it apparently already is." He nodded in half agreement, and somehow Rachel knew this would be no different than relationships in the past. With a little smile, she said, "Edoardo's at 8:00?" Corey smiled too, and shook his head positively.

The rest of Rachel's morning was as inconclusive and upsetting as the beginning. Two clients canceled appointments and in the personal wardrobe building business, this wasn't something she could recover from easily. The humid temperatures of August didn't help. She briefly contemplated the visit with Amber and then went about developing Mrs. Longley's wardrobe, whose due date was fast approaching. The Longleys were part of the wealthier local gentry, and clients like these were not easily attained. Colored fabric swatches were strewn everywhere. Rachel's office looked like the remnants of a hurricane. "Pull yourself together, Rachel, ole girl. Adele Longley has been a wonderful client over the years, so you must come up with something magnificent for the Ambassador's Cruise shortly after Labor Day."

She sat down at her computer and keyed in "Longley." As she waited for her screen to come forward, she thought about a great color combination for Mrs. Longley that would camouflage a few unwanted pounds and yet give her some flair in the bargain. Hugo Longley, while not a very observant husband, was a most giving one, and he would be elated by this wardrobe simply because it would make Adele happy. Most of the elite gentry were not into such emotional admissions, but Hugo was an exception.

Teals, bright greens with white and yellow accents would do the job nicely. Accessories that were interchangeable, white, yellow, green, or metallic with costume jewelry that was a bit splashy could mold this wardrobe package into a real winner. Her concentration was broken by the telephone.

"Hi, Corey, gee, I haven't talked to you in, ahhhhh, it must be three hours," she said, laughingly.

"Well, at least you're smiling, kitten." He hesitated and thought, what the heck, he'd always called her kitten, and he couldn't possibly get himself any deeper in trouble than he already had in the past few hours.

"You're a sketch, Corey Davidson . . . a cartoon would be a better description. I suppose you're calling to confirm that we're still on for dinner tonight?"

"Well, as a matter of fact, I didn't call for that reason. I'm afraid I can't make it tonight, so we'll have to postpone destiny until tomorrow night if that's all right." There was a quizzical kind of ring in Corey's voice whenever he was trying to intimidate Rachel, and this sound had a familiar ring.

"No problem, Corey, I'm behind on this wardrobe for Adele Longley anyway. I think I might just call Amber tonight to see if her schedule will permit a brief visit."

Corey responded, somewhat disappointed.

"I would have hoped that your first question would be 'what's her name?' or 'gee, I'm sorry we can't continue this morning's melodrama.' But I know that either of those responses would have been great coming from me—they're not coming from you. In the best of all possible worlds, I would have even hoped for some obvious jealousy. But, alas, complacency will have to do, and a rain check is offered for tomorrow night, if you'll accept."

"I'd love to . . . and Corey, have a good time whatever you're doing tonight," she replied and smiled.

"Love ya, kitten." and he hung up.

There was a knock on the door, and Rachel wasn't really in the mood for visitors.

"Who's there?" she called out.

"It's your friendly neighbor with pizza and a bottle of chilled white wine."

Blaise! She unlocked the three locks on the door of her exquisite apartment to find Blaise with a pizza box in his left hand, a bottle of wine in the other, and several newspapers under each arm.

"Hey, Ray, what's trippin'?"

Blaise's phrases made her laugh as well as most everything else that he said and did.

"Only me," she responded kiddingly, "only me."

"Listen, lady, you've got to get out more and have some fun! You've had one too many relationships and not enough relating. How many times have I told you that I'd be honored to take you out on the town? I know you don't exactly cotton to or understand my lifestyle, but, Ray babe, I can look real straight in my tux and patent leather shoes. A night on the town with moi . . . dinner, dancing, and a good show, and a guarantee for no foolin' around afterwards might be just what you need." His smile was as captivating as his personality.

How dull her world would have been without Blaise in it for the past several years. To look at him, one wouldn't believe that all of that vision of masculinity wore pink, abbreviated briefs. It's the nineties, and everyone who has had to has come out of their proverbial closets. Not Blaise, he came out in the seventies while controversy and acceptance was still at a minimum. Coming from one of the most socially prominent families in Grosse Pointe didn't make his "entrance" into society much cause for celebration. His mother had a breakdown, and his father publicly disowned him. Blaise's only glimmer of family hope was his sister, Renna. She didn't care what anyone said. To her, he was her big brother, and nothing could or would ever change that.

"Pizza is every man's answer to alternative eating. It's better than not eating out and cooking in! Moreover, pizza with everything on it is tantamount to the nectar of the gods."

"Goodness, Blaise, all this over some pizza and wine."

"Well Ray babe, entrances and exits are the exciting parts of most of our dull and mundane lives. When you've aspired to be a part of the wonderful world of theater arts, entrances and exits are the ticket. Get what I mean?"

"As usual, Blaise, you've turned something ordinary into something special. Thanks for being my neighbor and, most of all, for being my friend."

Blaise put down his excessively topped piece of pizza and came over to Rachel. He put his arms around her and hugged her for what seemed like an eternal minute.

"If there were any reason for me to ever believe that I'd be happy on the straight side of this life, it would be to make you happy." Rachel hugged him back and insisted that all of this slobbering wasn't going to get the pizza eaten, the wine drunk, or her work done.

Two

Monday's are rough for most working people and this Monday wasn't any different for Rachel. Even though most of her work was done from her home, it exacted the same discipline as though she were performing the same work in another building in the high class, downtown Village of Grosse Pointe on the Hill. A cup of freshly brewed coffee provided the wonderful taste and aroma that aroused her senses and prepared her for the busy day ahead. Mrs. Longley was her first caller, and Rachel assured her that the wardrobe preparation for the upcoming cruise was just about completed. They would meet for lunch on Wednesday at the club so that Rachel could go over the final ideas with Mrs. Longley and tidy up any unfinished details that Mrs. Longley needed to make her feel comfortable until the project was completed.

The morning flew by, and at 11:00 A.M. Rachel remembered that Amber was generally home for an hour and a half to check on the kids and the refrigerator since dinner at the Domani household was almost a ritual. Tony's Italian background provided the daily agenda that Amber adopted shortly after their marriage, now some twenty years ago. While Rachel secretly longed for the closeness and tenderness that Tony and Amber had always shared, she was never able to see herself in all that domesticity.

JFK International Airport had always held a certain fascination for Rachel. Not only the cosmopolitan travelers and never-ending traversing of people everywhere, but it was the gateway to New York, the Big Apple, Broadway, Wall Street, the garment industry's home base for the United States, the Rockettes, the Statue of Liberty, the Empire State Building, and the magnificent World Trade Center. They were almost visions in a dream for Rachel, who did most of her traveling in books and through travel programs on the cable Discovery channel. So, visiting Amber was not a difficult choice.

The phone rang, and Amber scaled the three steps adjoining the family and living rooms in their suburban, quite lovely tri-level home.

"Domani residence," she bellowed. Rachel chuckled.

"Can you put up a friend in need for a couple of days?"

"Shellie-baby," Amber responded, "where are you, and if what you need is a friend, you know I'm always here for you, doll." Time had a way of melting whenever these two pals since childhood found the time to converse.

"It's been a while, Amber, since I've seen you, Tony and the children, and I am primed for some good late-night chats, a couple of good shows, huggin' those two great kids of yours and imploring your husband to consider taking on another wife."

Amber was always amused by the humor that she'd come to know and love.

"I think Tony's probably ready for a trade-in, and the only things my kids are hugging these days are the telephone and trashy novels."

Rachel paused for a moment and was suddenly caught up in all of the seriousness surrounding her. Her face grew somber and she continued, "Amber, all kidding aside, if I can impose on you for a few days, I'd be in your debt eternally!"

"Then pack your bags, kid, call a cab, if you can find one in that preppy town, and get yourself to the airport. When you arrive at JFK, Shellie, we'll take it from there."

"Gracie, mi'amica!" she replied, with a sigh of relief and her eyes welling with tears. "Thank you, Amber, for not asking me questions, and thank you for being your usual understanding self."

Amber picked up on the emotion in Rachel's voice that wasn't there initially.

"See you soon, doll. Call us with the flight number and your ETA, and we'll be at JFK with bells on. Ciao for now, baby."

Rachel placed the telephone on the cradle and wept quietly. Her emotional level was fraying quickly. She sat down on the recliner that had become more her bed than a chair recently and laid her head back to rest, and just like the key to the flood gates of her mind, images and memories rushed in. Neil Radcliffe was as real as could be. He was standing in front of her, looking at her, pleading without speaking, searching without seeing. He was groping and reaching for her, and as he touched her arm, she awakened. Beads of perspiration ran down the sides of her forehead, and the recollection of their last encounter played like a rerun during TV's off-season.

She spoke aloud, as though he were really there. "I'm sorry for the hurt I've caused you, Neil. I'm sorry that I didn't fit into your world and that you tried so desperately and futilely to fit into mine." These memories were painful and draining. Rachel never handled endings well, and Neil wasn't going to make it any easier.

She could hear Neil's voice clearly. "I can't begin to imagine how other husbands handle a moment like this. I guess the gentlemanly thing to do is to bow out quietly." His hands were clammy, and his voice broke slightly. "I've heard it said that when you really love someone, you should let them go if they so wish; however, it makes me question my love for you, Rachel, since it's killing me to let this happen."

She wanted to put her arms around him and hold him just as she did many times in the past. She wanted to tell him it would be all right and suggest ways and things they could do to make it better. But this time was different. This time, it was really over. "Neil, this isn't about what someone else can or cannot do. It's about you and me and our relationship. We just never were able to achieve that place called 'oneness' that every married couple I've ever talked to longed for. Some achieve it . . . and others, like you and me, weren't that fortunate." She continued softly, "Perhaps if I had been more candid and honest with you in the beginning, I might have spared us both from this terrible grief."

Neil put his head down, and then, as he raised it again, his eyes met hers. "Rachel, I only know I love you, and while I realize it's not the kind of love you need and were looking for, it's all I have to give and the only way I know how to show it." The tears in his eyes and the devastation in his glance would haunt her forever.

A pounding noise in the distance shook her from this daydream, and she was aroused by Blaise's voice.

"Ray babe, are you all right? Open up. It's Blaise!" She rubbed her eyes and brushed back her hair as she went toward the door. "Whew, lady, don't do that to me. I was ready to kick this door down, and you know how much I hate to ruin a new pedicure."

She hadn't noticed it right away, but he was standing there with an open bottle of nail polish in his hand, cotton spears between each of his toes and a chartreuse silk robe wrapped around his very languid form. Rachel began to laugh and apologized profusely.

"Blaise, I'm sorry. I guess I must have drifted off into a sound sleep." Blaise looked at her quizzically.

"Did Corey-poo shed some more pain in your path, Ray babe?" He hesitated, anticipating her answer, "Why don't you accept my invitation for a night on the town?"

Rachel laughed even louder. Here was Blaise with cream on his face, cotton between his toes, and a copy of *Vogue* under his arm, and he was talking about a night on the town.

"Let's do it!"

She and Blaise agreed to meet in one hour—dressed to the nines and ready to party—Grosse Pointe Style.

Even though it was Monday, the cars and limousines streamed past the sentry gate of the Grosse Pointe Yacht Club. Taillights for as far as the eye could see lined the winding road down to the Lake Saint Clair entrance. Of course, Blaise instructed the limo driver to drop them off at the door. Martin, the long-time doorman for the club opened the limo door and extended his hand to Rachel who held on tightly as she exited the back seat in her very sleek, black crepe evening dress. Blaise followed, looking strikingly handsome in his tuxedo with matching tie and cummerbund. As they stood there waiting for other attendees to move ahead in front of them, Martin approached them and complimented them on being such a "stunning" couple. This comment and Blaise's resolve to ensure that Rachel would enjoy this evening prompted him to walk even taller than his six feet four inches.

"Your arm, sir." Rachel smiled and Blaise, in a manner befitting the would-be suitor of such a lovely lady, extended his arm, under which she looped her own, and they walked as if on air down the carpeted aisle and through the magnificently ornate doors of this august club. Music filled the air and familiar faces passed back and forth as they proceeded toward the ballroom. Some acknowledgments were pleasing.

"Good evening, Rachel, my dear," uttered Mrs. Longley, "I'm surprised and . . . uh . . . delighted to see you."

"Thank you, Mrs. Longley. I don't believe you've met my escort, Mr. Blaise Kinley."

Mrs. Longley who was the epitome of social graces and diplomacy at all times, extended her hand to Blaise with a warm smile and a nod of her head. Blaise responded by taking Mrs. Longley's hand and kissing it ever so lightly. He expressed words of praise about Mrs. Longley's dress.

"Thank you, kind sir. I'm certain you must know that Ms. Radcliffe is my wardrobe coordinator, and with such impeccable taste and knowledge of today's fashion world, I couldn't possibly be happier with her lovely choices."

Rachel was always a little uncomfortable with such glowing compliments, but she graciously thanked Mrs. Longley and reiterated that she would meet her in the club's dining room on Wednesday at noon.

As they mingled and exchanged socially acceptable utterances with other attendees, Blaise stopped dead in his tracks upon seeing his mother and father conversing with another couple across the room.

"Perhaps this wasn't such a great idea after all," Rachel chided.

"Don't be ridiculous, Ray babe. While I admit I didn't know they'd returned from Hawaii, I did promise you an evening of dining and dancing, and no one, not even my very elite parents, will prevent that from happening."

The rather large club orchestra, which played nightly, started to play a set of old tunes that Rachel loved and held dear. As the familiar, romantic "Stardust" permeated the rather large ballroom, Rachel recalled Mama and Papa DeRoca dancing together at every family function.

"May I?" asked Blaise, and he gently took Rachel's hand and led her to the dance floor. He was very tall next to Rachel's five feet four inches; she had to stretch her arm to the max so she could put her hand over Blaise's right shoulder. Her head rested on his chest, and as if made for each other, they began to move to the beat of this memorable song. Blaise hadn't deceived Rachel; he was a great dancer. Since she had always secretly aspired to be a professional dancer, her ear for music was keen and her movements were smooth and exact. They chatted and laughed about this somewhat curious date, and with all the flair he could exude without exposing his true character, he twirled Rachel around the floor as though no one else were in the room.

Later that evening, exquisite chateaubriand and well-chosen wine picked by the club's oenophile provided a scrumptious repast, and the cherries jubilee and the crème de cocoa aperitif were all that Rachel could manage for one dinner.

"I'm stuffed," she uttered, "but I feel wonderful. This has been an enjoyable evening, Blaise, and you've been dear. I'll never forget this special evening, my friend."

"Madame flatters me, and besides being so gracious, she's right. I am charming, even in this element." Rachel smiled and thought about how fortunate she was to have people like Blaise and Amber in her life. "I bet Corey would have needed a change of underwear if he saw us here tonight," jested Blaise. "It's too bad we didn't ask him to join us. I bet we could have really tripped the light fantastic, *ha ha ha ha.*"

"Oh, Blaise, you're too much," Rachel responded.

"That's even funnier," said Blaise, "most of my life, women have been accusing me of not being enough.

"Rats." Their limo was waiting. The ride home was as enjoyable as the rest of this marvelous evening. Now, Rachel would have to get about her business and wrap up this week so she could be in New York by the weekend.

As dawn crept between the slats of the miniblinds in her bedroom, Rachel suddenly arose with a start. "Daylight," she exclaimed. "What time is it?" She groped for the clock on her night table and winced when she saw 8:00 A.M. "I'm two hours late." She stumbled out of bed, shedding her "I Love Michigan" nightshirt as she rushed into the bathroom and jumped into the shower. Her shower routine each morning paid off, since in moments like these, each almost mechanical movement would provide the speed she so desperately needed. As she turned off the water, she was already reaching for her toothbrush and toothpaste, when she heard the telephone ringing in the other room. With a towel thrown around her wet hair and a towel semiwrapped around her still-dripping body, she opened the door and grabbed the phone.

"Hello," she gasped.

"Kitten, is that you?" queried Corey.

"Of course, it's me, Corey. Who did you expect to answer the phone, Michelle Pfeiffer?" Corey chuckled.

"It didn't sound like you. Are you all right?" he responded.

Rachel tried to catch her breath and compose herself all at the same time. There was definitely something about Corey's tone of voice and personality lately that was more than just a little unsettling and unnerving to her.

"I just got up late, that's all. I've got a million things to do before I leave for New York this weekend, and of all days, I overslept."

Corey paused for a moment. "My, my, whoever he was, he must have really worn you out." Corey said, in a manner only befitting Corey.

Rachel's reaction was immediate. She lost all sense of composure and threw politeness to the wind.

"You know, Corey, I really don't like the insinuations linked to that statement, nor do I appreciate what it implies; however, coming from you, it's not really too surprising. You are the only man I know who believes 'four on the floor' has nothing to do with a car!"

Realizing that recovery from this jab was in the same range as miracles, Corey sighed, lowered his voice, and in the softest possible way, tried to apologize for the inconsiderate and admittedly uncalled-for statement.

Unfortunately, her fuse was lit and her heartbeat elevated and her breathing became labored. Rachel unsuccessfully tried to control this rage spawned by the man who knew exactly what buttons to push when he wanted to put her down and just be blatantly nasty.

"Not that it's really any of your business, Mr. Davidson," she blurted out, "what I do at this moment, given the present situation of this ridiculous relationship, I did go out last night, and for your additional information, I enjoyed myself immensely. In fact, Blaise and I were the center of attraction at the club last night."

Now, Corey was the one finding it difficult to compose himself.

"You went out with that . . . with that—"

"Careful, Corey," she warned. "You're already on very shaky ground, and I won't tolerate any of your sleazy remarks about Blaise." Corey was fuming.

"Well, Rachel, I guess you must have been pretty desperate if you consider that half-and-half idiot to be your idea of a 'great time.' "

That was the proverbial straw for Rachel.

"I should just hang up on you, Corey Davidson, but before I do, let me tell you that Blaise is possessed of more gentlemanly traits than you'd ever hope to attain if you lived to be two hundred. Furthermore, the only issue that prevails in that pea brain of yours is your libido, which I've been meaning to tell you, is slipping lately. So, please don't—"

A dial tone was the last thing Rachel heard before she could finish that sentence. As she put down the receiver, she was more upset about not being the first one to end that crazy conversation than she was about the messy situation that had evolved since early this week. She did know, though, that any comments that would cast aspersions on Corey's sexual prowess would be met with such behavior. Since her decision to end this relationship earlier this week, nothing seemed to go well for her except maybe Mrs. Longley's check for payment in full for her hard work in her behalf and, of course, her evening with Blaise. She thought that if the measure of the man is his capacity for truth and sensitivity, then Corey Davidson would look a lot like Tom Thumb.

"Calm yourself," Rachel whispered, "he's not worth this upset and all the added energy it takes to perpetuate this anger. I will be done with him once and for all." Those words echoed in her head. She had thought them many times before and said them aloud, as well, but then he'd break down her defenses, apologies would be exchanged, and, after a short time, they'd be right back in that same old rut. "Not this time," she confirmed. "This time, it's over!"

The toothpaste had long since dried up on her toothbrush, and her hair was now partially dry and wild. So with quiet resolve, she went back into the bathroom and into the shower. She prayed that the rest of her day could be resurrected into something productive and meaningful.

Her first stop this morning was Jacobson's, and then onto the "shops on the Hill." Her wardrobe for Mrs. Longley's cruise was a chain belt away from completion. While chain belts weren't really in vogue at this time, one would go very well with the afternoon navy shift that was one of the basics that Mrs. Longley could dress up or dress down during the cruise. Another nice touch were the gold topsiders she'd purchased while visiting friends on Grosse Ile recently. The metallic touches of the belt and shoes would set off this simple, but classy, dress. Pleased with her accessory choices, Rachel thought how true it was that accessories make the wardrobe.

The travel agent's office was crowded, but when the agent recognized Rachel walking in the door, she merely picked up the envelope from her desk and handed it to Rachel with a "have an enjoyable trip" and Rachel was on her way. Somehow, holding the tickets in her hand reminded her, figuratively speaking, of the final application of superglue on a favorite project. It was "sealed," and suddenly, this trip became a reality. This coming Friday, she'd be in the Big Apple!

Packing wasn't going to be a problem for her this time of year, since summer in New York was pretty much like summer in Michigan. A couple of dress-up/dress-down shifts, jeans, a pair of neutral shorts and slacks, a silk jacket, some tops, along with the usual jewelry, nightclothes, shoes, bag, and sundries, and she'd be ready to leave.

Wednesday's lunch with Mrs. Longley went without any surprises. Mrs. Longley was pleased with her wardrobe package, as usual, and was also very ready to settle this account right after their brief soup and sandwich buffet lunch. The $10,000-check as payment in full would work very nicely towards cleaning up some bills, picking up a few last-minute things at the drugstore, and keeping the rest for whatever her needs would be during her visit. When she walked into the bank, it was relatively empty. She went to the manager, whom she knew, and after exchanging some pleasantries, Rachel asked if she could get about $5,000 worth of travelers' checks. This process usually took anywhere from half an hour to an hour to complete, so Rachel poured herself a cup of coffee at the customer service stand and waited as the checks were prepared for her signature.

Rachel checked her things-to-do list, which was ever present in her briefcase-like purse. As she crossed off several items, she smiled. She was always pleased at her ability to accomplish those somewhat ambitious tasks in the time frame allotted.

Since she had already purchased the "I Love Michigan" shirts for all the Domanis, the list was dwindling quickly. The rest of Wednesday and Thursday went relatively smoothly. Rachel had an opportunity to visit with Blaise and let him know her plans vis-à-vis her staying with the Domanis, whom Blaise knew. She asked, though she knew it wasn't necessary, that he look after her mail and check the house periodically.

"No problem, Ray babe. I'm ecstatic that you're going to the City of Dreams. New York is an exciting city, and I know your stay will be eventful." She embraced him and once again, thanked him for his invaluable support during this horrendous week.

When Friday morning arrived, there were still a couple of things left on Rachel's list; one of which was to call Corey. Even though she felt rankled, remembering their Tuesday morning discourse, she felt the need to try to settle some of their differences before her trip. She'd call him later on in the day. So after her usual shower routine and the time it took to pick out her clothes for the upcoming flight, she jumped into her Chevy and was on her way, first to the hair salon for a shampoo, trim, and style and also for a much-needed manicure. Afterwards, she stopped at the bookstore to see if there were a couple of good magazines or a new novel that she could read either during the flight or during the visit.

Traffic on the Hill was heavier than usual, and while she stopped to wait for a few pedestrians to cross, her thoughts turned to Corey and the phone call she intended to make when she got home. On second thought, she mused, his office was not too far away from where she was at this time, and when the traffic cleared, she headed for the street on which his office was located and parked about two blocks away. As she proceeded toward the very uniquely modern building that housed the architectural firm of Davidson & Jacoby, Rachel rehearsed in her mind how this scene would play out. Unfortunately, her gait was too quick and the distance from her car to Corey's door was too short for her to prepare for this encounter.

Tricia, the receptionist, smiled when she saw Rachel through the beveled-glass doors.

"Hi, Ms. Radcliffe. How have you been? I haven't seen you for quite some time."

Rachel approached the desk.

"Just great, thank you, Tricia, and yes, it has been a while," she responded.

Tricia answered her endlessly ringing telephone and advised Rachel that Corey and Bill were with a client and asked whether she could wait for a few minutes, and that she let Corey know that she was waiting. Rachel again thanked her and sat down in one of the more opulent chairs in the reception area. This little bit of time presented some opportunity for Rachel to think about how she and Corey could possibly settle their differences and still be friends. A half hour passed, and now Rachel was becoming nervous about the time constraints of getting everything done by flight time at 6:30 P.M. this evening. She stood up, and while walking toward Tricia, she noticed Corey as he entered the lobby. *He is handsome!* she thought as she watched him interact with his client and business partner. After all, it was his intellect and charm that had drawn Rachel to him at the beginning of their relationship.

"Thanks for your ongoing business, Jack," said Corey. "Bill and I will get back to you when the first set of prints are completed." They shook hands, and Bill and Corey, noticing Rachel, approached her. Bill spontaneously hugged Rachel and placed his hands on both sides of her face to look at her.

"It must be thrilling to wake up each morning knowing you're gonna be more beautiful than the day before."

"As the lucky man who's been there, I can attest to the truthfulness of that statement, Bill," Corey interjected.

There he goes again, thought Rachel. Not that it was a secret that they'd lived together in the past, but it was Corey's snide and uncomplimentary way of shedding a bad light on Rachel's character that really got to her.

"Thank you, Bill," she said and grinned, "for always making me feel like Liz Taylor, and thank you, Corey, for not telling Bill the truth about how I really look in the morning." All three laughed.

When Bill excused himself from the trio, Rachel and Corey walked toward Corey's rather large and opulently furnished office. He closed the door and swung her around and kissed her. She pushed him away in a tone of sheer disgust.

"You know, Corey, you're so sure of yourself. I didn't come here to nuzzle and play kissy face with you, nor did I make this stop to make you think that I had bypassed last Tuesday's telephone episode."

Being spurned by anyone was not something Corey handled well under any circumstance, and this latest falling out with Rachel made him more angry and desperate.

"Darn it, Rachel," he exclaimed, "once you make up your mind to something, there's no changing it." His tone was nasty, which his facial expression matched. "If you wish to settle this situation once and for all, let's get to it. But since I consider myself to be the victim, I'd like to state my case in this entire mess first!" Rachel was now out of time and out of patience.

"Sure, Corey, I wouldn't have expected you to do anything out of character at this time, even in the face of the possible end of our relationship."

Now, armed with a full head of steam to match his defensive attitude, he yelled.

"I'm sick of your criticism and tired of this whole melodramatic exchange. You know, Rachel, you haven't exactly been the perfect partner in this relationship; in fact, my having to cajole, beg, and plead to get anywhere near you of late hasn't been my idea of an enjoyable time. There was a time when everything I did was right and wonderful. Then, one day this week, you made the unilateral decision to end it, and I'm supposed to pick up my marbles and go home." The intensity of the conversation was electric. The energy that cross-fired between the two of them could have provided enough power to keep that building lit for a month.

"It's futile to continue this diatribe, Corey, and since I'm leaving for New York tonight and you appear to be so totally disenchanted with my performance, and I yours, why don't we just call it a day?" Controlling her emotions and holding back any possibility of tears, Rachel turned from him, opened the door, and left his office. By the time she reached the lobby, she was running and didn't even think to say good-bye to Tricia, who was left midsentence. "Good-bye, Ms. Radcliffe, it was nice to see—" and Rachel was out the door and down the street.

As he looked at the place where she just stood moments ago, Corey didn't feel too victorious. In fact, he was alarmed and concerned that he may have planted seeds of destruction regarding any resurrection of the relationship he once shared with his precious kitten. But being Corey Davidson, it didn't take too long for him to recover and think. "She'll be back," he whispered. "She'll be back when the novelty of new beginnings, new relationships, and New York wears off. I'll give her a couple of weeks to get this out of her system and to spend some time with her friends, who believe she could or would do nothing wrong, and then I'll be ready for her return." Everything that happened in the past during their somewhat tumultuous relationship told Corey that he was right. This was just another Rachel tantrum. What else did he have to do but wait and be there?

Of course, in the meantime, he didn't see anything wrong with staying "in circulation," just in case. With that, he picked up the phone and dialed a number that was very familiar to him.

"Hi, doll," he mouthed smoothly. "How's my Felicia today? How about some dinner, dancing, and a little entertainment at my place afterwards?" After an affirmative response, he ended with a few details about time, dress, and a few niceties, and Corey was off toward another weekend of fun and frolic.

As she drove down Kercheval, Rachel fought more tears and thoughts of retribution. Here she was at yet another ending. Once again, her mother's words rang clearly in her mind. "No one ever said it was easy, Rachel." She really didn't need that consolation and so decided, "I don't care what Corey Davidson does after today. I hope he'll make the other fourteen women in his life very happy. His ego, demeanor, and overactive sex drive should be ample enough for the immediate female community, and I'm glad to be rid of him and off the list."

However, if this were true, why wasn't she happier? "Enough of this sputtering. Enough of this negativity! I'm about to embark on an exciting trip to New York to see old friends and enjoy a few days of rest and relaxation, and maybe just a little diversionary day or two just for fun," she concluded.

Three

At 33,000 feet in the air, it was difficult to be concerned about anything other than the pilot announcing to the passengers that they would be encountering a thunderstorm just before landing in New York City and his asking all passengers to keep their seat belts on and the overhead lights out.

The thunder rumbled through the air, and lightning streaked the skies like thin cracks of light in the blackened sky. The turbulence was more than average, and the attendants, who were in seat belts themselves, tried very hard to console those passengers closest to them. Rachel's attention to this hopefully temporary crisis was briefly broken by a popping sound close to her. She turned and looked at the youngster sitting next to her and discovered that he was chewing bubble gum and blowing bubbles. He returned her glance. He was a good-looking lad, and his T-shirt was amusing. It read, "My parents are Great . . . as nominees for the Smithsonian." Rachel initially thought that that was a little brash, and she had just about had her fill of bratty and precocious kids living in Grosse Pointe.

"Are you frightened of thunderstorms?" she asked.

"Nah," he replied. "I've studied the phenomena of meterological forces and effects, and for me, it's just another bad weather situation. Living in Michigan all my life, I've grown used to this stuff," he said assuredly.

"Oh, I see," responded Rachel. "And just how many years would that total be?"

"Not quite twelve, but don't think that the relatively small number of my biological anniversaries has anything at all to do with my ability to comprehend and respond to the inquisitiveness of your somewhat curious inquiry."

"Whew," said Rachel, "that's quite a mouthful. Let's try something a little bit simpler. Where do you go to school? Or have I erroneously assumed that you are in school? You don't have your master's yet, do you?" she toyed with him. The bubble that he was blowing and was growing when she asked that question suddenly broke and was stuck to his nose, cheeks, ears, and eyelashes. He was quite a sight. Rachel could remember very well similar incidents in her young life and the embarrassment that went along with it. However, he recovered quickly.

"University Liggett, and no, I don't have a degree...yet," he responded.

Rachel wondered if God had blessed her by not giving her the opportunity to bear a child like this one, possessed of such intellect and indignation. Now it was his turn to ask questions.

"Do you have any children? Are you married?"

Funny about the order of those two questions in today's world and curious that at eleven years old, he certainly didn't see anything morally wrong about it.

"No, to both. How about you?" she joked.

He laughed and, oddly enough, he sounded like a little boy.

"I like you, lady. You're pretty cool." Rachel was pleased that she hadn't lost all her ability to make someone laugh and perhaps even make a new friend.

"Ladies and gentlemen, your attention, please. This is Captain Morley once again, with an update on the turbulence. While it appears to be over, we are approaching JFK International Airport in New York City and request that you keep your seat belts fastened until we have landed and have received permission to deplane at the terminal. Our attendants will come by one last time to pick up any discards before we land. The temperature in New York at 7:30 P.M. is a balmy eighty degrees, and the weather's clearing. On behalf of myself and the crew, I'd like to thank you for flying American Airlines, and we look forward to serving you again in the not too distant future. We hope you enjoy your visit to America's most populated city. Good evening!"

The landing was smooth, and taxiing the runways of this enormous international airport seemed unending. Finally, the terminal was in sight, and Rachel began to feel butterflies in her stomach as she anticipated her visit to this exciting city. When the airplane finally came to a full stop, Rachel's heart began to pound and the adrenaline began to flow. Thank goodness she was seated on the aisle about midway on this 350-passenger 727 transport. Once having stood up and gathered her purse and overnight bag from the top compartment, she began to inch her way slowly to the front of the plane. She hadn't realized that Master IQ was directly behind her, but as she turned to see what kind of line was developing behind her, she noticed him.

"Are you with anyone?" she asked.

"No, my parents are inside the airport. After I meet them, we're going to visit my maternal grandparents in Connecticut."

"My, how lovely," Rachel replied. "I do hope you enjoy your stay and don't run out of bubble gum, okay, sport?"

"Randy's my name. Randy Markham, Jr.," he emphasized. "My dad's the chief of surgery at Saint John's Hospital. What's your name, cool lady?" Rachel was amused by his description of her.

"Rachel Radcliffe, and it's a pleasure meeting you, Randy," she responded. Suddenly, she was through the door of the airplane and walking through that funny portable hall that leads into the terminal.

"Shellie" called Amber. "Shellie, over here."

Amber was waving her hands anxiously and jumping up and down at the same time. In what seemed like a split second, Amber was embracing Rachel, and then, placing both of her hands on the sides of Rachel's face, Amber asked the same question she'd asked Rachel ever since they were young teenagers.

"What's shakin', doll?" Rachel grinned.

"My world, Amber, my world."

Amber hugged her again, and Rachel finally noticed Tony standing right behind Amber, sort of waiting for his chance to greet her.

"Listen, Shellie, I've had an idea that perhaps with the new liberal freedom of husbands and wives these days, you know, time-sharing, condo-sharing, that maybe we could initiate husband-sharing. What d'ya think? Any interest?" Tony chuckled as he, too, hugged Rachel.

Rachel heaved a big sigh, and a little tear ran down her cheek. It felt like home."

"Oh, Tony," she exclaimed, "you don't know how wonderful it is to be here and to listen to all of your comedic babblings once again."

"Aha," replied Tony, "I see nothing's changed. You still think that I'm kidding." And with that, Rachel looked around again, trying to see if anyone else was there to meet her.

"Where's Carlo and Marisa?" Rachel asked.

"Well, there's bad news and good news," responded Amber laughingly. "The bad news is that they couldn't make it tonight. And the good news is they couldn't make it tonight." Rachel laughed as well and listened intently as Amber explained and confirmed that two teenagers in one house was tantamount to residing at Bellevue Hospital for the mentally disturbed.

"Let's get her luggage," said Tony, "and then we can talk in the car on the way home."

Rachel and Amber, still holding each other, agreed, but never dropped a syllable of their conversation during the entire time. There was a lot of catching up to be done, and it looked like late-night chats were going to become the rule, not the exception. If you had to guess how many passengers got off that plane by the amount of luggage, you'd have to guess at least 500 people. There were tapestry-type bags, matching garment bags, trunk-like pieces and just plain cardboard boxes tied with string on a seemingly never-ending conveyor.

"How many pieces of luggage did you bring, sweetie?" asked Tony.

"Just three, and I'm holding one," Rachel showed him. "The other two are a garment bag and a suitcase that matches this overnight case. With the way age is creeping up on me lately and borne out by my facial appearance during the last couple of years, I would have been better off putting all of my beauty aids, makeup, etcetera in the large suitcase and my clothes in the overnighter."

"And what's changed on that beautiful face, doll? You're just as gorgeous as ever," commented Amber. "If I had your looks, I'd have been married to Robert Redford," she mused.

"Yeah, I know, honey, and remember, if you *had* married Robert Redford, Liz Taylor would have had her wish come true. Me." They all laughed as they continued to wait for what seemed to be hours.

"There's my garment bag, Tony!" Rachel suddenly blurted out. "And I think it's resting on my other suitcase." Sure enough, they were the ones that had Rachel's name tags affixed to them. Tony swooped them off the conveyor.

They each carried a piece, and Tony led the way through the enormous American Airlines terminal housed in the famous John F. Kennedy International Airport. Rachel's head seemed as if on a swivel as she turned from side to side drinking in all the magic and electricity in one of the world's most exciting cities.

Amber observed her friend curiously and finally shook her hand.

"Hey, sweetie! You'd think this was the first time you'd ever been in an airport."

Rachel turned to Amber.

"It's my very first time in New York, Amber, and it's as wonderful as I had imagined."

Since people had always been of interest to Rachel, she enjoyed seeing international people, dressed in their ethnic garb, either greeting or bidding fond farewells to incoming and outgoing passengers. She couldn't help but think about how wonderful it was to know someone in this massive city. It must be very lonely to arrive in this airport and not know a soul.

The one thing that JFK Airport shared with almost every other airport in the world was the distance from the parking lots.

"When we get home, doll, we'll get you set up in the guest room, maybe you'll take a nice shower, and then we'll take you to one of our favorite haunts for dinner. Nothing fancy, just great food and people," Amber explained. The ride to their Westbury home was as exhilarating as the entire journey, so far. Rachel sighed almost in disbelief that she was finally here, in New York, the city of her dreams and with her very best friends in the entire world. *Life, if frozen at this moment, could hardly get much better,* she thought.

As they entered the driveway, Rachel saw that the house was pretty much as Amber had described it to her many times. Trilevel, three-car garage, twelve rooms spread out on a very nice piece of property in what appeared to be a very affluent suburb, and enormous by New York City standards. Rachel felt at home with the first step into her friends' home, and as she glanced around the beautifully decorated foyer and looked beyond at the groupings of furniture and wall hangings that they'd accumulated over the years, she was quietly filled with joy. As she looked further, her eyes stopped at a rather large photograph of Mama and Papa DeRoca with Amber and Rachel when they were children at a beach near Grosse Pointe Shores about thirty years ago.

"My Lord," Rachel exclaimed, "I've always loved that picture, and I didn't know that you had one." She walked over and stared at the happy faces looking back at her. Her recollection of that day brought tears to her eyes, and she turned to Amber.

"There are times when I fantasize about their being alive. I can hear their voices and their laughter, and it brings me such joy and sorrow. The joy of remembering and the sorrow of such devastating loss."

Amber purposely distracted her from the photograph by suggesting that she would have plenty of time to see the house later, but for now, Amber wanted Rachel to get settled in the guest room and then they'd go out for dinner.

In another section of New York City, in a car heading down the expressway system, young Randy Markham was sitting in the back seat of his Uncle Christian's Cadillac, telling his mother and father about the cool lady he had met on the airplane.

"She was cool, Mom, and pretty," he remarked. "She could almost be like a girl I might like when I reach the age of majority." The adult passengers in the car laughed.

"Pray tell, young Randall, what other of this cool lady's qualities dissuaded you from considering her as your eventual dream girl?" his uncle asked.

"You know, Uncle Christian, in your world, a pretty face and an eloquent speaking voice would be two characteristics that would get your attention." Randy then continued. "For me, I like a girl who can take care of herself and, like I, never admits to fear."

Estelle Markham put her hand on young Randy's arm.

"What was this lady fearful of, Randy? Flying?" she asked.

Randy frowned.

"I don't know about that, Mother, but she was certainly afraid of thunder and lightning." He continued, "I tried to allay her fears by explaining that this sky show was nothing more than that, a meteorological condition of which the thunder and lightning were a result."

"Well," replied his Uncle Christian, "that answer should have relieved her immensely." He smiled. "I know it would have for me." Christian nudged his brother-in-law, Randall, Sr., who was sitting in the front seat with him.

"Girls!" young Randy exclaimed. "Girls need a lot of security, don't they?"

"Enough of this Randall," Mrs. Markham responded, "it's time to enjoy our reunion and visit with Grandma DeDe. We've got an entire week or so to relax, have some fun, and get ready for the return to school right after Labor Day."

"Okay," answered Randy, "but I think Rachel would be a good candidate for me if she wasn't that old and frightened." Now it was Dr. Markham's turn to intercede.

"Randall, you heard your mother. Her suggestion that we get on with this vacation sounds like a great idea, and I think we can dispense with any further conversation about this lady that you met on the plane. Okay, son?" Dr. Markham smiled, and they proceeded toward their destination.

As Christian observed the traffic congestion increasing since they left JFK Airport, he suggested that they make a stop at his brownstone apartment in Manhattan, freshen up, grab a bite to eat, and then proceed to Grandma DeDe's home in Connecticut in the morning. It was easy for the other travelers to agree, and with that, Christian exited the expressway and headed for his home. As they pulled up in front of Christian's rather large house, it began to rain. Everyone had to scurry quickly with their luggage in order to get into shelter before the deluge.

Christian opened the door and was met by Trevor, his butler of many years.

"Good evening, Mr. Avian. I see you gathered up your family successfully."

"That I did, Trevor, that I did," he replied. "If you'd grab these bags and put them in the guest suite, Trevor, I'll call and make a reservation for dinner at the Club Intrepid."

Estelle smiled at her brother lovingly, for it was there that she met Randall Markham, Sr. some fifteen years ago. Randall had just received his medical degree, specializing in internal medicine, from Columbia University, and Estelle had just received her masters in theater arts. The Avians were a close-knit family; only she, Christian, and Mom and Dad. Grandma DeDe and Grandpa Joe were in vaudeville many years ago, and Christian's interest in the stage was evident very early in life. When Estelle was born, ten years later, she quickly became the shining penny in that family, a feeling that had never changed.

Estelle and Randall's wedding had made social page news in Grosse Pointe, where they were married, and her acceptance into this rather intricate community was almost immediate. Their early years were filled with one social event after another. Randall was asked to join the staff at Saint John's Hospital, and his career rocketed as his surgical skills became world renowned. When Estelle told him the news of her pregnancy, Randall was elated and ready for this new dimension in their lives. Their love for one another was never a surprise to anyone, for all one had to do was to look at them when they were together to see the much-talked-about glow that lovers emit when that emotion is true.

Estelle never regretted for a moment that she had put aside her aspirations for the theater so that she could be the kind of wife that Randall needed in order to gain the much sought-after position in his career. And now, a baby! What a joy. When Randall, Jr., was born, there was quite a celebration within the Markham–Avian families. He was the first grandchild on both sides, and from all appearances, he could very well end up being the only one. Christian and Tia never had children during their twenty-five-year marriage, and with her untimely death nearly eight years ago, Christian had pretty much given up on his ever being a father. Estelle had some ongoing problems after Randy's birth which led to an early hysterectomy. Young Randy, consequently, received all the attention of parents and grandparents and soon became the apple of his Uncle Christian's eye, as well.

The Domani household was filled with the excitement of Rachel's visit, and when she had unpacked, showered, and changed into something a little more casual than her silk blouse and linen slacks, she was hungrier than she'd been in a while. As she left her room, she could hear more than just Amber and Tony's voices down the hallway. Walking toward their family room, she observed Carlo and Marisa engaged in a heated exchange about their college of choice, and when they spotted their Aunt Rachel, as they had always called her, they jumped up and ran to hug her. Rachel's arms were suddenly filled with both Carlo and Marisa, and she was overcome with joy upon seeing these two lovely children, now as teenagers, quickly approaching adulthood.

"My, my, Marisa," exclaimed Rachel, "you're even prettier than your last school photograph and so much more sophisticated." As she looked and observed Carlo, she noticed the likeness to his father, Tony, and remarked, 'You're quite the handsome young man, as well, Carlo. And even on short viewing, it appears that you've acquired your father's good looks and his charm, as well." Carlo was a gentle young man, still given to blushing and did so when he acknowledged those wonderful compliments coming from his dear Aunt Rachel. She hugged them again, and as they exchanged brief catch-up questions, Amber and Tony interrupted.

"Well, guys, how about some dinner?"

No one disagreed. Amber told Rachel that she had made a reservation at the Club Intrepid for 9:00 P.M. It was already 8:30, and so they picked up their bags, jackets, and whatever else they needed and went out and into Tony's van.

The Club Intrepid wasn't too far from their home, but it was closer to Manhattan than Rachel had expected. When they arrived, the parking lot was filled with a potpourri of cars, vans, bikes, and a couple of stretch limos.

"I thought you said this was a casual place, Amber," Rachel stated.

"It is, sweetie," responded Amber. "It's a place where the old, young, rich, poor, successful, and failures meet to enjoy the food, share their experiences, and even dance a couple of sets if the spirit moves them."

Tony went up to the hostess and asked about the Domani reservation.

"Yes, sir!" she replied. "Right this way." As they walked into the rather large dining area, the DJ started to play some familiar tunes of the sixties, the conversations of several groups of diners blended into a cacophony of sounds. Rachel was suddenly caught up in the very New York atmosphere that permeated this dining place of choice. A round table set for five was situated near a window slightly to the right of the DJ, and as they walked past him, he acknowledged them and said that he would be happy to take requests once they got settled at their table. Just as Rachel was about to sit down, she heard someone calling her name.

"Hey, Rachel!" she heard, "Over here, cool lady." She turned toward the direction of the voice and saw her young friend from the airplane.

"Hello, Master Randy. What a small world," she said.

Dr. and Mrs. Markham were trying to quiet Randy down, since his yelling could be heard over the strains of the music and conversation.

"She's the lady I told you about," he explained to his parents.

Rachel waved to him and proceeded to explain to her friends who he was and how she met him. Amber was trying to be polite by listening to Rachel and not stare at the young boy and his family, but Marisa, who was less concerned about manners, spoke rather loudly.

"Never mind the little guy! Who's the hunk sitting across from him?"

"Marisa," said Amber, "please don't be so obvious and boisterous. You're embarrassing your Aunt Rachel." With that, Marisa was seated, and the waiter proceeded to take a drink and appetizer order. While only a couple of tables separated the two groups, it was difficult to hear any conversation regarding either situation, and it wasn't until the DJ announced that he was taking a break that anyone moved to go anywhere.

Several people from the two intermediate tables got up for various reasons, which provided a large enough opening to allow for a clearer view of young Randy and his family. Because Marisa had made such a point singling out the gentleman who was sitting directly across from Randy, Jr., Rachel tried to focus on him as she scanned the room nonchalantly. When she finally did manage to get a clearer view of him, she was startled to realize that he was looking at her as well. She smiled coyly, and he nodded as though to acknowledge her, but no sooner did she begin to notice specific features, when people who were absent from the intermediate tables began to return to their seats and once again blocked her view.

Concentrate on surf and turf, she thought. *The last thing you need on the first day of liberation from Corey Davidson is to begin another relationship. That's lunacy.* And with that, she dug her fork into a juicy piece of filet mignon and enjoyed each morsel of the exquisite repast. After dinner, Tony asked Rachel to dance. As they positioned themselves and began to twirl around the rather small area, Randy, Jr. watched them intently and observed every step. As they passed the young man, Rachel extended her hand in a high-five position, and Randy accommodated it with a slap.

"Cute boy," said Tony. "I think your short relationship on the plane had a definite impact on him, Rachel."

"Well," Rachel responded, "you know me and kids, Tony—none of my own, but there's something about me that children are drawn to." Tony laughed.

"Maybe they just recognize that you're a kid, too."

Christian watched Rachel move to the music so comfortably in the arms of this man, and he was curious about the relationship. His profession made his eye keen for those who could dance well and who appeared to have a sharp ear and natural sense for music. He thought Rachel was blessed with all these qualities.

The evening passed by too quickly, and before they knew it, the Club was announcing that they'd be closing in a short while. Amber was pleased that her friend was enjoying herself so immensely.

"You look like a weight has been lifted off of your shoulders, sweetie," Amber remarked.

"I guess it's all of this TLC that's always so heartwarming whenever we're together," Rachel responded.

"Well, bella," Tony added, "like all good things in life, this time has come to a close."

"*Boohoo*," cried Rachel, "do we have to leave?" Tony chuckled, since she sounded so very much like Carlo and Marisa.

"Yes, sweetie, we hafta!" said Tony, once again assuming his papa role.

"Come on, Aunt Rachel," called Marisa. "We've got lots to do and see while you're here. I don't know if Mom has told you, but Carlo and I are trying out for parts in the Theatre Youth Company next Tuesday, and we'd love for you to be there."

"I'd love to, honey," responded Rachel, "and I guess we'll just have to tuck this evening in our pocket, metaphorically speaking, and be on our way."

As Rachel turned around to look toward Master Randy's table, she saw his father almost carrying him out of the Club. It had been a very long day for Rachel, and she was an adult, so she knew Master Randy had to be exhausted. She didn't see the good-looking gentleman who sat across from the boy, and it all seemed too impermanent and fleeting. She sighed and took her friend's arm, and they walked out of the Club.

It was almost 1:00 A.M. when they got back to Westbury, and everyone was ready for some much needed sleep. Tony, Marisa, and Carlo were the first to head for their bedrooms, leaving Amber and Rachel alone sitting at the kitchen counter. With only the night light shining from the stove, they sat down on two of the captain-type swivel stools. Amber's days were long and filled with all her wifely-motherly chores. Rachel, on the other hand, was the consummate career woman with days just as long but filled with very different chores. Still, here they sat, very much on the same wave length.

"You know, Amber," Rachel confided, "I probably would not have come to see you on my own at this time. It's odd that Corey Davidson, of all people, was responsible. He was the one who suggested it."

Amber knew Rachel very well, and over the years, she'd come to learn just how to deal with her ups and downs. Early on in their relationship, Amber failed horribly when her friend would come to her with a problem. Back in those early years, Amber would huff and puff, any blow dealt to Rachel felt as her own. Two emotional people who never found any possible way to achieve a sane solution. Now, with a parent's experience, Amber would allow Rachel to fully explain the problem and possible solutions. Amber learned to listen, and usually Rachel would solve her own puzzle.

"Come on, sweetie. This volcano inside of you has been boiling for some time, and you and I know that there won't be any resolution until it erupts or it's quelled in some other way. In either case, I'm here for you, so why don't you just tell me what happened," asked Amber.

Rachel sighed and, with her head bowed, thanked Amber for her patience and soft shoulder.

"It's coping with another ending, Amber. Another relationship is over, and I just can't continue to live the lie that's now eating away at my very fiber," Rachel exclaimed. She continued. "After Mom and Dad died and Neil and I finally went our separate ways, Corey seemed to always be there for me, and I took full advantage of his assistance and friendship. I guess I always felt that if I waited long enough, he might become the love of my life. Neil wasn't that, and I hurt him terribly. The other men I dated were either too old, too young, too dumb, or too smart, and I tired of the search quickly. Somehow, since I had known Corey, even before Neil and I married, I felt a sense of comfort and assuredness with him." Amber had poured some iced tea for the both of them, and Rachel continued. "With my career on the upswing and having no real demands on my life from Corey, other than an occasional dinner date and show, I lulled myself into believing that this was what I wanted. No overtures, no commitments, no more hurting!

"Then as Corey became more demanding of me, I began to view it as complimentary. I thought he was interested in me because of my talent and my ability to keep our relationship on an even keel, but I was wrong. He really wanted much more of me than I eventually could give. The first time we made love, I remember being 'present and accounted for' every single second. Not once was I ever so passionate or thrilled by the experience that I lost myself in it. I thought that, with time, I would become closer to him and more involved in the love that he had felt and that seemed to be developing for me as well." Rachel hesitated and looked at Amber, who by now was sitting with her chin capped in both hands.

"If it's getting too late, sweetie, tell me," said Rachel. "I can always finish this tomorrow." Rachel was wound up by the recollection and description of it all, but she could see that her friend was just plain tired. Amber gave her her famous half-smile.

"I'd like to hear a little more before we call it a night. I think you'll feel better telling me, and I'll feel better hearing it," answered Amber. "Don't worry about my looking particularly tired, doll. That's something I can't change and that I've learned to control over the years, and right now, I'm more interested in hearing about what happened to you to get you into this state of mind."

Rachel smiled at her dear friend and continued.

"Somehow, I was never able to meet Corey's needs, and I found myself pretending to do so. I asked myself many times why I would continue to perpetuate this falsehood. Was it because I didn't want to hurt Corey? Or was I just plain afraid that I couldn't handle being alone again? In any case, I prolonged and avoided the inevitable."

Rachel's eyes were as intense as Amber remembered them. Her commitment and resolve were as she remembered them, and she listened with the same interest and commitment, since it was part of what made them such good friends. Rachel went on.

"As you know, this relationship went on for quite some time, and every once in a while, my friend and neighbor, Blaise Kinley, whom you know, would ask me such riveting questions, like, 'Why do you waste your time with that guy? You're not the only name on his dance card, Cinderella.'

"Because I trusted Blaise's opinions and respected his thoughtfulness and caring nature where I was concerned, when that seed of doubt was planted in my brain, I began to see Corey as he really was, not as I perceived or wanted him to be, and his shortcomings in our relationship became crystal clear. As an example, last minute cancellations of dinner dates. The long weekends away from Grosse Pointe with no explanation as to where or why. It all began to add up. When I was finally convinced that Blaise was right, I struggled with how I could ever continue in a relationship that could very well put me and others at risk."

Rachel sipped on the tea and her breathing became labored.

"Then . . . then there were the recurring nightmares—"

Amber interrupted.

"What nightmares? Are you still having them?"

"It's well over a couple of years now."

Amber was alarmed by this admission, and her concern heightened as she began to sense some real problem with her friend other than just the ending of another relationship.

"Tell me about the nightmares, sweetie." Amber inquired. Rachel's expression changed and her eyes became filled with fear and emotion.

"It's always the same," she began. "It's raining and I'm walking in a strange place. There are a lot of people, but they're faceless. I feel like I'm the only person in the whole world who doesn't know anyone." Rachel gasped and tears fell down her cheeks and splashed on the counter. "When I awaken, I can hear the rain and a voice speaking someone's name, but I can't discern or understand who or what. Then I experience this terrible sense of loneliness and desperation that feels so very real.

"Oh, Amber, I know it's prophetic. It's my destiny. My future will be lonely and devastatingly sad because I can't, for the life of me, seem to hold on to anyone. Why can't I feel love, and why do I have this terrible sense of distrust? I don't think I'm a bad person, but for some unknown reason, I can't seem to find that one true person who will make me whole."

Amber reached for Rachel and embraced her, trying to console her and soothe some of the obvious anguish being experienced by the one person in the world who Amber always felt would never have a problem.

"Now, now, doll, the wonderful thing about life is that it changes." Amber took a tissue from the box of Kleenex on the counter and dried Rachel's tears. "As much as we fear change, sometimes, it's the open window when doors in our lives have closed." Amber went on. "I don't presume to know all the answers as to why, for some us, relationships are easy, timing is perfect, and we live happily ever after. Yet for others, it's more difficult to develop a lasting relationship. and then to keep it, if it's worth having." Amber drank some tea, and Rachel had quieted down a little.

"All, I do know, sweetie, is that we cannot forecast what's going to happen in the next five minutes, much less in the next five years. You're much too young to be looking at your life as one big closure. Remember that God is merciful. He only gives us our lives one day at a time, and today is the only day we can count on or deal with."

Amber got off of her stool and with all the enthusiasm she could muster at 2:30 A.M. said, "Look at you, now. You're in New York, and the bulk of your problems are in Grosse Pointe, Michigan. Take a few days to let your mind and your body rest. No one here is going to pressure you, and I've a few things on my schedule that I'd like you to do with us. " Amber looked at her dear Rachel and whispered, "Listen, doll, I don't have all the answers for you or me in this crazy world, but I do know that only in giving do we receive, and so you must give your life a chance. If you want love, Rachel, you must give it."

Rachel's love and respect for Amber increased immensely, if that were possible, and now with both of them droopy-eyed and stuttering, Amber said good night to Rachel, pointed her in the direction of her room, and they both retired for the night.

Four

A few days in New York and already Rachel's attitude was upbeat. Being able to see Amber and Tony interact, both in their personal and business lives, was therapeutic. Rachel had been thinking about giving Blaise a call, even though he had Amber's telephone number and would call if he needed to. Curiosity about home was natural, and Amber understood Rachel's anxiety to make this call. The house was pretty quiet at this time of the afternoon, and since Blaise worked out of his home, Rachel was certain she'd catch him right about now. The phone rang only twice when Blaise picked it up.

"Kinley residence, Blaise here," he answered. Rachel grinned and responded.

"Hello, Blaise, it's Rachel." He was happy to hear from her, which was evident by the litany of questions he uttered without taking a breath.

"What's trippin', Ray? How's life in the Big Macintosh? Are you getting some rest?"

"Whoa!" Rachel interrupted. "I'm fine, Blaise. Amber, Tony, and the children have been marvelous. I can't believe I've achieved this sense of calm in such a short period of time. Other than being anxious to talk to you, dear heart, I haven't had a moment's anxiety since I arrived."

"Hey, Ray," he answered, "neato. I certainly hope that Mr. D hasn't bothered you. He hasn't, has he?" inquired Blaise.

"No, he hasn't, and he'd better not," she replied emphatically. Blaise was elated that Rachel had arrived at this decision and resolved to end that relationship once and for all.

"Listen, Ray," he went on, "if CD gives you any problems at all, I'll handle him."

Rachel had seen her share of confrontation and rage between families, friends, and business rivals in her lifetime, and she was definitely not in favor of any settlements that involved physical violence at this stage of the game.

"You know how much I appreciate your caring and protective actions on my behalf, Blaise, and I would never want anything that I've done to cause you to be in danger of physical harm." The mere thought of it turned her stomach, and she reiterated. "Do you hear me, Blaise? Nothing is worth risking your safety or endangering yourself in any way." She chided him a little by remarking, "Besides, Blaise, we don't have to worry about Corey taking on anyone at this time, he's much too involved in keeping up his image of sexual supremacy to risk his masculinity."

"Yeah, Ray, you're right on," said Blaise, "and I gotta admit, he's a fox when he gets angry. *Errrrrrh,*" he roared.

"Now, now, Blaise, let's be serious, all right? I know you think Corey is attractive, but remember, any interest on your part would only add fuel to a fire I cannot quench, so please, Blaise, don't provoke anything more at this time. Okay?" she pleaded. With just the slightest hint of disappointment, Blaise agreed to keep within the boundaries set by Rachel. At least for the time being. "Other than that, Blaise, how are things with you?" Rachel inquired. "Work okay?"

"Yeah, well, you know me, Ray. A little work provides some big bucks for me, so I do my stuff and take my pay. Not a bad gig for a few paintings and wall hangings," he concluded.

"Maybe if I'm really lucky, my mom and dad will call me for some decorating advice." He laughed softly and then added, "Of course, that would happen on the same day the moon turned blue, hell froze over, and Kevin Costner said he'd move in with me." Now Rachel laughed out loud.

"Thanks, Blaise, for always providing a little laughter in my life and for just being a great friend. I luv ya, and I miss ya," Rachel said.

"Yeah, well, me, too, Ray. Just hang loose, see some flicks, stroll Central Park and grab some Z's, and, uh, chew the rag with Amber baby," Blaise suggested. "What else could be better right now for my Ray babe?" Rachel chuckled and thanked Blaise again.

"Be good, dear heart. I'll call you again real soon, and you have my number here if you need me," she said.

"You got it, Ray. Be happy, sweetness. Tata for now," and he hung up. *How could 600 miles and a few days make such a difference so quickly?* thought Blaise.

Rachel was now anticipating an evening with Amber, Tony, and the children at a gathering of promising young actors and actresses at the school auditorium. This wasn't just any gathering of hopeful thespians, but one that would be attended by successful directors of Broadway plays and musicals.

One of New York's finest would be there as well, Christian Avian, Tony Award winner for Best Director of a musical production three years in a row.

Amber was more nervous than usual, but Rachel figured out quickly that it was on Carlo and Marisa's behalf, not her own.

P.S. 126 in Westbury was about as typical as any New York school could be—thirty-five to forty kids in a classroom, understaffed, and always on the brink of having to give up some cultural or theatrical program. It was the sacrifice due to millage drain somewhere in the midst of any school year. The New York Directors' Association for the Advancement of Youth in the Theater Arts consisted of a group of dedicated, world-renowned directors who volunteered their time and efforts toward inspiring the talented youth of New York to pursue the theater arts.

Tonight, Carlo and Marisa Domani would perform in front of this group as Fred and Adele Astaire. They had danced together since they were little children. They were always ranked highest in their class and best in their competitive group.

Most of the late afternoon in the Domani household was centered around the three and a half bathrooms, which would be used every minute by someone for the next three hours. Tony and Carlo used the bath and a half to shower and shave, shaving in the half, and showering in the full. The other two bathrooms were taken up by the three females. Showers, hair dryers, and mirrors galore for styling and makeup. When everyone was dressed and ready to go, they looked at one another and smiled with pleasure at their visible success.

Carlo and Marisa, in tuxedo and gown, brought tears to Amber and Tony's eyes.

"My, my, they're good-lookin' kids," said Amber. Tony joined in.

"And why not, with such great lookin' parents." It was all Rachel could do not to burst with happiness, seeing this show of family unity and love.

"Bravo!" she yelled. "Bravo to all of you before the show begins. You're already winners to me." After they all exchanged hugs and words of well-wishing and encouragement, they left for the school and the performance that would ultimately affect all of them, including Rachel.

The parking lot at P.S. 126 was filling up when they arrived, and Tony, in anxious anticipation of this evening's events, acted as valet, dropping everyone at the front door.

"Thank you, sweetheart," Amber said.

"Thanks, Dad," from Carlo and Marisa, and Rachel joined in as well.

With all the beautiful costumes, makeup, and hair styles everywhere, it was difficult to believe that some of these youngsters were only sixteen and seventeen years old. Moms and dads, sisters, brothers, grandparents, and any other conceivable relative were in attendance tonight. Rachel stood back for a moment taking it all in. Suddenly, she heard someone calling her name. Could this be? Yet another person who knew her in New York? But when she heard her name again, she turned, and lo and behold, it was young Randy Markham, again.

"So, we meet again, cool lady," he said. "We've got to quit meeting like this."

"What are you doing here, Master Randy?" Rachel replied with a big smile. "I thought you were going to Connecticut to visit your grandparents."

"I am visiting with them, but my Uncle Christian is a director and member of the association responsible for this performance tonight. Now, it's my turn," he laughed. "What are you doing here? Is your uncle a director, too?" Rachel grinned at the repartee they had developed over such a short period of time.

"No, no, as a matter of fact, the children of my best friend in the whole wide world are performing here tonight, and they're about as close as I'll ever get to a niece and nephew. I have no siblings." She shrugged her shoulders. People were beginning to enter the auditorium, find their seats, and wait for the show to begin! "Listen, Master Randy, why don't you meet me here in the lobby after the show. I'd like you to meet my friends, the Domanis." Randy said yes and scurried off among all the other attendees who were rushing to their seats.

Rachel found Amber and Tony and was seated just as the lights dimmed. You could almost hear a pin drop as the spotlight illuminated the stage and focused on the man who was the master of ceremonies for this occasion.

"Good evening, ladies and gentlemen. It is, indeed, a pleasure to see such a full house. For those of you who are attending for the first time, I'd like to introduce myself. My name is Christian Avian, and my profession brings me to this exciting place tonight. I've been a director on Broadway for many years and the fortunate recipient of three Tony Awards up until now." The audience responded with loud applause and cheering. "Thank you." He continued. "As thrilling as receiving those awards has been, I hope I can assure you that nothing is more inspiring or heartwarming than watching the youth in this community study and practice their craft in order to achieve a place in the wonderful world of the theater arts." He hesitated and reviewed the program.

"Tonight is no exception. We have several very talented young people who will entertain and enthrall you. As the program proceeds, I will explain how our association reviews and judges all the participants and what part we, as a group, play in developing not only their talents but their lives in the performing arts." He paused briefly and announced. "So, before we go any further, I'd like to introduce to you a couple who are very special, indeed. They have danced together since childhood and have won every major contest in this area for the past five years. Ladies and gentlemen, it is with a great deal of pleasure that I present to you, Carlo and Marisa Domani dancing for you tonight as Fred and Adele Astaire to a tune I'm sure all will recognize, 'Puttin' on the Ritz.' "

As he walked offstage, the curtains opened, and Carlo and Marisa were posed in the middle of the stage and ready to perform. The orchestra began to play and Carlo and Marisa danced as though they were born dancing. The tempo and excitement of this piece were captivating. Everyone in the audience was awestruck by the proficiency and timing displayed by this pair. Carlo and Marisa smiled beguilingly as they performed each move. They were happy; they were in sync; they were perfect!

Amber and Tony were always amazed at the maturity and grace their children had developed over time. Tony reached for Amber's hand, and Rachel turned to look at her friends, who by now were crying tears of joy. As Carlo and Marisa concluded their musical piece, the audience began to cheer and applaud and when Carlo twirled Marisa around the stage toward the finale, the audience rose to its feet. The two youngsters were overwhelmed as they bowed and threw kisses to this appreciative and loving audience.

"Bravo!" cried Rachel. "Bravo!" she called out.

The applause continued even after they left the stage, and Christian returned to the microphone and spotlight center stage.

"What did I tell you? Are they marvelous, or what?"

With that, they applauded again until Carlo and Marisa returned to acknowledge the accolades, each bowing humbly and then extending their arms up over their heads to wave to this wonderful crowd.

The entire program was pretty much like that, and anyone watching Christian's reaction to each performance could easily see that he loved these youngsters; he loved children. Rachel couldn't remember the last time she attended something as entertaining and inspirational. Her hands were actually hurting from all her clapping. She stood up and sat down so many times, she was getting a little tired from the sheer energy she expended in the participation.

The three-hour performance flew by, and when the doors of the auditorium reopened to the lobby, everyone was talking and exchanging compliments and best wishes. Amber told Rachel that they'd wait for Carlo and Marisa in the lobby, and so Rachel began to look around for Randy. She finally saw him jumping up so he could see over all the tall adults, and he smiled when he saw her.

"Here I am, Ms. Rachel. What did you think about my Uncle Christian? Nice guy? Huh?" he asked.

"Gee, Master Randy, I thought you were going to ask me about the performers," Rachel responded in a surprised tone.

"Nope," he said. "They're not looking for a pretty woman who's nice and funny. He is." Randy smiled.

"Oh, is that right. What's that supposed to mean? Are you a matchmaker, too, Master Randy, besides being one of Michigan's upcoming meteorologists?" She waited for his response.

"I happen to think he's a very nice man, and when my Aunt Tia died, my mom said he wanted to die, too. And ever since then, all my mom and grandmother ever talk about is their hope that Uncle Christian will find a nice, pretty lady who's blessed with a keen sense of humor." Randy was looking around as the people came pouring out of the auditorium, and Rachel was equally distracted by the crowd to answer Randy with any kind of sensitivity and just put her hand on his shoulder and pressed it as a gesture of understanding. "There he is," exclaimed Randy. "Hey, Uncle Christian, over here," he yelled.

Rachel finally got a better look at this man who Marisa so correctly described as a "hunk." Everyone was shaking his hand and congratulating him and his association for such a grand performance. Christian managed to extract himself from the well wishers and came directly over to Randy and his newly found friend. Randy was beaming as he introduced his Uncle Christian to Rachel.

"How do you do, cool lady," Christian grinned.

Rachel couldn't help but smile, and Randy's elation was obvious.

"It's Rachel, Uncle Christian." Randy blushed.

"Oh, said Christian. "While I like the name Rachel very much, I really like 'cool lady' much better; it truly does suit you."

Now Rachel could feel herself blushing, but she composed herself.

"Mr. Avian, this is indeed a pleasure on two counts; first, having the honor of meeting someone like you, who has invested so much of his time and talent supporting and promoting the future of our children, and second, having the opportunity to meet members of young Randy's family." She continued. "Our short time on the plane last week and our brief interlude at the Club Intrepid have convinced me that he's quite a guy."

Christian smiled and responded graciously.

"Your compliments are deeply appreciated, Rachel, and I hope that the joy of participating with these kids is as evident as the commitment I've made in doing so." His expression coupled with the lowering of his eyes and his head after he spoke, showed a humility that was even more attractive to Rachel than his contribution. "There's something else . . . " Christian went on ". . . if, in fact, my work has earned me such favor in your eyes, may I ask that you call me Christian?" He smiled again.

Rachel's eyes lit up, and she bowed her head as though to accept this request and responded.

"All right, . . . ah, . . . Christian. How's that?"

As he stood by, observing this interaction between his uncle and his newly found friend, young Randy thought to himself, *Wow! He likes her; I know he does. This cool lady is going to be my aunt.* Now, everyone was smiling, and as though they had known each other for a long time, Rachel and Christian began conversing. Scores of people passed by and acknowledged Christian's efforts. Congratulatory remarks and expressions of gratitude from others didn't seem to interrupt this conversational exchange that permitted them to get better acquainted.

Before long, Amber, Tony, and the upcoming "dance team" joined them. Young Randy managed to find his mother and father, as well. This group presented quite an involved exchange of introductions, which to young Randy seemed endless. He finally interrupted.

"I'm hungry." There was a brief silence and then a few chuckles. His expression gained the agreement of the rest of the group, and he was pleased as he thought, *This is going to be the best trip to New York in my whole life.*

The Club Intrepid was filled with a lot of people who had attended the performance. When Tony asked for a table for nine, the hostess smiled as if to say, "Sure and what other miracle would you like me to perform?" But with a little patience and some maneuvering of tables, they were accommodated and served almost immediately. Amber had asked Rachel a few questions in the van coming over about Christian and their meeting. Rachel appeared to be enthused about this new meeting, but she was also reluctant to lend much credence to its future development.

"For one thing," Rachel said convincingly, "he lives in Connecticut and works in New York." She sighed, "I live in Grosse Pointe, Michigan, and unless I've lost my mind totally, that's about a 600-mile commute." Tony smiled.

"It would probably take you as long to get to New York from Grosse Pointe as it does for me to get to New York from Westbury."

Amber loved Tony's humor and was happy that they all had a chance to laugh a little. This had been quite an evening for the Domanis, and having Rachel along to share in this wondrous event was more than Amber could have hoped for. Amber then held up her glass of water and proposed a toast to Carlo and Marisa.

"To my kids . . . ahhh . . . excuse me, . . . to our kids, whom we love dearly. May you always be as happy as you are tonight."

"Here, here." responded Rachel, and they all sipped on their ice water, which was the only thing served since they sat down. Tony motioned to the waitress and asked if they could get a couple orders of appetizers while they waited for the remainder of their party to arrive.

"What would you like, sir?" the waitress asked she poised her pen on the tablet. "We have cheese sticks, nachos, zucchini, wing dings, and potato skins."

"Uhmmm, they all sound great," said Carlo. "Let's have one of each."

"You heard the gentleman, one of each would do just fine," Tony added.

Marisa was sitting next to Rachel and telling her about her plans to continue with her dancing, which included trying for a scholarship at Juilliard. Carlo, upon hearing his sister's enthusiasm, put his head down. Rachel noticed his reluctance to share in this conversation about Marisa's career.

"What's wrong, Carlo?" she asked him softly. "You don't seem to be as enthusiastic about a dancing career."

Carlo couldn't lie, and it was not a secret to his family that he had aspirations of becoming a lawyer, like his dad.

"You're right, Aunt Rachel, I'm afraid that my dreams are of the law and not dance." He then got up and asked if he could be excused for a while and left the table.

"Well," said Rachel, "sometimes our wishes come true in strange ways. Who would have thought that Carlo would want to follow in his father's steps? You didn't, but here he is knocking on your door." Rachel grinned.

Tony was so proud of both of their children, and he knew that it would take time for Carlo and Marisa to accept and adjust to this split in their career goals.

Rachel made an attempt to get past this brief period of silence.

"Well, at least none of those plans will be solidified tonight, so I suggest that we get on with this celebration and have some fun. What do you think?" Everyone agreed, and all at once, it became noticeable that almost forty-five minutes had passed and there was still no sign of Randy and his family.

Rachel excused herself and walked toward the entrance of the Club. As she looked out the huge French doors, she could tell it was raining. Most of the people coming into the Club were running or carrying an umbrella to protect themselves from getting too wet. She stepped outside and allowed the rain to splash lightly on her face. She loved the rain, but somehow, it always seemed to leave her a little sad. Maybe because when she was very little, Mama DeRoca explained that rain was caused by angels' tears. As she looked further down the path leading up from the parking lot, she could see a man walking toward her, holding a huge black umbrella and whistling. As he came closer, he lifted the umbrella in an effort to get a gauge on how close he was to the entrance. Rachel gasped. It was Christian. He smiled and apologized for startling her and for being tardy. Evidently, there were many friends and admirers to talk with after the show and time simply got away from him.

"Where's Master Randy?" asked Rachel.

"He and his parents should be right behind me. We came in separate cars this evening. I'm staying in town for a few days, and my sister, Estelle, Randall, Sr., and young Randy will be returning to Connecticut to visit with my folks in the morning." Rachel couldn't get over how quickly she had become acquainted with someone previously unknown to her.

"I see," said Rachel. "Then, they'll be staying with you tonight?"

"Yes," responded Christian. "I have a brownstone in Manhattan, and it's convenient to my work and a nice stopover when family comes to town or decides to go on to Connecticut." They both realized that they were standing and talking under Christian's umbrella.

"Well, I do suppose we could go inside rather than continuing this conversation under my umbrella," Christian politely offered. Rachel agreed, and they went inside. Christian checked his coat and umbrella, and he and Rachel went to their table, where the Domanis applauded him as he approached.

"Wonderful show, Mr. Avian," said Amber. "I'm so elated with our children's performance and grateful to you and others like you in the arts who take the time to care and encourage them in theatrical careers."

Christian looked at Rachel, and somehow, she knew what he was going to say.

"Please call him Christian," she interrupted.

And with that, Christian thanked her.

" 'Mr. Avian' always sounds much older than I would ever admit to," he explained. "Also, I believe that I'm more casual and informal, so I enjoy and appreciate the comfort and warmth of first names." He extended his hand to Tony and Carlo and acknowledged Marisa and Amber by kissing their hands and complimenting everyone on the talents of this young brother and sister dance team.

"One other thing," Christian continued, "please forgive me if I ask again what the relationship is between the Domanis and the 'cool lady'?" Rachel delighted in the chance to explain about her long friendship with Amber and how she happened to be in New York at this time.

Christian listened attentively as Rachel skimmed over the rocky relationship which ended just prior to her visit. She apologized for openly imposing what seemed to be much too much about her own problems to a group who was supposed to be celebrating a happy event.

"Please don't apologize, Rachel. I've dealt with some pretty devastating endings myself, and whether they're by your choice or not, they still hurt and can even leave some pretty deep scars." Rachel could not believe how easy it was to talk to him. He seemed to fit right in. The appetizers were served just as young Randy and his parents arrived.

"Boy," expressed Dr. Markham, "traffic is a bear no matter what time of day or night you happen to be driving around in New York City. I missed an exit on the way here and then managed to get lost. Sorry, we're so late."

Young Randy was happy he didn't have any explaining to do. He was more hungry now than before, and he proceeded to try one of everything on the table. With nine people chatting next to one another and across the table, it was difficult to get a word in edgeways. Young Randy managed to talk with Carlo and Marisa about school and other young interests. Rachel and Christian conversed as though they'd known each other for a very long time.

Christian observed every feature of Rachel's beautiful face. Very large brown eyes, a small and somewhat chiseled nose, and lips that were full, expressive, and enticing. All these features were framed by tresses of unbelievably shiny, brunette, natural curly hair, which appeared to be sculptured to fit her face. Her smile was infectious, and her eyes reflected the truth of her emotions. He imagined that he could get very lost in them if he were ever allowed that luxury. His attention was not unnoticed, neither was it unreciprocated, for Rachel, as well, was doing her share of dissecting Christian in much the same manner.

She almost sketched his face in her mind, and her eyes moved slowly around it. His features could be described as square with rather distinctively high cheekbones, deeply set blue eyes, a tanned skin tone and what appeared to be premature salt and pepper hair. She wouldn't even venture to guess how old he was, although it was apparent that that face had experienced much emotional expression. His eyes exuded a sort of warmth that was both comforting and penetrating. She observed that when he looked at her, he truly did see her, a feeling that she had never experienced with Corey. This man had depth, and he conveyed it in his every move, expression, and word.

Rachel found herself captivated by the mere thought of any further involvement with this man, and the possibility of a relationship with him started her heart racing. Funny how Mama DeRoca's advice rang through her mind when she thought of possibly being involved with a man. "Never be too obvious, bella," said Mama DeRoca, "it's unladylike, and men want to be the pursuer, not the pursued." Rachel sighed and thought how different today's world would be for Mama DeRoca. In any case, this time, she was more than ready to totally ignore that advice. As the evening progressed, Rachel thought about the many days and nights in her life that she didn't want to end—this one was definitely going to be added to that list. As dinner was consumed and last drinks ordered, the conversation quickly turned to departure. Christian advised that it would be his pleasure to pick up the tab, explaining that the celebration of youth and new friendships were a good investment.

Rachel searched her purse and scurried to put her name and telephone number on a paper napkin and placed it in her pocket for dissemination before they left.

As it turned out, Master Randy was as vocal as usual.

"Ms. Rachel, I think it would be nice if you and my Uncle Christian would exchange telephone numbers, just in case there was something you forgot to say in all of the confusion here tonight." Young Randy smiled and was extremely pleased with himself. Everyone laughed and agreed that that would be a fine and friendly gesture and a good place to end this pleasant evening.

Christian walked over to Rachel and handed her one of his business cards. He then extended his hand, and she gave him hers.

"It's been a most enjoyable experience meeting you Rachel, and I know we will meet again." Rachel felt as though there were no one else in the room but her. She could also feel herself blushing.

"Thank you, Christian, and I'll certainly look forward to the next time." He pressed her hand in his, and when she released it from his, she felt a sense of loss. It was instantaneous and mysterious and a feeling she'd remember and relive many times in the near future.

The drive back to Westbury was one of wonderment. The images of this day flashed through Rachel's thoughts like a videotape. Christian's face reappeared frequently, and the memory of his touch sent chills throughout her body. *Can this be happening to me?* she thought. *Was I destined to come to this place at this time to encounter this wonderful man?* Her thoughts were jam-packed and unsettling. This uneasiness was almost exciting. It bode of adventure and romance, something that Rachel Radcliffe had not yet experienced. The image of young Randy waving frantically as they drove off in their separate directions left her a bit sad and eager for the next time she'd see this little guy who was so instrumental in arranging this act of destiny.

"Earth to Rachel," Amber murmured as they pulled into the driveway. "My, my, doll," Amber continued, "for someone you've just met, this man has had a serious effect on your consciousness. I do believe you've been daydreaming since we left the parking lot."

Rachel blushed and very awkwardly apologized for her behavior that was so out of character. Amber then reassured her that she could feel comfortable in just being herself, whatever that happened to be.

Carlo and Marisa were sleeping and Tony and Amber looked equally exhausted from all the excitement of the evening's events. Their "good nights" were brief, and an exchange of hugs had them all ready for some much deserved sleep.

Rachel went to her room and undressed quickly. She put on her favorite nightshirt and slipped between the cool cotton sheets. Propping the pillows up behind her head, she lay back and closed her eyes for a moment, trying to visualize Christian's face, hear his voice, and then she clasped her two hands together as she tried to recapture that I moment of his first touch. With her hands behind her head, she looked upward and began to pray. "Please, dear Lord, let this be a meeting you've designed for me and him." She continued, "and if it is your will, let it be a happy relationship. Thank you for your love and your guidance, as always." She bowed her head as if at the end of the prayer and turned off the light. Soon, she drifted off to sleep. It wasn't too long after that, in a deep sleep, the recurring nightmare began.

The rain, the black umbrellas, and the faceless people came charging at her and through her. She moaned and stirred, and as she tried to ward off the endless persistent dream, she awoke. "Oh, no, not again," she cried. "Will I never be free of this tormenting dream?" She sighed and, almost sobbing, uttered in a low voice, "Is this a sign—is there a message in this dream? Please, God, free me of this tormenting nightmare. Clear my mind, my heart, and my soul of any fear and anxiety. Show me the way to the peaceful and loving life I so long and pray for." She didn't realize it, but she had tears on her cheeks, and her nightshirt was damp from perspiration. She was physically exhausted by the dream. She got up from the bed and changed into a pair of pj's. She immediately got back into bed. She was so exhausted and ready for sleep, and this time, her sleep would be uneventful and restful. At least for now, Rachel was at peace.

Five

Mornings in the Domani household were always different and a lot of fun. The smell of fresh coffee, the noises of water coming from the shower, the radio broadcaster telling the latest reports of weather and traffic, and Amber singing:

"When the moon hits your eye lika bigga pizza pie, that's amore . . ."
For Rachel, these were the sounds of happiness. Anxious to join in on these activities, she jumped out of bed, almost totally forgetting about last night's restlessness. She shed her pj's and took a quick shower and was dressed and ready to face another day in this marvelous city. As Rachel approached the breakfast room, she overheard Amber and Tony talking about Christian and his seemingly wonderful effect on Rachel.

"Uh, hmmm," Rachel coughed so that her friends would know that she was approaching, "Good morning!" she sang out as she walked over and planted a kiss on the foreheads of both Amber and Tony. "It's a beautiful day, and I feel like a youngster." Rachel expressed almost jubilantly.

Amber grinned.

"Would we—could we dare to assume that Mr. Avian might be just a bit responsible for your elation this morning?" Rachel wasn't one for playing games and responded quickly.

"Most definitely, dear friends, you may assume, and correctly so, that I am enthralled by him, and this excitement is quite exhilarating, to say the least!"

Amber noticed the change in her friend's expression in the brief few days that she'd been with them.

"Listen, doll," said Amber, "if this new relationship can provide you with some much needed happiness, then I say—go for it."

"Ditto," replied Tony.

"Tony and I talked about how strange our destinies can be," Amber continued, "and we believe that it was your destiny to travel here to meet this man, sweetie."

"You know, Amber," Rachel responded, "when I first saw him at the Club Intrepid, I initially felt something I'd never experienced before. There was a connection or chemistry between us, and I could tell it was mutual. At first," she went on, "it was a bit scary, and then, it was unbelievable. Today, it's more exciting just thinking about the prospect."

The last word no sooner came out of Rachel's mouth, when the telephone rang.

"That's Christian—I know it!" Rachel stood up and said.

"Hello," Amber said, and the male voice on the end of the line responded.

"Hello, Amber, this is Corey Davidson." Amber frowned, looked at Rachel, and rolled her eyes upward.

"Oh, hello, Corey, how are you? she said politely.

Rachel's balloon was burst by the sound of Corey's name. Should she speak to him or not? Probably should, since he would only pursue her until she did. Amber handed the telephone to her.

"Hello."

"Hi, Rachel, I hope you don't mind my calling you, but I've been concerned about you. if you will recall, our last encounter was interrupted by your abrupt exodus."

Rachel couldn't believe the audacity of this man, but she collected herself and responded as calmly as she possibly could.

"Yes, Corey, I do recall, and I'm a little confused about your expressed concern for me," she responded. "I told you a couple of weeks ago that our relationship had to change, and probably easing the intensity was a definite means of doing so. Your abhorrent behavior from that point on is what ultimately led to my leaving your office so hurriedly. You'll also recall, Corey," she went on, "that my coming to New York was your idea."

"I can tell by the tone of your voice and the tempo of this discussion that you haven't gotten off the pin on this decision," Corey responded.

It was difficult to carry on this conversation in front of her friend, so she offered a compromise.

"You know, Corey, it's not polite for me to discuss this in front of my friends, so may I suggest that I call you later at your office so we can continue with this conversation?" She waited for his response.

"Suits me just fine, kitten," he replied.

"Ugh—Fine, then, I'll call you at 11:30 this morning, and Corey, no runaround, please. If you're not there, don't call me back. Is that clearly understood?" Corey mumbled something under his breath, but Rachel didn't bother to ask what he said; she merely said good-bye and hung up the telephone.

Her mood changed rapidly afterwards; she became nervous and irritable. When Amber saw her as she came out of the living room, she asked Rachel if she was all right.

"No, I'm not all right! I'm certain you can tell that I'm not all right!" she snapped. Rachel began to cry and Amber rushed to give her friend a much needed shoulder to lean on. "It will never be over," sobbed Rachel. "He will pursue me until . . . uh . . . until I'm dead!"

Rachel was shaking so badly that Amber led her to a chair and insisted that she just sit down and let all those tears come out. Amber tried to console her.

"It would serve Corey Davidson right if you never returned to Grosse Pointe," she said in righteous indignation. Amber went on in an even sharper tone, "That idiotic, pessimistic, womanizing excuse of a man . . . " Rachel was sniffling and smiling now as she listened to the babblings of her friend.

"This is like old times, Amber," Rachel uttered with periodic sobs. "I'd get upset, and you'd get more upset than me trying to help me out." Rachel held her friend.

"Some things never change, and thank God for that," she whispered.

A few minutes passed, and when Rachel had finally settled down, Amber fixed them a cup of hot tea, and they chatted about the best possible way to cope with and eventually resolve Rachel and Corey's differences.

Rachel explained that she truly did not wish to ever see Corey again. However, there were things about Corey that she liked. For instance, he never turned away from her once during the terrible and somewhat devastating divorce proceedings with Neil. In fact, there was even a time when she thought she was in love with him. But now, as she recalled the entire relationship, she realized it never really felt right. Making Corey understand this was going to be virtually impossible. It was almost 11:30, and Rachel could already feel the tension and anxiety building up inside her. However Amber was holding steadfast to her suggestion that Rachel stay in New York for a longer period of time, thereby letting Corey know she would not return just for his sake. It was all too depressing, and for an instant, Rachel thought about running—perhaps running to Christian—pouring her heart out to him and letting the chips fall where they may. Unfortunately, in Rachel's real world, she would never even consider such irresponsible behavior, and she certainly did not wish to risk losing the possibility of a deeper involvement with Christian, if that were in her future.

Rachel looked at Amber and said that she'd have to make this call, regardless of her uneasiness. It was inevitable. She couldn't shirk the responsibility. She had to keep her convictions intact and her resolve firm at this time. Amber excused herself and left the house to run a couple of errands. Rachel was alone and ready to deal with the next round with Corey Davidson. She dialed his office number from memory promptly at 11:30. Tricia answered the telephone in her usual manner.

"Jacoby & Davidson, how may I direct our call?"

"Hello, Tricia, it's Rachel, Rachel Radcliffe; how are you this morning?" she asked politely.

"Oh, hi, Ms. Radcliffe. I'm quite well, thank you. Mr. Davidson, I believe is expecting your call. One moment please and I'll connect you." And with that, Rachel waited until Corey picked up the telephone.

"Will we ever get back to a time when we at least can care about each other's feelings?" he asked in his own inimitable way and continued. "I so dislike this animosity that's developed between us, Rachel, and I'll do whatever you want me to to get back to the way it was before this whole mess started."

This is vintage Corey, she thought. But she had dealt with him before and would do it again.

"The way it was, Corey, doesn't exist any longer. And as much as it may hurt you to hear it, I cannot any longer—no, I will not—continue to hurt you or me by leading you to believe that it can be mended or resumed." Rachel's convincing and softer tone definitely got Corey's attention, and she continued. "I've always considered us to be too mature to stoop to gameplaying and much too intelligent to try to mastermind the other." She could feel her confidence building, and even her voice echoed a sense of assuredness. "If you can be true to yourself, Corey, you know, in your heart of hearts, that you never really considered anything more binding in this relationship. At best, it was comfortable, and I think over time, the assumption was why go for the real commitment. I can't remember you ever once mentioning marriage, and I must admit now that I'm happy you didn't, because I know now that I could have made another serious mistake and accepted that proposal." Rachel stopped briefly and asked Corey if anything she had said in the last ten minutes made any sense at all.

"I'm afraid it makes a lot of sense." Corey sighed deeply. There was a long pause before he continued. "You know, Rachel, when I first met you, you were already engaged to Neil, and when you married him, I knew that I wanted to continue to be your friend, and if nothing else, I believe I achieved that goal." His words were more deliberate and direct now. "I never stepped over that friendship line the entire time you were married to Neil, although, God knows, I was tempted—many times! It killed me to watch you try to make that marriage work. Year after year, you certainly tried everything humanly and sometimes almost divinely possible to make it work. I had convinced myself that I would stand by whatever your decisions were in that regard," he continued, "and when, after eight years, you couldn't handle the futility and the frustrations, I was there for you when you called it quits."

Rachel interjected at this point.

"Corey, do we have to rehash all those hurtful times?"

"I'm afraid we do, kitten . . . uh . . . ," he stuttered. "I'm sorry, Rachel . . . force of habit, I guess. We have to do this because there's a basis and a foundation for our relationship that I think you've forgotten." Now it was Corey who got Rachel's attention, and he was determined to make her see his side of the issue. "The next few months after the divorce were horrendous ones for you. The guilt, the recriminations, the misplaced blame, and the endless searching for any rhyme or reason to the whole situation, that it had to happen to you. While you may not have seen it, I was suffering along with you. My role was also changing, because my commitment to you as a friend was turning into love, but I could tell, it was not so for you." Rachel listened intently now, and the tenseness seemed to fade.

"At first, I thought it didn't matter that you couldn't return my feelings." Corey went on. "God only knows, you were an emotional basket case, but I inwardly felt and hoped that with time and understanding, you'd grow to love me too. Without getting too maudlin, Rachel, I wore my heart on my sleeve for you for a very long time. I never asked anything of you that you weren't willing to freely give, and I waited for you to come to me." Corey's voice weakened a bit, and he excused himself to get some water. When he returned to the telephone, he apologized. "I'm sorry, I hadn't intended to get this lengthy, but I think this has to be said, and I may never get another opportunity." Rachel agreed and listened as he continued.

"Then, our trip to Chicago four years ago, when you had to meet with one of the designers you felt could assist you in developing Christine Ford's wardrobe, was to be the turning point in our relationship. Remember, Rachel, it was late one evening, after all-day meetings and lunches and brunches and designer shows, that we decided to take a walk along Lake Michigan. I recall very vividly that one of the Midwest's most beautiful moons was suspended in that dark and clear star-filled sky. You were somehow reflective and perhaps a little melancholy that night, so I put my arm around you to console you. Holding you close to me like that was never easy for me, Rachel and it didn't take very long for my feelings to grow.

"Before I knew it, I was kissing you and much to my surprise, kitten, you were responding." Now Corey breathed deeply, almost as though he were reliving that very romantic moment. "It was happening, and I was lost in the ecstasy of it all." Rachel closed her eyes and remembered it, as well. Corey went on. "For most, a kiss is usually the first step toward a more close and even passionate fulfillment. For me, it was enough just to know that you might even consider some higher level of intimacy at some point. I was cautious, and I certainly didn't want to push you into something you couldn't handle or that you may have regretted in the light of day. Finally, I couldn't risk even the merest possibility of losing you." They were both silent now, and because Rachel was caught up in this description of a relationship she thought was never anything special to Corey, she listened quietly as he continued.

"Rachel, I know that the events that followed that magical night had to have meant something to you. As time passed and our relationship grew more deeply, I told you that I was falling in love with you and that my heart and my soul were yours. Then, from out of the blue, you decided to go to Paris for a convention of haute couture international designers. I begged you not to go; however, you explained that your career was at a crucial point, so I, once again, put my feelings on hold and waited for the next move, which was definitely yours. You were gone six months, Rachel. Six months! To this day, I never truly understood what took you so long to obtain whatever knowledge the Parisiennes had to offer and was feeling somewhat left behind and rejected. I got involved with a friend of a friend of mine.

"When you eventually returned and learned of this relationship, things between us began to deteriorate. No matter how many times I explained that the relationship was strictly platonic, and no matter how fervently I professed my love for you, as far as you were concerned, it was over. After a few months, you decided to partially forgive me and advised that we could be 'friends.' While it was another step backwards for me, I decided to take whatever time you've give me in the hope that I could somehow rectify the rending our relationship had suffered. And now, we're once again at this extremely uncomfortable place." This was a draining experience for Corey and he was emotionally spent, exhausted in this last-ditch effort to hold onto this apparently lost relationship.

Rachel now breathed deeply and began to respond.

"Oh, Corey, I know how you felt about me back then, and I remember the walk along Lake Michigan and your terrible hurt when I decided to go to Paris shortly thereafter. I've always tried to be honest with you and with everyone else in my life, Corey, and perhaps somehow during our frequent communicative exchanges you heard something you wanted to hear and not what I said. I don't believe, since Neil, that I ever told you that I was looking for love. At least, not in the sense that you've indicated. I was, however, looking for trust. It was one of the most important traits my mother and father tried to instill in me. 'Trust is the cement of any relationship,' I could hear my mother say. 'Without it as your foundation, your relationship and your love will fail.' " Rachel swallowed and held back the inclination to cry or to display any sign of emotion right now.

"I trusted Neil when he said he loved me. I trusted him when he promised that we'd have a family, but he lied, Corey. He lied on both counts. You'll remember, Corey. Neil didn't love me; he idolized me. He put me so far up on a pedestal that he never touched me. So the family he promised me was as much a lie as his professed love. If there's anything you should have remembered and learned from my past experiences, it was that I needed to have the trust first. The love would follow. You see, Corey, I married Neil because I trusted him when he said he loved me, and I was wrong.

"Then you said you loved me. I trusted you, too, Corey and bolstered with that feeling of security, I went to Paris. For some reason, probably some shortcoming of mine, you didn't trust me, because you couldn't wait to love somebody else. A fact that was borne out upon my return home after a six-month stay. It's the lack of trust that has destroyed our relationship, Corey. Initially yours, Corey, and ultimately mine. At that point, I couldn't even trust myself anymore. I was going through the motions of love, but my heart and soul were absent. When I explained to you that I felt outside myself when I was with you, that's what I meant. I was losing sight of me and who I am. Now, my coming to New York was somehow destined, and believe it or not, you were the motivation. For that, I will be eternally grateful to you, Corey!" Again, there was silence, and Rachel finally said, "So, where do we go from here, Corey?"

"I truly don't know, Rachel, but at least I feel somewhat better having had the opportunity to tell you how I got to this uncomfortable spot with you, and I'm still not ready to give up on it, but I will defer to your decision for the time being. The last thing I ever wanted was to be the cause of more pain in your life, kitten and I hope you know and can believe that."

Rachel was a bit relieved, and she responded contritely.

"I hope and I pray that my believing that will help us both toward an amicable solution to this entire situation, Corey." Rachel could hear the key in the door as Amber returned home from the couple of errands she had completed. They bid each other good-bye and, with that, hung up their respective telephones.

Amber found Rachel sitting at her kitchen counter staring into space. Obviously, the conversation with Corey had given her cause for some additional reflection. Rachel tried to understand Corey's viewpoint and to put it into proper perspective with her own. As she recounted their long and almost confessionlike conversation, she became even more confused. If he were right about her mixed signals along the way, then she was in deeper trouble than she could possibly comprehend. Why was it so difficult for her to end any relationship? Others she had known seemed to handle it quite well. Why was she so different in her assessment of what constitutes a deep and abiding love relationship? Had she analyzed herself out of ever being an active participant in any future commitment? These questions came slamming at her and only compounded her unsolvable dilemma. If Mama DeRoca could have told her more, counseled her less on behavior and more on participation, perhaps she'd have been better prepared to let herself . . . to let herself love.

But somewhere in the deep recesses of her mind, there was a blockage. Was it caution? Was it ignorance? Was it fear? It's almost as though Mama wanted her to figure it out on her own. But why? She was so free with instilling all she knew into Rachel's young and absorbing brain—literature, opera, drama, music, dance, foreign cultures, world environment, a sense of color and design—but nothing about love and how to build a loving relationship. She and Papa DeRoca were very happy, or at least it seemed so. What then was missing? How could she have overlooked something this fundamental, something this wonderful? Mama used to say, "Intelligence is the key to success. Knowledge is the light through the darkness of ignorance, faith is the road to tomorrow."

Now that Rachel thought about it, Mama never once mentioned anything about love. Perhaps it was too private. Perhaps she didn't know how to relate on such a personal topic with her precious Rachel. But whatever the reason, it would leave a blank spot in Rachel's mind that she would have to fill. Her failure to do so would increase, and any success at this stage in her life appeared futile.

Amber came up to her friend and hugged her just as Rachel thought out loud, "How desperate can I get just sitting here and pondering my fate? And how long will I continue to blame Mama for my awkwardness and inability to establish a loving relationship with a man?" Amber answered her, comically.

"At 1:00 P.M. it's too much to determine, and we've got greener pastures to survey that will take less energy out of my apparently exhausted friend. And as I was talking just now, I remembered that I forgot to pick up Tony's dry cleaning on my way home. So if you don't mind, Rachel, I'll run out again, and believe me, it won't take me too long."

"That's all right, Amber, and I think I'll just go to my room for a half-hour or so and take a brief nap, if that's all right," Rachel added.

"Sounds fine to me, doll. You just make yourself at home, and if you sleep past the half-hour, who cares. You probably could stand some rest anyway. Yours hasn't been a leisure schedule recently." Amber embraced Rachel and then pointed her finger toward the hallway leading to Rachel's room and exclaimed, "Andiamo, or get going, or words to that effect." Amber then picked up her car keys, which she'd thrown on the counter, and walked out the front door, locking it behind her. Rachel went down the hallway to her room, opened the door, and walked directly to the bed and lay across it. She was really exhausted, mentally and physically. The thought of her telephone conversation was disturbing, and the "what ifs" and "what fors" raced around in her head. Finally, without much strain, she drifted off to sleep and rested peacefully for what ended up being more than an hour. She was awakened by the telephone and, forgetting where she was for a brief moment, picked it up.

"Hello."

"Hello, is this the Domani residence?" the voice on the other end asked. Rachel just barely recognized Christian's voice.

"Yes it is. Is this you, Christian?" she asked.

"Quite right," he said. "I'm flattered that you recognized my voice; we've not really conversed that much, and I was even half-afraid that you wouldn't remember me." Christian smiled, and appeared pleased, as he waited for Rachel to talk again.

"I happen to pride myself in being able to recognize distinctive voices after relatively short periods of acquaintanceship, and your voice is definitely distinctive, Christian. How very nice to hear from you." Rachel was more than a little delighted to hear from him and extremely anxious to find out the purpose of his call.

"You flatter me, cool lady, and I'm happy that you're pleased to hear from me. As a matter of fact, I hope you don't think me too presumptuous, but I was wondering if you'd have dinner with me this evening?" He hesitated as though anticipating a negative answer and continued. "I realize that it's short notice, but I felt it was worth the risk."

Rachel's first inclination was to blurt out, "I'm ready now. Come right over." But she composed herself.

"I'd love to have dinner with you tonight, Christian." Her heart was throbbing in her chest, and her hands beginning to tremble. *For goodness sake*, she thought, *he's only asking you out for dinner.*

"Wonderful," he answered. "What's a good time for you? And, oh yes, I'll need directions." He smiled broadly as he waited for her response.

"Well, since it's two right now, how about seven? Is that all right with you?" she asked.

"Seven is fine with me. Now, what about directions?" He had pen and pad at hand to jot down whatever she relayed.

"Sorry, Christian, I'm afraid I'll have to call you back with those. Since I'm not from here, I'm afraid I don't know any of the roads or expressways. Are you in town or in Connecticut?" she asked.

"I'm in town at the brownstone, and I believe you have my telephone number I gave you at the Club Intrepid."

"One more thing, Christian. Where are we going for dinner? I'd like to dress accordingly, particularly since wardrobe development is my career. I like to practice what I preach in that regard." She laughed coyly.

"Did you bring something formal with you?" he asked. "There's a wonderful restaurant at the top of the World Trade Center, and the view is magnificent. What do you think, cool lady?" He grinned.

"I think I'll be ready at seven, and dressed to the nines."

He already liked her style and her succinct manner. Nothing protracted. Short and sweet.

"Then I'll see you at seven—uh, oh, first I'll need those directions. Is there anyone else at home now who could give them to me?" he asked.

"Why didn't I think of that?" Rachel laughed. "Just a minute. I'll put Amber or Tony on the phone. They can tell you how to get here." With that, Rachel placed the telephone on the night stand and walked out of her room through the hallway and into the kitchen, where she observed Amber sitting on their sofa in the family room, mending a pair of blue jeans.

"Sweetie," called Rachel, "sweetie, this is Christian on the phone, and he's going to take me out to dinner tonight, but he needs directions on how to get here from Manhattan. Can you tell him the best way?" Rachel was almost babbling, she was talking so quickly.

Amber chuckled and nodded her head positively.

"Give me the phone, doll. I'll tell Mr. Avian exactly how to get here from the city." With that, Rachel handed her the other telephone and proceeded to almost dance around the room as Amber was giving Christian directions to their home. When she was finished, she called Rachel and handed the phone back to her.

"All set?" Rachel asked.

"Yes, ma'am," responded Christian. "According to those directions, I could probably get there with my eyes closed." He chuckled briefly and then said, "I guess I'll see you at seven, cool lady."

Rachel was so excited she could hardly respond with any kind of composure, and when she hung up the telephone, she walked to the kitchen counter where Amber was sitting.

"He likes me, Amber. I think he really likes me."

Amber smiled at her friend.

"And why are you so surprised, sweetie? You're probably the freshest, most intelligent, and beautiful gal he's encountered in many a moon."

Rachel was curious as to why Amber said that and questioned about it.

"Now, whatever would make you come to that conclusion?"

Amber explained that at dinner, the night of the performance, Estelle, Christian's sister, imparted a little background on the loves and pursuits of her brother.

"Evidently," Amber said, "Christian had become weary of all of the young actresses, local debutantes, and this year's socialites pursuing him at every juncture. Initially, it was complimentary, and eventually, he found he was just 'going along' for the fun of it." Amber's face then lit up like a Christmas tree. "Rachel, if he called you, he must really be interested—I just remembered that Estelle said he hadn't called anyone in a very, very long time."

Rachel's elation hit a new high just thinking about that possibility. The rest of the afternoon was spent preening and preparing for the big date. Rachel and Amber laid Rachel's formal wear on the bed and then proceeded to match up the accessories that would accentuate every beautiful feature. Her gown was off-white with an illusion neckline trimmed in miniature pearls, her shoes, a soft pearlized material with an evening bag to match. When the time finally arrived for Rachel to start getting ready, she quickly showered and washed her hair. Thank goodness, it never took long for her hair to dry, and with its beautiful, natural curl, a few brushings and a quick combing would make her look like she'd been sitting in a beauty salon for the last couple of hours. Her hair was shoulder length. She pulled both sides and brought them together into a pearl clasp to rest on the top of her head. She looked like a Roman goddess lost in time. She smiled approvingly and continued to dress.

When she was done, she opened the door to her room and walked down the hall toward the living room, where Amber, Tony, Marisa, and Carlo were waiting. When they saw Rachel, they all gasped in unison.

"Oh, sweetie, you look absolutely magnificent," cried Amber. Tony smiled as he added his humorous comments.

"If I were he, I'd never bring you home."

Marisa's expression was one of approval and delight.

"Wow," she said. "How neat. The hunk gets the cool lady. If I didn't believe in fairy tales before, I do now."

Carlo was sort of on the sidelines, and when asked about Rachel's dress, he was quite emphatic.

"Awesome!"

Having heard the unanimous approval, Rachel was more sure that this would be an evening to remember.

By now, it was 6:45 and so quiet in the Domani household, you could virtually hear a pin drop. So when the doorbell rang, everyone jumped up, but it was Rachel who rushed to open the door.

Christian was speechless as he looked at Rachel when she opened the door.

"Hello, Rachel. You look absolutely exquisite. You're beautiful."

Rachel smiled broadly and motioned for Christian to come in.

"Thank you, Christian." Her heart was racing and her eyes were just about rimmed with tears of joy.

"You look pretty handsome yourself, and as I think about it, I've never really seen you in anything other than a tuxedo except for the brief time at the Club Intrepid."

Christian was, by nature, an extremely gracious person, and so it didn't take him too long to feel comfortable in the Domani home. He was particularly happy to see Marisa and Carlo, once again.

"Have you kids had any calls since the show the other night?" he asked.

"No, Mr. Avian," responded Carlo, "but Marisa and I didn't think we'd hear anything right away."

"Well," Christian answered, "I think you should be a bit more aggressive in pursuing some auditions. You possess a talent and should definitely market it." Marisa was pleased to hear his encouraging words.

"Thanks, Mr. Avian," Marisa interjected. "We really do appreciate your kind words of praise and encouragement and your advice and vote of confidence."

Rachel went into her room and did a final check on her hair and makeup, picked up her evening bag, and announced that she was ready to go.

Christian took that opportunity to address Rachel's friends.

"Amber, Tony, it's been wonderful to see both of you again, and I hope we have another opportunity to visit real soon. Good night, Marisa and Carlo," he continued. "Let's keep in touch about some future auditions, okay?"

Marisa and Carlo nodded affirmatively and told them to have a great evening. With that, Christian extended his arm to Rachel, and they walked out and to his car. She loved Christian's gentlemanly manners, and for a fleeting second, she thought about Blaise and how he would approve of this treatment.

Christian's car was as meticulous as everything else about him. Nothing but the best. Rachel saw early on that if he couldn't go first class, he wouldn't go at all. The attractiveness of this trait was enhanced by his unassuming and somewhat casual approach to it all.

The evening came seeping in around them, and the glitter of tiny lights everywhere made the ride even more magical. At first, there was almost a deafening silence, but when Christian began to ask her some questions about her business and personal life, Rachel began to pay attention quickly.

"Before you came to New York, were you seeing anyone seriously?"

Rachel's eyebrows rose and she thought, *Wow, how will I field this question? It's a pretty direct one, and I must be truthful.*

"No, not really. As a matter of fact, I had just severed a relationship that had been waning for months."

Christian could almost sense that he may have proceeded too quickly with this line of questioning and apologized for perhaps stepping over some lines that were taboo at this time. He assured her that he would not be offended if she said she didn't care to discuss anything at this time.

Rachel adjusted her seating position and then turned to look directly at Christian.

"At this moment, Christian, I can't think of one thing in my life that I couldn't discuss with you."

Christian was slightly taken aback by her candor and felt an immediate sense of self-confidence by her response.

"I'm flattered that you feel that comfortable with me in such a short period of time. May I ask why?" He smiled as he awaited her response.

"To be perfectly frank, I really don't know either, except it could be that we're just two simpatico people who like one another's company." She sat back and from a side glance, she could see that he was very pleased by her response.

"Simpatico . . . Hmmm . . . I rather like that word." He almost chuckled as he continued. "As a matter of fact, right at this moment, I like that word a lot."

Rachel was pleased that they interacted so easily. The ride, however, was longer than she had imagined, and once again, a silence set in. Only this time, Christian turned on the radio. The music was soft and comforting, and it set an atmosphere of such peace and tranquility that Rachel feared any conversation at this time could break the spell. The subsequent pieces were romantic, and the pause between each song left them waiting for the next to continue their mutual enjoyment. At one point, the time lag included a station break, just long enough for Christian to reach across the seat and grasp Rachel's hand. She was thrilled by this gentle and loving gesture. She held his hand tightly and gently stroked the side of his wrist with her thumb. The simple connection of two hands was turning out to be an extremely stirring moment for Rachel, and she could sense that he felt the same.

Tony Bennett's recording of "Yesterday, I Heard the Rain" began to play. The violins were sweet. He pulled Rachel toward him and soon she was sitting up against him. He put his arm around her, and she didn't resist him at all. As Rachel listened to the lyrics, she was enthralled by the words that seemed to mirror her recurring dream. She hadn't divulged these dream episodes to Christian, so he didn't realize that she was almost in a trance as she listened to every word. When the song ended, Rachel spoke as though awakening from a dream.

"I've always loved Tony Bennett, and I don't believe I've ever heard that song before. But I know, Christian, that whenever I hear that song again, I will always think of you and this beautiful evening." She turned to look at him. He was so close, she could almost reach his cheek if she puckered her lips very slightly. When he turned his head to meet her glance, his eyes said more to Rachel than words could impart. As difficult as it was for Christian to take his eyes off her, he had to keep his mind on the business of driving. And when he turned at the next corner, Rachel looked ahead and gasped when she saw the twin towers of the World Trade Center in front of them.

"They're magnificent, Christian, and so high," she exclaimed. "Does one take a helicopter to the top?" she joked. He laughed.

"I'm afraid nothing that extravagant. A common elevator makes it to the top quite nicely," then they both chuckled. "But first, we must park this vehicle in the underground garage of the complex." When he entered the parking garage and began to search for a place to park, Rachel could tell that he had been there before. "Well, maybe we're early enough to find a space on one of the lower levels." He drove to level A, then B, and then on C. He finally found an open space. He pulled in and said with a smile, "Remember C level, by the door to the stairway."

Rachel replied quickly.

"No problem. C for Christian—hmmmm. C for Cadillac—how can I miss?" She chuckled. He turned off the ignition and got out of the car and came around to assist Rachel, who sat and waited for him to open her door. He offered her his hand. She put her hand in his and stood up as if propelled from her seat. He found himself staring at her.

"You're very beautiful, Rachel, and I'm afraid you'll be hearing that phrase again and again tonight. I can't remember when I've met someone as stunning."

Rachel could feel the blood rush to her face and hoped he couldn't see the blush or feel the heat that she was exuding as a result of those words.

"I can't imagine being upset hearing you say such wonderful things, and even if I felt uneasy, I'm certain I could get used to it quickly." She smiled at him, and he led her to the elevators. He began to read aloud.

"Elevator A to Level 4. I guess that's us." He pushed the button indicating level 4 and the doors opened.

She stepped in, and as she stood there, she thought, *Were all elevators this exciting?* She couldn't remember. Nonsense. She'd been on hundreds of other elevators, but this one was different—Christian was in it. When they reached level 4, the doors opened and they stepped off and walked toward the next bank of elevators. Rachel noticed that one said: "Skylight Room–Floor 100" *Wow,* thought Rachel, *1 hundred floors up—no wonder they call it the Skylight Room—it's in the sky!*

As they stepped into the second elevator, other people similarly dressed also got on. Christian and Rachel moved as far to the back as possible, and Christian stood in front of Rachel in order to shield her from being squashed. When the doors closed and the elevator began its move upward, Rachel closed her eyes tightly. Christian had no way of knowing of her apprehension of heights, but he immediately asked if she were all right. She nodded and uttered a very meek yes. He leaned down and whispered in her ear.

"This isn't nearly as high as the 33,000 feet you flew to get here and the airline people couldn't possibly have provided the lovely dinner and view that I promise when we get to the top."

Rachel smiled and opened her eyes. His attempt to make her laugh worked. As Rachel looked around, she noticed other couples nuzzling one another and stealing a kiss whenever they thought no one was looking.

"I've always secretly envied people who were so in love that they could share a kiss or a hug and not be intimidated by the observing public. Kind of like their own private world. As much as most people may seek fame, I guess anonymity does have its privileges."

As though on cue, Christian lowered his head and kissed Rachel's forehead. She was surprised by his spontaneity and looked up at him with what he perceived was an approving glance. The angle of her face toward his was much too tempting to pass up, so he bent his head a little lower and kissed her again—this time, on the lips. His mouth was cool and his cologne sensual. She was almost frozen in time. She didn't know if she should respond. But it didn't matter. The decision and dilemma were taken out of her hands, since they reached the one hundredth floor and the elevator came to an abrupt stop. He lifted his lips from hers and kissed her quickly on the forehead. She smiled and watched everyone getting off the elevator. It was only because she had learned how to walk from childhood that she was able to do it so automatically and appear to be composed and under control.

The chandelier overhead was probably the largest collection of crystal prisms that Rachel had ever seen. The ceiling was textured and painted to look like the sky. Offset track lighting directed at the chandelier plus the glow from its own lumination caused a glittering and sparkling spray of rainbow-colored reflections everywhere. Everyone was clad in what could have been appropriate for the president's inaugural ball.

"Who are these people?" Rachel asked. "They look like movie stars and models, but I don't recognize anyone."

"This is not uncommon in New York, Rachel. In fact, at night, it's pretty much the dress code, no matter what club or dining room you choose. Might be just the place for you to accelerate your career, wouldn't you say?"

Rachel smiled again. Boy, he was fast on the uptake. She liked that about him. Not only that, but it appeared as though he was trying to give her some subtle hints about how he felt. She was enjoying that immensely.

"Thank you, kind sir. However, as good as I am at what I do, this is beyond anything I've ever dreamed of doing. Saying it's incredible would be the understatement of the century, and I'm afraid these people are more than a little out of my league, at least right now."

"My lady is too humble, and since I've not known you long enough to argue the point, I'll just say that as uncomfortable and uneasy as you may feel in this setting, I'm equally confident and positive that they have never feasted their eyes on such a goddess as you. For they are mere mortals and possess only human qualities. Whereas you, lovely lady, are certainly among the divine."

No one had ever touched her so quickly and so deeply. Her breathing was irregular, and once again her heartbeat accelerated.

"I'm speechless, Christian. I don't think I've ever heard such wonderful praises from anyone in my life. And while I don't measure anywhere close to your definition of divine, I can tell you this is the closest I've ever been to living a dream." And with that, she reached up and kissed his cheek.

His reaction was swift as he embraced her tightly. He suddenly felt as though he were just awakening from a long and deep sleep. He felt invigorated and excited—he felt alive!

The maitre d' checked the table reserved for Christian Avian and led them to the rim of the dining room next to the windows that overlooked Manhattan. It was all too breathtaking for Rachel, who oohed and ahhed as each new sight appeared before her very large and beautiful eyes. When they were seated, Christian hesitated a moment and then extended his hand for Rachel to hold. She took his hand in hers. They stared at one another, and he looked deeply into her eyes.

"Am I moving too quickly for you, Rachel?" he asked quietly.

She wanted to yell out, "No, I've been waiting a lifetime for you, Christian Avian, so speed it up. I'm ready." But instead, she repressed the humor and became serious and contemplative in her response.

"I must admit, Christian, that I'm overwhelmed and flattered by your sudden and candid expressions of affection, but I'm not afraid or confused, since they match my own feeling for you."

He smiled that marvelous smile that Rachel had seen a couple of times during their short relationship. Once when he first saw her at the Club Intrepid, another while announcing and hosting the performers just a mere two nights ago. It was a smile that touched her heart and her soul. It was a smile that promised a new beginning that would lead to the love she had yearned for for such a very long time.

Six

The dinner selection was delectable. Christian made certain that every course was as exquisite as the previous. Vichyssoise to begin, followed by a light shrimp and tomato salad. A thin linguini with oil and basil sauce and a smattering of grated Romano pecorino started the third course. Escargot came next, prepared so magnificently, Rachel, who ordinarily disliked them, savored every morsel. Finally, Veal Marsala that melted in the mouth completed the entree. Rachel could not believe how wonderful each new taste tingled her palate and satisfied her taste buds. The wine that Christian chose was not sweet, but compatible with all that preceded it.

Dessert was the clincher for Rachel. Chocolate covered raspberries in a vanilla cream sauce with a hint of rum. She sighed when Christian announced that dinner was over.

"I couldn't eat another bite without fear of bursting, Christian. Your choices were exciting and scrumptious."

He was happy she was so pleased and so willing to venture into this style of eating that for him had become customary.

"You did extremely well, m'lady," he chided. "I was a bit apprehensive initially, but when you didn't complain and appeared to be enjoying this repast, I was overjoyed with your enjoyment."

A small aperitif followed by a welcomed cup of coffee was all Rachel could handle, and sipping on each was a delight.

All during dinner, she watched as other couples danced and talked and cuddled fondly. Her desire to be in Christian's arms was overwhelming, but she had become quite good at composure since she met him, and tonight was no exception.

When he finally asked her to dance, it seemed as natural as everything else in their relationship. She stood up, took hold of his extended hand, and followed him to the edge of the dance floor. As he placed his arm around her waist and drew her toward him, she knew he could feel her heart beating so frantically in her chest. She rested her arm on his shoulder and cushioned her face next to his neck. The music tempo was slow, and moving around the floor seemed so simple. His dance steps were exact and easy to follow, and she was certain she could follow him anywhere.

"I believe dancing is one of the neatest ways to find out how well two people fit together, don't you think?" He laughed.

"Couldn't agree with you more."

There was a slight pause. Rachel asked slyly, "And how do I fit in your arms, m'lord?"

Christian was seldom off guard under any circumstance. He paused before answering.

"Better than I could have imagined, and I hope better than you had imagined."

"Nicely put, sir, nicely put."

"Would you like to see more of the New York skyline? There's a walkway around the outside of the restaurant. It's quite safe, I promise." He grinned.

"Safe from whom?" she inquired, laughing a little.

"Safe from falling mostly."

"Ah ha," she said. "Then I should love to see this wondrous city from 1,000 feet in the sky." Rachel forgot her fears and reveled in a new-found courage with Christian. When the music stopped, she took his arm, and they walked to the door leading to the circular walk. It was quiet and glass-encased. The lights of New York were everywhere. So much so that they blocked out the light from the stars. It was like nothing she'd ever seen. They walked slowly, and Christian pointed out the spots of interest.

"If you'd like to see the Statue of Liberty and the Empire State Building, we could do some sightseeing another time."

"That would be wonderful, Christian. I'm afraid, though, I must start to think about returning home to Grosse Pointe. I only planned to visit with Amber and Tony for a few days, and it wouldn't be considerate of me to overstay my welcome," she said softly.

He was captivated by her humility and consideration. Since Tia died, several years ago, he was cast into an arena of women who only knew how to take. Rachel was definitely different; her giving nature was totally disarming.

"I know this may sound forward and presumptuous, but would you consider staying with me?"

All of Rachel's defenses were being tested. It would have been easy to agree. Somehow, all the old cautions drummed into her young head by Mama DeRoca came front and center. Her head must steady her reeling heart.

"Thank you, Christian, I'm flattered that you would ask me to be a guest in your home. But while I may be comfortable with the speed of our relationship, I don't think I could in good conscience take a step that serious at this time." She looked at him intently for a glimmer of understanding.

As much as he had hoped for a positive response, he was secretly pleased that she declined.

"Can we get on with this evening and not talk about good-byes?" she said. "I've never handled endings of any kind very well, and good-byes are a very specific difficulty for me." Rachel lowered her head and continued to walk alongside Christian. Like the rest of this wonderful new and developing relationship, they were in step, and in sync. When their walk had been completed, Christian stopped and turned to Rachel.

"This beginning is so strange to me at my age, because I find myself floundering over simple language and notice a confusion in my thinking. I was always so much in control. After Tia died, I had resigned myself to a life of being alone. I dedicated myself to my craft and never for a moment suspected that would change. Then only a few short days ago, I met you, and I knew—no, I felt it from the top of my head down to my toes—that nothing in my life would ever be the same again."

She sighed and stared at that marvelous face before her. Could she, could he, have found what each felt would never be happening again? Could this possibly be the beginning of love?

Rachel put her hands on his arms, and with the gesture that he had come to know and understand, touched one side of his face with her hand.

"My dear Christian, I can see in your eyes the depth of feeling that lives within you. Losing the love of your life is as devastating as never finding it. I'm a strong believer in destiny, and along with that, I have a deep and abiding faith in God, whom I know has a master plan for all of us. Even if none of this were true, you and I are here now, and my life, like yours, will never be the same again. The sadness would be to not act on this chance for the happiness we both felt was lost to us. For me, I don't want to see it end, and as uneasy as I might be, I have a feeling in my heart that it's right and I'm ready."

They embraced and held one another as though to confirm the words just spoken, and as they returned to the dining room, instead of going directly to their table, they automatically went to the dance floor and resumed their smooth and fluid movements once again.

It was past 1:00 A.M. when they left the Skylight Room. The ride down the elevator had a somewhat depressing impact on Rachel, and she hung on to Christian's arm. He clasped her hand and assured her that it was all right.

As she looked up at the light showing the floor numbers, level 4 showed up brightly, and the doors opened. Elevator A would forever be etched in Rachel's mind as the place that Christian kissed her for the first time.

"C for Christian, C for Cadillac," she said briskly, "and by the door to the stairway."

"My, my," he replied, "your memory is like a steel trap. Have you taken courses to develop its excellence?" He chuckled, and when they spotted the elegant vehicle just where they parked, which seemed like a lifetime ago. He opened the door for Rachel and went around to enter the driver's side. He was confused and excited, with a new feeling of impulsiveness and joy in his very planned and regimented life. Christian reached for Rachel and cradled her face close to his.

"When we started this evening, Rachel, I told you how beautiful you are and that phrase was going to be said many times during this evening. But now, I can't go a moment longer without telling you that I'm falling in love with you. And as overstated as that expression may sound, I mean it from the depth of my heart, my soul." He kissed her, only this time it was a more passionate and revealing kiss.

She, as well, was falling in love and into the maze and wonderment of this new emotional tidal wave. They were as one, and at that moment, Rachel felt a connection and union she had never before felt with anyone. It was the last conscious moment she could remember before totally letting go of all of her past inhibitions and defenses. She was his.

"Must you go back to Grosse Pointe?" he implored. "Can't you wrap up whatever affairs, both personal and business, and stay here in New York?"

She would have done that in a heartbeat, but it was not in Rachel's character to simply walk away and abandon her commitments. She was too responsible and involved. Not only that, but her roots were deeply steeped in Michigan, and it would be difficult to extricate herself so quickly.

"I must return home, Christian," she responded. "I can't just pick up and sever my life in Grosse Pointe. With the exception of a bad marriage and a couple of ill-fated relationships, life in Michigan was always fulfilling. My neighbor, Blaise, would be devastated if I never returned. Not to mention my having clients who have entrusted me with the responsibility of creating and managing their wardrobes. They would be lost if I didn't at least give them another way to go. Do you see how difficult this would be, Christian?"

Christian sighed, as though admitting that he did realize the serious circumstances that could develop from such a rash and somewhat selfish decision. Not only that, but he could see that this woman who was so tender, caring, and sensitive to the feelings of others close to her, would never abandon her principles and her friends. She could not act so totally out of character. He held her again and conceded that he should not have asked her to even consider such an irresponsible move.

But what could he do or say now to let her know how he dreaded losing sight of her for even a brief period of time? He had told her he was falling in love with her, and she admitted to the same feelings. He would have to trust the outcome to the destiny she so totally believed in.

"All right, my beautiful cool lady, return to your Camelot, but know that I will not rest until you're back in my arms and in my life," he said, with a sense of concession.

"Christian," she murmured, "if we cannot bridge a separation of short duration and trust each other strongly enough, how will we ever be able to build on a foundation of security? It's better to find that out now before we commit ourselves to a relationship based on possessiveness. Believe me, we'd both be smothered, and our love would die in the meantime. Mama DeRoca, being of Italian heritage, always said, 'Che serà serà,' what will be, will be." She smiled a smile that melted every defense he could wage against such logical and well-placed thinking.

"Such wisdom from one so much younger than I. It's frightening in a way," he continued. "I feel as though I'm the one who should be counseling you, and here we are at opposite ends of that spectrum. Only understand one thing, my darling, I shall defer to this logic somewhat reluctantly, and if I see anything stand in the way of our one day being together, I will move heaven and earth to get you." Before Rachel could respond, Christian kissed her. "That's so you'll remember I'm serious, and this is so you'll remember that I will spend my life loving you and making you happy." He kissed her again, and as she slumped back into her side of the car, he started the motor, put it in reverse, then proceeded to exit the World Trade Center garage. The smile on Rachel's face was so curious and continuous, Christian asked, "Since you haven't replied to any of my comments, may I presume that you're in agreement?"

She loved his use of language, and she loved his dynamic approach to their relationship. The more Rachel thought about it, the more she loved everything about Christian Avian. However, if this man was truly the love of her life, he would be no matter where she was physically domiciled. If he was to be the love of her life, they would have to know a lot more about one another, and that would take time, precious time.

Even though she wouldn't be returning to Grosse Pointe within the next couple of days, her eyes were filled with tears at the prospect of leaving Christian. She moved toward him, and when she once again was sitting up against him, he put his arm around her, and she reveled in the comfort and security of this new love.

It was just past 2:00 A.M. when he walked her to the door.

"My beautiful Rachel," he whispered, "the image of your face will accompany me during our separation, and I hope you will take something of me back with you so you will think of me until we meet again." He kissed her with as much emotion and deep commitment as he could, knowing this could be the last time for a very long time.

She clung to him and thrilled to the loving sensations that filled every fiber of her being. She wanted to etch this moment in her mind and heart.

"I'll miss you, my love, and I pray that we will be together soon," she whispered as she moved away.

"I love you, Rachel, crazily, deeply, and as passionately as I know how. I will ache every moment you're away from me. Please hurry back, and call me every hour while you're away," he said, reluctantly letting her step away from his grasp.

"Good night, my darling, until next time," she cried as he walked down the path away from her. Almost in an instant, the taillights of his car disappeared into the night.

The closing door awakened Amber. She arose and tiptoed into the front room to observe Rachel, her back against the door and tears streaming down her cheeks.

"Oh, my, sweetie. Don't tell me you didn't enjoy the evening. Why? What happened? Was he nice to you? Why are you crying?" blurted Amber, who by this time was face to face with Rachel.

"He's the one, Amber. He's the love of my life, and crazy as it may sound, I'm so in love with him, I can't even remember my name or anything else that makes any sense in my life. These tears are tears of joy and gratitude. Gratitude to the dear Lord who has guided me to this place, where I finally found love. It is so exquisitive and so meaningful," she uttered softly. "I'm so happy, I'm frightened." She cried openly. "It's so precious and so special, Amber, I would die if anything ever happened that would cause me to lose it."

Amber listened intently, and when she finally sensed a little calmness, she spoke.

"Well, doll, it's only the beginning, so let's not sing any sad songs if they're not necessary." She looked to see if this got a glimmer of a smile. It had. "Listen, my friend, if this is love, and I have to believe you already know that it is, enjoy it, my dear. You've spent a lifetime searching, and the road has been bumpy, to say the least." Amber was on a roll now. "Matron of honor, nothing less, understand me? I'll handle the caterer, and Tony can be the bartender."

"Whoa," said Rachel, "before this scenario is finished, you'll be requesting that you and Tony be godparents, too." She chortled.

"Oh, oh, Rachel, what are you telling me here? You're not saying this could be a shotgun wedding, are you?" Amber said teasingly.

Rachel now laughed out loud and then apologized for her boisterous response.

"Not hardly, Amber, not hardly," she assured her friend. "I think you know me better than that. I've been through too much to complicate my life and his with something as marvelous and special as a baby. Rachel's breathing again became irregular. "My God, Amber, a child. I just alluded to the possibility of having a child." She smiled.

Amber was as humorous as her friend and responded.

"Well, I wasn't thinking about a lamb, sweetie." They both laughed, hugged, and went to bed.

By the time Rachel got into bed, it was 3:00 A.M. and she didn't feel sleepy at all. She placed her fingertips to her mouth, as if to recapture the feeling of Christian's lips on hers. The images of the evening's many pleasures flashed like a film in her mind. The last thing in her mind as she slipped into the arms of the sandman was Christian telling her that he was falling in love with her. The smile on her face challenged that of the Mona Lisa.

The sunshine creeping between those now familiar miniblinds aroused Rachel from a deep and very restful sleep. She opened her eyes and was very conscious that she was smiling. How wonderful to greet a new day with hope and joy and love. As she sat up and stretched her arms high into the air, she yawned a deep sigh and exclaimed aloud, "Thank you, Lord, for this wonderful day and for this newly found happiness. I love you, and I love Christian."

The shower was more invigorating than usual. Even brushing her teeth was a joy. She looked at the just-scrubbed image in the mirror and spoke. "I hope he thinks I'm still beautiful with toothpaste on my nose, and hair so wild it looks like an invading army marched through it," she frowned. "Well, only time will tell, and at least for the moment, I don't have to worry about it. Then, perhaps by the time I do, it won't make any difference." She smiled.

Breakfast—she could smell bacon, toast, fresh coffee. As she left her room and moved down the hall toward the kitchen, she could once again hear Amber singing, "When the moon hits your eye like a bigga pizza pie, that's amore."

"Don't you know any other song, dear friend?" Rachel asked.

"Oh, and a good morning to you, Cinderella." Amber laughed. "How is your highness this morning?"

"Exquisite, only exquisite, thank you. However, this newly found love, which is absolutely divine, has increased my very human appetite for food. I'm famished," Rachel exclaimed.

"M'lady will have her wish," Amber responded and bowed. "The vittles are comin' up. Oops, wrong time frame. Your repast will be served at once, whatever that means." And again, they both laughed.

They sat and finished a whole pot of coffee while Rachel shared with Amber her evening with Christian and her joy with her newly found introduction to love.

"Sounds like you're both pretty serious, doll," said Amber. "What will Christian be doing in your absence?"

"Wow," said Rachel, "that never even came up during the entire evening. You know Amber, I know he's a Broadway director, but we never discussed anything about his work." Rachel was surprised that she never thought about it. "I don't even remember a point when that would have come up."

Amber remembered briefly that Estelle mentioned a new Broadway show that Christian was working on, but she didn't mention any details.

"Why don't you call him and ask, Rachel? It would certainly be a logical question, and if not that, then the perfect excuse just to call."

"You're right, as usual, Amber. And it wouldn't hurt to hear his voice to confirm that last night was real."

It didn't take much coaxing. Rachel went to her room to find Christian's business card. Master Randy was so prophetic so early in life. How could he have known there'd be such an early requirement for his Uncle Christian's number. She found the card tucked away softly in a zippered section of her neatly arranged Coach bag and finally looked at it. It read, "Avian Productions, Inc., Christian Avian, President, 350 Broadway, New York City, NY 10010, (212) 555-6777." Rachel reached for the telephone and dialed.

"Avian Productions, Heather Venable speaking. May I help you?"

"Good morning, I'd like to speak to Mr. Avian, please."

"Who may I say is calling?" Miss Venable asked.

"Ms. Radcliffe."

"Thank you, hold on please."

As she waited to hear Christian's voice she found herself a bit nervous, but the thought of talking to him was exciting.

"Good morning, my darling Rachel. I was thinking about calling you. It must be true that great minds and lovers think alike." He laughed.

"Christian, good morning. I hope I haven't disturbed you at your work this early in the day."

"Not at all. I was hoping to be interrupted, since my mind wasn't on my job at all. I could only think about you since I left you last night."

Rachel almost forgot why she called, but she didn't want to take up too much of his time.

"Christian, in all of our many exchanges last night, we never once talked about your work and what you'll be doing while we're apart. I do apologize for being so remiss."

"Nonsense. Certainly I was not thinking about work last night, and if we didn't touch on it, it was by coincidence, not by design." He chuckled. "However, since your call denotes some curiosity in that regard, I'll satisfy it by telling you a bit about my present undertaking." He took a drink of ice water, which was always available on his somewhat massive desk, and proceeded.

"For years, I've been captivated by the big screen and the many stars it made or broke over time. Of course, being a musical director, those feelings were the ones that caught and held my interest. About two months ago, another director and I collaborated on an idea for a musical production that we'll call 'Cinema.'

"We managed to find an angel or two." He paused then explained, "In case you're confused by the term 'angel,' it's Broadway jargon for money backer." Rachel smiled, and he went on.

"We hope it will be this season's big hit, maybe even tempt the possibility of yet another Tony Award. It's about all the great musical actors, actresses, Fred Astaire, Gene Kelly, Ann Miller, Eleanor Powell, Vera Ellen, Cyd Charisse, and a host of others. Sid, that's Sid Goldstein, my friend and partner in this production, thought that there must be a youngster somewhere in this world who aspires to be like one of those stars, and we've set out to find them. That's why I'm so active in the Directors Association, which presents shows like the memorable one you attended a few nights ago." He went on. "You should really encourage Carlo and Marisa to audition for my new play. They are good. I know, I've seen a lot of young talent in my day."

Rachel loved listening to him talk; his voice echoed sweetly in her ears. His deep and rich tone possessed a softness that made her feel calm and excited at the same time.

"It sounds exciting, Christian," she said. "There's an awful lot we don't know about each other. We have a lot of ground to cover sometime soon."

He agreed.

"How about tonight?" he jokingly hinted. Rachel caught the humor of his statement but also a hint of anticipation.

"I love you, Christian," she said softly. "I wish I could; however, I think I'll be returning home in a couple of days, and I want to be a good guest and visitor and spend some time with my dearest friends. You understand, don't you?"

"Of course I do, Rachel, and I love you for all your caring ways toward all whom you know and love. Is there any reason why we can't talk by phone just a little each day?"

"Wild horses couldn't stop me from doing that. And Christian, I promise when I return to Grosse Pointe, I'll do some serious thinking and planning about you and me and our future."

"I like the sound of 'our future.' I'll be marking time until we're together again, my darling."

When they hung up, Christian stood motionless for a brief moment. Sid Goldstein walked by his office door and noticed him in a semi-state of inertia.

"Earth to Christian, Earth to Christian," Sid called out as he knocked on the door.

"Sid," exclaimed Christian, "I guess I was far away for a brief moment."

"More like light years, I'd say," he responded, looking quite sheepishly at his friend and partner. "You know, Christian, if I didn't know better, I'd say there's a woman in your life."

"Sid, if anyone would have told me even a week ago that I would meet the lady with whom I may spend the rest of my life, I would have had them committed." Christian responded and smiled slyly. "But, here I am, like a kid again, thinking about a kiss, a moment of passion, and the possibility of everlasting love. Can't help but wonder, though, what I could have done to deserve this second chance to live and to love?"

Sid, being a man of deep faith and conviction, put it nicely.

"What goes around, comes around, my friend. No man—no, no husband—was ever as understanding, devoted, and loving to a wife whom he loved totally and watched as she died such a terrible death. Never once during all of your years with dear Tia did I ever hear a disparaging word come from your lips. You loved her and fulfilled your commitment to be there in sickness and in health until death stole her away. You've paid your dues, dear friend, and the good Lord is rewarding you with his best gift—the ability to love and be loved." Sid approached a very humble Christian and patted him on the back. "Enjoy this opportunity, enjoy this blessing, Christian, it's your turn, it's His will!" Sid nodded affirmatively and left the office.

Christian sighed deeply and held back the tears that welled up in his eyes after listening to Sid's kind words. "If Sid is right, dear God, let me be worthy of this blessing. You know I love her with all my heart and soul." Christian bowed his head as if finishing a prayer.

On the other side of the town, a few miles from Broadway, Rachel was explaining to Amber the phone conversation she had just had with Christian. Amber became excited when Rachel mentioned Christian's expressed interest in Carlo and Marisa possibly appearing in his new Broadway musical, "Cinema."

Suddenly, Rachel's thoughts turned to Master Randy. She wondered how the young lad was enjoying his visit with his grandparents and whether he and his family would be returning to Grosse Pointe soon. Rachel was already thinking about how to keep in touch with the guy who made the introduction to Christian possible. Perhaps she could call Estelle Markham and inquire about the next University Liggett auction. In the past, Rachel had always donated her time and efforts to charitable and educational efforts. Her motives here, though, were really geared toward getting to know Christian's sister and family better.

After Amber and Rachel munched on a great salad and exchanged some conversation about Rachel's return to Michigan, Amber suggested that she call Blaise to find out if everything was all right with her business and things in general.

Blaise Kinley was never at a loss for activity. Between his business and personal life, his calendar was filled with various and sundry activities. As he checked the calendar today he had written across the entire week—"Ray babe—Ray babe—Ray babe!"

I wonder how she's doing? he thought. *I haven't heard anything for a couple of days. Maybe I should call Corey-poo's office to see if he's in town and behaving himself. Nah, I'd only antagonize the suit, and he'd only get all hot and bothered. Well, if I don't hear from her by tonight, it will be my turn to reach out and touch someone—ooah, I love those ads.* He brushed aside the thought of making that call for a while and continued to create a piece of pottery he had been commissioned to complete for the Annual Heart Association Ball coming up at the end of the month. No matter how intently he pursued the completion of this piece, his thoughts strayed to Rachel and her recent upheaval with Mr. Macho Davidson.

When the phone rang in Blaise's apartment some hours later, he was not too surprised to hear Rachel's voice.

"I've missed you, Ray babe," said Blaise. "Are you winging it back to Grosse Pointe soon?"

"Yes, Blaise. In fact, I wanted to find out how things were going at home and to let you know that I'll be coming home this weekend."

"Best news I've had since you left, Ray! Haven't had a good pizza or a good bottle of wine since you left; however, Ray I sure do hope your trip to the Big MacIntosh did you some good." Rachel laughed.

"Only you, Blaise, could say that."

"Specifics, doll. Life is full of generalities, but it's the specifics that separate the men from the boys, or something like that." He smiled. "How are my favorite Italian family, the Tomorrows?"

"Stop it, Blaise," cried Rachel, "you're making me laugh so much I almost forgot the real purpose of my call." Rachel composed herself and asked if Blaise would be kind enough to pick her up at the airport when she came home.

"Course I can, Ray," Blaise responded. "Give me the flight and time. I'll be there."

"Thank you, Blaise, you're always so accommodating, and I do so love you for it."

"My pleasure, Ray babe, my pleasure."

"Well, listen, Blaise, that's pretty much it for now. Everyone here sends you their best. I'll call you with the details of my flight home as soon as I know. Take care, dear heart, see you soon." And with that, they both hung up.

Amber was a bit pensive today, and Rachel knew why.

"I know you're sad because I'm leaving sooner than I had expected, Amber, but I think you understand why, don't you?" Rachel inquired.

"I guess when friends live miles apart, it's understood that hellos are wonderful and good-byes are too quick and very sad." Amber sniffled. "Are you certain you can't stay for a few more days, Rachel? I think you're still pretty fragile from the breakup with Corey, and I'm afraid this new relationship with Christian may cloud your judgment and lead you to do something rash and risky when you get home." Amber sighed.

"Rash and risky? My Amber, whatever would lead you to come to that conclusion?"

"You remember, doll," Amber went on, "When your mom and dad were killed in the car crash ten years ago, you were so devastated. That's when you believed that marrying Neil was the best thing for you, and we know what happened after that fiasco. You're an emotional time bomb, sweetie, when you're dealing with an amalgam of emotional solutions. This recent breakup with Corey, and now Christian, I'm just afraid for your mental and physical well-being."

Rachel could see the concern on Amber's face and knew she was right.

"But isn't life all about taking risks?" Rachel asked. "Even though we get burned, we always pick ourselves up and get back into the race, knowing full well we may get hurt again. What are the alternatives, Amber? I'm going to be forty years old very soon, and I can't become complacent or reluctant about putting some order in my life before it's too late. Christian is the man I've fantasized and dreamed about. He's not a paragon of virtue or a Greek god, but he's a truthful and loving man, and we've hit a responsive chord quickly in our relationship." Rachel hesitated and then finished, "If this is opportunity calling on me with one final knock, then I'm opening the door." She sighed.

"Oh, baby," cried Amber, "I'm not trying to discourage you from living your life with someone who loves you, I'm only trying to make certain you don't get hurt again in the process."

Rachel mulled over Amber's concern, and it was as though those very words pushed Rachel back in time.

She could hear her mother saying quite clearly and succinctly, "You listen to me, Rachel, I forbid you to ever see him again. Do you understand? I don't want you to get hurt." Mama DeRoca couldn't have been more demanding. Rachel recalled thinking at that moment, how could Donald Ramchek hurt her any deeper than she was here and now "You'll thank me someday, sweetheart, for preventing this relationship that could only end up in heartbreak for my baby."

"But I love him, Mama," Rachel cried out.

"Love him?" repeated Mama DeRoca. "At fifteen, you can't tell me you even know what that word means! Enough of this nonsense. I've made up my mind, Rachel, and you will accept my decision. All right?" She stared a hole right through her, Rachel recalled.

No, it's not all right, Mama, Rachel thought but would never say out loud. *I will never forgive you for this, Mama,* she thought.

The next day after school, Rachel beckoned to Donald as he left the building. They stood off to one side of the entrance. Rachel was already crying when she told Donald that her mother would not allow her to see him anymore. Donald was fifteen, too, and not old enough or brave enough to stand up against Mrs. DeRoca. He took her hand and responded.

"When we're of age, we'll be together, I promise, Rachel, then no one will ever keep us apart again." They hugged. Rachel remembered how firmly she believed Donald's expression of love and commitment. It became her secret and the anchor that would get her past any further discomfort and unpleasantness at home. Her attitude changed from a lovelorn, forlorn teenager to an inspired and happy sophomore. *He loves me,* she thought, *and I know he'll wait for me.*

It was difficult to not speak to him in the hallway or to meet at the corner shop for a soft drink and a stolen kiss. She'd known Donald since they were five years old, and even in kindergarten, they were always paired off. *But this was true love, and I trust Donald,* she had thought, convinced.

The day after graduation, Donald and Diane Ainsworth ran off and eloped. The news was devastating, the humiliation unbearable. If she ever heard the phrase, "I told you so" one more time, she knew she'd die.

Mama DeRoca was relentless in her bragging about being so right and thereby preventing her precious Rachel from getting hurt by this ne'er-do-well friend.

"Okay, Mama, okay!" cried Rachel. "I hear you. I didn't want to believe you. I trusted Donald. How could he break his promise? Why did he hurt me so badly?"

Mama DeRoca was as sympathetic as she could be under the circumstances. When addressing the issue of trust, she responded.

"Trust is based on reliability and truth. It is the glue of a long and loving relationship. Without it, you're walking on quicksand, and when the trust goes, so does the love, in that order."

Seven

Those words rang in Rachel's ears, so long ago, she had forgotten about that terrible unrequited love. As she came back to her present frame of mind, Amber was sitting, looking at her, and wondering where her friend's mind and attention were.

"You know, Amber, as I think back to my teen years, that's all I can remember Mama saying: 'Don't get hurt; don't get involved; don't trust anyone.' I wonder if all of those 'don'ts' haven't been partially responsible for my ill-fated relationships. What do you think?" Rachel asked.

Amber tried to comfort Rachel and explained that she didn't have the answers to all these questions, but she did know one thing for certain, the past was gone, Mama DeRoca was gone, and Rachel must deal with her life now. Even if Amber's fears and concerns could not stop Rachel from taking the risk of ending one relationship and heading into another one so quickly, Amber had to make her friend aware of her own concerns.

Rachel was overcome by the caring nature of Amber's interest.

"You'll always be my best friend, Amber, and I'm so happy that you care for me in spite of my repetitious stumbling in and out of relationships."

"But Christian is different, Amber," Rachel affirmed. "He's honest, trustworthy, and loving. This time I may have grabbed the brass ring, and, Amber, no one's gonna take it away." Rachel paused and began to read the evening paper for a while.

Tony, Carlo, and Marisa arrived home at the same time, and Amber had a wonderful hot dinner ready to be served, as usual.

"Uhhm, something smells good," said Tony. "Could it be meat loaf, I hope?"

Amber had an infectious smile, and Tony and the children could make her smile faster than anyone.

"Yes, sir," she said. "Let's sit down and have dinner." Carlo and Marisa helped their mom put on a fine dinner, and everyone sat down at the dining room table.

Tony said grace. "Bless us, O Lord, and thank you for the bounty you have placed before us. And, Lord, thank you for bringing us all together at this place. In the name of the Father, the Son, and the Holy Spirit, amen."

Everyone said "amen," and Tony passed the first plate to their beloved friend, Rachel.

These were the times that Rachel cherished. Chatting about the good ole days and the not so good ole days. Watching Carlo and Marisa hanging on every word as Tony and Amber recalled their meeting, their first date, and a future that was unknown, scary, and wonderful. You didn't have to know Tony and Amber long to see how very much in love they were.

It was so relaxing that when the doorbell rang, moans and groans filled the dining room.

"Who could that be?" sighed Amber.

"I don't think we're expecting anyone, so I'll solve this mystery and answer the door," Tony replied.

When he opened the door, he didn't expect to find that person standing there in front of him.

"Hello, Mr. Domani. I hope I haven't disturbed anything by coming over unannounced." It was young Randy Markham.

"Not at all, Randy, isn't it?" said Tony.

"Yes, sir."

Tony asked him in. Rachel and Amber were left with their mouths open when they walked toward the foyer and saw that bright smiling face looking at them.

"Hi, cool lady, I mean Rachel, how have you been?" Randy asked.

"Just wonderful, sport," Rachel replied and smiled happily upon seeing him again. "And what may I ask are you doing here so far away from home? Where are your parents? How did you get here, Randy?"

"My uncle drove me. He's waiting in the car because he didn't want to intrude on your evening with your friends, but I'm leaving with my parents on Saturday, and I wanted to say good-bye and thank you," said Randy.

"Christian is in the car waiting for you?" asked Rachel, looking frantically out the window and straining to get a glimpse of him.

"Yes, ma'am," he said.

"Thank me? What did I do that would warrant your thanks? I didn't do anything."

"Oh, yes, you did. You made it possible for me to talk with my mom and grandmother without their once talking about or mentioning the possibility of Uncle Christian finding a pretty nice lady with a sense of humor. He found you, and now they can go back to just talking about me and where I'm going to college, how much of a trust fund I'll need to carry me through to graduation, and where we should all vacation next time. I love being the focal point, and I have you, cool lady, to thank for it."

Rachel and Amber, even Tony, Marisa, and Carlo laughed. Rachel excused herself and ran out to the car. Christian leaned over and opened the door and was ready as she jumped in the car, threw her arms around him and proceeded to kiss him all over his face.

"Wait a minute," he said, trying to contain himself and yet not interfere with this spontaneous, affectionate moment. "No, on second thought, don't wait a minute. Come here." He enveloped her in his arms and kissed her. His hands longed to touch her, his passion quickly going out of control. He lifted his lips unwillingly from hers and looked into those eyes he adored.

"Say something, you beautiful lady," he beseeched her.

"I love you, I love you, I adore you, my Christian," she repeated over and over again, and out of the blue, "What are you doing here?"

"I . . . " he stuttered. "I couldn't refuse young Randy's request to see you. I do hope you're not upset with me, Rachel. I've missed you horribly," Christian blurted out.

"Upset? Of course I'm not upset. Come with me. Come in, I know Tony and Amber would love to see you again," Rachel prompted. She hugged him again and whispered softly in his ear, "I love you, my darling," and he was once again in trouble.

"Do you have any idea, my little vixen, how difficult it is for me to control this fire inside of me when you tempt me so wildly with your expressions of love?" and his eyes confirmed his words. Rachel's temperature had also risen a couple of points, and if they were ever going to get out of his car, it had better be soon.

When the door of the car opened, Rachel and Christian got out, looking very composed and in control. Thank goodness, Rachel thought, that no one could see her knees "liquefying" as she held on to Christian's arm as they approached the house. Amber was waiting at the door.

"Welcome, Christian. I'm so happy to see you again." He embraced Amber fondly and thanked her for asking him in.

When they were all back inside the house, Amber invited Christian and Randy to sit down and enjoy some of that fine dinner. Master Randy never said no to food. After dinner, Carlo and Marisa sat down at the piano in the family room and led the group in some songs they all loved to sing. Rachel was amazed at how comfortable all this was. She was bewitched by the magic of Christian's presence and intrigued by young Randy Markham, whose boyish charm and interfering curiosity brought this group together.

"Well, Uncle Christian, I'm so happy that my plan worked out so well," Master Randy stated.

"What 'plan,' Randy?" asked Christian, casually.

"You know, looking for Ms. Right for you, and then coming up with Ms. Perfect. I'd say I aced it, don't you think?" He laughed.

Rachel couldn't contain herself.

"Well, besides being the matchmaker of the decade, you're running for Mr. Humility, as well." She giggled.

"See what I mean, she *is* cool. Always knows just what to say, and she's pretty, too," Randy bragged.

Christian didn't know whether to be embarrassed or incensed by his nephew's incorrigible behavior, but since no one seemed to be offended by Randy's remarks, he just sat back and reveled in the humor of it all.

This was something unplanned and totally unexpected for Rachel, and she felt as though someone was truly guiding her destiny, only this time, she seemed to be heading for some much overdue happiness.

Tony and Amber suggested that Carlo, Marisa, and Randy go into the breakfast nook for some ice cream, thereby leaving Rachel and Christian alone for a while.

They were sitting on the appropriate piece of furniture, the love seat, when the silence was broken by Christian.

"I can't remember a more enjoyable time in a very long time. You have brought such joy into my life, and your friends are just wonderful. Am I under some spell, or is this truly happening?" he asked.

"It's a spell, my darling, and one I wish is never broken," Rachel responded. "All my life, I've heard that timing is everything, but it always seemed to work for someone else, never for me. I used to feel as though I was out of step with the entire universe. Then, a few days ago, I met you, and all of a sudden, I feel like I belong and that the timing is right for me and for us."

"Rachel, I can't help but be mildly concerned about something that we've not discussed." Christian uttered softly. "Our age difference . . . it's—" Rachel pressed her hand against his lips.

"Hush," she said, "Let's not question anything. I think we should be grateful we met and not analyze the whys and wherefores. Do you agree?"

"Yes, my darling, I agree with you." They were wrapped in each other's arms for what seemed to be a short period of time when they heard knocking.

"Hello," said Amber. "Excuse me, but I think you should know Randy has fallen asleep in the playroom."

Christian got up, checked his watch, and apologized for the lateness of the hour.

"I must get him back to the apartment. He's had a very long day." He hugged Rachel tightly, and she responded in kind.

Christian picked up a very sleepy and somewhat limp Randy, nodded good night to everyone and left. Rachel accompanied them to the car and assisted Christian in putting Randy in the back seat.

"Please call me," Christian whispered, "and I'll be thinking about you until we meet again, my love. I'll call often, and don't forget for a single moment how much I love you."

Christian got in the car, and once again Rachel watched those taillights disappear into the night. Somehow, she wasn't as saddened this time, and the smile that graced her lips reflected the happiness she felt in her heart.

After helping Amber tidy up the kitchen and prepare for the next day's activities, the two friends sat down at their familiar spot at the kitchen counter and enjoyed a nice cup of tea.

"Isn't he wonderful?" queried Rachel.

"Yes, he is. For such a young boy Randy is wonderful," Amber said and grinned. Rachel almost choked on her tea and on that note, they chuckled and bade each other good night.

Each night, Rachel's room was a bit more comfortable and a little less strange. The blinds that covered the window to the front of the house allowed the slightest glimmer of light from the street lamp and the moon. Rachel's prayers were the same. "Give me the strength to do your bidding. Show me the way, dear Lord, and thank you for the blessings you've bestowed on me in my friends and, more particularly, thank you for Christian!" She bowed her head reverently and suddenly opened her eyes wide. "And, oh yes, Lord, thank you for Randy Markham, Jr. What a blessing he's been. Nice touch, Lord." She smiled and found a nice spot on the pillow and drifted off to sleep.

In the middle of the night, Westbury was hit with a terrible thunderstorm. Lightning flashed through the shades and illuminated Rachel's room. The shadows of the night now bounced around in a kind of frenzied movement. The thunder was loud and sometimes caused the house to shake. Rachel was deep in sleep, moving around in the bed, and her restlessness led to the old nightmare.

Black umbrellas over faceless people walking through her as though she was invisible. She kept searching for a familiar face and listening and straining to hear the name echoing in the background. Perspiration broke out on her forehead, and her thrashing about suddenly awakened her. As she sat up, a clap of thunder broke loudly overhead, and she screamed. She was afraid, and as she looked around, she couldn't remember where she was. There was a knock on her door and someone came in.

"Rachel, it's Amber, are you all right, sweetie? We heard you scream."

"Oh, Amber," cried Rachel, "it's the nightmare again, it's so frightening, and I don't know what it means." Rachel gasped and sobbed on Amber's comforting shoulder.

"It's all right, baby; it's okay. The storm is almost over, and I'll sit here until you fall asleep, Rachel." Amber tucked her in and sat on the chair next to the bed until Rachel fell back to sleep. Amber returned to her bedroom, explained to Tony that Rachel had a nightmare, but was all right now, and they, too, went back to sleep.

It was more difficult to get ready to return home than Rachel had imagined. This trip that started out to be a visit with her best friend so she could sort out her feelings about Corey and the rest of her life without him had blossomed into yet another new chapter in Rachel's ever-changing life. This time, being without Christian was yet another test. It almost seemed as though she was constantly leaving one situation only to end up dealing with another.

Mama DeRoca's words came flooding back into her thoughts. "Those things only happen to the living, bella." It took Rachel a long time to understand its true meaning. *How simplistic,* Rachel thought—*no, how trite.* Back then, she would never have expressed those thoughts to Mama.

When the initial packing was over, Rachel looked around the room that had become hers during this brief stay. She examined each feature as though to implant them in her mind. Very soon, she'd be back in her own bedroom, and the memories of her friends' home would act as gentle therapy when she was missing New York so terribly.

"Well," Amber, exclaimed, "how about the Club Intrepid for dinner tonight? Sort of coming full circle with Rachel's visit?"

"Sounds great to me," replied Tony. "How about you kids, are you game, as well?"

"Sure," said Carlo, and Marisa agreeing, "Why not? It's the weekend, and a lot of cool people show up there on Friday night." He laughed.

"Yeah, Carlo, you mean like Aunt Rachel, Westbury's official 'cool lady.'" Rachel couldn't have been more pleased, and they all agreed to be ready in a half-hour in order to avoid some pretty heavy traffic.

"Well, maybe the hunk will have the same idea, Aunt Rachel," said Marisa, who developed the directness and charm of her mother. She looked searchingly for any glimpse of a blush in her Aunt Rachel's cheeks.

"I don't know, Marisa," Rachel added, "I've already said good-bye to him twice, and I'm not really up to having to do it one more time. However, there are worse things in life, and I probably could deal with it if I had to." And when everyone had finally changed clothes, used the bathroom, and combed the last lock of hair in place, they were ready to get underway.

Tony opened the conversation in the car.

"You know, Rachel, another attorney at our firm mentioned that there's an article on Christian's new Broadway show 'Cinema' in *Variety* this week. It sounds like another winner," Tony added. "Auditions start in two weeks, and Christian has done everything possible to entice you to attend—What do you think, are you interested guys?"

This time, Marisa spoke up on behalf of her most understanding brother.

"You know, Dad, Carlo has a couple of tests coming up this semester in prelaw, and I don't know how he, or I, for that matter, will have the time for it."

Rachel spoke up only because she remembered how talented they were, and that this could be the beginning of something very exciting.

"Christian truly believes that the two of you can pass that test. This may be a chance of a lifetime. Think long and hard, dear hearts, before you pass it up." The expressions on Marisa and Carlo's faces were ones of surprise and wonderment. Anyway, at least Rachel spoke her piece; the final decision would be theirs.

Almost in unison, Marisa and Carlo thanked Rachel for her advice and show of confidence in their talent.

"Okay, people, andiamo! The Club Intrepid awaits," cried Amber, and everyone knew it was time to get on with the business of taking Rachel to dinner.

The parking lot was full, and Tony left them off at the front door.

"Déjà vu?" Marisa cried out. "I wonder what else will be a rerun of last week's dinner performance." The words no sooner left her mouth, when she shrieked, "I told you so, I told you so," and after shamelessly pointing her finger in the direction of the sidewalk, Christian, Estelle, Randy Sr., and young Randy came into view.

"Fancy meeting you here," said Marisa as she came face to face with Christian.

"If I didn't know better, I'd say this was some grand plan and scheme. Only thing is I don't have a clue as to who could have devised it," said Tony, who by this time was helping everyone out of the van so he could park the car. Not only that, but impatient drivers in the cars behind him were beginning to honk their horns.

The young man who was in charge of valet parking approached Tony's window and asked if he could be of assistance. Tony sighed.

"Why not? Let's go whole hog tonight," and he stepped out and gave the keys to the young man.

It had been one week and one day since the lives of these people had blended, people who didn't even know about each other eight days earlier. Some were happy, some were skeptical, some were suspicious, and some were in love. What an emotional roller coaster this combination could create. However, the atmosphere was mostly friendly and often humorous, thanks mainly to the pronouncements of young Randy.

Looking at each of the people sitting at the connected tables, one could see only one face that was never really smiling or joining in on much of the gibberish that was taking place. It was apparent that Estelle Markham was having a difficult time adjusting to this whirlwind romance between her brother Christian and this divorcee from Michigan. *Isn't it odd*, thought Estelle, *that everyone thinks she's so wonderful? I'll just bet there's more to this Pollyanna than meets the eye. Grosse Pointe is known for its very extensive and active grapevine.* Surely, someone she knew would have some insight into Ms. Rachel Radcliffe, and if there was anything to be known, Estelle would find out. She owed it to her late sister-in-law, Tia, to protect Christian, even if it ended up protecting him from himself.

Theirs was a special relationship. Since the beginning, Tia and Christian were the best of friends, then lovers, and finally, they became husband and wife. The only sad part of that union was that they weren't able to have children. Tia insisted that Christian not be subjected to the extensive testing necessary to determine the cause of this unfortunate infertility. On the other hand, Tia subjected herself to every conceivable test in a desperate attempt to understand and somehow correct this inability to procreate. Twenty years is a very long time to sustain all the disappointing reports, sleepless nights, self-recriminations, and utter despair, but Tia and Christian were one, and if children were never to be their own, they mutually agreed, so be it!

They were the envy of all of their friends in New York. Christian always gave Tia the credit for his creativity for the Broadway stage, and it was Tia's love for vaudeville and the old movies that spawned "Cinema" as a production.

Up until now, Estelle always felt that "Cinema" was a memorial for Tia and a testimonial of Christian's undying love. Could anything happen that might change Christian's commitment to Tia and the show? Yet, as she thought more realistically, how could she expect her brother to remain loyal and faithful to a memory? He wasn't that old (he'd kill her if he heard her say that). But perhaps this wasn't what was bothering Estelle at all—maybe Rachel was more of a threat to her relationship with Christian since Tia's death.

The elder Mrs. Avian always expressed her concerns over Estelle's possessiveness of Christian of late—maybe she was right. In any case, Estelle's assessment of her brother's apparent infatuation was, at best, cautious observance. She would assume a wait-and-see attitude.

Young Randy broke the silence by asking his mother to invite Rachel over for dinner sometime soon. Not exactly a welcomed request, but Estelle knew that young Randy was somewhat smitten with the obvious possibility that his "cool lady" could become his new aunt.

"I think that's very thoughtful of you, Randy, and I will call Rachel soon to spend an evening with us." Randy smiled broadly at his mother's perfect answer and then insisted that it be soon after they returned home this weekend.

In another part of the room, there sat two people whose world was obviously light years away from anything going on with the rest of this group. Together, hands clasped on the table for all to see and staring at one another as though in a trance.

"If you wish, Christian," said Rachel, "I can return in a couple of weeks to see some of your auditions." He hesitated as if in awe of this suggestion, but in reality, he was kind of daydreaming, and when suddenly he returned to earth, it was as though he subconsciously heard Rachel's voice.

"Uh, I'm sorry, did you say something, Rachel?"

Rachel realized how difficult these brief meetings had become for her, so she could empathize with Christian's inability to handle yet another upcoming good-bye as well.

"All I said, Christian, was that I might be able to come back in a couple of weeks after you've started auditions." She smiled coyly and stroked his face with her hand. Christian clasped her hand in his and brought it to his lips and kissed it. Rachel's heartbeat increased a couple of points, as did her blood pressure.

"That would be the best gift you could give me, darling, and I promise not to nag you for a return date when you return to Michigan," Christian said sincerely.

While it was not on everyone's mind, September was at the halfway mark, and the holiday season would be fast approaching. Mama and Papa DeRoca always began planning the holidays as soon as Halloween passed. Rachel thought about how this time of year was never the same since they died. The thoughts of all this were swirling around in her head. How could she recapture that happiness, those special times? Were they gone forever with her mom's and dad's passings? *I hope not—no, I pray not,* she thought. *My spirit has been rejuvenated during this trip and I feel as though . . . I'm coming alive again!*

"Then, my dearest, I shall return next month and see just what kind of work you do." She smiled, and so did he.

"I must be doing something right," Christian exclaimed. "I've received the highest award my industry can give, and it was because my peers in this wonderful world of live stage saw fit to honor me so. I've been blessed many times in this life of mine. Certainly recognition of my work ranks high amongst those blessings."

A good deal of Rachel's admiration for Christian was spawned by his humility. It captured most everyone's attention and endeared them to him almost immediately.

"You've added so much to my life, Christian, in such a short period of time. I feel as though someone up there has ordained that it's my turn to experience some of the quality of life for which I've been searching such a long time." Rachel sighed and looked lovingly and gratefully into those deep and magnetic eyes.

Young Randy whose consumption of food was not obvious in his somewhat lean image was observing every move made between Rachel and his Uncle Christian.

Am I lucky, or what? thought he. *I bet with a little gentle persuasion and some absolute interference, I can have a new aunt by next year.* He smiled gleefully. "Yes!" and he motioned with his arms up and down, *"Yes!"*

"What on earth are you doing?" his mom asked rather sternly. "Randy, are you aware that you're talking to yourself?"

"Yes, ma'am," he respectfully replied. "I was thinking about a project I'm working on in school and the formula just came to me," he responded. Thank goodness, thought Randy, that his mom couldn't see the slight blush that was always an indication that Randy was telling something less than the truth. *Whew!* he thought, *I'm going to have to be more cautious if I'm going to pull off this whole matchmaking business.*

Amber and Tony were on the dance floor, and as they spun around, they motioned to Carlo and Marisa to join them. As they arose to obey their mom's gesture, it was obvious that even their walking had taken on an artful blended grace when they were together. Rachel and Christian looked on with joy as the brother and sister team began to dance. Slowly, but surely, others on the floor became aware that something special was happening here as, one by one, dancing couples stepped aside and walked to the side of the dance floor to watch this magnificent couple.

Eight

When the band noticed what was going on, their music accompaniment changed to match the tempo of Carlo and Marisa. As they performed one step after the other, the music changed again to a piece that they had danced to many times before. The strains of "New York, New York" suddenly had everyone in the club on their feet, circling the floor and clapping in time to the beat as this dance team rose to the occasion.

"You could be witnessing my first audition," said Christian quietly to Rachel, who was standing next to him amidst everyone else who could manage to find a place.

Rachel beckoned Christian to bend down so she could whisper something in his ear.

"I've been trying to get them interested in the possibility of auditioning for your show. I'll keep trying," said Rachel. "They're outstanding."

As the song finally drew to a tumultuous crescendo, the audience went crazy. There they were, Carol and Marisa at center floor, bowing and responding to an overwhelmingly pleased audience.

"Bravo!" they cried. "Bravo! "Encore, Encore!"

With these calls and the continued ovation, Christian excused himself from Rachel, walked up to the bandleader and introduced himself. He then asked if he could use the microphone. The bandleader was most accommodating, and Christian began to try to get the crowd under control.

"Ladies and gentlemen, please may I have your attention? Please. Thank you." As the applause subsided and only a few "encores and bravos" remained, Christian's distinctive voice almost demanded a certain silence. "Thank you, ladies, gentlemen. First of all, let me introduce this wonderful couple to you. They are Carlo and Marisa Domani, who just last week dazzled a crowd much like yourselves with a performance before members of my association The Directors Association for the Advancement of Youth in the Theater Arts. Uh, oh, yes, perhaps I should introduce myself. I'm Christian Avian, director of Broadway musicals, some of which you may have heard of, 'Long Time Friends,' 'Summer's End,' and my upcoming show, 'Cinema'." The audience responded positively with more applause and whistles. "Perhaps, we might be able to have Carlo and Marisa do another number for you." The applause resumed, and Christian went over to Carlo and Marisa, who were almost overcome by such adulation.

"What do you think, kids?" he said. "Will you do another number for your appreciative fans?" Christian smiled, his eyes shining brightly. The response came from Amber, who looked at her children with such loving pride.

"How about 'Singing in the Rain,' kids? You do that so well!"

"Okay," they said in unison, and Christian asked the band if they were prepared with an arrangement to do this.

"Sure are," responded the leader. "Okay guys, number 52 in the blue book," and with little else remaining to be done, the band started the intro to "Singing in the Rain," and Carlo and Marisa were center stage once again.

Watching this entire evening develop into such a wonderful event put a new bent on Estelle's feelings about Rachel and her New York friends. Dr. Markham was always the easiest man to please, and when Estelle and Randy were happy, so was he. He could tell that Estelle was reevaluating her earlier perceptions, and while it may take some additional time, he could also see the change had already begun.

"Aren't they great, Mom!" cried Randy, and he looked once again for his Uncle Christian and Rachel who were still holding hands and enjoying every bit of this unforgettable moment.

"Yes, they are, dear. Yes, they all are," Estelle said reassuringly.

When Estelle focused on her brother and Rachel looking so happy and holding each other so tenderly, tears came to her eyes. Estelle could feel that he was content with his new love. Why would she be suspicious of something so wonderful and exciting for him and the rest of the Avian family? More than one audition happened here tonight, and perhaps the revitalization and reintroduction of new love was the big winner. Even though she had previously questioned this new devotion for Christian, Estelle could feel a calm and a happiness in her heart that felt right, and it definitely felt good. The smile that came to her face as a result of this revelation came as a ray of sunshine to Christian, who caught his sister's eye. He could see the approval in her expression. He, too, was filled with such incredible joy.

Excusing herself from her husband, Estelle worked her way through the enthusiastic crowd. Getting around people in chairs and unattended tables was more difficult than she had expected. For a moment, she grabbed the first available chair and sat down to rest. Suddenly, a hand on her shoulder made her turn around to observe her one and only brother, Christian, who held out his hands to her. She responded, and he hugged his baby sister tightly, stroking her hair and whispering quietly in her ear.

"Thank you, Stellar," he grinned. Stellar was a name he gave her early on in her young life because every time she smiled, someone would say, "she shines like a star." So, instead of calling her Estelle, he called her Stellar. Christian went on. "I know this new relationship has caused you to be concerned and, honey, don't think for a moment that I've forgotten how much you loved Tia and still do. You weren't only sisters-in-law, but you were best friends." There was a lump in his throat as he recalled the grand times they had had before Tia became mortally ill. "It's time to move on, sweetie. It's time—"

"I know Christian, but I'm so torn between my loyalty to Tia and my deep longing for your happiness." Estelle confided. "We've gone through so much, Christian, that I feel a twinge of jealousy toward Rachel, and I apologize if it seems selfish and possessive." She took a deep breath and looked again into her brother's eyes. "Go for it, big brother. I know she loves you; you'd have to be blind not to see it." Estelle chuckled. They embraced.

"Bless you, Stellar, bless you." Almost simultaneously the orchestra concluded their song, and the applause started all over again.

"What an evening," proclaimed Rachel. "Is everything done in such grand style in New York?"

"Only when great things happen," Christian was forced to respond. As the comments and compliments circulated around the table, the beginning of a new mutual admiration society was born.

Rachel was involved in some pretty heady conversation at the table, and so she really wasn't aware that Christian had gotten up and was talking to the bandleader when she noticed he was missing from her side. She watched him return to the table. He stopped in front of her.

"I believe this dance is ours, m'lady," and as though on cue, the band began to play "Yesterday I Heard the Rain," hers and Christian's song.

As she stood up to respond to her love's request, the melody had the same effect on her as always. Tears filled her eyes as she put her arms around Christian's neck, nestled her head in his shoulder and thrilled to the touch of his arms around her waist.

"Someday Rachel, I'll bring you Tony Bennett singing this song just for us, but for now, this will have to do."

Randy, his chin cupped in both hands, almost swooned as he watched his uncle and the cool lady move to the strains of that beautiful song.

"They've got the formula, Mama, don't they?" Randy inquired.

Estelle was somewhat confused by young Randy's question.

"What formula, son?"

"You know, Mama, you and Gramma are always talking about people who have chemistry. Well, since it's basic science, all chemistry is related in formula style, so I think Uncle Christian and Rachel have found a good formula," he said.

Estelle shook her head, and Dr. Markham did as well.

"How about you and I putting together a little formula on that dance floor, Mrs. Markham?" Dr. Markham asked.

"Why not," responded Estelle, "maybe we'll get a standing ovation, too." Dr. Markham laughed out loud as they proceeded to the dance floor, hand in hand. The evening had developed into one that each of them would long remember.

"No more good-byes, my darling," Christian whispered in Rachel's ear as he held her one final time before her departure for home tomorrow.

"Just temporary 'so longs,'" Rachel responded.

Christian pressed her to him and held her so tightly, Rachel was certain they were fused together by some magical intervention.

"No matter where you are, sweetheart, I'll be with you in spirit and with love," Christian uttered. "I love you, my dear, sweet cool lady, and I'll count the seconds until you're back in my arms again."

Rachel could not control the surge of emotions that finally erupted into tears.

"Oh, my God, Christian, please don't let us lose this wonderful moment ever," she cried. "I thought my life would be played out alone, and now I feel as though I could not live another day without you in it."

He raised her head and looked into those beautiful eyes. Softly, he kissed each lid and finally their eyes met. For seconds, they were lost in the thrill of that special oneness that happens only to a precious few, if ever.

"You and I have a date with destiny, my darling," he said quietly.

"We will be as one very soon," Rachel acknowledged quietly as well.

"Yes, my darling, yes."

It was over—the dinner, the dancing—and the heart-rending time had come once again. They must say "so long." Amber, Tony, and the children bid a fond farewell to everyone, and Amber approached Rachel slowly and urged her to come along.

"It's been wonderful," Rachel exclaimed to Christian, Estelle, and the senior and junior Randys, "No, it's been magnificent, and I thank you from the bottom of my heart for every moment we shared during my all too brief visit. I hope to see you in a couple of weeks, and until then, stay safe, be well, and God bless." And with her hand up to her mouth, she blew them a kiss and whispered, "Luv ya."

The last image she had of Christian was this paragon of a man standing with his arms around his sister and nephew, smiling, with one lonely tear too obvious not to notice and too precious to forget, running down his cheek.

As they left the club, a light rain was falling, and Rachel could hear each drop whispering "Christian." She was so overwhelmed with the emotional separation that it took Amber and Tony a few minutes to get her to turn around from facing the club as they drove off into the night.

Back in Grosse Pointe, Blaise was scurrying about making sure that Rachel's duplex was cleaned up and ready for her return. There was a bit of a problem, however; Blaise didn't know where he could put all the floral arrangements that had been arriving since Thursday. If you didn't know for sure, you'd think their homes had been mistaken for a funeral parlor.

"Wow," exclaimed Blaise, "Ray babe has either met the richest man in New York or he owns a local florist. I don't know which would be better." He heaved a big sigh and stood almost in a state of inertia. "What if this is Mr. Right for my Ray babe?" he thought out loud. "What if she moves to New York? What if I never saw her again?

"Stop it," he said. "Stop this nonsense. How could all this take place after such a short visit to New York?" He was trying to convince himself that this was not the case. A mere infatuation. No one in his right mind sends forty-two floral arrangements. Maybe he's an escapee from Bellevue? He cringed! "Oh, well, this speculation would come to an end tomorrow night, and once Ray babe was home and back to work, it would be like old times.

"Uh . . . Oh, no, old times is why she left. I forgot about Corey poo. I wonder what that devil has been doing lately, as if I didn't know!" Blaise sighed. "If he causes Rachel any more problems, I'll, I'll, I'll do something. But what, I don't know."

Blaise, by nature, was not a violent person. But it did make his heart race thinking about it. His blue eyes shone and the grin on his face foretold of some scheme only Blaise could conceive.

Anyway, Ray babe would be home tomorrow, and Blaise already had her favorite pizza ordered and a six-pack of beer and, oh, yes, champagne, of course. How wonderful it would be to have her back.

Somehow, JFK Airport didn't exude the same electric excitement as it did when Rachel arrived there nine days ago. It seemed like everyone was involved in some stage of good-bye, and she dreaded the familiar ending associated with departures like these. She wasn't alone. Amber, Tony, Marisa, and Carlo all looked like they just lost their best friend. Perhaps that description held more truth than fiction.

"Don't forget to call me as soon as you walk in the door, sweetie, okay?" Amber blubbered.

The tears were now flowing freely on both Rachel's and Amber's cheeks. Only two people in the group weren't adding to this tear pool, Tony and Carlo. Crying wasn't macho, so they just stood there and coughed.

"I will. I promise, Amber," Rachel sniffed. "I can't tell you how much being with all of you has meant to me. You're the only family I have since Mama and Papa died, and I didn't realize how much I needed all of you in my life. Life can deal you some pretty devastating situations, and if you don't have anyone with whom to share these experiences, I do believe they could drive you mad." Rachel sighed deeply and then proceeded to hug each of them with a special thanks to each for their part in making the trip such an enjoyable and memorable one. "Ciao, my sweet and loving friends. I love you with all my heart," cried Rachel as she presented her ticket to the airline attendant. "I'll call. God bless you," she murmured as she waved and walked out of sight.

As she stepped into the airplane, the attendant noticed the tears on Rachel's face.

"Are you all right? If you need anything, please let me know once you're seated."

Rachel was grateful and thanked the attendant for the warm and thoughtful gesture. She sat snugly in her seat next to the window, and as the 727 took off, Rachel looked out the window. The craft climbed high into the sky. Below, buildings, roads, cars, and people were shrinking by the second. Soon they were thousands of feet in the air. Rachel was on her way home. Even as she thought about Christian and their precious moments together, there was a spark of excitement about the prospect of getting home to her work, her friends, and hopefully, the resolution of the problems she left behind.

She closed her eyes and lay back in the seat. *What will I find when I land in Detroit?* Rachel thought. She hadn't heard a peep out of Corey since their last telephone conversation, and Blaise hadn't heard anything about him either. *He'll understand*, she mused. *It's my turn, and Corey has to understand, But would he?* Was she deluding herself in order to find some comfort in the midst of this terrible dilemma. She snacked on half a club sandwich and a salad that the flight attendants served almost immediately upon leveling off at about 32,000 feet. The two seats next to her were empty, and she reminisced about seeing young Randy's face for the first time, all covered with pink, sticky bubble gum.

As she finished her snack and wiped her hands and face with the cool wet napkin, she looked up just in time to see the "fasten your seat belt light" go out. She thought she'd go to the restroom, put on some fresh lipstick, and then rest for the remainder of the trip. Rachel was very slender, consequently she never had a problem with narrow aisles. She sort of walked from side to side, and the occasional movement of some turbulence caused her to stand still and wait until the motion stopped.

About halfway to the restroom, which was located between the galley and the business class section, she heard a familiar popping sound and quickly passed it off, thinking that other children chew bubble gum, and also, other noises could be responsible for that same sound. But just as she got to the door of the restroom, young Randy stood up since he, too, had to use the facilities, and there they stood once again.

"This is kismet," sighed young Randy. "That's the Arabic word for fate, cool lady."

Rachel gasped in disbelief.

"This is also incredible, sport," she exclaimed. "I didn't know you were returning home tonight."

"Well," said Randy, "initially we were going to stay for a few more days, but my dad was called back to perform a surgery that only he can handle."

By this time, Estelle had become aware of her son's conversation and recognized Rachel's distinctive and beautiful voice.

"So we meet again, Rachel," said Estelle. "I guess there is some sign of divine intervention going on here; it's unbelievable that we didn't even know one or the other was returning home, much less when."

Rachel noticed that Dr. Markham was dozing, and so she spoke softly to Estelle and young Randy.

"Maybe we can meet when the plane lands so that we can make some arrangements to get together soon," Rachel suggested.

"Great with me," expressed young Randy exuberantly. "Great with you, Mom?" he inquired of Estelle.

"By all means," Estelle responded, and with that, Rachel went to the restroom, returned to her seat, and closed her eyes, hoping to take advantage of this next hour or so with a nice nap.

Her lids were hardly closed when she drifted off into a somewhat deep sleep. It was so peaceful, so relaxing, and then, suddenly, her nightmare replayed. Faceless people scurrying about running through and around her. She searched for a face, for a familiar voice, and a clap of thunder shook her and she could feel the rain splashing on her face as she ran aimlessly looking, searching. She was stirring in the seat, and other passengers became aware of some moaning, so they rang for the flight attendant.

"We think that woman is experiencing some difficulty breathing," said the lady across the aisle from Rachel. The attendant leaned forward, standing over Rachel and gently putting her hand on Rachel's arm.

"Miss, are you all right?" she asked. "Are you okay?" She shook her arm gently. Rachel's face was wet with perspiration, and the attendant got a Kleenex and wiped her face. "Miss, Miss," called the attendant. "Wake up, you're having a bad dream." At that, Rachel awakened, surprised and confused about her whereabouts.

"Where am I?" she asked.

"It's all right, Miss," said the flight attendant, "you were having a bad dream. You're on an airplane heading for Detroit, Michigan.

"Do you recall taking this flight, Miss?"

Rachel replied a drowsy yes. She breathed deeply and finally began to focus on the face that was attached to that distant voice. As she became more conscious of the situation, she wiped her eyes firmly as though to assist in correcting her blurred and somewhat dimmed vision. Finally, Rachel saw the distinct features of the woman who was trying to help her.

"I apologize for my behavior," Rachel said softly. "Unfortunately, I have little control over these recurring sleep-related episodes."

"I'm just pleased that you're feeling better, Miss, uh, what is your name?" asked the attendant.

"Rachel, and yes, I'm feeling immeasurably better. Thank you for your kind assistance and concern." She smiled and began to straighten herself out. "My, my," she inquired, "how much further before we land in Detroit?"

"About another thirty minutes or so. Still plenty of time for me to get you some hot tea if you like."

Rachel declined graciously and again thanked her for being so wonderful during this whole situation.

"You're most welcome, Rachel. Please keep your seat belt fastened for the remainder of the flight. If you *do* need anything, just ring for one of us. Okay, Rachel?"

"You've been wonderful, and yes, I shall remain seated." And with that, Rachel looked out the window just in time to see the lights of the beautiful Detroit skyline. "Home," Rachel whispered, "I'm almost home," and she laid her head back and prepared herself for the landing.

Blaise was standing at the assigned gate making his usual observations of the number of the airport's coming and going passengers with their respective families and friends. He was as obvious as a pair of brown shoes in a room filled with tuxedoed men. His two-way reflection sun glasses coupled with an earring and coral Levi suit made it difficult to miss this tall image of a man. The smile on his face was beguiling, and almost without exception, every woman and child could be seen taking a second look at this striking person leaning up against one of the pillars. On the other hand, most of the men tried very hard not to look at him. And the more Blaise perceived this avoidance, the more visibly pleased he became. *It's a macho thing,* he thought. *I love it*, and he listened as the arriving flight from New York City was announced.

As they taxied toward the terminal, Rachel smiled when she saw the familiar surroundings of Detroit Metro. She began to ready herself to deplane. The attendant approached her and advised that she had asked for a wheelchair to get Rachel off the plane and into the terminal. At first, Rachel objected, but when she tried to stand up, her knees were noticeably shaky, and so she accepted the offer and sat back down to wait for the attendant's return with the chair.

Rachel knew that Blaise would be upset seeing her get off the plane in this manner. She thought about having him paged in order to prepare him, but it all happened so quickly once they got her in the chair, she didn't have time to control or prepare for the exit.

Blaise was probably the only person at the gate who didn't have to strain to see who was coming off the plane. A couple of parents with young children and then the flight attendant pushing a wheelchair with—with—oh, my God!

"Ray babe," he said loudly, as he excused himself, moving past several other waiting people. He got through them quickly and knelt beside the wheelchair and his returning friend. "Ray babe, what's wrong? Are you all right? What happened?" he blurted out with a look of terror on his face that brought immediate tears to Rachel's eyes.

"I'm all right, Blaise. I'm all right dear heart." And she hugged him and breathed a sigh of relief that she was once again in the care of her loving friend.

The flight attendant asked if Blaise would like to wheel her to wherever his mode of transportation was located, and over strong objections from Rachel, he agreed it would be best. The attendant filled him in briefly on what had transpired, and Blaise was most appreciative for their great care of his precious Rachel.

"Cool, that's what you are, Ms. Flight Attendant."

He reached in his pocket and pulled out a fifty-dollar bill and proceeded to hand it to the attendant, who refused it and assured Blaise that what she and others on the flight had done for Rachel fell strictly within the framework of their duties.

"I know and I'm grateful, but I'll bet good money that there's nothing in your service manual or code of ethics that prevents you from accepting a gift from a very grateful customer" He grinned and put the bill in her hand. "Believe me, Miss, it's little price to pay for such a good deed." Blaise thanked her again, and Rachel also expressed her gratitude for all the fine assistance.

For some of the other people standing around waiting for the passengers to deplane, this was a real show. This guy in a pink suit picking up a beautiful woman in a wheelchair would provide some great conversation for all of them.

After Blaise picked up Rachel's luggage and managed to situate her in a place where she would be comfortable until he got the limo up to the closest door, he scurried about, making certain that all was ready for her to just step into the car, and then he'd have accomplished what he set out to do from early that morning.

As Rachel sat and watched the people pass in front of her, she looked at the faces of as many people she could, trying to possibly match a face with that of Christian. It never worked, and she then decided that it wouldn't ever happen, since his face was unique, so handsome, so expressive. Obviously, she was seeing him through the eyes of love.

Soon, Blaise returned and exuberantly exclaimed that their limo was waiting. He pushed her toward the exit door, which opened as they broke the field of the automatic eye. The weather was balmy for September, and a gentle breeze passed softly over her face and through her hair. Blaise and the limo driver were now both at her side, assisting her out of the wheelchair and into the back seat of that luxurious limo. She sighed and leaned back into the plush cushions. By then, Blaise had taken the wheelchair back into the airport, tipped the sky porter for handling the luggage and placing it in the car and then folded himself into the limo alongside Rachel.

"There, Ray babe, we're all set for the trip home." The limo driver closed the window between him and his passengers and drove away from the airport and toward the Ford Expressway, which would take them eastbound to Grosse Pointe. The ride home was relaxing and quiet. Because Blaise sensed that the departure from New York plus the continuing recurrence of Rachel's nightmare was more than enough for her to cope with tonight, he didn't ask about the trip or Rachel's plans now that she was back home.

When the limo driver pulled up to their Grosse Pointe duplex, Rachel smiled and heaved a sigh of relief upon seeing her home and the neighborhood she loved so dearly. Blaise was his usual attentive self and all but carried Rachel from the curb to her front door.

"Welcome home, Ray babe. Welcome to your waiting abode. You'll be happy to see that everything is as you left it. Neat, clean, and exceedingly organized. Only a few additional items are missing," he said slyly.

"Missing?" mused Rachel as she looked around at each piece of furniture and wall decoration. All of which appeared to be present and accounted for. "I don't see anything missing, Blaise; whatever are you referring to?"

"Well," responded Blaise with his usual flair. "Only a few dozen floral arrangements from some religious fanatic in New York who just signs, 'yours always, Christian.' I mean, gee whiz, Ray babe, where did you meet this pedestrian? Obviously, he must have some heavy bread, because you don't buy those posies he sent with a few sous."

"Oh, Blaise, you're too funny. Christian is his name not his religious conviction." She grinned. "What posies are we talking about? And for goodness sake, Blaise, please talk English—'heavy bread?' 'a few sous?'—if you want to know the facts, just ask me!"

His striking blue eyes lit up, and a great smile developed across that marvelously handsome face.

"So you like this dude?—a gentleman, huh? Is that what you're trying to tell me, Ray?" He cocked his head to one side and raised his eyebrows waiting for her response.

"Yes, dear heart, I like this gentleman, and in fact, I'm in love with him," she said with a certain degree of assuredness that Blaise had never before witnessed.

"Really, Ray?" he quizzed. "The big L word at this stage of the game?

How long an acquaintance are we talking? A few days? A few hours?"

"I know it sounds a bit impulsive and, oh, so incredibly quick, but after just a few hours and a couple of brief conversations, I truly felt like I knew him for a very long time. You'd definitely like him, Blaise," she said proudly. "You and he are perhaps the only first-class men I've ever met in my entire life."

Blaise's eyes lit up, and he looked at her with such affection and appreciation. He stammered as he proceeded to address that compliment.

"Ray babe, everyone should have someone who views them in such high esteem. Your description of me in comparison to your new love is just about the most wonderful and touching thing anyone has ever said about me, and I luv ya for being that special someone for me."

He bent his head as though overcome by overwhelming emotion, and Rachel responded by interjecting that these feelings should not come as a shock to him; she had always held him in the highest esteem.

"It's not every woman who's fortunate enough to have Sir Galahad as a neighbor, and I'm just a little surprised that you never realized my high regard for you before this, Blaise!" She looked to see if he had contained himself enough to at least smile a little at the comparison.

Blaise was always up for the magnificent humor that Rachel displayed when things got either too serious or too emotional, and he responded likewise.

"Well, Ray babe, I'm not exactly sure what dude said it, but it goes something like this: 'Once a king, always a king. Once a prince, always a prince, but once a knight is enough!'" He laughed and she joined in, and they hugged each other like the good friends they'd always been over the years.

When the excitement of being home calmed down a bit, Rachel told Blaise about Christian Avian and her enjoyable time in New York. The pizza and six-pack of beer was soon consumed, and as so frequently happens, time passed very quickly and before they knew it, it was midnight.

"Thanks, Blaise for picking me up at the airport earlier this evening. Thanks for the pizza and beer, and thanks for letting me bend your ears with my exaltations of love and romance. I hope I didn't bore you to death, sweetie!"

"This guy's pretty wonderful from the way you've described him to me. My only concern, Ray, is that maybe it's happening too soon after Corey." He chose his next words very carefully. "I just wouldn't want you to get hurt again in a situation that looks a lot like a rebound relationship."

Rachel wasn't upset with Blaise's perceptions at all, since she had thought strongly about that possibility and even discussed it with Amber.

"You're right on about how wonderful he is, Blaise, and I guess, I'm describing him in the best possible light because I love him. However, I've looked at the possibility of a rebound situation, and, Blaise, I can honestly say I've never felt about anyone the way I feel about Christian. Certainly, I've never even come close to these feelings with Corey."

"Okay, doll, I hear ya loud and clear, and I just hope that he sees the same happy ending that you do. I'm more than a little weary of yet another disappointment in your life, Ray babe."

"I guess only time will tell, and you've got to know, Blaise, I'm giving this relationship my best shot. This time I'm not only going for the brass ring, I'm going for the gold," she insisted.

"Then do it, go for it, and I'll be there to see that you succeed. Your happiness means the world to me, Ray babe, and if orange blossoms and turtle doves are what you're aiming for, I'm the copilot who'll get you to that target whenever you say it's time."

"You're one in a million, dear heart," Rachel continued. "My life these past few years would have been a living hell without your support and guidance, Blaise." She reached over and embraced him. He hugged her back, and suddenly, there was an awareness that was new—and strange.

Rachel, for the very first time in her and Blaise's long relationship, felt a glimmer of excitement in his embrace, and as though she transmitted her thoughts directly to him, Blaise found himself holding her more tightly and began to place his face in the soft curvature of her neck. His heart was beating furiously, and in a moment of clear sanity, Rachel pushed away to look up at her friend's somewhat confused and fearful expression.

"What's going on here?" asked Rachel as she broke the silence that hovered around them.

"Beats me, babe, I think we're both caught up in the emotional excitement you've been describing. Sorry, Ray, if I got a little carried away. Uh, I don't know what came over me," he stuttered.

"Well, Blaise, you certainly don't have anything to apologize for. I'm equally guilty for this bizarre episode. I can't imagine how we got to this point, but I think we should step back and return to my finishing up about the New York City saga. What do you say, Blaise?" she asked.

"Sounds all right to me, Ray babe," he stammered, "but first, I think we should pop the cork on this bottle of champagne and toast your new found romance."

The events of the trip and her return home were more than a bit draining, and when Rachel apologized for all of the imposition she had put Blaise through, he was quick to retort.

"Nonsense, Ray babe," he said. "I said I'd be here for you, and here I'll be whenever and for however long you need me." He smiled. "But I'm getting ready for a few z's myself, and I think it's time we put this day and ourselves to bed? Agreed?"

"Thanks, dear heart, I'll talk to you in the morning. I don't think I'll get right back to work. I'm going to rest a bit before I jump back into work again."

After Blaise kissed her forehead and uttered some last-minute comments about a hot bath, hot tea, and bed, in that order, he was out the door and Rachel was, once again, alone. Alone, but not lonely, for certainly, her immediate thoughts of Christian provided all the company she'd need until their next meeting.

Blaise entered his apartment with his hands filled with empty beer cans, a half-bottle of champagne, and six pieces of some now rather old looking pizza. He couldn't forget about all the floral pieces that he hadn't given to Rachel, since they smelled like a floral shop or conservatory.

After he had disposed of all the paraphernalia left from their rather bohemian-style dinner, Blaise sat down on his Corinthian leather sofa and observed each floral piece and its attendant card. *What an appropriate name*, he thought—*Christian! Well, it's certainly better than Messiah or Allah.* He chuckled to himself.

But the humor he tried to add to this situation was defused by his puzzled underlying feelings of rejection, or maybe even twinges of jealousy.

He leaned back and scratched his head. As he stared almost unfocused into space, he replayed the embrace of Rachel a few short minutes ago and wondered what it all meant. Was this the time he would share his well-kept secret with Rachel? Was he ready for the problems this declaration would unleash? *Timing, in life, is everything*, he thought *and if I wait any longer, I may miss the very opportunity developing at this moment.* "Oh, Rachel," he exclaimed, "how will I tell you I've been deceiving you? When I explain why I had to carry out the facade, will you understand the reasons why and the hoped-for outcome?"

He could feel her in his arms, and this time it wasn't the usual huggy-kissy embrace they always shared; he felt her excitement, or at least he thought it was excitement. The worst thing that could happen would be his misreading her feelings and gestures. A wrong move at this time could lose her to Christian or someone else, forever!

He took off his coral Levi jacket and looked in the huge mirror that covered three-fourths of his living room wall. "Who are you really, Blaise Kinley?

"Right now," he continued, "you're two people: the person everyone thinks you are, that is, the good-looking, successful, wealthy Grosse Pointe homosexual and the person you really are. Blaise Kinley, designer, heterosexual, and one very much in love with your next door neighbor, Rachel Radcliffe—although only I and my shadow know it.

"This is craziness," he uttered. "If I profess my feelings and disclose my true sexual preference at this time, I may lose her because I lied, or I may lose her because the declaration was too late. It seems like she really does love Christian."

Maybe this very well-kept secret should remain just that—a secret. This relationship that germinated and grew so quickly might fall equally as quickly. In any case, it was much too late to do anything about it tonight. Ray babe was home and well, and tomorrow always had a way of assisting in the decisions of design and destiny. "Enough, is enough!" he exclaimed. "To bed and to rest." And with that, Blaise shed the coral Levi's and hopped into the freshly made-up bed between two cool and crisp cotton percale sheets. With his hand resting on the extravagant down feather cushions, he drifted off into a deep and most welcomed sleep. "God bless us one and all," he mouthed in prayer. "Please direct me on the path of Rachel's love." He bowed his head and was asleep shortly thereafter.

As Rachel awakened to her very familiar surroundings, she missed those miniblinds in Amber Domani's home that let in only a smattering of light and she missed the detectable smell of freshly perked coffee and toasted English muffins. Still, it was good to be home. She bounced out of bed, motivated by the thought that she would have to arrange to get her Grosse Pointe life in order and determine what changes would have to occur if she and Christian were going to get together some time soon.

Why, Rachel mused, *can't I use the word "married?" Oh boy, Mama, I'm having a real hard time trying to accept that possibility at this stage in my life. You and Papa seemed so unified always. Why didn't some of that closeness rub off on me?* She could hear Mama DeRoca pontificating about how everything that she and Papa had accomplished was because they did things "according to the book." Rachel could remember vividly thinking, *What book? Was there a journal of how to live that only grown-ups had access to?* Mama would smile and say, "Anything worthwhile in life is worth the sacrifice."

Boy, how I wish I could have understood the analogy and reasoning for all of those sayings! Rachel thought. *Maybe if I had asked more questions, I would be better prepared now to accept this new role developing in my life. But Mama was always citing plaudits and adages which made sense to her, but never to me. Mama would always end one of these sessions with "you understand, don't you sweetie?" And I was always too ashamed to say no. I think Mama believed I was possessed of adult comprehension shortly after I turned ten, and from that time on, dealt with the awkwardness of being socially accepted and a menstrual cycle that Mama called "puberty." What a terrible sounding word. All in all, every time I get anywhere near a close relationship with a man, a certain apprehension rears its ugly head, and the analytical process begins!*

What was different about Christian and this relationship? she thought. For one thing he was so totally independent. His success was most attractive and the air of security and first-class opulence presented a comfort she'd never experienced. Rachel had always taken care of herself. She had graduated from college and the sacrifices and disappointments still lived vividly in her memory. Perhaps their independence put them on common ground initially. As she analyzed Christian's other attributes, she certainly couldn't overlook his sensitive and caring nature where children are concerned. His nephew, Randy, was an excellent example of that, as were her own personal observations of his interactions with Carlo and Marisa.

And there was this magnetic quality about Christian that intrigued Rachel. One couldn't discount his handsome face and the tall and lean body that represented everything she'd always imagined of her dream man. The one thing that certainly couldn't be denied were the number of years' difference in their ages. Twelve years was a lot for some couples, but she always felt she was older than her years, which made for equality in their maturity level. Bottom line, though, was an excitement in the chemistry they shared from the first moment their eyes met.

Even now, as she thought about being in his arms, feeling his closeness, and even smelling his fragrance as she snuggled her head in his shoulder, caused her heart to race and goose bumps to rise all over her. She could only imagine anything else more intimate, and her temperature rose as those thoughts crossed and lingered in her mind. Once again, she recalled their hands touching for the first time and the sparks she felt that she had never before experienced. This must be love.

As she then began to think about all that must be done before any future with Christian became a reality, she thought about the unfinished business with Corey. Then, though she tried desperately to quell any thoughts about what happened with Blaise earlier tonight, she focused on those brief moments in Blaise's arms. Was something going on between her and Blaise? Why wasn't she ever aware of anything like this before now?

"He's always been gay since the day we met," she said out loud. "although, in all the time I've known him, he's never once mentioned a lover or even intimated that he was involved with anyone." She sighed. "what about all of those trips to New York and San Francisco? Were they merely business trips?" All of a sudden Rachel began to realize that the only persons who'd ever mentioned his homosexuality were Blaise and Corey. Strange that she never paid any particular attention to it before. But then, he said he publicly declared that he was "coming out of the closet" at a social function attended by his parents, which caused the riff between them. However, Rachel wasn't there. Blaise told her about that episode.

Why must everything in my life supposedly be coming to a head all at one time? she thought. Perhaps this was a midlife crisis of sorts and not that unusual at all. She was getting more tired by the moment and finally donned her "I Love Michigan" nightshirt and got into her own very comfortable bed. It didn't take long to drift off to sleep. She needed rest, and it looked like this would be the night for it.

Back in New York, in his brownstone Christian lay awake staring at the moon that shone so brightly through his bedroom window. He too reminisced about the past ten days and fantasized that Rachel was there beside him, holding him close to her as they slept. His emotions intensified, and he smiled as he thrilled to this newly found excitement in his life. He continued to think about her until he too fell asleep.

This night had presented peace and tranquility for almost everyone. But Corey Davidson was not sleeping. He had been upset over the last conversation he had with Rachel and could not understand why he hadn't heard anything further from her since their last phone conversation. This was not what usually happened in the past, and this change in Rachel's behavior was causing him some uneasy and uncertain days. He tried to call the Domanis several times but only got their answering machine. He knew the only other person who would know anything about Rachel's plans was Blaise, and he'd die before he'd call him.

"If I don't hear anything tomorrow," he said. "I'm going to get in touch with that fruitcake! Enough is enough. I've played Mr. Nice Guy long enough, and now I'm ready to play hardball." Corey was more than angry, he was frustrated and stressed out. None of his other "friends" had been available, and Mr. Macho was getting a bit uptight. *Not for long,* he thought. *I'm not giving you up without a fight, kitten!* "You loved me once, and I'll make you love me again," he said confidently. He sat down to watch some TV and finally gave up and went to bed.

The new day and week in Grosse Pointe was as uneventful as any other recently, except Rachel had developed a new resolve, and her approach to everything in her life was changing dramatically. She was glad she had decided to take Monday off. A glass of orange juice and an English muffin spread lightly with raspberry jam tasted scrumptious; the instant coffee, however, could never match the freshly perked coffee served daily at the Domani residence. Rachel no sooner thought that, when the telephone rang. She answered it after the second ring.

"Hello," she sang out.

"Good morning, doll," Amber responded. "How's my girl today?" Rachel was so happy to hear from her.

"Oh Amber, I do miss you so already."

"Well," Amber replied, "I was just beginning to put my schedule together for today, and I suddenly thought back to last week when you first arrived. You were so upset about the breakup with Corey and so anxious just to get away from everything for a few days. Now, it's almost two weeks, and I can't believe how much has happened during that time."

Rachel sighed deeply and agreed with her friend on all counts.

"It's strange, Amber, how closely you and I still think. It's almost as though I transmitted those very thoughts to you earlier this morning." Amber smiled and then asked Rachel if she'd heard from Corey since she returned to Grosse Pointe.

"No, I haven't and I'm surprised that I haven't. Blaise hasn't heard from him either. But Corey wouldn't call Blaise unless he thought I wasn't ever coming back. I thought he would have called me at your house, Amber, so I'm puzzled but really relieved. I didn't want to get involved in a rehash before I left for New York. And while Corey's rather sympathetic call while I was in New York really got me to think about my own contribution to the failure of that relationship, I'm still too vulnerable to him, and I don't want anything unpleasant to disturb all my wonderful and new-found feelings for Christian." Rachel summed up briefly her return to Grosse Pointe and then told Amber that there was an unexpected episode with Blaise.

"Unexpected? What?" asked Amber. "Is Blaise all right, Rachel? I don't know what I'd do if something happened to him. He's been your protector and my secret insurance policy for your security and well being."

"No, he's fine, Amber, and I thank God for his presence and caring nature. But something happened yesterday that gave me pause, and perhaps you may be able to shed some light on it for me." Rachel told Amber about the events that led up to the embrace that seemed so natural, so right at the time. She told about the excitement that occurred when Blaise evidenced a distinct sense of urgency during their shared moment of closeness.

There was a pause in the conversation, and Amber expressed not surprise, but rather amazement at it all.

"You know, Rachel, I guess I've always perceived that Blaise's feelings for you were deep-rooted, and I must admit that when you made me aware of the fact that he was gay, I never gave it a second thought; however, there was always this glimmer of doubt since I never heard or saw him involved with anyone at any of our functions over the years. Until your mentioning it just now, I just believed that he'd be there for you if you needed someone. How did this whole situation end up, Rachel?"

Rachel's response was not any different than what Amber anticipated.

"It went nowhere, because when I became aware of the difference in this particular embrace, I asked Blaise what was going on. Problem is, Amber, he wasn't the only one participating. Why did I suddenly feel this emotional stirring within me?" Rachel asked, almost desperately.

"Well, I'm certain it was all very innocent and occurred because of the intensity of your recap of the events that led you to a wonderfully new and exciting romance"

"I do hope and pray that that's all it was," Rachel admitted, "because if I've inadvertently led Blaise to believe that there was anything more to my feelings for him, then Corey Davidson would be totally justified in making me aware of the mixed signals he was receiving from me during our rather long and somewhat arduous relationship." Rachel sighed deeply, but Amber was not going to permit her friend to conclude that these so called "mixed signals" were somehow a part of her interaction with the males in her life.

"Look, doll," Amber stressed "because of the very traumatic course of events over the past several months, anything is possible. Corey could have desired you so much that he envisioned only what he wanted to see, and we all know it wouldn't be the first time that he manipulated or devised a set of circumstances that forced you, either intentionally or otherwise, into a position you may not have chosen had you had more time or felt freer to express your opinion.

"What you have to guard against, sweetie, is letting Corey continue to direct your movements or make you suspicious of your recent motivations and involvements with other interests in your life. I think you should sit down with Blaise while this is fresh in both your minds and ask him directly what he was thinking about or, at least, what events led up to this moment."

Rachel was nodding her head in agreement with her friend.

"You're right on, Amber, I will ask Blaise, and in the meantime, I, too, will do some soul-searching about my part in all of this."

"Before we go any further, doll," continued Amber, "what if Blaise were not gay, and what if you did not meet Christian and fell in love with him? Have you ever thought about that?" Amber sat back and waited for Rachel's response.

"That's ludicrous, Amber, if I can't even make a distinction between my friends and lovers, then how will I ever be able to make any distinctions about anything? I can't believe I wouldn't have picked up on something in Blaise's behavior that would have signaled a change in the relationship. Am I that naive and unobservant about these things? I don't know, Amber, I'm beginning to question all my relationships, romantic or otherwise, and the possibility for doubt is crowding my ability to think clearly."

"That's nonsense, Rachel and I doubt that you should be feeling all these negative things just because of one unexplained incident. My God, Rachel, he didn't seduce you. Did he? It was, for all intent and purposes, a moment shared by two people who are friends and very sensitive to one another's feelings and emotions. Let it go at that, and be done with it!" Amber concluded.

"You're absolutely right. Why should I analyze every move and every feeling in a relationship of such long and predictable experiences?" Rachel appeared convinced that any further pursuit into this situation could compromise her and Blaise's relationship. "Thanks, Amber, for once again being my voice of reason." Rachel was satisfied with their mutual explanation. She then asked about Tony, Carlo, and Marisa.

"They're all just wonderful as ever, and, oh yes, doll, Carlo and Marisa are scheduled to audition for 'Cinema' next week. Christian has called twice, and I think they're convinced that they shouldn't pass up this wonderful opportunity."

Rachel was ecstatic on hearing this news and decided that it would give her a good reason to call Christian, not that she needed one, but she would do so right after her conversation with Amber was over.

Monday of the new week had started off with a bang at Avian Productions. The announcement in *Variety* about the upcoming auditions for

Christian's new play "Cinema" had caused a stir in theater circles, and the phones were ringing off the hook with calls from hopeful actors, some seasoned and others, aspirants in this career. The struggle was extensive and the opportunities minimal. Only a few would be cast, and while rejection becomes a part of any actor's life, the acceptance and adjustment was never easy.

As Christian paced the floor of his downstairs office and looked seriously at the lists and sketches drawn the day before, his thoughts were mixed. This show, no different than any of his others, would demand his total focus and commitment. Yet, this time, he seemed to be more energetic, more enthusiastic. In fact, his whole demeanor had changed since he found himself in the grasp of that mystical, magical thing called love. Even the people closest to him noticed the obvious lift in his spirit and voice. For Christian, it was therapeutic as well, for he no longer dwelled in the sadness of the past eight years after losing Tia.

He thought more about his nephew, Randy, and his sister, Estelle. The family unit took on more meaning with the prospect of starting one himself. And of course there was Rachel. "Oh, Rachel, my darling Rachel, the distance between us, though temporary, strongly emphasizes and increases my intense longing for you to be at my side," Christian whispered to himself. "Think of me, my love, and hopefully our thoughts will blend until we're together again." Even the thrill of just thinking about her energized his resolve to embark on putting together this new show.

Nine

While school was always a snap for young Randall Markham, he found a great deal of joy in both the education process and the ability to add gobs of knowledge to that holding tank, called his brain.

University Liggett's revered reputation was augmented by its staff and its hallowed halls. Young Grosse Pointe children were being prepped for all the major universities in the world. The plan for Randy Markham was no different; however, this young man's brain was extraordinary, and the university and its immediate environs took on a new bent with this young man in its presence.

Randy jumped off his ten-speed bike and parked it next to his friend Mitch's spot.

"Hi, dude," the salutary chant around the campus.

"Hey, man," was Mitch's response.

"What's up?" asked Randy.

"Nothin', man," responded Mitch. Randy and Mitch walked toward the entrance, zigzagging in and out of the constant stream of cars, which were dropping off other students.

"Whatcha do on your trip?" asked Mitch.

"Primo thing is I think I found myself a new aunt."

"Were you on a picnic or something?" asked Mitch "I didn't know you were into entomology." Randy laughed out loud.

"Not ant," he explained. "Aunt that's opposite of uncle, you know!"

"Oh, said Mitch, "I didn't know you were looking for one."

Randy refreshed Mitch's memory about his Aunt Tia dying when he was very small. He briefly described his one and only Uncle Christian and then proceeded to fill Mitch in on his encounter with "the cool lady."

"She sounds like a fox," said Mitch, his eyes rolling.

"She is, my friend, she is, and I think I did a masterful job of getting them together."

By this time, they had arrived at their respective lockers and checked the bulletin board for any schedules that involved either their swimming or soccer teams. They agreed to meet after school and ride down to the park afterwards and practice some soccer moves.

Randy's concentration in social studies was distracted by yet another plan, the scheme to keep Rachel Radcliffe in the family spotlight. University Liggett's annual auction was coming up in a few days, and Estelle Markham was the cochairman this year. If Rachel were to contribute some of her Wardrobe Coordination Services as a major prize, that would give Estelle Markham more than enough reason to invite Rachel to their home and perhaps even prompt a weekend lunch or two.

The biggest part of this grand plan was to somehow get his Uncle Christian to attend the auction ball at the Grosse Pointe Yacht Club a week from Saturday night. Randy knew the only thing he had to entice his uncle with was the cool lady. So after school, he'd ask his mom to call Rachel and solicit her contribution and participation in this worthy cause. The proceeds from this annual auction were donated to Mott Children's Hospital in Ann Arbor.

Rachel finally got a moment to sit and ponder her call to Christian. She had the perfect entrée. She missed him. Add to that the news that Carlo and Marisa had accepted his invitation to audition and she was motivated enough to pick up the phone and began to dial.

"Avian Productions," the receptionist answered.

"Mr. Christian Avian, please."

"Thank you," responded the receptionist.

"Christian Avian here, may I help you."

"You certainly may," responded Rachel laughingly. "You may help me to get past this terrible emptiness in my life since we parted a couple of days ago."

The expression on Christian's face reflected his excitement at hearing Rachel's voice.

"Certainly, madame, may I suggest a quick trip to the airport, a short flight to JFK, and a very long and passionate embrace followed by your own personal fantasy!"

Rachel half smiled and half-yearned to drop everything and follow his directions to a tee.

"Perhaps that will happen sooner than you think. With the auditions now scheduled to start in a couple of weeks, it won't be long until I get on a plane and fly to your side," Rachel answered. "Until then, my love, the telephone will be the 'tie that binds' and our very own way to reach out and touch one another."

"Bravo, dear heart, methinks, besides being blessed with a sharp wit, you've got promotional talents as well. Shall I call my friend at AT&T and advise him that my love overtures have been 'prone to please' lately?" Christian was amused at his own poetic comedy.

"Oh, oh, now," Rachel responded. " 'Tis you, m'lord, who's a poet and know it." They laughed, and Christian was happy to be able to have some fun and kid around again. It was invigorating and wonderful.

"You're getting more beautiful by the minute, Rachel," he chided.

"Okay," she responded, "just how could you say that? Do you have caller identification and video transmission capabilities?"

"Of course, my love," he continued, "while you were here I had my secret agents in Grosse Pointe install a minicamera on your telephone."

"Well, it mustn't be working too well, because I've got an inch of cream on my face and my hair's up in rollers. I don't exactly look like Scarlett O'Hara," she mused.

"To me, my love, you will always be beautiful no matter what you're wearing." There was a brief pause and then they both broke out laughing.

"Is this conversation for real, or what?" Rachel asked, with a grin still on her lips and a lilt in her voice.

"I think these lines were spoken in a play I wrote once a very long time ago," Christian added. "But as corny as that must sound, I do truly mean every word. You are and will always be my cool and beautiful lady."

Rachel's heart sang with joy. She was elated to be so blessed with this wonderful man in her life who only saw her through the eyes of love. *This has to be the pinnacle of my life*, she thought.

"I love you, Christian Avian, for a million reasons that I'll enumerate one by one some time in our future. Among these are your most complimentary praises of my looks and the expressed depth of your capacity to love little ole me."

Christian's eyes became blurred with the joy and emotion that Rachel evoked in him. His body and soul were alive again. His senses were keen, and his desire for her was intense and anxious.

"I'll look forward to that time when you and I can both enumerate the things we love about one another, but I must be honest, my darling, my first thought is of our opportunity to make love and to be able to express totally our commitment to that deep and abiding love." Christian's desire was rising quickly, and he chided her about the safety of 600 miles.

"This is my dream as well, and while you may describe the 600-mile distance between us as some safe haven, I can assure you, my darling, that being in your arms is the only haven I'm seeking!" Rachel could feel the heat in her face as she blushed listening to herself. "Well, Christian, I will let you return to your show. I must get going and return to the world of the gainfully employed. I miss you and love you."

"And I love and miss you, my darling. I'll call you real soon," he said.

"Whew," she gasped, "conversations with Christian certainly can produce a lot of energy and heat." *He's a fox!* she thought. *No one else can inspire and stir such passion in me.* Her imagination was getting way too active, and she went into her kitchen, took a glass from the cupboard, filled it with ice and then water. She drank the entire glass of water and sat down as the cool water quieted some of the inner warmth. "A glass of ice water to quell these feelings is like using a squirt gun to put out a raging inferno." As she sat and reveled in this new emotional tidal wave, she calmed herself by saying things to herself like, "It's all right, Rachel, it's the middle of the day, stop this nonsense. Cool it! cool lady, let's not start something you can only imagine—let's wait for the whole enchilada." She laughed and went about the business of tidying up and making up a new to-do list for tomorrow's return to the real world—a work day.

Corey's disposition had only gotten worse during the past few days, and he was upset that Rachel had not seen fit to call him after his candid declaration of love during their last phone conversation. The one high in his life was the increased business at Davidson & Jacoby. For whatever reason, new business was suddenly in vogue, and word of mouth traveled quickly in the megabuck circles of Grosse Pointe. Many of the residents who lived in the Farms and Shores were bankers, professionals, and just plain wealthy people, who no longer worked, but merely invested in money-making propositions. The professional office and industrial plazas had multiplied with the exodus from Detroit in the late sixties and early seventies, and the relocated businesses were now expanding and spreading their markets. If Corey's personal life were a bit more settled, yet exciting, he would be the perfect example of a man who has everything.

"I'm going to try her at home one more time before I have to talk to that powder puff next door," he exclaimed. He dialed Rachel's number and listened to the first and second ring.

"Hello," Rachel sang out.

"Kitten," uttered Corey half-surprised that she was home, "you're home. When did you get back?"

"Oh, Corey, I got home yesterday," she replied. "How are you?"

"How nice of you to be concerned," he responded curtly. "Why, may I ask, did you not see fit to let me know you were returning?"

"Well, so many things were going on, and when I made the rather spontaneous decision to come home, I called Blaise and he met me at the airport. You sound a little perturbed, Corey. Are we still at odds with one another?" she asked sternly.

"I guess as much as I wanted to believe that this falling out we had a few weeks ago would pass, it really hasn't and I'm finding myself always on the defensive for something I didn't do."

"You know, Corey, I don't believe either of us has had enough time to examine our feelings with respect to that incident, and I'm not totally strong enough to continue this exchange. So, if you'll forgive my abruptness, I don't wish to offend you, but I'm going to end this conversation while I can still be civil."

"No, wait, Rachel, don't hang up," he said almost pleadingly. Rachel listened and said nothing. "I can't seem to do anything right in this situation, and I want to be able to get it straightened out! Do you not wish to talk to me at all anymore, kitten?" He didn't care that he slipped and called her that, and Rachel's nature to be sympathetic toward any such expression of dismay made her calm down.

"No, Corey, I'm not saying I never want to talk to you or see you again. I'm merely saying that we need time to think and let this situation calm down. I hear the anxiety and anger in your voice, and I can't handle the negativity. At the risk of being repetitious, you know how these things affect me. I'm sorry you're struggling with the separation, but I can't keep rehashing the whys and wherefores any longer." She paused and held back tears. "Please, please, Corey, give me some time and space. But also understand, I want to get on with my life, and what we shared once is no longer there for me. I can't be anything other than truthful with you, Corey, so please don't make it any more difficult than it is for both of us. Let me go."

He hung his head and sighed deeply.

"All right, Rachel, I'll give you some time and space, but I don't know if I can let you go. I love you, kitten." With that Corey began to weep. Rachel could hear his sobbing and could not then hold back her own emotions.

"Please don't do this, Corey. I'm sorry for the hurt I've caused you. I'm sorry for all the things I should have said and didn't, and I'm sorry that we're not going to end up as you imagined, but it's just not there for me." She coughed a little and excused herself.

Corey had had a few moments to compose himself.

"I've always admired your honesty, Rachel. Even during the toughest days with Neil, you were always consistent in your direction and what it would take to reach your ultimate goal. I never imagined that your honesty would somehow cut me so deeply," he said. "I guess I've been deluding myself into believing that you'd change and eventually would love me as I love you. It's very difficult to imagine my life without you in it."

"It doesn't have to be like that, Corey," Rachel explained. "I never suggested we couldn't be friends. Do you think we might still be friends, Corey?"

There was an even longer silence and, finally, Corey spoke.

"If that's what you want kitten, and that's all I can expect, I guess it will have to do. Can we, at least have dinner some time and just chitchat?"

"I don't see why not," Rachel responded, "but let's give it some time, okay, Corey?"

"All right, then, I'll call you next week, kitten, and in the meantime, I hope you'll try to find it in your heart to forgive my outbursts and bad behavior, which, obviously has lost any possibility of love for us," Corey said apologetically.

"Corey," Rachel said, "I can forgive, if you will as well, and let's leave it at that, okay?"

They agreed, said good-bye, and hung up the phone.

Corey put down the receiver and put his head into his cupped hands. Defeat and rejection were things he never handled well. This man rarely lost at anything. Coping was one thing. Failure, as it would be seen by others, was something altogether different. His overtures about how he and Rachel would marry someday were like bitter pills that he'd been forced to eat, and he'd do it. For Corey, winning was always the only option. The means never bothered him. This time would be different. The only confidante that Rachel would have now was Blaise. Corey's stomach turned just thinking about this so-called man next door. As he thought about this the enmity between them riled him all over again.

Back at Rachel's apartment, there was a knock on her door.

"Who is it?" she called out.

"It's only me, your friendly flower-covered neighbor," Blaise responded.

Rachel opened the door to a flower-filled hallway and Blaise's face amongst a bunch of mums and sunflowers.

"These, dear lady, are the ones that lived for four days in my somewhat oxygen-drained living room!"

Rachel laughed and began to look at the many cards attached to twenty or so arrangements of every size and species imaginable.

"I like this one the best," chuckled Blaise, as he read the card.

" 'Roses are red,
Sunflowers are yellow.
You'll recall what I said,
I wanna be your fellow.'

"Really, Ray babe, *this* from a man who is the director of the year? Puleeeze!" he chided. "And this is the pièce de résistance.

" 'You're like a carnation,
So fragrant and pretty.
I hate this separation,
Hurry back to New York City.'

"Be still, my heart; this man will never be a threat to Shelley or Keats."
Rachel hadn't stopped laughing. Blaise was always at his best when he could make her smile. Finally, she raised her hand.
"Stop it, oh, please, Blaise, that's enough. My goodness Blaise, when you mentioned a few floral arrangements, I had no idea there were so many," she remarked, almost apologetically. "Whatever shall I do with them?"
"I have an idea," responded Blaise. The smile on his face and the expression in his eyes led Rachel to believe that it wasn't nice.
"Now, now, Blaise, let's not be nasty. After all, Christian was just trying to let me know how much he misses and loves me."
"Well," Blaise said in an exasperated manner, "he could have flown here and been waiting on your doorstep for a heck of a lot less, or how about skywriting? It worked well for the witch in the Wizard of Oz."
"All kidding aside, Blaise, perhaps you and I could take some of them over to Saint John's children's ward and to a few nursing homes. How about it?"
"Sounds like a wonderful idea. Maybe I'll be able to wake up one morning without feeling like I've been transported to the Garden of Eden. Let's do it, Ray babe. I'll get the car, and we can start right now."
"All right, but not before I remove every card and take a look at each and every one, so I'll be able to thank Christian for them soon."
"It may be Thursday by the time you finish, but I'll finish my glass of chardonnay and take one last whiff of all those hundreds of roses before they're gone forever." Blaise put his hand to his forehead and walked, as

though offstage, to his adjoining apartment to wait for Rachel's completion of this card-gathering task.

She couldn't believe how many times she read "I love you" on all these cards. This overabundance of beautiful floral arrangements made her heart swell.

As Blaise sat on his leather sofa, sipping his chardonnay, he felt a twinge of jealousy as he looked, hopefully for the last time, at all of these arrangements and wondered what they had to mean to Rachel.

I guess, I'm too late, he thought. *One trip and one romance too late.* Blaise sighed and thought about all the opportunities now past and lost to him forever. His secret may forever remain just that. A half-hour or so passed, and Rachel came rushing to Blaise's door!

"Hellooo," she called out. "I'm ready, Blaise. Can we go now?"

"Certainly, Ray babe. I'll bring the car around, and we'll take as many arrangements as will fit in the back, and do it again, okay?"

"You're wonderful dear heart. What would I ever do without you in my life?" she echoed from down the hall.

Oh, boy, thought Blaise, *that's a real interesting observation.* But he came right back.

"Well, let's hope neither of us ever have to find that out."

Rachel peeked around the apartment door leading outside.

"I'd never let it happen," she affirmed.

Blaise looked at her from the sidewalk and gave a thumb's up sign and went to the car.

The afternoon flew by for both Rachel and Blaise. Missions of mercy were always better done if they were short and sweet. With their heads still filled with the thank you's and other statements of gratitude and appreciation, Rachel suggested they stop for a snack somewhere.

They stopped at Sparky Herbert's, one of the local pubs and indulged in a Reuben and a glass of draft beer, favorites of both of them.

"Hmm," sang Rachel, "does it really get any better than this, Blaise?"

"I don't think so, and besides, even if it did, who'd tell us?"

Rachel agreed, and when they raised their glasses to toast their agreement Blaise stopped quite suddenly as he spotted Corey Davidson sitting in a booth directly across from them. His eyes were locked into Blaise's and a cold chill went through Blaise's body, and a sense of fear caused him to drop the glass. As it shattered on the table and splattered in an area that seemed to cover half of the establishment, Rachel jumped back and seemed shook up as she asked Blaise what had happened.

By this time, the waitress and bartenders had run over to their table and proceeded to clean up the mess. Blaise was apologizing profusely, and Rachel kept cautioning everyone about the shattered glass. She asked the waitress to remove the sandwiches, which were dowsed with beer and most likely bits of glass. As Rachel looked at Blaise, she noticed blood on his hand and became upset that he'd been hurt.

"Oh, Blaise, you've been cut," she said. "Let's see if someone has a Band-aid. Is it deep?"

"I'm okay, Ray, I'm okay. It's just a nick," Blaise responded. "How silly, all this because Corey Davidson is here." Rachel looked up in total surprise.

"Where?" she asked.

"Right here" said Corey. "My, my, isn't this cozy. And I wonder who made this mess. Could it have been Ms. Kinley?" With that, Rachel stood up and slapped Corey hard across the face.

"Enough, Corey, you've had too much to drink," said Rachel. "Go home." But to no avail.

Corey continued his demeaning comments about Blaise, and when he insinuated that it was obvious that they must deserve each other, Blaise punched Corey in the mouth. He fell back through the chair directly behind him. His fuse was ignited, and the only target he could see was Blaise. Corey bolted from the floor, and with a leg of the chair lunged at Blaise, striking him on the side of his arm.

Rachel screamed at Corey to stop, but the rage inside him exploded. He was a man out of control. Blaise was holding his arm and trying desperately to hold back the fierce blows, which seemed unending.

Patrons were now pushed to the wall, watching this brawl, almost in a state of disbelief. This was Grosse Pointe; something like this never happened, well, almost never. Blaise pushed at Corey whenever he could dodge either Corey's fist or the jagged piece of wood that became a bludgeoning weapon.

"Someone call the police," screamed Rachel. "Call 911; please, help him."

She was pulling at Corey's shirt trying to stop him. Finally, Corey grabbed Blaise by the neck of his shirt and hit him hard with his fist. Blaise fell backwards and hit the rail around the bar with his head. The thud as he hit the floor was horrendous. Rachel ran to Blaise's side. There was blood seeping from the back of his head.

"Blaise, Blaise," she called frantically. "Can you hear me? Oh, my God. Call an ambulance, hurry, please someone call a doctor!"

The bartender called 911, and within minutes, sirens were screaming down the street as they approached the pub. Rachel was holding Blaise in her arms when the paramedics and police arrived. They ushered her away from Blaise and began to examine him for vital signs.

"He's alive," said one of the medics, "but just barely. We've got to get him to Saint John's emergency. Call ahead, and tell them we may need a surgeon on hand for major internal head injuries."

"No," screamed Rachel. "Oh, no. Oh, Blaise, I'm so sorry." She was almost hysterical. "This is all my fault," she sobbed.

After the medics had placed Blaise on a gurney and secured him for travel in the ambulance, they asked Rachel if she'd like to accompany him; she did. As she proceeded alongside the stretcher, one of the policeman asked what happened.

"It was him," Rachel blurted out and pointed to Corey. "He did this and I want him charged with felonious assault."

Corey was drunk and in a stupor. He tried to talk to Rachel, who could only scream at him.

"If Blaise dies, Corey, I'll see that you spend all the remaining days of your life in prison."

The police took Corey into custody and left the pub while reciting the Miranda warning to him. They put him in the backseat, and the police car and the ambulance left the pub at the same time.

Rachel's mind traveled quickly back to when she had been notified that her parents were in a car accident. The high pitch of all of those sirens remained in her head long after her parents' deaths, and now the sound and the fears had been reactivated. As she looked down at Blaise," who was lying there unconscious and very pale, she held his hand and prayed fervently.

"Please, God, not Blaise. Oh, please God, not Blaise." It didn't take long to get to Saint John's emergency, and the medical team was ready and waiting when they arrived. From that point forward, things happened very quickly, and Rachel's mind became one great blur.

She was asked to sit in the visitor's waiting room while Blaise was being examined. Her head was pounding with the worst headache she could recall in recent memory. With her head in her hands, she was barely aware of voices and movements. Other emergencies arrived almost every five minutes, and she could hear muffled sounds and sobs. Crying people sat everywhere nearby. The waiting was interminable. She heard a loudspeaker.

"Paging Dr. Markham, please come to the ER, stat." Rachel lifted her head when she heard this familiar name. Randy's dad—chief of surgery—it must be serious, since he's only called in on life-and-death situations. Rachel stood up, trying to see through the small windows of the swinging doors that led to the examination room. Her attention to those windows was broken by a voice.

"Excuse me, miss, are you with the gentleman just brought in by ambulance?" asked the triage nurse.

"Yes, yes I am. Is there any news on his condition?" Rachel asked anxiously.

"Not yet, but I'd like some information, if you could come over here with me." Rachel automatically followed her.

"Information? What kind of information?" she asked.

The nurse explained that she'd need a name, address, and any past medical history, etcetera.

"Oh, I can give you some, but I don't know anything about his medical history," she explained.

The statistics all seemed so cold, so calculating. *Couldn't this be done later?* she thought.

"Any communicable diseases?" the nurse asked.

"Are you kidding?" Rachel exploded. "Blaise is lying there, maybe even dying, and you want to know if he's ever had measles? I don't know," she sobbed. "I don't know," and she broke down helplessly. The nurse excused herself and went to get Rachel a glass of water. She offered her a box of Kleenex.

"I apologize for the seemingly insensitiveness of all the questions. What is your name?"

"Rachel, Rachel Radcliffe," she sighed.

"I'm certain, Rachel, that you know our doctors are doing everything possible to help Mr. Kinley, and all of this information assists them in their total evaluation," the nurse explained.

Rachel wiped her eyes and blew her nose.

"I must look a wreck." She noticed the blood on her sleeves and slacks. She tried to wipe it off but couldn't. "Doesn't matter, though, if anything happens to Blaise because of me, nothing matters." She just sat and shook her head and stared into an endless space.

"You can return to the waiting room, Rachel. We'll let you know as soon as the doctors have finished their examination," said the nurse.

Rachel got up and walked back to a row of seats, now almost filled with other people whose plights were the same as hers—endless, empty waiting. The last time she looked at her watch, she thought it had stopped, for it seemed never to move. The magazines that lay on the appropriately spaced tables were old and dog-eared. Many had been torn, with more pages missing than not. *Popular Mechanics* and *U.S. News & World Report* of months earlier didn't really appeal to her, and the conversations of others were too strange and excessively loud. She began to feel closed in and decided to walk to the entrance for some fresh air. Suddenly the swinging doors opened, and Dr. Markham walked out into the waiting room.

"Is there any family here for Mr. Blaise Kinley?"

Rachel walked toward him. He was surprised to see this familiar face.

"Rachel, do you know Blaise Kinley?"

"Yes, Randall, he's my neighbor and best friend."

"This is a surprise to see you, Rachel, and I'm afraid the news about your friend is not too good." Rachel's heart skipped a beat.

"Oh, no, he's not— he's not—dead, is he, Randall?"

"Oh, no, no, but he's in critical condition. I'm afraid we're going to have to operate immediately. He has a massive hematoma, or blood clot, that has to be removed immediately. The concussion from when his head hit whatever object caused the damage, and we're working against the clock," Dr. Markham. said. "Do you know any of his family members, Rachel?"

"No, I'm afraid I don't. His mother, father, and sister live in Grosse Pointe, but I don't know where."

"Well, we'll proceed without permission in this instance. Time is not on our side at this moment. Will you be here?" he asked. "Or can you leave your phone number? I'll let you know ASAP when the surgery is over."

"I'll be here. I'll be right here," she said, and with that, Dr. Markham went back through the swinging doors and the waiting began all over again.

Rachel's thoughts were scattered. She was thinking about poor Blaise lying in that ER bed, fighting for his life. Also running around in her mind was the plight of Corey Davidson. How could he do this? How could he inflict such pain on another human being? This violent side of the man whom she'd known for so many years was frightening and devastating. Her anger began to swell, and the vengeful side of her began to work feverishly. *I'll make him pay,* she thought. *He'll be sorry he ever laid a hand on Blaise.*

She was fidgeting with the piece of Kleenex that the nurse had given her earlier. *What if Blaise dies? Oh, my God.* She shivered! "He can't, please Lord, don't take him, please," she moaned softly. She was distracted by other patients being rushed into the ER section of this very large hospital. How many times she'd passed by and never thought much about the daily life and death situations. Other than going to the hospital to identify her mother and father after their fatal accident so many years ago, Rachel could not identify with its ongoing heart-rending situations.

She remembered when she was about eight or nine, Papa DeRoca had to have his appendix removed. Mama DeRoca was so calm, and yet, Rachel remembered clearly seeing the tears sit fragilely on her eyelids. She could remember the fear of all those people dressed in white and green, running up and down the halls. Back then, you had to stay in the hospital at least three or four days after surgery to make certain that the healing process had begun without infection and that the bodily functions were all working well. Papa DeRoca was such a loving father, and it upset him to see his little Rachel standing so close to her mama, not really knowing or understanding why her daddy couldn't reach for her, pick her up in his arms, and give her a big hug and kiss. *Nothing good could happen in this place*, she thought. *Everyone is either sick, or dying.* Not a very good place for an eight-year-old or her daddy.

As she came back to the present, she thought, *This isn't a particularly good place to be at any time in your life.* She looked at her watch, and it was only 11:00 P.M. It felt as if she'd been there all day. A little thirsty now, she began to look around for a vending machine.

She walked slowly and deliberately around the visitor's room and paused to look out the window at the parking lot. How she longed to be leaving there and going home to a nice cup of tea and her warm bed. But reality, at least for now, was that she'd be there until she had word on Blaise's condition after the surgery.

Suddenly, she thought about calling Christian but it was so late, and why should she upset him with something whose outcome would not be determined for quite some time? Maybe Amber was still up. She needed someone to talk to, and Amber knew Blaise and Corey. So she sat down and started going through her purse, looking first for Amber's name and number, which she always knew from memory, but not now. Then she looked for her AT&T credit card. As she dialed the number, her breathing became irregular, and she tried to calm herself when Amber answered.

"Hi, Amber, it's Rachel," she said quietly.

"Hey, doll, what's wrong?" said Amber. "You sound like you're upset. Are you all right, Rachel?"

"Yes, yes, I am. It's Blaise, Amber. Blaise has been seriously hurt and is in surgery right now."

"Good Lord. What happened, sweetie? Was he in a car accident?" Amber asked anxiously.

"No. No, it was Corey," Rachel said, and again the tears began to well up in her eyes.

"Corey?" said Amber. "What's he got to do with this?"

"He hit Blaise at a pub we were in tonight. He'd been drinking, and when he spotted me and Blaise together, he lost it. Oh, Amber, it was ugly. Blaise is suffering from severe head injuries, and pray, Amber, please pray that he makes it through the surgery."

"Listen, doll, I can catch the red-eye tonight and be there in a couple of hours."

Rachel thought for a moment.

"Oh, no, Amber, please don't do that, not now. If something were to happen to you, too, because of me, I'd die." She sobbed.

Amber consoled Rachel and asked her to call back as soon as she had some news about Blaise, no matter what the time.

"Hang in there, doll."

"Thank you," responded Rachel, and she hung up.

Rachel's thoughts were now focusing on her lifelong memories—and endings. She quivered at the sound of the word and what it meant. Here she was again, fearing she might experience yet another ending. Blaise was always so good to her. Why was this happening? Perhaps there was some hidden, cryptic message in all of this. Did she complain too much about her lost romances? Was this somehow meant to show her once again how serious endings could be when there's loss of life? It was more than she could bear, and now the guilt about her protestations. What if her involvement with Christian led to some harm for him? Her ability to rationalize this evening's event as nothing more than a liquor-induced jealous rage tainted her ability to reason with anything else in her life.

"Christian," she uttered, "Christian, I can't do this to you. I love you too much to cause you harm. If you get involved with me, you may be risking bodily harm or worse."

At this moment, Rachel's psychological confusion led her to believe that she was somehow responsible for all the endings in her life. Mama and Papa, Neil, Corey, and now Blaise may pay the ultimate price for her folly. She never considered herself a selfish person, but she could see nothing else at this time. Her selfishness was the reason for all the pain in her life. As she walked by the huge windows, her reflection became repulsive to her. She walked faster in order not to look at what she was convinced was the basis for all this suffering. When she came to a dead end in the hallway, she turned around to return, but her whole body seemed too tired to do so. She slumped down in an attempt to rest for a few moments. She was so tired, but she couldn't sleep now. Too much was at stake. She had to stay alert, for if she slept, others she knew may suffer as well. She suddenly stood up and started back to the visitor's waiting room.

There's nothing worse than being selfish in one's life, she thought, *except self pity. Nothing is as nonproductive.* Rachel's survival mentality finally clicked into high gear. "Enough of this nonsense!" she affirmed. "I'm not the master of the universe, and I don't control destiny."

"Phew," she said, "I need a donut or a candy bar. My energy level is at a low, and it's causing my brain to short-circuit." She bought a Snickers bar and consumed it as though it was her last meal. When she went back into the waiting room, the sofa in the corner was unoccupied. It looked inviting, so Rachel sat down, took off her shoes and curled up in the corner cushions and lay her head back and immediately fell asleep.

Ten

Dr. Markham and his seasoned surgical team worked diligently and expertly on Blaise's injury. The sweat on Randall Markham's brow increased as the risk of removing the blood clot became more dangerous.

"Wipe," exclaimed Dr. Markham, and the efficient surgical nurse in attendance mopped his forehead quickly. "Syringe" was his next command and as he engaged the rather large clot, he expunged it, and gave the syringe to the nurse next to him. "Check," and he and the assistant surgeon reviewed the gaping incision to ensure that all foreign matter and all parts of the clot had been evacuated.

Comfortable that the incision was clean and that the affected area was free of damage, Dr. Markham asked his assisting surgeon to close, and the stitching process began.

When he left the operating room and entered the adjoining clean-up room, he took off his surgical gloves and cap and rested his hands on the sink and bowed his head. "Thank you," he said softly. "Thank you, Lord, for your guidance during this young man's surgery. I've done all I can, and now the rest is in your hands." His head stayed bowed for a few minutes before he began to wash up and prepare himself to advise Rachel about the outcome of the operation.

Rachel was sleeping all curled up in a corner of the waiting room sofa, when Dr. Markham arrived.

"Rachel," he called, "Rachel," he called again as he gently put his hand on her arm and shook her ever so gently.

"Uhmm," moaned Rachel as she began to awaken. Then, as she recognized Dr. Markham through her sleepy, slitted eyes, she was wide awake and jumped up. "What is it? How's Blaise? Is he all right?"

Dr. Markham quieted her down.

"Rachel, he's all right. He came through the operation beautifully. He'll be in recovery soon and then in his room in about one and a half hours."

Rachel was so happy to hear that wonderful news, she burst into tears.

"Thank you, God!" she exclaimed. "Thank you, sweet Lord, for saving Blaise's life."

Dr. Markham advised her that the next forty-eight hours would be crucial and that Blaise wasn't out of the woods yet.

"Is there a problem?" asked Rachel. "Will he be all right?" She was sobbing almost out of control.

"Well," said Dr. Markham, cautiously, "He has a very good chance of coming through this without any complications, but I'll know more when I examine him and do some further tests later on today!" He paused. "I would suggest that you get a bite to eat, go home, freshen up, and come back around noon, Rachel." His smile was comforting, and she didn't need much of a push to get out of those clothes. And as she thought about it, she hadn't eaten anything in almost thirty-six hours, since she and Blaise's dinner was so terribly disrupted.

"That's great advice, Randall," she sighed, "and I think I'm going to take it. Perhaps I might even be able to take an aspirin for this nagging headache." Dr. Markham asked how long she had it and whether or not she had somehow been hurt in that rowdy fracas.

"Oh, no," said Rachel grinning. "This headache is the product of some pretty heavy worrying after this whole mess came to such a frightening conclusion. I'm sure after I've eaten, freshened up, and taken a couple of Anacins, I'll be just fine!" Dr. Markham's concern only confirmed Rachel's initial feelings and impression about him. "You've been wonderful, Randall," she remarked. "I really think this situation would have been more of a nightmare without you." He extended his hand to her.

"Well, Rachel, I thank you for that expression of confidence, and I hope we're both feeling better this afternoon when I check in on Blaise." They left one another.

As Dr. Markham continued his rounds during this unending day, Rachel pushed through the exit doors of the front of this enormous hospital. She breathed in the crisp autumn morning air and began to look up and down the street for a cab.

It wasn't too long before one came along. As she got into the back seat and sat down, she experienced a sense of relief that she hadn't felt in a very long time.

"Fifteen Bedford!" she exclaimed, and as the meter began to tick away, she rested her head back on the seat and was dozing in an instant. It only took about fifteen minutes to get to her home, and as the cab came to a stop, she awakened.

Her home was always such a welcomed sight, but today brought mixed emotions as she stood looking at the duplex that was half hers and half Blaise's. His half was now unfortunately empty.

The light in the answering machine was blinking as she opened the door and entered the living room. She pressed the indicator on the answering machine, and the first playback was from Amber.

"Hi, doll, I'm going crazy waiting to hear from you. Please call me as soon as you get this message. Luv ya, sweetie, hang in there. We luv ya, and we're all praying for Blaise's recovery." Rachel sat down in the wing chair next to the telephone, then listened to the second message.

"This call is for Ms. Rachel Radcliffe. My name is Detective Marsh with the sixteenth precinct. We're holding Mr. Davidson here pending the issuance of formal charges for felonious assault. Please call me at 555-2370 when you get this message."

"Corey!" she exclaimed. "Corey's been in jail overnight, and I don't know what to do." She thought for a moment. *I should let him sit there for a while and think about the trouble he's caused. If anyone at the* Grosse Pointe News *gets hold of this, his reputation won't be worth a plug nickel. Randall Markham believes Blaise will be all right, but until I know for certain, I'm not going to let Corey off the hook!*

She couldn't believe the dilemma she found herself in. Only a few weeks ago everything and everyone in her life was doing relatively well. Now, her best friend is fighting for his life, and the man with whom she shared a degree of love and passion was in jail responsible for this incident.

Several times through the night in the waiting room, she thought about calling Christian and finding comfort and solace in the thought of his warm embrace. She also felt totally responsible for all the unhappiness in her life. The sudden loss of her parents, the divorce from Neil, the breakup with Corey and now the near loss of Blaise—dear Blaise.

Her thoughts became a maze as she looked and searched for a way to accept what she couldn't change, adjust to what she could change, and be content with both. *Prioritize,* she thought. *You've got to put all of this in its proper perspective.* "Blaise is lying in the hospital fighting for his life, and Corey is in jail pending my decision to file formal charges." She put her head in her hands. "Well," she sat up, "I'll take a shower and freshen up, go back to the hospital, and then I'll deal with Corey, in that order."

She moved quickly, ridding herself of those wrinkled and bloodstained clothes. The shower was warm and relaxing. The longer she languished in the comfort of this almost medicinal spray, the stress and tension was washed away and a sense of newness and enthusiasm filled her head and her heart.

She donned a crisp white shirt and navy slacks. She gazed in the full-length mirror of her closet door and was pleased with the image of the Rachel who was ready to embark on a project or activity that grasped her mind and heart so totally. As she finished the last touch of blush and a final brush of her hair, the telephone rang. She wasn't expecting any calls and was a bit anxious about getting back to the hospital to see Blaise. Her uneasiness resounded in her somewhat loud and perturbed hello.

"Is this you, my darling Rachel?" she heard come from the receiver.

"Christian?" she blurted out gleefully. "Oh, Christian, darling, yes this is me."

"You sound upset, Rachel," Christian responded. "Are you all right?"

Rachel was overcome with emotion at the sound of his voice and his concern for her well-being.

"Yes, my darling, I'm all right; however, I've been through a virtual nightmare these past few hours," she explained. "I don't believe I ever mentioned my friend and neighbor, Blaise Kinley, to you, Christian, but he's in the hospital after undergoing some pretty serious brain surgery."

"I'm sorry, sweetheart. Will he be all right?" Christian inquired. "Is there anything I can do for you during this waiting period?"

"Thank you, Christian for your thoughtfulness, but Blaise is in very good hands. Believe it or not, Randall Markham was the doctor who performed the surgery, and he has assured me that Blaise is going to be all right."

"This is ironic, isn't it," Christian interjected. "A few short weeks ago, none of us knew one another, and here we are now with all of our lives so inexplicably entwined. Perhaps I could come down for a couple of days to see you, and I could stay with Estelle and Randall. What do you think, Rachel?"

Rachel's eyes lit up at the prospect of seeing Christian and having him near during this somewhat stressful and uneasy time in her life.

"Oh, darling, that would be wonderful, but I wouldn't want you to disrupt your production schedule, and I'm truly doing just fine now that I know that Blaise will be all right."

"How was your friend hurt? Was he in a car accident?"

"No," said Rachel. "He was injured in a fight last night at one of our local pubs." Rachel confided. "There's a lot more to this story, Christian, and I'll tell you all about it when next we speak. However, I must get back to the hospital and I hope you won't be upset with this hasty good-bye, my darling."

"No, not at all, sweetheart. Please do go about your business and promise you'll call me later this evening so we can talk a bit further about your friend's unfortunate injury." Christian hesitated and then spoke in the soft tones she had become so accustomed to hearing. "I love you, my beautiful Rachel, and I'll always be here for you, you know that."

"And, I love you, my darling," Rachel whispered. "I will talk to you later and, Christian, thank you for your concern and thoughtfulness on my behalf. Your love has given me such strength."

They exchanged a few more loving thoughts, and when she hung up the phone, Rachel sighed and smiled. Christian Avian provided all the support she needed to get through this tragedy. She prayed as she went out the door that everything would work out well.

Saint John's was always a busy hospital, but it looked twice as busy to Rachel, with all daytime activities in progress. It seemed more difficult to obtain the information she needed to find out about Blaise's condition and his new room.

The intensive care unit was noisier than she had expected. However, as she observed the quick and exact movements of everyone there, she quickly understood that being quiet wasn't their first priority. The monitors and sophisticated equipment were very foreign to her.

"May I help you, miss?" The young nurse asked. Rachel apologized for staring at all of the emergency situations taking place in this unit.

"I'm here to see Mr. Blaise Kinley," she said.

"Mr. Kinley is in Unit D on the right. Are you a relative?" Rachel was taken aback by that question but responded quickly.

"No, I'm his friend and next door neighbor." The nurse directed her to Blaise's bed and asked that she stay only ten minutes.

"He's still critical, and until Dr. Markham examines him and changes that condition, you'll only be able to visit ten minutes on the hour, every hour."

The nurse left Rachel standing at the foot of Blaise's bed. She looked at him lying there with his head fully bound in bandages. She gasped and tried to hold back the emerging tears. To no avail. She sobbed quietly as she approached his side and gently took his hand in hers. He was cool and Rachel was alarmed. She looked around to see if anyone could explain this condition, but then she just stood and observed that marvelous face, feature by feature. The face that she had rarely ever seen without a smile. An aide passed by and noticed Rachel's tear-stained face.

"He's doing just fine," he said. "It's always a little frightening to see those we love in these surroundings and in life-threatening situations."

Rachel thanked him for stopping by. She queried him about the coolness of Blaise's hand. "It's not unusual after surgery, and it's nothing to be alarmed about. When he awakens and his blood pressure and other vital signs begin to function more normally, his body temperature will rise as well." Rachel noticed the young man's I.D. and was surprised that he was a nurse.

"Do you have any idea when he'll come out of the anesthesia?" Rachel asked.

"Probably another three or four hours, but Dr. Markham will be here soon to check on his progress."

Ten minutes had flown by. Rachel patted Blaise's hand and left the ICU area. As she was walking toward the visitor's waiting room, Dr. Markham got off the elevator. He smiled when he saw her.

"You look much more rested, Rachel. I'm glad you took my advice!" Dr. Markham was well liked by his staff and everyone else. He had a manner and demeanor that put everyone at ease, and his gentle, understanding ways made his patients and their respective families feel more comfortable.

"Thanks, Randall," Rachel replied. "While I was home freshening up, Christian called and I told him about the incident and that you were the operating surgeon. He sends you and Estelle his love."

Randall smiled and asked Rachel if she'd like to wait while he examined Blaise.

"Oh, could I, please." Randall showed her where she could wait and went directly to Blaise's unit and began his examination. Two nurses assisted him as they checked each monitor and Blaise personally.

"Looking good," said Randall. He said it loud enough for Rachel to hear, and she grinned.

"Thank you, Lord," she whispered.

Randall approached Rachel and told her that all of Blaise's vital signs were good. The seriousness of the surgery was still cause for concern, but his age and general good health were definitely in his favor.

Christian entered the stage door of the Palace Theatre and checked the audition and rehearsal schedules. Two names jumped out at him on the audition list—Carlo and Marisa Domani.

"All right!" exclaimed Christian. He was elated that these two youngsters had finally agreed to follow their God-given talent and pursue a career in the theater. He looked at his watch and saw that he had about four hours of good rehearsal time before auditions this afternoon.

As Christian fixed himself a cup of coffee in the cast cafeteria, he noticed Jan Welmer, *The New York Times* theater section editor, and Leo Theilman from *Variety* sitting at one of the tables chatting with Roman Navarro, the choreographer of his new musical. They waved when they spotted Christian and beckoned him over to their table.

"Hello, Jan. Hi, Leo," said Christian as he shook hands with both of them. "I suppose you're trying to get some early insights into my latest production. Well, Roman's the guy to talk to, he's really created some great dance numbers for the recreation of Adele and Fred Astaire's numbers. Also, the routines with Gene Kelly and Leslie Caron is spectacular."

Jan Wilmer, who was about Christian's age, attractive, intelligent, and single, always made it obvious to anyone who would listen that she'd take Christian on in a heartbeat, but Christian never felt the same way, and so this unrequited affection lived on to no avail. Still, she admired his talent and success and would take every possible opportunity to interview and feature him in her column.

" 'Cinema' is going to be your best work, Christian—I feel it," Jan remarked.

"I guess, by now, I should believe you, dear Jan, since you've said that about my last three shows."

"And, my friend, my predictions have been borne out by three Tony Awards, right?" she retorted.

"Flattery will get you anywhere," he joked, but as he looked at Jan's expression, he modified his statement slightly. "Well, almost anywhere," and they all grinned.

Leo Thielman wasn't as pro-Christian as Jan, but he did admire his unique ability to produce musical hits.

"Can we expect to see some superstars in this new musical, Christian, or will you go with some unknowns?"

Christian finished his coffee and responded quickly.

"You know, Leo, since 'Cinema' represents a revue of past and present movie hits, I've been thinking about both. There's a lot of talent out there just waiting to be discovered and since musicals are not exactly being written every day, it would be good for all of us to inject some new blood into this somewhat dying performance in hopes of rejuvenating the excitement and entertaining possibilities that musicals have always given their audiences."

"Mr. Avian," called Jack Farrell, his production manager. "We're about ready to start rehearsing the opening number."

"Thanks, Jack," Christian acknowledged and bade his newspaper friends a final adieu and asked Roman to join him for the start of the morning's workouts.

Sitting in a dreary jail was not Corey's idea of a great place for some R and R. The look on his face spoke more words than he could have uttered at that moment. His stern mouth and apparent clenched jaw showed only a part of the anger and frustration he was experiencing. This whole incident was incredible. Rachel out with that wimp! Blaise's further attempts to match the strength of Corey's well-developed brawn. Add to that his eventual arrest and being charged with felonious assault by the woman he loved. It was all too bizarre. But very real.

"How much longer do I have to sit in this place?" he asked a passing guard.

"Someone should be filing formal charges this morning," was the response.

"Did I call my attorney last night when I was brought here?" he asked.

"Sorry, I don't keep a diary of all your movements," was the brash response. "But if you don't remember, I can tell you, someone would have been here by now if you had."

No sooner did those words leave the guard's mouth than two men, a police officer, and another man dressed in a three-piece suit approached Corey's cell.

"Corey Davidson?" asked the man in civilian clothes.

"Yes," answered Corey.

"Come with us. I'm Jim Slatter from the prosecutor's office. Ms. Radcliffe is here to press formal charges."

"Wait a minute, formal charges for what?"

"The guy you had a fight with last night had brain surgery early this morning, and if he dies as a result of his injuries, you'll be facing manslaughter."

Corey's expression changed quickly from anger to shock to fear.

Corey was handcuffed when they brought him into the courtroom. The only people there were the judge, his clerk, the arresting officer, and Rachel. Her eyes were ice cold as she stared at him.

As he stood in front of the judge, the clerk read the charges and asked Rachel if she wanted to proceed with this matter. Her glance went from Corey to the judge as she began to speak.

"Your honor, I've known Mr. Davidson for quite a while, and this fight started because of me. The injured man, Blaise Kinley, is my neighbor and best friend. Although we're not the typical 'triangle,' even though one might presume that to be the case. But Mr. Davidson was under the influence of alcohol and in a jealous rage." She breathed deeply and continued. "I just left Mr. Kinley at Saint John's Hospital, and his doctor has assured me that he will survive the surgery and the injuries caused by Mr. Corey's despicable actions. Because of our past relationship and my own contributing fault in this matter, I would like to drop the charges against Mr. Davidson."

Corey breathed a sigh of relief and smiled.

"However," Rachel continued, "I would like an injunction issued against Mr. Davidson preventing him from getting anywhere near me or Mr. Kinley in the future."

Corey could not believe the variety of emotions he had experienced in the past few hours. He was so overwhelmed by Rachel's request.

"An injunction? he blurted out. "Rachel, I would never hurt you, or Blaise for that matter. I was drunk last night, and I misunderstood the whole situation."

The judge dropped his gavel on the desk.

"You're out of order, Mr. Davidson. Given the series of events that have been represented here today, and because of the unknown condition of the victim, Mr. Kinley, I see no reason not to grant your request for the issuance of an injunction, Ms. Radcliffe, and will have my clerk draw up the necessary paperwork." The judge then looked directly at Corey.

"Mr. Davidson, I'm going to ask the bailiff to release you from the handcuffs and give you back your personal belongings so you may be dismissed. However, this injunction I've just issued against you is in full force and in effect now. If you come anywhere near Ms. Radcliffe or Mr. Kinley and you are reported, I will have you arrested on the spot and returned to this court for punishment consistent with that violation."

Corey looked at Rachel almost pleadingly. She asked if she could leave, and the judge asked one of the officers to escort her to her car. He also advised that he would detain Mr. Davidson one-half hour to allow her to return to her home.

The injunction was more devastating to Corey than doing more time in this despicable place. He was no longer angry. He felt only hurt and utter shame. How did he come to this spot in a relationship he valued and treasured so highly? Could this damaging consequence ever be righted and what, if anything, could he ever do to make this up to his little kitten?

Rachel was crying as she got into her car and drove homeward. She was caught between her concern for Blaise and her pity for Corey. If there was a resolution for everyone in this mess, she certainly didn't have a clue at this moment. Perhaps the best thing to do right now was to get to her office and make a few phone calls. Mrs. Longley was high on her list. She'd check her answering service to see how many calls she could handle before she returned to the hospital to see Blaise later on.

She stopped at the coffee shop close to her office and got a cup of coffee and a cinnamon bagel. Eating wasn't very much of a priority these past couple of days, and her stomach was grumbling from the neglect. As she opened the door of her office, the phone was ringing. She rushed to pick it up. It was Bill Jacoby, Corey's business partner.

"Rachel, is that you?" he asked.

"Yes, oh, hello, Bill, how are you?"

"Well, I'm just fine, but I just got a call from Corey, and I can't believe the story he just told me. Is it true?"

"It depends on what he told you, Bill. Why don't you repeat what he said, and I'll either confirm or deny it?. How's that?" she snapped.

As Bill began to relate, verbatim, his conversation with Corey, Rachel almost in an unconcerned manner, proceeded to go through some paperwork on her desk.

"Well, Rachel, is that really what happened?"

She thought for a moment and responded.

"You know, Bill, everyone has a different opinion and bent in a situation like this. Corey's vantage point was not mine; however, he has a right to his perceptions. Basically, this whole mess could have been avoided if I had been more explicit when I told Corey that our relationship was over." She hesitated. "On second thought, this happened because Corey is an egotistical bore who's never put anyone before himself and was armed with too much scotch; his judgment got blindsided, and he acted like a jackass. Only problem is, a nice guy named Blaise Kinley had to pay a terrible price for Corey's arrogance and stupidity."

There was a silence, and Bill Jacoby was most conciliatory with Rachel.

"Of course, Rachel, I had no idea about any of this, and I'm sorry that you've had to be a part of such an inconsiderate and tragic episode. I hope you know how much I've respected your somewhat heroic behavior to have sustained a relationship with that friend and business associate of mine for as long as you did. You also know if you need me for anything, I'll be happy to oblige."

Rachel sighed and thanked Bill for his understanding and offer of assistance. Bill and Corey had been childhood friends, and she knew it had to be difficult for Bill to consider her feelings over those of his friend in this instance. Rachel made sure to mention that an injunction against Corey had been issued and that she would appreciate anything that Bill could do to make certain that Corey did not violate that order.

"For a person whose career is to erect edifices and monuments to last a lifetime, you'd think that some of that talent would have rubbed off on how he handled his relationships." He promised to help as much as possible and again asked Rachel to call him if she needed him.

Rachel finished her coffee and bagel and dialed Mrs. Longley.

"Welcome home my dear," exclaimed Mrs. Longley, "I hope you enjoyed your trip to New York. I've been anxious to tell you how marvelous the cruise was and to thank you once again for the lovely wardrobe ensemble you put together for me."

Rachel was pleased that her number-one client was happy; it made her realize how gratifying it was to provide her service for others.

"Thank you, Mrs. Longley, for making my day. You've certainly given me the nudge I needed to get me back into the swing of things." Rachel described just a bit about her trip to New York. Describing her first visit to the World Trade Center brought a blush to her cheek and some wonderful thoughts about Christian.

Mrs. Longley mentioned an upcoming trip to Australia and asked Rachel to start thinking about some wardrobe ideas for this exciting jaunt. Rachel thanked her for the new commission, and they agreed to meet sometime soon to discuss details and have Mrs. Longley share her ideas of some specific items before Rachel began to work on this new job. As usual, her day flew by. It was already past 4:00 P.M. when Rachel decided to go home, change, and get to the hospital in time for visiting hours, 7:00 to 9:00 P.M.

When she left her office, it was raining and she'd forgotten her umbrella. As she waited in the small doorway of her office entrance, she watched as the passersby scurried to and from their cars and in and out of the shops on the avenue. The dark clouds overhead looked as though they were permanent, so she decided to make a run for the van, which was parked about one block away. She tried desperately to avoid the growing puddles and people coming at her with umbrellas covering their view of where they were going and bumping into her. She was looking quickly to see if she knew anyone, but they were all strangers, trying to get out of the rain and disgruntled that she had gotten in their way.

As she opened the door of the van and jumped inside she was soaked.

She'd have to do more than just change her clothes. Now, she'd have to wash her hair as well.

The drive home was uneventful, and if it wasn't for this unexpected rain, she'd have been changed and ready to go to the hospital in about half an hour. Once she got home and commenced to remove those wet clothes, she felt a little less anxious about the delay. The hot water spray in the shower was medicinal. She felt relaxed and refreshed as she stepped out of the shower stall. *Thank God for my natural curly hair,* she thought. No sooner had she dried off and began to go through her closet, her hair was already beginning to dry, and with a few minutes of blow-drying, she looked like she just left the beauty salon.

The potpourri of colors displayed on her silk blouse truly reflected the artistic talent of Rachel Radcliffe. Guided by her mood and critical eye, her choices generally displayed her temperament for any occasion. This evening she wanted to look pretty and professional. Two adjectives that Blaise used constantly to describe his longtime neighbor.

The teal-blue silk was easy on the eyes and enhanced Rachel's flawless ivory skin. Pearl earrings and a single strand of pearls added the final touch to her ensemble. It wasn't quite 7:00 when she grabbed her floral-lined cape and matching umbrella and drove to Saint John's for the long-awaited visit with Blaise.

At the hospital, she waited for the elevator that would take her to the fourth floor intensive care unit, and she sighed deeply as if to prepare herself for any surprises. When she walked into the ICU, she was pleased to see Blaise sitting up and sipping on some broth being fed to him by the attending nurse. For a moment, she smiled at him and she felt a lump in her throat.

"What's trippin Ray babe?" he raised his hand and uttered.

Rachel was overcome with excitement that he recognized her and that he was still able to express some humor in his state.

"I'm well, Blaise, and a whole lot better now that I see you awake and taking sustenance."

"Hunger is a compelling beast, and I'm not in any position to argue."

The nurse managed to feed him most of the broth and some famous green Jell-O when he expressed the inability to handle anymore.

"I wish you would have eaten just a bit more, Mr. Kinley, but you did pretty darn good for this first time," the nurse said and grinned.

"I'll be happy to eat more next time if you promise to bring me some real food." Blaise responded without any hesitation at all.

Rachel laughed and was encouraged by his winsome nature. She slowly walked to his bedside and leaned over to kiss his cheek.

"I was so worried about you, dear heart," she said. "I would have died if anything had happened to you as a result of my relationship with that jerk."

"Oh, oh, no apologies and no recriminations, promise?" Blaise said. "Besides, Ray babe, you can't die. What would our neighbors think about Blaise's continued relationship with a good-looking corpse? Not a fun idea." They both sighed, and a sense of warmth crept over Rachel as she sat and held the hand of her dear, dear Blaise.

"Just so you'll know that something has been done about Corey's irresponsible actions, Blaise, I initially pressed charges against him for felonious assault, and then I waived those charges and I asked for the issuance of an injunction against Corey so that he can't get within two miles of us without penalty and punishment."

Blaise picked up his thumb in the okay position and thanked Rachel for her responding so quickly in his behalf.

"I just hope, Ray babe, that Corey doesn't disobey this order, since I won't be next door to help you, if he does."

"Don't worry, dear heart, I've made it clear that I wouldn't hesitate to have him hauled off to jail if he so much as thinks about violating the order. I don't think Mr. Davidson is too ready to tempt fate right now, and as a little bit of additional insurance, I've asked Bill Jacoby to keep an eye on him. Now, Mr. Kinley, I think I should leave and let you get some rest," Rachel said quietly. "Are you feeling all right?" Blaise nodded affirmatively and agreed that some rest sounded like a great idea.

"Will I see you again tomorrow, Ray babe?"

"You most certainly will. In fact, sweetie, you'll probably get tired of seeing this face before too long," she jokingly replied.

"Never happen," he said as she leaned to kiss her friend good night.

"Pleasant dreams, dear heart, until tomorrow." Rachel walked toward the door and turned to blow a kiss good night to Blaise. She was smiling when she left the unit and headed down the hall toward the elevator.

She pressed the down button and the elevator door opened immediately. She then pressed the first-floor button. She felt the elevator move slowly downward. Ever since the World Trade Center elevator ride, she somehow felt close to Christian whenever she rode one anywhere. As it came to a soft stop, she was smiling as she thought of Christian. The doors opened and she found herself face to face with Corey Davidson.

She was stunned. She maneuvered herself to the side and then looked him directly in the eye and spoke.

"Have you completely and totally lost your mind? You're incredible, Corey!" She was floundering, trying to think about what she should do. By this time, other people were walking around them in an attempt to get on the elevator before the doors closed.

Corey put up his hands in a conciliatory manner.

"Rachel, please, please, calm down. I know this is crazy, but I had to see if Blaise was all right. You may not believe me, but when you asked for that injunction, I felt like my head had been hit with a sledge hammer." Rachel was looking at him in total disbelief, but she remained silent as he asked her indulgence. "We've got to bury this hatchet that was spawned when our relationship began to decline several weeks ago. I know," he said apologetically, "I know it's mainly my fault, and the series of events that followed have left me in a whirlwind. Just give me a couple more minutes of your time, and then, if you wish, you can call the police. I'll even give you the twenty cents for the call."

Rachel couldn't help but be cautious; she had been lulled into a false sense of comfort with Corey in the past only to be tricked again by yet another scheme. Somehow, this time, he appeared to be different. She listened as he went on.

"First of all, I want to make things right with Blaise," Corey explained. "I'm going to pay for the doctor and hospital bills and any other damages that Blaise feels are due and owing. Then I'm going to promise you, in a signed and notarized document, that I will never, ever be the cause of another discontented moment in your life." Rachel almost laughed about the document part, but as she continued to stare at this new incredible expression, she recognized it as the truth.

"You mean this, don't you, Corey?" she inquired. "This isn't just another patch-up and then continue to go about your merry incorrigible way? Then what, Corey? I'm afraid this scenario is a new area for me. I must admit, I'm pleased that you've decided to pay for Blaise's medical costs. But I must be totally honest, Corey, I cannot believe that you could be held to a voluntary document you describe when you just blatantly violated an injunction. What punishment do you believe I could exact if you violated your Sir Galahad document?" She grinned.

Corey wasn't at all surprised by Rachel's reaction to his peace offering and went on to explain.

"I guess I've been a lot of things in my life Rachel, and I'm not going to start to defend things I've done which I cannot now correct or change. But

I'm not a fool. In the first place, I truly do have deep feelings for you. I know you don't want to hear that, but that doesn't change my feelings. I don't want to lose you completely. And I know I'm pretty close to that point now. Second, this injunction just doesn't fit my lifestyle or my professional life. It's made me ashamed of my recent actions, and I know for certain that I want all this to be over. I need you to release me from this terrible situation.

"Third and lastly, whatever Blaise may be to you, I really do not have an ax to grind with him. I could have killed him, and for that I will beg his forgiveness, because whether you believe it or not, Rachel, I'm not a killer either."

By this time, the emotions of the past couple of days caught up with Corey, and Rachel crumbled as she saw two very large tears stream down Corey's cheeks.

"Forgive me, kitten, please forgive me," he uttered in a last attempt to gain her trust.

Rachel, now unable to stand another second, sat down on the chair directly behind her. She, too, was close to tears, and suddenly, she looked up at Corey.

"All right, Corey, all right. I'll give you another chance, but I certainly can't speak for Blaise. For right now, I think you and I should go directly back to the downtown police station and see if we can get this injunction dropped."

Rachel agreed to meet Corey at the police station, and they went their separate ways. As she drove, she couldn't help but want this emotional roller coaster to stop. She would have to get this situation resolved once and for all and for all parties, particularly Blaise.

As for Corey, he wasn't as sure of himself lately and was hoping that Rachel believed his plea for resolution and her assistance in quieting this terrible upset. He'd be tested, and he knew it. This would be his last chance to have any association with Rachel at all. It was important to him, he'd make it work!

The rain had stopped while Rachel was visiting with Blaise, and Rachel always loved the freshness that permeated the air afterwards. As she stood and watched for Corey's car to arrive, her thoughts about how to solve this seemingly unending situation rumbled through her mind. She still could not believe the incredible gall it must have taken for Corey to ignore the injunction and proceed with the scene that took place moments ago. He was possessed of such a lyrical syntax, it was almost hypnotic, especially when he was trying to absolve himself of wrongdoing. This wasn't any different than the heart-to-heart conversation they had while she was in New York visiting with Amber.

She felt then that Corey would accept the inevitability of this separation. But here she was, not even two weeks away from that poignant and touching time, when Corey once again emerges in that tyrannical and machismo manner.

Perhaps he has a split personality. A Dr. Jekyll and Mr. Hyde psychosis and wasn't even aware of it. The frightening part, when she followed this theory to its fullest conclusion, was that she may be the trigger for his evil side to erupt. She shivered at this thought and was now pacing in front of the police station not quite understanding what was taking Corey such a long time to come the same distance. Could he have backtracked and gone to see Blaise without her? What if he hurt Blaise even more?

Oh, these thoughts were unending, and her uneasiness and uncertainty about Corey's roller coaster behavior were compelling her to return to the hospital. As she began to walk toward her van, the headlights of Corey's car pulled up and he exited the car, apologizing—again.

"Sorry, Rachel," he began, "I ran into Bill Jacoby in the hospital parking lot. He was on his way to see Blaise and will perhaps catch up with you, as well." He seemed a little out of breath. Rachel was glad he was here but bewildered because Bill Jacoby didn't even know Blaise Kinley. Why would he go to visit him?

Rachel stopped in her tracks and grabbed Corey's arm to turn him toward her.

"Corey," she blurted out, "Bill Jacoby doesn't know Blaise Kinley, so why on God's green earth would he go to visit a complete stranger?" She looked totally exasperated.

"Good question, kitten, and I asked him that myself.

"I guess when you told Bill about the background of this mess, he thought a visit from a friend of mine might help ameliorate some of the hostile feelings that kept burgeoning from this altercation." Corey sighed. "Secondly, he has an overwhelming amount of admiration and respect for you, Rachel, and he was so moved by your deep emotional involvement at the time, he wanted to be there for you, if only to sit in the lobby if you so desired."

Rachel's sorrow from all of the negative and confusing thoughts brought tears to her eyes once again.

"This is a merry-go-round Corey, and I'm so fatigued with having to figure out who's doing what and why. I'm sorry, but I still believe you are the source for a major part of this discomfort and suspicious manner I find myself in. Let's get on with this dismissal, and then, once and for all, I want to be done with it."

She was resolute in her statements of discontent and frustration. Corey, too, began to understand and see that the hurt caused from his side would perhaps never heal for Rachel.

They walked up the stairs and into the police station. After Rachel explained the cause for the injunction, a very unconcerned and somewhat puzzled police sergeant advised them that a dismissal or removal of an order of the court would have to be handled by the same court. Rachel explained that since the police were the reinforcement body explicit in the injunction she wanted to make certain that Corey would be released from any possible threat of apprehension.

The sergeant nodded as though agreeing and reiterated his previous advice. He did take their names and said he would put this information "in the system" just in case.

As Rachel and Corey looked around at other things going on in the station, they could well understand why the priority of their request would be at the bottom of the station's list. Handcuffed men and women were being interrogated and booked. Rachel looked at Corey and, for a split second, realized that in spite of whatever had happened in the past seventy-two hours, she didn't want him exposed or included in this part of life that was so frightening and pitiful.

"Let's get out of here," she said, and they left quickly.

As they stood by their respective cars, she felt absolutely spent, and the only thing she wanted to think about now was getting home and going to bed.

Corey could see that Rachel had taken just about all she could handle, and while he wanted to see her home and maybe even talk with her for a while, he didn't want to tempt fate and somehow push her any closer to her limits.

"Good night Rachel," he said, "I hope after a good night's rest that we can try and resolve our differences. I really want us to be friends, if that's all it can ever be."

She looked at him and smiled ever so softly.

"We'll see, Corey, we'll see, good night." She got into her van and drove home.

When she slipped between the cool percale sheets and rested her head on the inviting down pillow, her thoughts were of rest and some much-needed sleep. But deep sleep eluded her, and as she tossed and turned, trying to shut down her mind, the uneasiness and fear returned. Back again, in her subconsciousness, she relived the tragic occurrence in the pub. The smashing noises of the glass and broken furniture echoed in her ears. She squeezed her eyelids tightly, trying to avoid the images, and then there was that loud thud as she recalled Blaise falling against the bar's brass rail. And suddenly there was silence. The deafening, almost abandoning, sound of stillness. She grimaced and fought this recollection. But the picture of Blaise lying on the floor so brutally injured was framed in her head.

She sat up, brought up her legs to her chest, and wrapped her arms around her knees and she nestled her head in the crook of her arm. She breathed deeply and just sat quietly, trying to calm herself. When she turned on the lamp next to her bed, she was surprised to see that she had only been there an hour. She got up and went into the kitchen and poured some milk in a small pot and heated it for a couple of minutes. Then she rummaged through some of the cupboards looking for the jar of honey she knew she had placed there. A couple of teaspoons was all she took.

As she stirred the elixir that her mother always prescribed when she was a child, she sat at the counter and placed both hands around the warm glass. "You'll fall right to sleep, sweetheart, when you've finished your milk and honey. It will warm your tummy and scare away all your fears of the night." As though Mama DeRoca's voice was whispering in her ear, Rachel grinned and tried to remember if that were true. It must have been, since she continued to use this remedy through most of her life. She returned to her room convinced that she would rest now. She put her head on the pillow and surrendered to the mysterious world of sleep.

Eleven

The next morning in another Grosse Pointe neighborhood, Randy Markham was brushing his teeth vigorously, and as usual, he pulled way too much floss out of the small dispenser. He rushed to get this necessary part of his morning routine over with. Estelle Markham was preparing breakfast for her family and listening to the morning news and weather forecast. Dr. Markham was reading the *Free Press* and something in the paper reminded him about Rachel and her recent incident involving her neighbor.

"You know, dear," he said, breaking the silence of the morning breakfast routine, "Rachel Radcliffe's neighbor was involved in a skirmish in one of the pubs here locally night before last."

As she directed her attention to her husband's comments and put down the ladle she was using to make pancakes, Estelle responded.

"Is Rachel all right, Randy?" was her first question.

"Yes, but her neighbor was injured quite seriously, and I was the operating surgeon who removed a rather large blood clot that he sustained when he fell."

"Oh, my God, did he come through the operation okay?" she asked.

"Yes, my sweet," Randall responded, "and, as a matter of fact, I think Mr. Kinley is going to be all right."

Estelle stopped for a moment.

"Did you say Kinley, darling?"

"Yes, do you know the name?" He looked at her quizzically.

"I believe I do, there's a Milly Kinley in my bridge group at the War Memorial, and if I'm not mistaken, she has a son, uh, although rumor has it that there was a major falling out some time ago when she found out that he was a homosexual."

"Goodness, Estelle," he exclaimed, "you certainly do gather some juicy tidbits at these so-called social gatherings." And Dr. Markham smiled broadly.

Estelle smiled as well, but she couldn't believe how coincidental life was and how small the circles of people we know gets as time goes by.

"Well," continued Estelle, "this gives me the perfect excuse to call

Rachel and find out how she's been. She was kind enough to offer her services at our next charity auction, and I promised Randy that we'd invite the 'cool lady' over for dinner."

"Great idea, sweetheart." He got up and moved toward her and leaned down and kissed her lightly on the tip of the nose and said, "I love you, you know that?"

She looked up at him with the same sparkle in her eyes since the first day she met him.

"I know, and I love you, my sweet."

Young Randy made his usual two-by-two trek down the stairs and burst into the kitchen, filled with his usual glut of energy.

"Good morning," he sang, "what's for breakfast? I'm starved."

Estelle and Randall laughed as they looked adoringly at their young son.

"Pancakes and fresh blueberries, vanilla yogurt, and a glass of freshly squeezed orange juice," Estelle responded.

"Yum, I'll have six, okay, Mom?"

Estelle shook her head in amazement, but was never surprised when he would ingest every bite of whatever amount he took.

This was one of the few times during the day when the three of them could sit and enjoy each other's company. It was a treat, as well, since Dr. Markham's schedule was so erratic, they never knew when he'd be called away at a moment's notice. Young Randy was growing up so quickly that they savored each moment he could share with them.

"I think I'm going to call Rachel later on this morning, Randy," Estelle said. "Your father told me earlier that her neighbor and best friend had been seriously injured in a fight at one of our pubs the day before yesterday."

Randy's eyes lit up when he heard the cool lady's name, particularly since he had been wondering when his mom was going to invite her over for dinner.

"Super," he responded. "I mean, not that her friend was hurt, but that you're going to call her. I do hope her friend is all right, and, Mom, don't forget to set a specific date, like this weekend, to have her over for dinner, okay?" He was pleased at the prospect of seeing Rachel again. Maybe he'd call his Uncle Christian.

He hadn't spoken to him in a long time. Randy would ask about his new show's progress and then just happen to mention that Rachel might be coming for dinner that weekend.

It didn't take much for young Randy to imagine a whole bunch of other things, as well. Like maybe Uncle Christian could come to Grosse Pointe this weekend. What a surprise it would be for his mom and dad, not to mention the cool lady. And when they left New York, his uncle did ask him to keep him posted about Rachel when and if he found out anything. He decided to call him after school when his mom and dad were both at work, and maybe by that time, his mom may have had a chance to call Rachel and explain the situation.

"Thanks, Mom, great breakfast!" Randy exclaimed. "I'll see you after school." He gave Estelle a quick kiss on the cheek, ran into the half-bathroom and washed his hands, grabbed his school bag, and was out the door.

Estelle sighed and began to clear the table. As she filled the dishwasher and tidied up, Dr. Markham came downstairs and went over to give her a kiss good-bye.

"Have a super day, sweetheart," she uttered as he, too, rushed out the front door to begin a very busy schedule at the hospital. When everything was put away, she went upstairs to take a shower and get ready for her day. She thought she'd try Rachel at home before she left for work.

Estelle checked her organizer and found Rachel's phone number. She dialed and waited as the phone began to ring.

"Hello," she heard.

"Good morning, Rachel, this is Estelle Markham, how are you?"

Rachel was surprised to hear this familiar voice and responded in kind.

"Good morning to you, Estelle. It's been a while, and I hope you are well. I suppose Randall has told you about my situation recently." She waited for Estelle to respond.

"Yes, as a matter of fact, Rachel, that's one of the reasons for this call. First of all, of course, I wanted to send along my best wishes and sincere hope that your friend will recover from this terrible injury. Secondly, I had been meaning to call you and extend an invitation to have dinner with us, perhaps this weekend?"

Rachel thought for a moment about what day it was and how far away the weekend was.

"Thank you," she responded, "that would be lovely, and I don't believe I have any plans as of yet for the weekend." Rachel paused and sipped some of her coffee. "I suppose Randall has told you that he saved Blaise's life with his masterful surgical techniques. You know, Estelle, Randall and I mused at how strange life is, in that a few short weeks ago none of us knew one another and here we are pretty involved in each other's trials and tribulations that we've all come to expect on this journey called life."

Estelle was always proud of Randall's professional expertise and expressed that very sentiment to Rachel.

"He's a dedicated physician and surgeon, and the same qualities that make him so are the very ones that I love so dearly. His compassion and caring for everyone, not only his patients, but our friends and family members, endear me to him more each day."

Rachel couldn't help but wish that she had developed a relationship like theirs. Belonging so totally to one person and living that commitment must be the most secure feeling in the world. For her, the search continued, and she hoped she may have found it in Christian.

"It's wonderful to hear such glowing compliments about a good marriage. They're few and far between these days." They continued their conversation for quite some time. Just chitchat initially, and then Rachel asked about Master Randy.

"How is that charming son of yours, Estelle?" Rachel smiled. "He comes to mind every so often because he was so instrumental in pursuing me and making certain that I would somehow become a part of his world. I'm so happy his persistence succeeded."

"Well," Estelle replied, "he is a youngster, but he has a good eye for beauty, and he's blessed already with good, sound judgment when it comes to people." Rachel gleamed and thanked her for the nice compliment. "He'll be thrilled, as we all will be, if you can come for dinner on Saturday next."

"Saturday it is," replied Rachel. "What time and how shall I dress?" she inquired.

"Seven for a cocktail before dinner, and casual would be just fine. We have to dress up so much of the time in our respective careers that it's a treat to dress down and relax whenever the opportunity presents itself." Estelle paused. "I don't believe I gave you our address while we were in New York, Rachel, but we live on Lake Shore Drive. It's kind of tricky to find, since the address is not seen from the road. Call me on Saturday afternoon, and I'll give you exact directions then." Estelle concluded.

"I'll do that, Estelle, and needless to say, I'm really looking forward to it."

"Me, too, Rachel, maybe we can have a good long talk about my brother, as well." She chuckled.

Rachel's excitement grew, and again she thanked Estelle as they said their good-byes and hung up.

In Manhattan, Christian sat in his rather large breakfast nook while

Trevor, his butler, fixed him a cup of hot tea with lemon and honey. He had obviously contracted the nasty virus that was flagrantly romping about from casting director to choreographer and managed not to miss one of the chorus line dancers. It was unusual for Christian to be sick. He was just someone who always enjoyed good health, up until now, that is. He was sneezing and coughing and grumbling all at the same time.

"This is the most miserable cold I've ever had," he bellowed. Trevor, was truly a gentleman's gentleman, and he merely ignored his master's utterance and proceeded about his business; that being making certain that Christian ingested enough fluids, took his prescribed medicine, and rested as much as possible. None of these were easy tasks, but Trevor had been with Christian for almost twenty years, and he knew that gentle persuasion and stubborn persistence would get the job done.

"This is—This is"—and he sneezed again. He was out of breath and more annoyed than before. "This is awful," he gasped and sneezed again. The telephone rang, and Trevor answered.

"Avian residence."

"Hi, Trevor." It's Randy Markham. Is my uncle there?"

"Why, yes, Master Randall, he is, but I'm afraid he's a little—no, very much under the weather," responded Trevor.

"Who is that?" yelled Christian from the other room.

"It's Master Randall, sir," responded Trevor. "Do you wish to speak with him?"

"Yes—ah, yes. I do—I'll pick it up in here." Christian cleared his throat and adjusted himself in the oversized, opulent velvet wing chair. "Hi, Randy—how are you, lad?" Try as he may, he couldn't camouflage the extremely deep and raspy voice that echoed from his lips.

"Is that you, Uncle Christian? You sound awful!" stated Randy, who was surprised to hear this unfamiliar and not too pleasant voice.

"Well," said Christian, "that's the precise adjective to describe this nasty malady."

"I guess," said Randy, "this pretty much answers the purpose of my call before I even ask and definitely eliminates a super idea I had for this weekend." Since the two of them had developed a close relationship ever since Randy was a baby, Christian was well experienced in dealing with these somewhat nebulous statements from Randy.

"And, what pray tell might that be? Perhaps a quick jet to the Big Apple so you and I can see the Yankees? A sail around the island? Or a Christmas walk through FAO Schwarz?"

Randy disliked having to disappoint his Uncle Christian, who was always so accommodating to his previous "super ideas," and he responded sadly.

"The cool lady is coming over for dinner Saturday night, and I just thought it might be nice if you paid us a surprise visit. She needs you, Uncle Christian, a friend of hers has been seriously injured, and she's depressed." Christian sat up, and had he felt just a bit better would have jumped at that suggestion, but with this blasted cold, he couldn't. No, he couldn't subject anyone else to it.

"Yes, I know, I spoke to Rachel just yesterday. You're right, Randy, it would have been a wonderful surprise, and if I were feeling better, you know I wouldn't hesitate a second to accommodate you. Perhaps there will be another time real soon for a visit, and I do appreciate your concern for Rachel. I share those concerns and will call her frequently." Randy understood totally why his uncle declined and was already thinking about the next invitation some time in the near future.

"Well, maybe I'll find out a little more when she visits, and then I can call you again. I hope you feel better, Uncle Christian. Please take care of yourself, okay?"

"Thank you, Randy, and I'm so pleased you thought about this wonderful possibility. I think Rachel is right," he chuckled. "You are a little matchmaker, aren't you? And I'm not complaining, either, I'm pleased and grateful that you were responsible for bringing Rachel into our lives, Randy."

"I like her, too, Uncle Christian, so my motives are a bit selfish, as well," and Randy grinned broadly.

They exchanged a few more pleasantries, and when Christian started to sneeze again, he apologized to Randy and said they'd talk again real soon.

When Randy hung up, Christian sighed deeply and thought how wonderful it would have been to see Rachel. He could imagine her beautiful face, and the thought of her close to him was comforting and much more exciting then he could handle. He would love nothing more than to be there for her during this troubled time, but all things considered, it was best that he be alone with the monster cold, and he sneezed again.

Back in Grosse Pointe, Randy had to figure out how he'd explain the long distance phone call to New York. He'd think of something; he always did.

At Saint John's Hospital, Blaise was lying in bed, staring at the other ICU units and wondering when he'd be transferred to another room, one with a bit more privacy and one that didn't have as many seriously ill people. The nurse and attending doctors had been wonderful. He admired their deep sense of commitment to, and efficiency at, their chosen craft. Dr. Markham had been most diligent in his observance of Blaise's progress ever since the surgery. His professionalism and reputation were impeccable, and Blaise was yet another living patient who bore the proof of Dr. Markham's successful surgical powers.

With the exception of an occasional minor headache, which was to be expected, Blaise had not experienced much discomfort since the operation. Of course, he knew he was being given pain relievers and other medications to help him through the initial healing process without too much pain. This was his favorite time of the day. Rounds were over, baths were finished, medication had been consumed, and the first blood-letting routine was over. Now he could rest and look forward to breakfast. He was hoping to have something a bit more delectable than Cream of Wheat, skim milk, and green Jell-O. He swore he'd never ingest green Jell-O again in his life once he left here.

His thoughts drifted now to a topic he enjoyed and loved to think about. Rachel. This recent near-escape from death brought things in clearer focus, and Blaise could no longer continue this charade about his homosexuality. He'd have to tell Rachel the truth. Even though he would risk her absolute rejection, he could no longer lie to her or delude himself any longer. He loved her. He had for a very long time. The problem was how to make Rachel understand the deception. The lies. She had always explained her need for trust. If he told her the truth, would the trust she had in him be destroyed. And if so, would it be irreparable?

Questions only led to more questions, but Blaise was convinced that it was time for the truth to be told once and for all. He breathed a deep sigh of relief and closed his eyes to doze for a while.

As Rachel pulled into the hospital parking lot, she was excited about the phone call from Estelle and anxious to tell Blaise about her upcoming invitation to dine at the Markham home on Saturday. She also wondered why she hadn't heard from Corey. Her attorney assured her that the injunction would be dropped as soon as he could get the order requesting it signed by the issuing judge. Among other things, she hadn't returned Amber's calls about Blaise's progress, and she hadn't spoken to Christian.

All of a sudden, she became a bit overwhelmed by all the things she had to do. Walking from the parking lot to the rear entrance of this large medical edifice, she was glad that she'd be seeing her friend, Blaise. He always put things in their proper perspective and would reassure her that she could successfully get everything on her list completed in good order.

The medicinal odor and general noisiness of the hospital interrupted Rachel's thoughts as she went to the elevator. She expected to be face to face again with Corey when the bell rang and the elevator door opened. She held her breath as she looked into the empty elevator. She got on and pressed "4." The doors closed slowly, and the ascent began. Today, unlike other times, she went directly to the fourth floor without a stop. As she got off, she looked quickly toward the ICU unit to see if she could see Blaise. "Yes," she uttered to herself, "there he is." But as she neared the entrance, she noticed that he was sleeping. The nurses on duty acknowledged Rachel, and so she took the opportunity to ask about his condition.

"He's coming along nicely," said one of the senior nurses. "He has such a wonderful attitude and an obvious will to live, two things people in this profession love to see and are grateful for. Dr. Markham will be here this afternoon to examine him and decide whether or not he can be transferred to a private room." Rachel thanked her for the encouraging update and continued down the aisle and into the unit. She stopped at Blaise's bedside and just looked at how much better he seemed. His color was eminently better. He stirred and awakened as he sensed someone's presence.

"Ray babe," he whispered, pleased. "What a glorious way to wake up, seeing that beautiful face."

"Well, Mr. Kinley, you're obviously feeling much better, and if I can believe you're telling me the truth and it's not the effects of some of your medication, I'm flattered." Blaise loved these exchanges with Rachel and responded as usual.

"Your beauty, my princess, is euphoric, and if I am drugged, it's only by your loveliness."

Rachel chuckled, and her eyes sparkled with joy and tears to see her dear friend able to joke and participate in this bantering she enjoyed so much.

"I surrender, kind sir." She laughed. "I surrender to the truth of your observations and with humility. I agree, I'm 'your-phobic.'"

Blaise now laughed aloud, but not without consequence; his head under the bandages reminded him quickly that the incision was still new, and any loud emotional bursts or movements irritated the needlework that was still quite sensitive. He winced, and Rachel's expression changed quickly to fear.

"Are you all right, dear heart?" she exclaimed. "Oh, Blaise, I'm sorry if

I've caused you any discomfort." She looked very upset and reached for his hand to try and comfort him. He recovered quickly and putting his hand on hers, assured her that he was all right. Rachel couldn't believe her behavior, certainly she was smarter than that, and to believe that he was up to a level where she could act so freely was incredible. It was just another instance where she questioned her judgment and displayed less than her usual good common sense.

"I'm fine, Ray babe," Blaise said emphatically. "Honest." He was now looking at her and trying to see if her eyes would see his sincerity.

Rachel patted Blaise's hand and, in a more quieting manner, suggested that they converse with as little emoting as possible. Her smile was beguiling, and all Blaise needed to know that she was fine. He scrutinized his friend's expression and wondered if now would be the correct time and place to express his love and perhaps risk the loss of their relationship completely.

Living this lie had taken its toll, and Blaise had convinced himself that no matter what the outcome would be, he must finally bare his soul and prepare himself for whatever the outcome would create. He hoped beyond hope for even a glimmer of understanding and forgiveness for the manner in which this revelation was dropped in her lap. His thought was interrupted by the sound of Rachel's voice.

"I spoke to Christian today, Blaise, and I explained to him in detail what transpired between you and Corey." She hesitated, and continued. "He was concerned about the whole situation but was happy that you were going to be all right." Blaise listened as Rachel went on! "I know you're going to like Christian. He's as caring and thoughtful as you are, Blaise. And I have thanked God so much lately for giving me two wonderful friends." She was holding Blaise's hand as she described this man who had become his rival.

"When I went to New York, Blaise, I was so confused and unsettled. I won't believe it was anything else than divine intervention that led me to Christian." She got up from Blaise's bedside and walked to the window overlooking the rear of the hospital.

"Now, that you're on the mend, dear heart, I feel even more grateful that you'll be coming back home in the near future. Back to our beautiful home and neighborhood! Maybe, Christian will be able to come to visit soon, and then you'll be able to see why I fell in love with him so quickly and so totally."

The look in her eyes could not deny what she was feeling as she talked about her New York romance. It was difficult to continue to listen, but he didn't want to interject anything that might upset Rachel and destroy any possibility of explaining his hidden feelings.

"You're so quiet, Blaise. Are you all right?" She looked at him and could tell that he was preoccupied! "Have I bored you with all of my blithering about Christian? If I have, sweetie, I do apologize. I guess sometimes its coincidence is a bit overwhelming." She looked sheepishly at Blaise, waiting for a response. The hesitation and silence created an atmosphere that could almost be seen. Blaise smiled and responded.

"You know Ray babe, I've always been concerned about, and interested in, anything or anyone who makes you happy or unhappy." He stopped speaking, took a deep breath. "I can't dismiss the memories of the developing nightmare you experienced or the troubled times that you and Corey sustained over the past few months. I've always believed in my heart of hearts that you would resolve these differences and get on with your life."

Rachel was listening intently as Blaise replied in a tone filled with compassion and understanding.

"You must know, Rachel, that everything in this life is not always what it seems or as it seems at any given moment. There are times when we do things to get past a rough time, walk around the truth to pacify someone's feelings, and remain silent when we should have spoken. Nothing in life is ever simple, and as imperfect humans, we are vulnerable, capable of things that we wouldn't do or say in safer moments."

Rachel's expression changed from one of listening to one of concern.

"Blaise, have I said something to upset you? It almost sounds as though you're getting ready to confess something or chastise me for something I've said or done."

He floundered and searched his mind for a direction, a hint of how he could proceed with this colloquy he initiated.

"No, Ray, you haven't said or done anything to upset me, but I may have done you a great disservice by not being totally honest with you."

"Oh, my God, Blaise, don't tell me you're sicker than we thought. Please tell me you're all right." She came to tears quickly and grabbed his hand once again.

He patted her hand and responded.

"No, no, Ray, it's not that. I guess I've appointed myself as your sole guardian and protectorate for so long, I just can't break the habit." She was trying to understand where Blaise was going with this, and now a tear raced down her cheek.

"Are you trying to say good-bye to me, Blaise? I don't understand where this conversation is going!" She brushed away the tears and waited for his response.

Dr. Markham walked into the room and excused the interruption of their visit.

"Sorry, folks, but I have to check on Blaise's condition today to see if we can transfer him to a private room later on."

Blaise and Rachel both recovered quickly from the intensity of the discussion, and Rachel excused herself as Dr. Markham proceeded with the examination.

"Well, Blaise, according to my examination, you're doing remarkably well, and I think we can transfer you to a private room as soon as I check our availability." Dr. Markham was writing in the required entries on Blaise's chart, when Blaise spoke to him.

"I have you to thank, Dr. Markham. Your expertise in the operating room has definitely given me a second chance at life, and I'm not quite sure if I'll ever be able to thank you for this precious gift." Blaise smiled, and Dr. Markham expressed his gratitude at hearing such high praise about his surgical skills. He left the area to see if he could effectuate Blaise's transfer before the shift change took place.

As Dr. Markham walked down the hall toward the nurses' desk, he could see Rachel sitting and waiting in the visitor's room. He walked over to her and advised her of the good news of Blaise's progress. Rachel's composure was intact, and she thanked Randall for his dedication and profound caring for his patients.

"This has been a banner day for plaudits and accolades." He grinned. "It's both encouraging and gratifying when the outcome of my labors is so wonderfully expressed by patient and family alike."

Rachel smiled at Randall's implication that she was one of Blaise's family members.

"So, Randall, you don't see anything that might stand in the way of a full recovery for Blaise?" she asked apprehensively.

"That's right, Rachel. He's come past all the critical phases, and his physical and mental conditions appear to be heading for normalcy at a fast rate." Dr. Markham then excused himself and told Rachel she could return to Blaise's unit for another little while.

Blaise smiled broadly as Rachel approached his bedside.

"I think Dr. Markham's interruption was most timely," he said. "I'm probably under the influence of too much medication, Ray babe, so please, let's disregard that last exchange and talk about more pleasant things. Like—Mrs. Longley."

Rachel laughed out loud. Only Blaise could bring them back to a more comfortable position. His mention of Mrs. Longley was amusing to Rachel since Blaise knew she was Rachel's most influential and wealthiest client. He, too, had the pleasure of doing a few sculptures and wall hangings for the Longleys.

"Right on, Blaise," she replied. "Mrs. Longley has been just wonderful, and she continues to challenge my talent and, more importantly, keep me from starving." Rachel grinned.

The familiar and light-hearted exchange they enjoyed was uplifting and just what they needed at this moment.

"Randall says your healing progress and prognosis are both wonderful, Blaise. This transfer to a private room is the next step toward getting you out of here once and for all."

Blaise's square jaw and angular face was as handsome as ever, and Rachel was encouraged to see the sparkle return to his smiling eyes!

"Do you think I could have just a little hug before you leave, Ray babe?" With somewhat of an effort, he extended both arms.

"Your wish is my command, kind sir!" She smiled and moved directly into his arms.

Blaise thought about her response, then, *Don't I wish! But at least for now, this hug will have to do.*

Rachel hugged him a little tighter and then planted a kiss on his cheek.

"Luv ya, dear heart," and she slowly backed away.

His emotions were erupting, and his ability to quell their expression was almost more than Blaise could handle. He may look incapacitated, but once again, looks were definitely deceiving.

"Love you, too, Ray. The next time you visit, I'll be in my private room. Maybe, if you're really good, I'll share some of my green Jell-O with you!" He chuckled.

"I can hardly wait!" She smiled. "Sleep well, dear. I'll see you tomorrow." She blew him a kiss and left the unit.

He watched her as she walked down the aisle. He had successfully avoided divulging his true feelings and, at least for right now, sighed a breath of relief.

When Rachel got home, she quickly changed her clothes. She then headed directly for the kitchen and put on the kettle for a nice, soothing cup of tea. She had decided to just lay back and spend a quiet evening at home. She'd call Amber, though, and fill her in on Blaise's upgraded condition.

Also, she'd explain about the surprising outcome of the injunction she had filed against Corey. For a moment, she couldn't recall if she had told Amber everything that transpired during the past few days. As she sat and began to go through four days of accumulated mail and stacks of newspapers, Rachel began to think about the conversation she had with Blaise just before Dr. Markham came into the unit.

She was curious about some of the things he had intimated. And in her own inimitable way, she began to self-examine all of her moves that led to it. The tea kettle began to whistle, and as she went into the kitchen to get the Red Zinger tea bags out of the cupboard, she could think of only one thing that might have initiated Blaise's mysterious discussion. Christian. Perhaps Blaise was concerned about the speed with which this relationship with Christian had developed. Blaise had certainly been there when she was at both her zenith and nadir with Corey. The tea was steeping, and Amber once again came to mind.

"My goodness!" she exclaimed. "If I don't get back to Amber tonight, she'll either disown me, or I'll find her at my doorstep for sure." She brought the piping hot teacup and saucer into the living room. She sat down on her favorite wing chair and dialed Amber's number. The phone rang only twice when Tony answered.

"Helloooo," he echoed.

"Hi, Tony, my dear. It's Rachel. I thought if I didn't get back to Amber tonight, she'd be on her way to Grosse Pointe tomorrow."

"Ah, my sweet, Rachel," Tony responded, "we've been very concerned about you and Blaise. And you're right, my friend, Amber has been pacing for a couple of days, wondering how Blaise is doing and how you're managing to cope with this whole messy situation." He stopped briefly and then continued. "But, you know, Rachel, it's only because she loves you so dearly."

Rachel was about to respond when she heard Amber's voice in the distance.

"Honey, is that Rachel?" Amber asked Tony.

"Yes, my sweet, it's she," he responded. "Well, Rachel, take care of yourself. You sound like you've got everything under control. Luv ya, babe. Here's Amber." Rachel bade him good-bye, and "love you, too" and Tony handed the receiver over to Amber.

"Hey, bella! What's happening?" Amber asked anxiously. "I've been going bonkers waiting to hear from you. And, quite frankly, if I heard Tony say 'no news, is good news' one more time, I was going to have to hit him."

Rachel laughed at her friend's usual comedic retorts. She then started to apologize for her tardy call and Amber interrupted.

"No need for apologies, bella, as long as you're all right. I'm fine. Only thing left now is my darned curiosity. You know me, sweetie, I want to know everything. The whole blow-by-blow description. First though, start with Corey rotting in some jail cell. I think I like that part the best."

Rachel grinned and sipped her tea.

"Well," she sighed, "that's as good a place as any to start. Because I never did press charges after all." Rachel began to explain what happened. She went over all the events leading up to the fight and how she dealt with the consequences thereafter. With Amber's counter comments as Rachel disclosed the entire situation, an hour and a half quickly passed. Rachel finally yawned and took a deep breath.

"I guess we should purchase some stock in AT&T. If we keep engaging in these long distance telephone calls, we should at least reap some dividends. Besides, my current stock portfolio could stand an injection of profit once in a while."

Amber was now finishing her third glass of orange juice and feeling one hundred percent better about her friend's well-being. Most of her earlier fears had been allayed, and she was ready to say good night and call it a day.

"So, doll," asked Amber, "when do you think you and Christian will get together again? If absence, in fact, does make the heart grow fonder, you'll both be chomping at the bit to see each other real soon." Then, right out of the blue, Amber asked, "You do still feel the same about Christian, don't you, Rachel?" There was a brief pause and more silence than Amber could handle.

"Of course I do, Amber. Our short moments together still live vividly in my mind and in my heart. He's made inroads into my heart that would be extremely difficult to extricate right now. Even thinking about him makes my pulse race and my temperature rise a couple of points." She sighed and walked over to get a cold glass of spring water from her refrigerator.

"Sounds like love to me," Amber responded. "With everything else happening in your life right now, doll, this love will get you through."

They had pretty much covered all the topics for one conversation, and Rachel yawned again and thanked Amber for having such an understanding ear and soft shoulder.

"What would I ever do without you, Amber?" Rachel sighed. "You're such an anchor for me, and I love you for it!"

Amber smiled and decided to leave her friend with a happy thought.

"If I don't quit eating like I have been recently, I'll look like your anchor," she chided. "Ciao, bella."

"Love to the children, dear heart. We'll talk again real soon," Rachel said and hung up the telephone.

Amber hung up, thinking that the news about Carlo and Marisa appearing in Christian's new musical, "Cinema," would be good news for yet another time.

Tony was waiting for Amber in their bedroom and teased her as she came through the door.

"I'm happy Rachel is paying for that call. We'd almost need a second mortgage to support that one."

"Oh, sure, Tony," she responded, "poor us. Maybe I'll get a job." And she laughed.

As Amber got into bed and snuggled up against her waiting husband, she thanked God for putting this wonderful man in her life. She also prayed that some day soon, her best friend would share in a relationship as precious as theirs.

However, back in Grosse Pointe, Rachel donned her U of M nightshirt and crawled into her cool bed. Quite alone and very tired. Sleep was beckoning to her and she surrendered to its call.

Twelve

A couple of weeks had passed and getting back into the routine of going to the office and working on the projects she loved made the time without Blaise pass a little more comfortably. He would be released tomorrow, and she still hadn't heard from Corey. His silence made her more than a little uneasy and uncomfortable. But she would wait.

The dinner with the Markhams was very enjoyable. Rachel was still trying to absorb the magnificence, the grandeur, of their home on Lake Shore. Success had its privileges, and the Markham's were living proof of that. She also felt a certain bond beginning to develop between her and Estelle. They actually spent more time talking about Christian, and Rachel was soaking up every bit of nostalgia that Estelle could offer. Most of her visit was spent with Master Randy. His love for the sea and the universe was borne out by the magnificent room that Randall and Estelle had built specifically for him. It almost paralleled the Cranbrook Planetarium. She was amazed at this youngster's vast knowledge of the solar system and its impact on the world in which they lived. His intellect was definitely beyond his twelve years. What a delightful mixture of youth, maturity, and eclectic humor. He was a joy, and she reveled in sharing time with him.

"I'm going to have a star named for you, Rachel. Of course, I'm going to call it 'Cool Lady.' "

Rachel was becoming more enamored with the whole family. And just thinking about the possibility of becoming a part of it made her very excited. The evening and the visit went by much too quickly for all of them, but they promised not to wait too long before it happened again.

In the meantime, Rachel became more concerned about Corey's very obvious silence. In the past couple of months, she had learned to accept different things into her life. And getting away from old habits, like wondering about Corey's whereabouts on a regular basis, was a nice change. She could feel the resurgence of life and vitality filling her very soul.

She had called someone to come over and tidy up Blaise's house. For dinner, she planned to fix a couple of Cornish hens, Blaise's favorite, along with some fresh asparagus and steamed red-skinned potatoes. Add to this a crispy romaine salad topped off with balsamic vinaigrette dressing, a chilled bottle of Chablis, and the feast would be complete. Since neither of them ate too many sweets, Rachel picked up some fresh fruit and had it already chilling in the refrigerator.

The day was whizzing by as she finished running last-minute errands, which included picking up a "Welcome home, Blaise!" banner. She bought a few multicolored balloons to place here and there. Blaise was coming home, and she reveled in the thought of his ongoing presence once again.

At Saint John's, Blaise was putting together his accumulated get-well cards, mostly from Rachel, and a couple of his clients. The bandages on his head had been replaced with much smaller pieces of gauze. And his hair had begun to grow back. One of his nurses came in his room and asked if she could help him with anything.

"As a matter of fact, Ms. Liz, there is," he replied. Blaise sat down on the chair next to his bed and looked up at the pretty nurse. "Do me a favor. Would you?" he whispered. "You must know someone in the billing department, don't you?"

She grinned slightly and responded rather hesitantly.

"Yes, as a matter of fact. I do, Mr. Kinley. Knowing that, how can it become a favor for you?" She'd been a nurse for about ten years, and there weren't too many questions she hadn't been asked. With the exception of a few, she had fielded them, up to now.

"Well, Liz, rumor has it that I have a fairy godfather, and I wanted to see if it's true that he paid my hospital bill." Blaise's eyes lit up as he smiled, and Nurse Liz found it difficult to believe he was telling the truth. But after a few more questions and some additional coaxing on Blaise's part, she conceded and left the room to see what, if anything, she could find out from her billing department friend.

As Blaise decided to rest for a while until Nurse Liz returned, he thought again about how he would divulge his true feelings for Rachel. He'd almost done it two weeks ago. But fate intervened, and he now felt that it was for the best. He had other hurdles to overcome, as well. This brush with death certainly brought this deception about being gay to a screeching halt. With this facade, he had already lost the respect of both mother and father. And while he never developed a relationship that anyone could point at as being "proof positive," he'd unfortunately found that the *presumption* was as damaging as if it were really true.

Obviously, recanting would be a slow process. This kind of revelation could almost be as disconcerting as the deception. In the meantime, he would try to maintain the same type of behavior patterns that Rachel had come to know and accept. His determination to finally tell Rachel the truth and nothing but the truth was more than a bit unsettling. These feelings that he had suppressed would no longer be denied. But timing would be critical. *First things first,* he thought. *Rachel's infatuation with Christian Avian. Is it infatuation? Or is it really love?* If it is love, should he risk telling her this stranger-than-fiction story about his incredible quest for her love? And putting all this into its proper perspective, what if she just decided to divest herself of him for the very same reason she dumped Corey—mistrust?

"Oh, well," he muttered, "what are the lines of that silly poem—'if ifs and ands were pots and pans,' la la, la la, la la, la la." He sighed deeply, and as he contemplated his plight, there was a tap on his door. He called out "come in," and there, as big as life itself, stood Corey Davidson.

Blaise's first inclination was to ring for the nurse's desk, but as he looked more closely at Corey's expression, he decided to hold back. Corey walked toward his bed very slowly, and with his hands held out in front of him, proceeded to talk with him.

"Hello, Blaise. First of all, I don't mean you any harm. Honest. I've just come to see for myself that you're all right. I've called every day for the past two weeks to check on your progress, and I was elated to find out that you're being released today." Corey stayed close to the door and was prepared to leave if Blaise asked him to.

"You're a real case. You know that, Corey." All of Blaise's pent-up fears and anger spewed out. "You've got more nerve than anyone I've ever met in my entire life. You mess up a relationship with one of the most wonderful women that ever walked the face of this earth. And when you decide that drowning your sorrows in a gallon of booze is the only solution, you add almost killing me to your list of stupid moves. My God, man, is there no end to your bad judgment and screw-ups?" Blaise breathed deeply and began to reach for the bell button attached to his bed.

"Please don't do that," said Corey. "You're absolutely right about me and my abhorrent behavior. I guess, if I were trying to justify any of these so-called stupid moves, my only defense would be that when I finally saw that I had lost Rachel, I went berserk! But, hey, I'm not looking for any sympathy or understanding. What I did was plain crazy, and I consider myself infinitely fortunate that Rachel dropped the felonious assault and injunction against me!" Corey's tone and direct response surprised Blaise. Even more, he was confused because he was actually believing him.

"I know," said Corey, "that I'll never be able to rectify my relationship with Rachel or my terrible actions that left you near death, Blaise, but I hope you will allow me to at least pay for the doctor and hospital bills. And I would be more than wiling to pay you whatever earnings you've lost and will lose in the future due to my horrible behavior!"

When Rachel had mentioned this possibility to Blaise initially, he really didn't believe it would happen. And this morning when he asked the nurse to check on that possibility, he was half-hoping and half-disbelieving.

"You are a conundrum, Corey," Blaise continued. "I guess on the one hand, I can almost buy this generous offering as some kind of redemption. But on the other hand, realistically, I'm a bit leery of accepting and trusting your behavior, given your past history with Rachel." Blaise kept an eye on the set of buttons that could bring assistance if he needed it.

"You're right to mistrust me and my motives because of what you just said. History would absolutely confirm that I shouldn't be trusted." Corey's expression was firm, and his jaw was clenched as he proceeded. "People change, Blaise. That's not any big revelation, but for me, there's been a remarkable change." Blaise was now listening with a little less apprehension but still with his hand close to the emergency buttons on his pillow. Corey breathed deeply and continued.

"It's remarkable because I've never ever once in my life felt that I should have to change. I was the incomparable Corey Davidson. Never had a lack of cash or the companionship of a beautiful woman. I graduated in the top three percent of my class, and my first architectural project was a smashing success. Everything I ever wanted was either mine for the asking or for the taking. Then along comes Rachel. I knew when I met her that she could be my total undoing, but I made certain that I couldn't be found out. For to be vulnerable to anyone would be a sign of weakness, and Corey Davidson couldn't afford to be weak."

Blaise was amazed at this revelation. It sounded more like a confession in order to save his immortal soul. But why now, and why was Corey doing this for him? Corey continued.

"Rachel was different than any other woman I had ever met. She was honest and sincere, and when she told me that she was going to marry Neil Radcliffe, I was devastated. Even though she was already seeing Neil when we met, I never believed she would accept his proposal of marriage. He was too needy. Every time I saw Rachel with him, it was she doing for him. I never really got a sense of any spark in their relationship. It lacked passion."

Corey stopped briefly and, looking almost embarrassed, asked Blaise if he could sit down.

Blaise had no earthy idea where all of this was leading, but by now, he was intrigued with this admission, and after offering Corey a chair, he asked him to continue.

"I knew right away that the marriage wasn't working. Rachel would go through long periods of silence and deep depression. The relationship that she had hoped would germinate never did. Neil idolized her and in this idolization, he never touched her. Eventually, after too many years of therapy and failed reconciliations, Rachel left him. It almost killed Neil, and the guilt almost killed Rachel."

"For a long time I was just there as a friend, lending moral support and a soft shoulder whenever she needed either. Then one day, she asked me to go to Chicago on a business trip with her and our relationship and our lives would never be the same." Corey was now sitting with his head in his hands.

"I don't really know when you came into the picture, Blaise, but I sensed when she started to mention your name that you could very well be competition for me. Our relationship was an up and down kind of thing. We'd stay together for awhile, and then something would happen, and we'd separate. But I always felt that even during the rough times, she'd come back."

When Corey stopped speaking, the clamoring of bed pans, the conversations of doctors and nurses, and the unidentifiable cacophony of hospital sounds echoed through the hallway. This potpourri of noise interrupted Corey's thought processes and brought him back to the present.

"This time she won't be back," he said, "and the finality of that realization is what drove me to almost destroy you." Corey heaved a sigh that seemed to come from the very depths of his soul.

As Blaise sat back and observed this man whom he thought he knew, he could see the similarities between them. His charade, in an attempt to win Rachel's heart, may, like Corey's, have been for naught.

There they sat in as unlikely a place as anyone could conjure up. So totally different one from the other, but so alike in their quest for the same woman and brought to this very same moment. What was it about Rachel Radcliffe that was so attractive, so appealing, and unique amongst women that it brought the men in her life into such an abyss?

Perhaps that question would never be answered to either man's complete satisfaction. But one man in that room was unwilling to give up the pursuit. Blaise's resolve now became stronger, and his willingness to risk everything would once and for all chart a path out of this labyrinth.

Blaise stood up and walked over to Corey. He looked down at him and spoke softly.

"This has been a gut-wrenching situation, Corey, and I've got to hand it to you for being able to bare your soul as you have. I don't know if you had planned to do that when you walked in that door, but for whatever reason, it's allowed me to see the human side of Corey Davidson. And while I would have preferred not to be the object of your ultimate desperation, I believe our mutual love for Rachel placed all of us in that destined situation." Blaise walked slowly around the room and continued.

"This offer to pay for my hospital and doctor bills is a generous one, and I'd be crazy to decline. But with my acceptance, I believe, I will somehow allow you to be free of the guilt, and maybe we can all begin to heal."

Corey was still recovering from the unbelievable admissions he'd made to Blaise. Perhaps, it was a purging of sorts. He couldn't remember ever making those admissions to anyone else or even thinking them, for that matter. But it felt good. It was as though someone had lifted a tremendous weight from his shoulders. A weight he himself had placed and only he could remove. Many times as he'd heard "the truth will set you free," and now it was working for him. Corey stood up and, with all of the composure he could muster, responded to Blaise's suggestion.

"I've said some pretty terrible things about you in the past, Blaise, and won't ever understand your way of life, but right here and now, I'd like to shake your hand and thank you for being man enough to defend the woman you loved. As puzzling as that sounds to me, given the things I know about you, I'm obliged and indebted to you for not bringing criminal charges against me." Corey stopped briefly, and then, reaching in his pocket, he brought out a blank check made out to Blaise Kinley. "Whatever amount will take care of the hospital, doctors, and personal damages is the amount I want you to fill in. I'm not the richest man in town, but I'll honor whatever figure you enter on that check, no questions asked." Blaise's surprised look brought a smile to Corey's lips.

"It's a good check, honest," he said.

Blaise sort of fumbled for the correct words.

"I really don't know what to say beyond thank you, Corey. I'm overwhelmed by your visit and this generous offer."

"Believe me, Blaise, it is I who will thank you for accepting this as my way of apologizing for my appalling behavior. Now," said Corey, "enough of this for one day. Good luck, Blaise. I hope your recovery from here forward is a speedy one." With that, Corey turned to leave the room.

"Thank you," said Blaise. "Thank you," and Corey was gone.

In another part of Grosse Pointe, Rachel tried desperately to make certain that Blaise's return home would be a happy one.

The dinner was his favorite. The decorations were festive, and his house was sparkling clean. She was pleased with herself as she bustled here and there in the kitchen. Steamed vegetables and wild rice with these delectable game hens would tickle the palates of most master chefs. The champagne was already on ice. Rachel was whistling as she prepared the salad ingredients. The asparagus was washed and ready for steaming. "Well," she remarked, "that does it for preparation. Now all I have to do is jump in the shower, get dressed, and get over to the hospital to pick up Blaise." As she took off her apron and headed for the bathroom, the telephone rang. She picked it up on the second ring.

"Hello," she almost sang the word.

"Hi Ray babe!" Blaise responded. "I'm ready to be picked up anytime now," he said happily.

"Oh, Blaise," Rachel replied, "how wonderful. I was just going to shower and change and come over to pick you up. Can you wait there for another forty-five minutes?"

"I guess so," said he. "I doubt if they'd throw out a guy who just paid cash for his release?"

There was a brief silence.

"Did, did you say you paid your bill in cash, Blaise?" Rachel said, almost stuttering.

"That's right, Ray, but that's a story and a half, and I'll tell you all about it over dinner tonight. You and I are going out," he said anxiously.

"Oh, no, we're not, Blaise Kinley," Rachel retorted almost definitely, "I'm bringing you straight home. I didn't slave over a hot stove in this kitchen all day only to go out and eat someone else's cuisine. Tonight, dear friend, you and I will dine at Chez Ray. How does that sound?" she grinned and waited for Blaise's response.

"You're the best, you know that, Ray. I'm flattered that you would go through so much trouble on my behalf and I'm pleased that we shall be dining alone. Now that I think about it, I've had enough people hovering over me and invading my privacy for the last couple of weeks. Some peace and quiet in your company has to be high on my list of what this doctor ordered!" The excitement stirred within him as he thought of the prospects of this timely occasion. "I've only got one other request, Ray," he asked shyly.

"What's that, Blaise?" she responded.

"Hurry up!" he blurted out, and they both laughed heartily.

"All right, dear heart," Rachel continued. "I'll be there as soon as I can. See you soon, Blaise," and with that, they bid each other good-bye.

The trip to Saint John's to pick up Blaise was short and sweet. No fuss. No muss. As she pulled the car into the driveway, Blaise expounded with glee.

"Yesss! I'm home. What a beautiful sight." He opened the car door and was at the entrance of his home by the time Rachel turned off the ignition and grabbed the single bag that contained what few personal articles Blaise had accumulated during his two and a half-week stay. She walked up to where Blaise was standing, put the key in the lock, and opened the door.

"Welcome home, my friend. I've missed you." Blaise stepped over the threshold and smiled as he observed the cleanliness and freshness that permeated the air in the home he loved so dearly.

"It looks grand, Ray, and I thank you for taking such good care of my place during my absence." He breathed a sigh and just walked from room to room, sort of soaking in every inch of the home he had worked so diligently to decorate and make his own. "I love this room," he exclaimed as he walked into the area that he called his studio. A very large skylight in the midst of the cathedral ceiling welcomed the rays of sunshine that broke through the clouds. This was the room where his creativity was born and where his talent was honed to perfection.

"This room has always been the center of my inspiration and the haven for my troubled brain. It beckons to me like an old friend, evoking my spirit to create a masterpiece. It challenges my heart and soul." Blaise sat down in one of the many comfortable chairs as he recalled his past when he began to develop the many works of art. Suddenly, he turned around to face Rachel, who had been watching. He walked over to her and put both arms out to her and they embraced.

"I have so much to thank you for, Ray. I couldn't begin to mention all the wonderful things I've experienced with you in my life." He put his hand softly behind her head and pressed it close to his chest.

His heart was racing, and as they stood there, almost motionless, Rachel felt a sense of calm in Blaise's arms. She nestled against him, and suddenly the beating of his heart was echoing in her head. This was the second time she found herself in his embrace. Brought there by a closeness they shared. She recalled the awkwardness of her movements the last time, but she was reluctant to destroy this moment, this time. For some strange reason, she could feel herself participating in this closeness and in an attempt to observe Blaise's mood, she lifted her head and slowly looked up into his revealing eyes. He stared into those eyes, which were searching, seeking, and almost longing for an answer, a reason or an explanation of what was happening.

"Blaise," she uttered softly, "what's going on here?" And while she was inclined to step back in order to pursue and determine the whys and wherefores, she didn't want to. This felt good, and it felt right.

Blaise was reluctant to speak for fear he'd say something to ruin this moment he dreamed of since the last time. He was almost mesmerized by her beauty and holding her this close, he could hear her breathing and smell the sweet fragrance of her hair. He lowered his head and opened his mouth slightly as she tilted her head back and raised her lips to his. There they stood, locked in each other's arms with their lips blending in a kiss that excited every fiber of Rachel's being. Blaise's arms were wrapped around her tightly, his mouth consuming and deliberate in its movements. Rachel was lost in the thrill of it all and surrendered herself to wherever Blaise would lead.

"Rachel, Rachel," he whispered her name as he slowly separated his mouth from hers. She wanted to hear his next words, for she was speechless. She clung to him because she felt weakened by his strength and the magic of that kiss.

He felt her wilt in his arms and reacted by lifting her to him once again, and as his lips followed the outline of her face, he found her lips waiting and inviting him to kiss her again. This time he gently held her as he sat down on the sofa in his studio. He laid her head on the arm rest and kissed her urgently and passionately. As she returned from the wonderment of the moment, she backed away and once again looked up at Blaise.

"This is incredible," she stuttered. She was trying desperately to recover, and after a safe distance from Blaise, she straightened her skirt, pushed back her hair behind her ears, and pressed the back of her hand to her lips.

"You were the one who suffered the head injury, but I feel like I'm the only who's losing my mind."

Blaise thought for a moment before he responded and then he uttered softly.

"No, sweetie, you haven't lost your mind, but I must tell you now that I lost my heart to you a long time ago." He sighed and then waited, anticipating her reply.

"Wait a minute, Blaise, this is me, Rachel, your good neighbor and trusting friend. I'm also your confidante, so I know things about you that make what you're saying and doing almost impossible."

Rachel stood up at that point and began to walk around the studio she had come to know so well. Suddenly, she was in familiar surroundings but with someone she really didn't know. Blaise watched her and could tell that her thought processes were working overtime.

"Blaise, my dear heart, when I thought I had lost you during that terrible fight that I caused, I thought I would die." She stopped at the remembered fear and desperation. Her eyes filled with tears. "I don't understand what's going on here and can't handle it," she said, and her voice broke ever so slightly.

Blaise stood up and approached her. He put his hands on her shoulders.

"I'm sorry, Ray," he pleaded, "sorry for causing you to be confused and uncertain about me. Please give me a chance to explain, and I hope and pray you'll understand what I'm about to say."

Rachel, whose sense of humor was always a resting place when tension and an uneasy situation occurred, looked at her friend.

"Well, if this is going to be a long story, may I suggest we not waste the superb dinner that I've made for your homecoming. And, since you've already got all my attention, believe me, I will be all ears." She smiled, and he smiled and agreed. Neither Rachel nor even Blaise would have believed how long it would take to tell the story that Blaise was about to reveal. The dinner was as scrumptious, as Rachel promised, and as they enjoyed each course, Blaise set out to describe the saga that brought them here.

Rachel was almost spellbound as he revealed his incredible and heartwarming story in pursuit of her love. Initially, she was complimented about the extreme manner in which he sought her attention and eventual affection.

That fateful night when she had finally left Neil and drove off to an unknown destination came to her mind. She could feel again the sense of guilt and total devastation as she told Neil it was over. Their marriage was a farce. To be married, by definition, was to be united in body as well as in spirit. Neither was the case for them, since Neil so adored Rachel, he couldn't bear the thought of defiling his perfect Rachel!

One evening while driving home, she saw the lights of a suburban club close to Grosse Pointe limits, she remembered needing desperately to see people who could laugh. She needed the distraction of concentrating on someone else other than herself, and what better place to find that someone but at a cocktail lounge. She'd always observed occupied bar stools, the men and women, who, after a few drinks felt a sense of relief in telling all their problems to a seemingly interested bartender. It didn't matter that anyone understood, only that they listened. When one of the bar stools became available, she sat down and ordered a glass of ginger ale. She could still see the quizzical grin on the face of the bartender.

"Anything else you'd like with that, miss?" he had inquired. Rachel responded sarcastically.

"Hemlock would do nicely, thank you!" Unfortunately, this bartender wasn't thinking of poison, but of the tree.

"Sorry miss, our stirrers are a lot smaller, but they work." Rachel laughed aloud, and it was that laugh that got Blaise's attention. He was sitting at a small table to the left of the bar.

That's where Blaise first set eyes upon a face he'd never ever be able to forget. As people left, Blaise managed to get closer to the bar merely by going to the restroom and upon returning, moving his drink to an available table closer to the bar. His last move brought him within earshot of the conversation between the lovely woman and the bartender. One thing was certain, she wasn't too enamored by the male population, and that was what Blaise needed to hear.

He, in an attempt to break away from affluent, materialistic, and selfish parents, declared that he was a homosexual. Waves of disbelief and downright nastiness left him renounced and exiled, which for Blaise, spelled paradise. Even though he would never engage in such relationships, it was all the shield he needed to keep a wide gap between himself and his disgusting family. Only Renna, his younger sister, was still his staunch supporter and only connection to a life he abandoned.

Now, once again, he would use this same declaration, in the hope of gaining an entry into this beautiful lady's world.

When one of the barstools next to Rachel became available, Blaise moved quickly to seat himself next to her. By this time, Rachel had graduated from ginger ale to straight scotch. A drink her father had always professed was the best choice if you had to imbibe alcohol at all.

As Blaise went on to explain their meeting, Rachel listened more intently. She was flabbergasted at the confession that rang through her ears.

Blaise not really a homosexual! This was only a facade to gain acquaintance with her. The duration of their eight-year relationship was an act? Rachel couldn't believe what she was hearing. Blaise capable of such a massive deception. She was stunned to the point of stopping him from continuing.

"Blaise, please, are you telling me that you pretended to be homosexual all these years as a ploy to gain my love and affection? Are you telling me that I poured my heart and soul out to an impostor?" She sat shaking her head back and forth. Blaise became concerned as Rachel's reaction to his story was disappointment.

"Ray, once I started I thought I could tell you the truth soon, and then one thing led to another, and weeks and months and, ultimately, years passed." He was scrambling for the correct phrases and praying simultaneously that she'd understand.

"Each crisis you encountered heightened your anger and disgust for men. I couldn't risk telling you the truth, and I didn't want to lose you." Blaise was beginning to tire, and Rachel noticed it. They sat in silence for a few moments.

Rachel's first thoughts of yet another untrusting relationship changed to wanting desperately to save whatever she could of the relationship she enjoyed and revered for so many years.

Blaise was trying to find the right words to smooth over any possible rift caused by his revelation.

"Ray babe, are you shocked, angry, or just plain disgusted with me and my hour of truth?" He never took his eyes off her. Rachel had ended many a relationship due to misplaced trust and misunderstanding She lost Donald Ramchek because of undeserved trust, left and divorced Neil, and severed her relationship with Corey because of his admitted unfaithfulness.

Now, Blaise? She was trying to rationalize the past few hours of this stranger-than-fiction story. Losing Blaise would exact too high a price, Rachel realized she cared much more deeply for him than she had realized.

"I don't understand a great deal of why we do the things we do, Blaise, but I can't and won't be your judge, Truth is, I'm not perfect, and we don't live in a perfect world. You did what you had to do to seek happiness. Who am I to say what you did or how you did it was right or wrong?" She was breathing a bit easier now and looked deeply into his eyes as she went on.

"How could I possibly dislike or hate someone who, from the first day we met, was so consoling and protecting? You have been the glue that has held me together and my rock when I needed the reassurance to go on one more day." She stopped and took a drink of ice water.

Blaise raised his hands to feel the surface of his head just under the bandages. He massaged his temples and asked if he could be excused to take some of his pain medication. Rachel offered her assistance and suggested that this episode be continued at another time. For now, her friend was noticeably tiring and after a long day of shopping, preparation, and serving that wonderful dinner, Rachel was ready to get some rest as well.

As they walked back to Blaise's unit, Rachel put her arm around his rather large frame in a minimal attempt to support him as he stepped very deliberately toward his bedroom. Once there, he turned and sat on his bed. His expression was one of relief and peacefulness. He smiled at Rachel, who was trying to put some of his things in drawers and appropriate closets.

"Please come here," Blaise beckoned her. "Sit by me for just a moment or two." Rachel responded to his request and sat down next to him. He took her hand and enveloped it in his. "I don't think you'll ever quite know what a relief this has been for me, Ray, to once and for all tell you the truth about me and my love for you."

He was really getting quite sleepy now, and Rachel suggested that he stop talking.

"Shhh," she uttered. "You need some rest and a good night's sleep, and I think, having exorcised some of those demons that were haunting your brain, you may achieve that state of slumber before too long." Rachel made certain that he was all right and then walked over to him and kissed him good night.

"Pleasant dreams, dear heart. We have changed the course of our relationship tonight, and I think we both need some time to digest this very large revelation. Then we can continue to pursue what it will mean and where and how we're going to deal with it. For now, sleep tight, and you know my number if you need me during the night."

"Good night, Ray babe, good night, my love," said Blaise. Rachel smiled and returned to her home.

Nighttime always provided the atmosphere for dreaming, and tonight would be no exception. For Blaise, it was whisking Rachel away to an island on the other side of the world, far from the memories and the forces that would keep him from her side. His last conscious recollection tonight was the vividness of the kiss that opened a new door for him and possibly a new direction for them.

Rachel put a cup of water in the microwave and made herself a cup of hot tea. As she sat at her kitchen counter and sipped the Red Zinger tea, it was almost medicinal in its effect. "Blaise loves me," she said. "No, Blaise is in love with me. Incredible! I've been searching for love most of my life, and it was right under my nose!" She finished the tea, slipped into her University of Michigan nightshirt and got into bed. "What now, Rachel Radcliffe? What on earth are you going to do now?" And with that, she punched up her pillow and placed her weary head into its waiting softness. She said her prayers and asked for guidance as she embarked on a new adventure, a new relationship. Another love? She shook her head and whispered "incredible" and fell asleep.

Possibly experiencing the deepest sleep Rachel had in some time, her dreams of the past and the recurring nightmares joined together and ran like a video in her mind. The strains of the music she first heard with Christian echoed melodiously and the words as though on a marquee flashed in her mind's eye . . . "Yesterday I heard the rain echoing your name, asking where you've gone . . . " Rachel stirred in her bed and winced as the haunting nightmare returned. Black umbrellas over faceless people charging at her. The rain was splashing on her face as she tried to edge her way through the crowds of people. She was searching for a familiar face, a friendly smile, a trusting love. She was moaning now, and as she ran faster in her dream, the umbrellas became larger and larger. Suddenly, she tripped,, and a hand reached to help her up. She grabbed it and hung on as the strength it possessed lifted her from the ground and, almost weightless, she stood up and looked at a pair of eyes she knew, but the rest of the face was obscured by a collar. She could hear her name being called in the distance. "Rachel, Rachel, I'm here," said the voice. It was familiar and urgent. "Rachel," it called. The hand that had helped her to get up was suddenly gone, and everywhere she turned, the people holding the umbrellas were moving away from her. She called out, "Don't go. Who are you?" but no one seemed to hear. She stood there in the rain, listening for the voice and straining to find those caring eyes. Then she awakened with a start. Her breathing was labored, and the perspiration on her forehead made her get up to get a damp face cloth to cool her face and neck.

She looked at the clock, and it was still the middle of the night. Her thoughts turned to Christian. It had been a couple of days since they'd spoken, and she suddenly felt very alone. She longed to see his face and hold him in her arms. She needed his strength, his support, his reassuring love.

This evening's surprising events were weighing heavily on her mind, and while she wouldn't hurt Blaise for the world, she was going to have to give this entire new set of circumstances some very serious thought.

"Amber," she uttered, "I'll call Amber in the morning, and perhaps she can shed some light in this labyrinth I've discovered and lend me some of her sage advice."

The discouraging part of this saga was that her decision to separate herself from Corey had only complicated her life. Now, she had Christian Avian, whose professed love was like an injection of hope. She was beginning to feel secure and comfortable in pursuing her feelings for this wonderful man. When she told Christian that some time back home in Grosse Pointe would allow for both of them to think about their rapid love relationship and determine whether or not it was infatuation or truly love, she didn't plan on the violent event that took place between Corey and Blaise, which ultimately led to Blaise's declaration of love. In fact, nothing in her recent life remotely resembled anything that she had anticipated or even fantasized about.

Looking at the positive side of things, which Rachel always tried to do, she thought herself fortunate to be so loved by so many wonderful people.

She got back into bed and laid her head down on the beckoning pillows. She didn't have a morning appointment, and sleeping in sounded like a great idea after being awake half the night. "And so to sleep . . . ," she quoted Shakespeare, "but not to dream . . . " She smiled and drifted off to sleep once again.

The next couple of days were filled with telephone calls, errands, and making certain that Blaise was doing well on his way back to better health. Obviously, the longest telephone call would be to Amber. Rachel poured out her heart, as usual, and Amber offered her usual advice and counsel. After all the bantering back and forth about how Rachel should handle the situations in her love life, they discussed Carlo and Marisa's rehearsal schedule for "Cinema." In fact, Amber was almost gloating over Christian's calling the Domani household on a very regular basis.

"It's my captivating charm, doll," bragged Amber. "Christian is enamored with my voice, my glowing persona, my children, and mostly, . . . my best friend."

"You are an imp, Amber, you know that? And I'm envious, even if you are only kidding. You live in his state, and your children see him on a regular basis. A far cry from my recent interaction with Mr. Avian since I left New York." Rachel sighed and whispered, "C'est la vie!"

Amber couldn't pass up this opportunity.

"Oh, puleeeze, darling, tell me you're seriously jealous of moi? Be still my heart," she chided. They chuckled, and then, Amber became more serious. "Listen, my dearest friend in all of this world, all of this rhetoric is for your entertainment only. Christian's mind may be on many things and certain people, but his heart belongs to you, bella. Believe me."

Rachel recalled the warm feeling she experienced when Amber emphasized and reminded her about Christian's affection for her. What was surprising to Rachel was the lack of any conversation about Corey. She hadn't seen him since their meeting in the hospital. Blaise's encounter with Corey proved to be a blessing in more ways than one, for not only had Corey fulfilled his promise to pay for Blaise's hospital and doctor's bills, but he even attempted to patch up some pretty deep wounds between himself, Blaise, and her. How different the priorities in her life had become. They had changed dramatically almost hour by hour for a while, and the latest revelation regarding Blaise only added to the dilemma of it all.

Rachel's conversation with Estelle Markham was consoling and comforting. Estelle had truly changed her attitude toward Rachel, and she was certain that Master Randy had a great deal to do with that.

If all went well with Blaise's recuperation this week, she had planned to take Master Randy to a movie and early dinner this coming Saturday. Even though he had the intellect of Einstein, he was still just twelve and found cartoon movies entertaining. *Little Rascals* was his choice for the movie and Taco Bell was one of his favorite dining places. As she looked over her calendar, she couldn't miss Randy's name spread out over the entire evening of this coming Saturday.

The two telephone calls with Christian were wonderful, as always. His cold was gone and that beautiful resonant voice returned. They talked about everything except Blaise. Rachel wanted to impart this to Christian, but she didn't feel that over the telephone was the proper way, nor did she wish to discuss anything with Christian that might impact negatively on his direction of "Cinema."

"I can't wait to see you again, my beautiful Rachel," he said softly. "I can feel you in my arms and see those gorgeous eyes filled with promise and love." He sighed deeply. "When, my darling, when will I see you again?" His question held a certain pleading and a sense of urgency.

Rachel tried desperately to explain the difficulties that surrounded her life at the moment, but reassured him that she, too, was longing to be with him. Her silence prompted him to continue.

"If you can't come to New York, sweetheart, I can certainly arrange to come to Grosse Pointe for a couple of days. My associate director has a pretty good handle on the show, and I could be on a plane this evening." Rachel discerned the excitement in his voice.

"Oh, my darling. As much as I would love to say 'come ahead,' I can't, Christian. Please understand. It's not that I don't want you to come here. It's just that the timing is all wrong. You do understand, don't you, Christian? Please tell me that you do," she pleaded.

He couldn't deny that he was disappointed, and he tried to erase the desperation he could hear in her voice.

"Yes, of course, I understand, Rachel. But that doesn't change my desire to see you. I love you, and I'm lonely without you. I miss holding your hand and feeling you close to me when we dance or just go for a ride in the car. I miss the sweet aroma of your freshly washed hair when I embrace you." He hesitated for a moment. "This is foolish of me. I apologize for acting like some lovestruck teenager. I shall attempt to exercise some control and patience here. Promise. I'll just have to be satisfied with our telephone calls until we can be together again."

"Thank you, my darling Christian. Thank you for understanding and for caring." Rachel didn't think about it right away, but she hadn't returned Christian's pronouncements of love. Something was different suddenly. She had not, in the past, hesitated to express her love. Now, somehow, she found herself almost guarded. And while she felt she had covered her uneasiness, she was not aware that Christian had noticed the lack of her spontaneous responses and viewed them as quizzical gaps. He wasn't new at this kind of thing, and the absence of responses that once came so freely left him questioning and a bit insecure.

At least for now, they ended the conversation with the same respect for one another's feelings as had been the case from the very beginning. However, each of them was aware that something was different.

Rachel's once simple existence had become an amalgam of situations she had not faced in the past. As much as she avoided thinking about the possibility, it could very well be that she was in love with two men—a frightening place for someone of Rachel's staunch beliefs concerning trust and honesty. How could this possibly be happening to her?

The telephone rang and managed to shatter those thoughts. She rushed to pick up the receiver.

"Hello, is this the cool lady?" uttered the voice on the other end of the line.

"Master Randy!" she exclaimed. "How are you, my friend?" Rachel was happy to hear his voice.

"I hope I haven't disturbed you," he said politely.

"Not at all, Randy. As a matter of fact, I've been thinking about our upcoming 'date' and I was going to call you in a little while," she replied.

"Great! I was hoping we were still on, but during breakfast this morning, my mother suggested it would be courteous to call to make sure that your work schedule would permit you take off some time."

Randy's manner was so adultlike that Rachel had to keep reminding herself that he was only twelve. Well . . . almost thirteen. "I wouldn't miss this for the world, Randy. And in fact, I was going to call you. Honest. Just in case you had decided to back out." Rachel grinned as she waited for his response.

"Back out?" he laughed. "No way. Especially since my Uncle Christian is coming for a visit this weekend." There was silence. "Oops! Sorry, cool lady. You weren't supposed to know that, and I'll be properly annihilated on the spot if he finds out that I've slipped and exposed his secret."

Rachel caught her breath.

"Christian is coming here?"

"Oh, boy. I'm really going to be in hot water now. Please don't let on that you know. Okay, cool lady?" Randy continued to backpedal, and Rachel observed that he had become very nervous.

"It's all right, Randy. I won't divulge your boo-boo, and I'll do my utmost to act surprised, too," she assured him.

"You're the best. You know that, cool lady? I have to hang up now, but I'm looking forward to Saturday," he said.

"Me, too," responded Rachel, "and, thank you so much for calling, Master Randy. Saturday at 2:30 P.M.—it's a date." And with that, they hung up their respective telephones.

"Christian is coming here," she uttered. There was silence and then she spoke out loudly. "Oh, my God. Christian is coming!" She plopped down on the sofa and tried to sort out the mixture of feelings rushing through her mind and body. "Christian's coming," she reiterated.

She sighed and put her head in her hands. As she moved them to cup her chin, she looked off into space, and the reverie of moments she had spent with Christian chased around in her thoughts. As usual, her heart began to race, and the excitement of it all became very real. As though he were sitting next to her, she could almost feel his breath on her throat, the warmth of his embrace, and her lips tingled as she recalled the magic of his kiss. "Whew!" she gasped. "I love him . . . uh, I do love him." Then she tried to shake herself out of this periodic meditational trance. She leaned her head back on the soft cushions and breathed deeply. "What about Blaise?" she whispered. Then, as though someone within her were listening, she heard someone say, "Yes, Rachel. What about Blaise?" It was startling to experience these kinds of thought gyrations. But Blaise had become closer to her in these past weeks, and his recent revelation about his deep and secret love for her gave her pause.

Still in a sorting-out frame of mind, she remembered her anger with Corey when she learned of his deception and the following mistrust. Her teeth clenched tightly, and her breathing became labored. The betrayal was too much to recall. She would rid herself of this would-be indiscretion. She would not permit a relationship that wasn't based on trust and understanding. Her body language portrayed the defenses built up in her as she crossed her arms over her chest and then crossed her right leg over her left. She had become almost adamant and recalcitrant about her resolve to find someone who would love only her and whom she would love, as well.

A few moments passed as she reminisced about her hateful exchanges with Corey. Again, the inner voice repeated. "But, what about Blaise?" Her arms unfolded and her right leg moved back to its sitting position. She closed her eyes and thought about Blaise's first day back from the hospital. The thrill of having him back home. The surprise when he confessed his facade about his being gay in order to gain an entrance into her life. And how could she forget that moment in his studio as they stood in an embrace that permitted their hearts to beat as one? That frozen moment when she raised her head from his chest to look into the eyes of a man who had just confessed his love for her. She could see his mouth coming toward her and her lips meeting his in a kiss that was tender, passionate, and welcomed. She recalled vividly participating in that expression of love, and it felt wonderful. It felt right.

Rachel sat upright on the sofa as though jabbed by a sharp object. "Oh, my good Lord. I love Blaise. I love Blaise!" She shrank back and put her hands over her face. "Okay, Rachel Radcliffe! Now, what?"

The next few days were spent in getting together with clients; in particular, Mrs. Longley. She had to make certain that her business continued to flourish. The only thing worse than losing yet another relationship in her tumultuous and transitional life would be to go bankrupt. While her financial footing was pretty sound at the moment, Rachel knew that only a continuous income would ensure the perpetuation of the position of security she had established for herself. Mrs. Longley still represented over fifty percent of her income, and their long business relationship could not be jeopardized at this time, or any time for that matter, if Rachel were to remain solvent.

As Saturday morning approached, she was trying desperately to rid her thoughts of Christian's arrival in Grosse Pointe. She did remember to tell Blaise, though, because she didn't want everything to blow up when Christian entered the scene. Blaise was not real happy about the visit. He tried to maintain his decorum and still make certain that Rachel remembered his recent disclosure of love.

"I guess the old Blaise would have come over and shared the news of Mohammed's coming to the mountain," he jeered.

Rachel chuckled, but cautioned him about any outburst along any of those lines during Christian's visit.

"And what's this approach about an 'old Blaise'?"

He looked at her as she smiled and noticed how her beauty shone so magically whenever she was elated about something. He tried to avoid her question.

"You know, you're drop-dead gorgeous even when you're throwing out the garbage at seven-thirty in the morning. Or drenched with rain as you run from the car to the door without your umbrella in the middle of a thunderstorm. But, there's something fantasylike about your smile that captivates me to the point where I feel like I'm living in some magical dream."

Rachel could see the love in his eyes and felt a bit shivery as he expressed his feeling so tenderly.

"In response to your earlier question, if I live to be a hundred, Blaise Kinley, will I ever truly know who the real Blaise Kinley is? Or will I be destined to seek and never find?" She was half-joking and half-baiting him to see if she could evoke a response from this friend who was vying for her affection. She was almost trying to test the sincerity and veracity of his professed love.

Blaise stood as though suspended in time. His thought processes were whirling. His response must be profound and the intrigue compelling. He must let his heart respond with the guidance of his head! His pulse was racing, and the mere closeness of Rachel set off sparks of passion within him that would not or could not be denied.

"The truth, m'lady is that I am what you see. I can be the answer to your problem or the problem in your answer. I may be the love of your life or the life of your love. However, no matter what you perceive, so long as what you perceive is what you want, what you long for, and what you'll have." He sighed deeply and waited for her response.

"My goodness. We're getting a bit profound, aren't we? Suffice it to say that you have opened a new door for me, shown me different roads to travel and possibilities to pursue. What I don't need is the confusion that could ensue if the solution remains a dilemma." She walked toward him and looked up into those adoring eyes!

"Blaise, will we be able to put aside our situation temporarily while Christian is here?" She asked coyly. "I realize that's a lot to ask of you, but, this will be Christian's first visit to Grosse Pointe since our meeting in New York, and because I'm really not certain of my deep feelings for him, I think it is only fair to see where this relationship is going, if anywhere. I won't lie to you, Blaise, your declaration of love left me in a quandary, and the only way that it could happen is if I, too, felt something for you. Having openly admitted that as a distinct possibility, may I ask that you at least allow me to see what kind of impact, if any, this will have on my feelings for Christian?"

The telephone rang, and Rachel, as though transported back to the present, rushed over and picked up the receiver.

"Hello," she sang out.

"Hi, cool lady. It's Randy, and I'm just checking to see if we're still on for the movie and dinner." He waited anxiously.

"We most certainly are, Master Randy. I wouldn't miss this date for anything," she exclaimed emphatically. Randy smiled one of his Cheshire-cat smiles and then asked what time and mode of transportation.

"I shall be delighted to drive by and pick you up around 2:00 P.M. if that's all right."

"That's perfect," responded young Randall. "Mom would like to talk to you for a couple of minutes earlier, before we leave on our date, if that's all right with you." As Rachel was about to reply, she heard him whisper. "Rachel, please say yes, and don't let on that you know about Uncle Christian, okay?" Rachel couldn't see him of course, but the urgency in his pleading left her no chance.

"Of course, Master Randy, don't worry. I'll be happy to come over a few minutes early." As she listened intently for his next words, she heard him yell out.

"Rachel said she'll be here early so you can talk to her, okay, Mom?" And with that he continued. "Thanks, cool lady. We'll see you at 2:00. I'm really looking forward to this date particularly since it's my very first official date."

Rachel had to steel herself from even sounding like she was amused by Randy's attempt to sound so mature about this whole thing.

"Then, it will be a first for both of us, Master Randy, because I've never seen *Little Rascals* or had the pleasure of having dinner at Taco Bell with such a charming escort."

Randy almost stood at attention as he tried to measure up to the image of the description Rachel just described.

"Then we're all set, and I'll see you at 2:00."

"Good-bye till then, Master Randy," acknowledged Rachel and they hung up.

Now Rachel was really in a quandary. Why did Estelle ask to see her before she and Randy departed on their planned afternoon? Was Christian there already? And if so, what would she do if it interfered with her plans with Randy? Her thoughts ran rampant, and when she assumed every possible "what if," she sat down and consciously brought her thought process to a halt. "Enough," she exclaimed, "get on with this, and whatever happens, just handle it."

On the other end of that telephone call, Master Randy ran upstairs and knocked on the door of his mother and father's bedroom.

"It's me, Mother," he said. "May I come in?"

Estelle had been reading up on a charitable organization fund-raising proposal, and when Randall, Jr. knocked on the door, she beckoned him to enter.

"Come in, sweetheart. Did you talk to Rachel?" she asked.

"Yes, I did, and she is going to come over early so that you will have a chance to talk to her. Are you going to tell her about Uncle Christian's visit?" Estelle looked up abruptly.

"Randall, you haven't mentioned Uncle Christian's visit to Ms. Radcliffe have you?" she asked directly.

"Uh, no ma'am," answered Randy, crossing his fingers behind his back.

"Uncle Christian plans on surprising Rachel when the two of you return later on this afternoon. His flight arrives at 3:00, and he's renting a car at the airport. So he'll be here by 4:00 if all goes well." Estelle then looked at her young son and commented, "You know, Randall, you're getting taller by the minute. I can almost look at you eye to eye." Once again this morning Randall almost stood at attention as he tried to grow another inch and live up to his mother's observations.

"Do you think I'll be as tall as dad when I'm fully grown?" he asked.

Estelle smiled in the most kind and loving manner possible.

"One is not measured in feet and inches, dear heart. We are measured by the respect, the love and demeanor we convey. Height is only a physical measurement. And while I know you look up to your father and aspire to emulate him, you already have so many of his fine qualities even at your present height."

This had been a wonderful day for Randall Markham, Jr. He wondered if another day could possibly get any better than this one.

"Thanks, Mom," he said, and with that, he reached over and kissed her on the cheek. "It's going to be an awesome day, and I am up for every single minute." He then turned and rushed out the door and down the stairs two at a time.

"Yes," said Randy as he landed at the foot of the stairs, "this is going to be a great day!"

Thirteen

Looking out the window of the Northwest 767 as it took off from JFK International Airport was always an exciting time for Christian Avian. Viewing the city he loved so dearly from thousands of feet as the aircraft climbed was still a thrilling experience. However, that feeling had been magnified one hundred times because of his destination, where he will see the woman he loved. He could hardly think about his arrival in Detroit without stirring those deep and passionate feelings that only Rachel Radcliffe could evoke.

In a couple of hours he'd be looking at that face he adored. Those compelling brown eyes and enticing mouth brought moisture to his brow and a pounding in his chest that set off emotions he hadn't felt since the last time he saw her, now some six weeks ago. If it hadn't been for his involvement in "Cinema," he would have gone crazy when she returned to Michigan. He remembered how agonizingly slow time seemed to pass when she was gone. If he had any doubts about the depth of his love for this woman, they were all allayed as he watched the plane leave the runway and soar into that infinite sky. But life does have a way of prodding you back into mainstream existence. He was thankful for his craft and the God-given talent he had honed to perfection over some twenty-five years of directing on the New York stage.

"Cinema" would be no different, and when he returned to New York after this trip, he would dedicate himself totally to the completion and opening of this latest Broadway musical. He thought about his last telephone conversation with Amber Domani and her exuberance about his surprise trip. She did, however, make him promise that Rachel would call her when all the excitement of the visit was past. He agreed to bring this message to Rachel, but he did not guarantee when that call would be made. He had some plans of his own for himself and Rachel during his trip, and talking on the telephone was not among them.

Traveling first class definitely had its privileges. The flight attendants never left these special passengers without a drink or a snack! Even at 2:30 in the afternoon, a nice chilled glass of Savignon Blanc was just what Christian needed to help him settle down and relax for the next hour. There would be lots of time for excitement once he arrived in Grosse Pointe and had Rachel in his arms once again.

When the doorbell rang, young Randall yelled out loud.
"I'll get it! It's probably Rachel." And after racing from the rear of the house to the front door Randy came to a screeching halt and opened it. He wasn't surprised to see Rachel's smiling face looking at him.
"Well," she exclaimed "are you ready for our date, Sir Randy?"
He smiled broadly and poised himself.
"Ready, I am, m'lady." Randy was about to yell out again that he and Rachel were leaving when Estelle came down the stairs.
"Hello, Rachel," she said graciously.
"How are you?" Rachel advanced to meet Estelle, and they embraced and exchanged friendly greetings.
Randy was more than a little excited about his and Rachel's schedule, and he didn't want to waste another moment.
"Okay, Mom," he blurted out, "I apologize for interrupting this tête-à-tête, but Rachel and I have a date with the *Little Rascals*, and as you've always taught me, punctuality is a sign of respect and discipline, and we can't miss the beginning of the movie." He then stood there while Estelle and Rachel chuckled over his comedic manner.
"You are a clown, Randall, and a charming one at that," stated Estelle.
"We'll not be too late, Estelle," Rachel assured her. "The movie and Taco Bell should get us back here by 4:30, if that's all right."
Estelle appreciated having a time that she could look for their return. It would help in making this upcoming surprise of Christian's visit easier to orchestrate.
"That's fine," responded Estelle. "Have a wonderful time, and I'll be anxious to hear about how you enjoyed the movie. Perhaps we can compare notes later.
"I always liked the original *Little Rascals* and will be interested to hear your observations, sweetheart." With that Randy gave Estelle a quick kiss on the cheek, straightened his jacket, and opened the door for his date.
As Estelle stood in the doorway, watching them depart, she reflected on the positiveness that Rachel's presence had brought to her entire family. She sighed deeply and watched the car disappear down the driveway and up the road.
"I didn't think we'd get out of there on time," said Randy. Rachel smiled and tried to calm his anxiety.
"Well, Randy, it's wonderful to come from parents, like yours, who are

so kind and gracious. It isn't every day that one gets to meet such wonderful people, and I'm pleased that your mother is as comfortable with me as I am with her."

"Boy," said Randy, "this is working out even better than I planned." He hesitated and then said with a smile, "It would be neat if you and my mom could also be best friends."

Rachel laughed and shook her head in amazement.

"You certainly have a vivid imagination, Master Randy. Perhaps you will follow in your uncle's footsteps and write stories for Broadway."

As Randy thought about that possibility, he didn't see why he couldn't do that and be a meteorologist, as well. With everything falling into place in regard to his plans for Uncle Christian and Rachel, who knows, anything would be possible.

The theater was filled with enthusiastic youngsters. To Rachel's welcomed surprise, just as many adults accompanied their sons, nephews, daughters, grandchildren, and neighbors. It was the first time in a long time that Rachel was excited about watching a G-rated movie. In fact, it was the first time in a long time that she'd been to a theater to watch any movie.

Nothing had really changed, she noticed, except for the cost of the movie and the unreal cost of a bag of popcorn and a candy bar. It's no wonder youngsters don't take their dates to a movie. Even the gainfully employed felt the pocket drain for this mode of entertainment.

Sitting midway down the aisle in seats that were cushioned and had rocking capability brought a smile to Rachel's lips. Her newly found friend, Randy, was scoping the other attendees. He charitably filled her in on the modus operandi of his friends and peers and was pleased when she inquired about any new and expected behavior on her part as an adult.

Master Randy smiled and assured her that she was not to worry, for she had already passed the cool-lady test with flying colors. In fact, it was he who felt like a fish out of water, for it was he who had a date with an older woman.

"Check it out," said one of Randy's friends observing his algebra classmate with an older chick. "Not bad," he continued. "The Randall has scored big-time in my eyes."

Finally the theater lights dimmed, and the show began. Rachel sat back and nibbled on her buttered popcorn. Oblivious of all other things going on in her life, she totally relaxed and enjoyed this fun movie. Listening to the audience laugh and joining in from time to time, she too was amused by the replay of the Rascals of old; it was almost therapeutic. How refreshing it was to just sit and watch a movie that was strictly entertaining. No violence, no porn, no profanity. When it ended, she felt a sense of sadness, because the fun had come to an end.

The house lights brought the audience back into view. The smiles were still present as the other attendees recalled particularly funny segments.

When she and Randy stepped out into the aisle to make their way to the lobby, she made a little promise to herself. It was simply that she would frequently take some time to partake of such entertaining and wonderful movies, whether it be in the theater or from a video rental.

The sun was still shining when they walked outside, and as Rachel slipped on her sunglasses, Randy thanked her for taking him to see this flick and for pretending to enjoy it, as well.

"Ahh," said Rachel, "I beg your pardon, Master Randy. I most certainly was not pretending in there. I truly enjoyed the movie and am so happy that you were instrumental in making this happen for me." She smiled and put her arm around Randy's shoulders.

"Gee, cool lady," he said excitedly, "that's all right. I was fearful that you might have found it to be too childlike and immature." He hesitated and waited for her response. "You wouldn't kid me, would you?"

"No way," responded Rachel, "I think when friends enjoy each other's company and share some special time together, they owe each other the honesty of true feelings and clear understanding of likes and dislikes." She hesitated and continued. "I like you very much, Master Randy, and there's no way I would ever deceive you or do anything that would lead you to mistrust or lose faith in me." She hugged him and waited for his response.

"You and my Uncle Christian are going to be very happy together, you know," he said right out of the blue. "He loves the movies and Broadway, and so do you. He loves popcorn, and so do you." And then he cleared his throat, and with a grin that could charm the skin off a snake, he said, "and you both like me. If that's not enough to have in common to talk about marriage, then I don't know what is."

Rachel chuckled at Randy's observations and, filled with all the new and exciting energy from that fun-filled movie, she was ready for step-two of this auspicious date.

"Onward to Taco Bell," she exclaimed.

"Andiamo," responded her short but attentive date.

"Si, mi amico, andiamo," and laughed even louder.

It was quite a sight. Rachel Radcliffe and Master Randall Markham sauntering down Kercheval Avenue in the center of Grosse Pointe Farms, laughing and joking. This was almost unheard of behavior in the Pointes, but Rachel was learning something new, and she didn't care if it fit the mode or not, she was having fun.

To look at Rachel Radcliffe, one would have to believe that she never ingested one ounce of fat, unsaturated or otherwise. She was lean and almost Olympic in stature. Though height was not her strong feature, her confident and graceful manner gave her an almost royal appearance. Laughing contagiously was uncharacteristic to Rachel, but like everything else about her, it was charming and most becoming.

Since the hallowed borders of Grosse Pointe did not house even one Taco Bell, it was necessary to get back into the car and head for a younger and livelier part of these environs.

Master Randy had already found the radio station listened to by others his age and was pleased to see Rachel tapping her hand on the steering wheel very much in tune and tempo with this new rap beat.

Two original tacos and a large Coke was all she could handle. The main enjoyment from this fast-food repast was watching her friend ingest almost one of everything on the menu. He finished and looked at her.

"If I were to die tomorrow, I would be a happy man," he exclaimed and grinned.

"Oh, my Lord, Master Randy, you do indeed possess a flair for the dramatic, and your choice of lines leaves me speechless."

Master Randy was quick on the uptake.

"Well, it was either that line or 'give me liberty or give me more tacos,'" and with that they both started to laugh all over again.

Rachel checked her watch; 3:45 P.M. had arrived very quickly, and she had promised Estelle that she'd have Randy home by 4:30 P.M.

"Come on, champ," she exclaimed, "time to get you back home. I did promise your mother you'd be back by 4:00, and we've only fifteen minutes to keep me from being a liar." She sighed and peered at her young escort.

"No problem, cool lady. It's been a blast for me, and I can hardly wait to tell Mom about our first date." He smiled happily, and after paying the bill, they got back into Rachel's Chevy and proceeded to return to the place where this fun-filled afternoon began.

Pulling up into the circular drive didn't appear to be any different than a few short hours ago, but somehow, Rachel felt a certain excitement and didn't know if she should follow him into the house or wait. She no sooner thought this than Randy came running out.

"My mom's not home Rachel, and my dad said she'd be back soon." He leaned over and put his head in the window near her ear. "She's picking up Uncle Christian, remember?"

"Yes, I do remember, and I think it best if I leave now and let this next episode take its normal course without me," Rachel replied equally as quietly.

"Good idea," said Randy. "I'm certain Uncle Christian will be seeing you later. Thanks again, cool lady, it was primo." And he planted a kiss on her cheek.

Rachel placed her hand along Randy's sweet face.

"The thanks are all mine, dear heart. It was 'primo' for me, too."

With that, Randy raced back into his house, and Rachel drove away, wondering what else this day would hold. Her heart once again was racing. Christian was near, she could feel his presence.

As Rachel drove home, she began to observe the changing colors of the leaves, and it was as though someone shook her suddenly. *It's fall* she thought, and along with everything else that made this season so special to her was that Mrs. Longley always started to plan a Christmas in Hawaii trip, which meant hours of wardrobe creation for Rachel. Feeling a little sentimental and still reveling in the enjoyment of the last few hours, she tuned on the car radio. The dulcet tones of Tony Bennett permeated the air, and she listened intently as the strains of the music and lyrics presented an almost déjà vu sensation:

"Yesterday I heard the rain whispering your name, asking where you've gone.
It fell softly from the clouds on the silent crowds as I wandered on.
Out of doorways, black umbrellas came to pursue me.
Faceless people, as they passed, were looking through me; no one knew me.

"Yesterday I shut my eyes, face up to the skies, drinking in the rain.
But your image still was there floating in the air brighter than a flame
Yesterday I saw a city, full of shadows, without pity,
And I heard the steady rain, whispering your name . . . whispering your name."*

Rachel was amazed how the lyrics coincidentally mirrored her night-

*"Yesterday I Heard the Rain," by Armando Manzanero and Gene Lee, © 1968 BMG Songs, Inc. (ASCAP). All Rights Reserved. Used by Permission.

mare recollections. She felt goose bumps as the music enraptured her very being. Her senses numbed, and she gave in to the romantic mood it created. What a sensation, what a thrilling sensation. Her thoughts went immediately to Christian, and then to Blaise. She sighed and once again, her mind was filled with conflicting thoughts. Would there ever be a time when she would be at peace?

Bedford Avenue was always the catharsis Rachel needed to bring her back on cue. This typical Grosse Pointe Americana street represented her entire personality, her values, and her sense of loyalty and commitment. It's where she lives. It's where Blaise lives. Her breathing evidenced her confusing excitement now about seeing Blaise.

"This is crazy!" she said out loud as she pulled into her driveway. The closing of the car door aroused Blaise from a short nap, and he peeked out his miniblinds just in time to see Rachel come charging frantically up the steps. He heard the door unlock and then close. He waited a few minutes and then walked to the common sun porch that adjoined their two homes. When he got to her back door, he knocked his usual knock. A few seconds passed and the door opened, and there she stood. The face he adored. The woman he loved so deeply. Her beguiling smile touched his very soul. His composure, as usual, was diminished, and he tried desperately to calm himself so he could speak without stuttering and sounding like a blithering idiot.

"Heh, Ray babe! You look ravishing as ever, but you appear to be in an enormous hurry. Can I even dream that it's because you could hardly wait to see moi?" He grinned.

Rachel opened the door wider and motioned her tall friend inside. She looked up at him, with his hair just growing back after the surgery, he looked almost childlike. His blue eyes were piercing hers, and she reached up to give him a hug.

"You know, I somehow never quite realized just how tall you were, Blaise." She smiled.

He took advantage of this wonderful moment and embraced her.

"You never hugged me before," he said. "Remember, you thought of me as 'one of the girls.' "

Now they both laughed, and as she moved away from him, she felt the same sense of loss she had experienced after Christian had kissed her for the first time. These feelings of closeness were becoming more quizzical and Rachel delighted in the wonderment of it all.

"Blaise," she said, "come in, we have to talk." She sounded almost dictatorial in her request, and Blaise's usual humor sprung forth.

"Yes, ma'am! Comin'!" he responded.

"Sit down!" was her next directive.

"Oh, oh," he said, "I have a feeling something's afoot here and that I may not like it!"

Rachel was always amazed at his unique perceptions about what she was going to say or do. It was kind of eerie; however, she had known him for a very long time, and he was certainly more sensitive to her every move. More so than anyone else.

"Listen, Blaise, I just wanted to remind you that Christian is in town. He's here in Grosse Pointe visiting his family." She looked at him and saw the concern in his expression. She extended both her hands to him, and he obliged her by grasping both of them in his hands.

"So," he said, "Mohammed has come to the mountain." His head was bowed now, and Rachel tried to allay his fears.

"Look at me, Blaise." she implored. "Please, dear heart, look at me!" Her voice almost cracked as she felt her emotions begin to kick in. She swallowed and spoke softly. "You knew this moment was inevitable. Please don't read too much into this, okay?"

His eyes rimmed with tears he could no longer hide.

"This is it, isn't it?" He struggled to keep his composure. "It's the moment of truth." He breathed in deeply and gasped as he continued. I've played my whole hand, my darling Rachel. I don't have any more trump cards left. My heart, my soul, and my life are in your hands." He picked up her hands and kissed them tenderly.

By this time, Rachel's emotional level had peaked, and a tear raced down her cheek. Again, she swallowed hard and smiled at him.

"Yes, I guess it is a moment of truth, but I don't think you should be as devastated as you appear. Do you not understand that I, too, feel the apprehension? Your declaration of love, Blaise, has touched my heart, and I feel a bond with you that I don't yet share with anyone else." She hesitated and looked for some expression to indicate that he understood.

He looked up at her, almost as though in shock.

"Really, Ray? Really?"

"Yes, my dear, remarkable friend. Yes. I'm in a quandary now, because I truly don't know what it will be like, seeing Christian again." She continued, "So much of that trip to New York has become almost dreamlike. And with all the events since I returned, I'm confused. Your near-death experience after Corey's despicable behavior and my just getting back to some semblance of everyday life in my home. It's given me cause to evaluate all aspects of my current life and what the future holds for me. But please, Blaise, don't despair. I do care about you, and if you don't already know it, I do love you, my dear, dear heart."

Blaise's response was almost volcanic in nature. He stood up, perhaps much more quickly than he should have, and reached for Rachel and picked her up in his arms and swung her around. Almost too effortlessly for Rachel's liking.

"Ohhhh," he blurted out. "Can this be happening to me? Is this reality or a dream?" He stood her up on the floor and cupped her face in his large hands and bent down to kiss her. She did not move away, and the excitement and tenderness of his kiss sent her reeling.

Recently, Rachel's involvements had given a new meaning to the word "dilemma." She was probably approaching the most decisive part of her life, and the outcome was going to depend largely on her ability to exercise sound judgment. Wrapped in Blaise's arms with his urging lips on hers was not the time for reasonable decisions. She put her arms around his neck and responded to his kiss that felt so right. So exciting, and, oh, so passionate.

When the plane landed at Detroit Metro Airport, Christian quickly recalled his last visit here. It wasn't very pleasant. He had just lost Tia, and Estelle had talked him into spending a few days with them. She, Randall, and young Randy were greatly responsible for helping him pull himself together after the worst year of his life. The onslaught of the ravenous cancer that attacked and ultimately claimed his beautiful Tia still sent shivers up his spine. It stirred the deep emotional sadness and grief he tried so futilely to inter in some hidden and almost lost recess of his memory. And now, here he is, years later, returning for very different reasons and pursuing perhaps yet another love in his life. The city looked so different—so alive and so vital. Time certainly does heal the wounds of the past and sometimes jettisons one into a new and invigorating zest for life.

As he flung his carry-on piece of luggage over his shoulder, the flight attendant wished him a pleasant stay in Detroit, and he thought "magnificent" would have been more appropriate. He was the first person to get off the plane, and as he walked through the connector panel adjoining the aircraft to the terminal, he smiled just thinking about his beautiful Rachel and this unexpected surprise. The next face he saw was Estelle's. She was vivacious as ever

"Stellar!" he called and picked her up in his arms and hugged her.

"You're looking more beautiful every day, sis." Estelle could not hold back her tears of joy at seeing her big brother.

"Sure, and I guess I'm supposed to reciprocate and say that you look more handsome every day." She chuckled. "Funny thing is, you do, Christian." They embraced again and then walked through the terminal to the baggage pick-up area, located on the lower level.

"They've really done wonders with this airport since the last time I was here. I'm amazed at the apparent expansion and upgrading." And he continued to look around.

"Well," responded Estelle, "while I'm not that conversant on the success and growth of this airport, I do know that Northwest Airlines' choosing it as their domestic hub has increased the traffic and provided more originating flights around the world. More than we ever had in the past."

"Hub city. My, my, sis, I'm impressed at your aviation jargon. You must be more knowledgeable than you are willing to admit," he said jokingly.

Christian identified and picked up the last piece of luggage off the conveyor and left the airport. Estelle had hired a limousine, which was waiting for them right outside of the Northwest exit door. Christian smiled approvingly as the driver relieved him of his luggage. They got into the luxurious limo and prepared themselves for a very comfortable but brief return trip to Grosse Pointe. Estelle had arranged for a chilled bottle of Savignon Blanc, one of Christian's favorite domestic California wines. She had also ordered a few light hors d'oeuvres, not too much, and definitely just what he needed. Estelle and Christian were always simpatico to one another, and their closeness over the years got them to a quick, comfortable place. It seemed as though only a few hours had passed since their last, brief visit in New York. After catching up on Randall's career and Master Randy's school activities, Christian couldn't wait any longer.

"So, tell me, Stellar, when's the last time you talked to Rachel, and how are we going to pull off this surprise?" Christian could no longer hide his excitement and anticipation to see his beautiful Rachel.

"As a matter of fact," she grinned, "I just saw her a few hours ago."

Christian turned to look directly at his sister now.

"She doesn't know that I'm coming, does she?" he inquired nervously.

"No, no, Christian," she responded and tried to calm him down. "No, she took Randy, Jr. out for an afternoon of movies and Taco Bell."

Christian couldn't contain himself.

"Taco Bell?" he bellowed. "My beautiful Rachel likes Taco Bell?

Amazing!" and he shook his head in near disbelief.

"Well, now," replied Estelle, "I didn't say that. Actually, as you know, your dear nephew likes Taco Bell, so Rachel indulged Randall."

"Okay," he responded, "I'm ready—what movie did they see? *Sleepless in Seattle?*"

"Close," she chuckled "How's *Little Rascals?*" She laughed and he laughed, as well. Christian was still laughing, and Estelle thought how terrific it was to see her brother so happy and excited. *What a wonderful visit this is going to be,* thought Estelle.

The ride to Grosse Pointe was just as Christian remembered it. Short and sweet. The trees that lined the circular drive leading up to the Markham mansion were almost at peak autumn colors. The hues of reds, russets, oranges, burgundy, and chestnut brown blended together to provide one of nature's more beautiful settings.

"I guess autumn in just about any state in the midwest has beautified mother nature's leaves in flaming color. There to wait and ultimately be swept away by the winds of winter. Swooped into the cycle of life and left only with the promise of rebirth when once again, the warmth of spring would give birth to her new and glorious life." Christian sort of balladized the words and, in an almost melancholy way, made the ever familiar analogy comparing the seasonal changes to our life span. The similarities had been alluded to by many a song writer, current and past; however, never did they ring as true for him as they did recently. As the limousine pulled up to the main entrance. Christian felt a sort of peace come over him. These portals certainly had seen a sadder Christian, and they had also allowed him the solitude and comfort he needed to heal and prepare to get on with his life. As he exited the limo, he extended his hand to Estelle, who already had the tip ready for the driver. They stood in the driveway for a while, watching the limo drive off. Christian put his arm around his sister's shoulder and spoke softly.

"Well, Stellar, here we are again at this familiar place. Does it feel like déjà vu to you as well? I don't know why, but at times, I appear to be entering into some midlife crisis. Experiencing such sensitivity and being aware of almost every little thing?" Estelle smiled.

"So, my dear brother. What are we alluding to here?" she asked rather firmly. "Are you talking about your past life, life in general, or the philosophical combination of both?" Estelle even grinned after posing that somewhat obtuse question.

"Oh, my," retorted Christian, "I fear that the lady is about to 'clean my clock.' What say, ye?"

"Not so, m'lord. I was only setting thee up for some comedic response, if one were there."

Then, she became quite serious and turned to look up at her handsome brother.

"Christian, don't live your entire life in one moment or one day. You can't change the past, so don't dwell on it. Let it rest. Let Tia rest. Life is for the living, no matter where we are on that scale." She was purposely urging him toward the door now, and he picked up his luggage and followed her.

"The comparison you've made goes on in life each and every day. There are segments which are seasonlike in every relationship and in each aspect of life itself. However, if you always look to dissect it and identify it, you may miss something. You must stop being so analytical and introspective." Estelle felt she was zeroing in on the real reason for making these analogies and finally she blurted it out. "This is all about Rachel, isn't it, Christian?"

By this time they were inside the foyer. Master Randy heard their voices and came running down the stairs to greet his favorite uncle.

"Hi! Uncle Christian!" He shook his hand and then embraced him. "How was your flight? Meet any cool ladies?" Randy loved to play around with his uncle, and now was no exception. They all laughed; it certainly helped to change the subject for Estelle and Christian.

"No, as a matter of fact, I didn't. I've been so wrapped up in the show and then preparing for this little get-away to see our own cool lady, that I completely forgot about the possibility of meeting any others." Christian's love for Randy was not difficult to see. Not having any children of his own, he always focused on Randy, who was much more than a nephew to him.

"I'm so happy you're here, Uncle Christian. I thought, perhaps, you and I could play some tennis at the Yacht Club and maybe even take Mom and Rachel along? Sounds like a capital idea to me."

Estelle shook her head.

"I think you should allow your uncle to at least settle down before you start creating his activities' schedule. And, Randy, when will you get past this interminable matchmaking idea?" she gasped almost exasperatingly.

"That's an easy one to answer, Mom." He grinned his Cheshire cat grin. "When Uncle Christian marries the cool lady. Then I can concentrate on pursuing a career and a mate of my own." He shook his head assuredly.

"I can't believe you've concocted such succinct plans for your Uncle Christian's future, and your own. I do hope that your father and I are incorporated somewhere in all of this, since, in case you've overlooked it, you're not of age to do much of anything just yet."

Randy was getting a little edgy with this conversational exchange and tried to soothe Estelle's concerns.

"Certainly, Mother. How do you think I could pull this off without you and Dad? None of my schemes—I mean plans—could have worked without the two of you. I know that I'm much too young to have acquired the necessary cash it would take to set the scene for these eventual nuptials." Estelle was astounded by his response.

"Randall Markham, Jr.!" she exclaimed. "That's quite enough!"

Master Randy knew he had crossed one of those "bad lines." His mom had told him that there were lines around every relationship that the participants must observe. They have to do with respect, integrity, and trust. Having felt as though he had just trespassed over one of those lines, he stood almost mum!

"Your uncle just arrived," Estelle continued, "and I really don't think it's polite to plan his entire future before he gets settled in and has time for a decent bite to eat." She smiled and patted Randy softly on the head.

Randy knew he had been properly chastised and lowered his eyelids and responded.

"I apologize, Mother—uh, and to you, as well, Uncle Christian, for my brash and inconsiderate behavior." He hesitated for just a brief moment and added, "Why don't we all have dinner—and then we can call Rachel?"

Estelle couldn't help but laugh, and so did Christian. He followed her upstairs as she led him to the west wing, which was used for visiting family and friends.

"Here's your room, Christian. When you've had an opportunity to settle in and make yourself comfortable, come downstairs. By that time, Randall should be home from the hospital and we can all enjoy our dinner together."

"Hmmm," replied Christian. "Sounds wonderful, dear. I'll be down shortly." He nodded to Randy, who politely reminded Christian that his own room was right down the hall to the left of the Grecian urn. Christian winked at him to acknowledge his subtle invitation. When Estelle and Randy left, he was alone.

"Alone" was a place that Christian didn't like. It was a circumstance in his life that he never truly accepted very well. It afforded him much too much time to think. And after Tia died, his thinking eventually led to sadness and the awareness of his virtual solitude without her. At times like these, he would strive to remember the happy times. But the agony and pain of losing someone he had loved so completely, so totally, would come rushing back. As hard as he tried, the bridge between those difficult times and getting on with his life never got any shorter or easier. Coping became the order of the day. And it became the thin thread that pushed one long day into the next one, plunging him into another tomorrow and forcing him to leave behind memories that would live forever in the never-to-be altered shrine called yesterday. Eventually, anticipating the possibility of ever loving again challenged all of Christian's reasons for living. The risk for happiness was great and the abyss of losing, once again, loomed vividly somewhere in his consciousness. If this rebirth and resurgence of body and soul is not a fantasy, then, perhaps he may know, once again, the oneness he had found with Tia.

He struggled with the possibility of such good fortune. Finding true love, for some, never happened. But imagining and even hoping for it to happen twice in one lifetime . . . might be asking for a miracle.

There was a sitting room in Christian's quarters, and the ringing of the telephone that sat on the small Queen Anne table brought him quickly back to reality. Someone else in the house had answered it, and he sighed.

"Well, nothing ventured, nothing gained, ole man!" He smiled as he thought about referring to himself as an "ole man."

"Perhaps, the more operative word would have been 'older man." In any case, hopefully not too old to grab that brass ring one more time!" He walked toward the dressing room mirror and almost stood at attention as he looked at his reflection.

"Not bad!" he said out loud. "You can do this, Christian. You can live again." He stopped and then added with complete certainty, "You can love again!"

By 8:30 P.M., Dr. Markham had returned home. He was delighted to see the preparation for a lovely candlelight dinner. Doria, their housekeeper of many years, was an excellent cook, and her knack for preparation was outstanding.

Young Randy was occupying himself with a good game of Super Nintendo. Situated in the sun room at the back of the house, he needed some time alone. He had honed his computer skills to a point where he was an expert game player.

Estelle and Randall were seated in the library adjacent to the dining room. They each held a magazine covering their respective interests. Randall was deeply entrenched in the current issue of the *J.A.M.A.*, and Estelle was skimming through the latest issues of the *People* and *Time* magazines.

The silence was once again broken by a ringing telephone, and Christian, who was well on his way down the main stairway spoke out.

"My, My, this is a busy household. Someone would think a doctor resided here."

Dr. Markham got up from his leather chair and walked over to shake his brother-in-law's hand.

"Good to see you, chap," said Randall, Sr. "I guess directing musicals agrees with you, since you always look so hale and hearty during the development and actual production."

"Thanks, Randall. I think you may be right. I know being a part of the medical fraternity, you must advocate that hard work never really killed anyone."

"Well," responded Dr. Markham, "I think we ought to add to that statement by saying, 'hard work, lots of rest, and proper diet may not kill anyone.' But you know, Christian, the variables are immense and the possibilities too diverse to nail any statement like that to hospital walls."

"Well, sis, you look ravishing this evening." Christian walked over to where Estelle was sitting and kissed her on the forehead. "I think I could get used to this suburban living. I like the casual and comfortable ambiance and the quiet that exists in this affluent hamlet that borders the Motor City." Christian fixed himself a glass of sparkling water, which was sitting on the grand piano in the rather large living room rimming both the library and the dining room. No one in the family was a big alcohol drinker, and with Dr Markham's careful scrutiny over the lives of those he loved, it wasn't missed. The Markhams enjoyed life and never needed the infusion of drugs or alcohol to either induce or reduce their zest for life.

Master Randy looked at his watch and wondered when and if Uncle Christian was going to call the cool lady. However, after this afternoon's near collision with his mother about his matchmaking antics, he wasn't really up to tempting fate.

Fourteen

In another part of Grosse Pointe, several miles away on the shores of Lake Huron, Corey Davidson looked out at the sunset over his favorite of the Great Lakes. The style of his home, which he personally designed and had built, allowed him some small glimpse of the water no matter where he was in the house, except, of course, from the bathrooms. He was sipping from a glass of Old Rarity scotch on the rocks and thinking about none other than Rachel. It had been weeks since he saw her last and the same amount of time since they had spoken to one another. His silence was almost penance in some respects, since he truly was devastated by his actions that almost killed Blaise Kinley, landed him in jail, and intoned the death knell of a relationship he almost single handedly destroyed by his selfish and arrogant behavior. Bill Jacoby, his friend and business partner, had convinced him to take off for a couple of weeks and just relax and regroup.

It was unusual for Corey to do both of these things without a woman. It's not that he didn't want to or because there weren't any available. It was because nothing seemed the same in his life without Rachel. Perhaps she was the one woman in his life who fulfilled his passions. She, he recalled, never demanded anything of him. She didn't try to control him or manipulate him. She listened probably better than anyone ever had to his incessant ramblings about one thing or another, and she expressed her feelings genuinely without coaxing and with great sincerity. No one else either in his past or in his future would ever fill all the areas of his life so totally again. Her stimulating intellect and her keen sense of humor combined to make her the date and the choice of every class and quality.

No matter how hard Corey tried to come up with something, anything, that would somehow bring them back to what they shared, he knew it was futile and most definitely over. If salvaging any part of this defused relationship were possible, he certainly was a day late and a dollar short.

He put the glass down on one of many marble-topped tables of his rather enormous terrazzoed patio. Should he risk a telephone call? What could he lose at this point? He did want to find out about Blaise's progress, and most of all he wanted to hear the voice that at once could soothe any discord, any apprehension that life could deal. Before he could give it a second thought, his hand was on the receiver and pressing the "memory" number one which was Rachel Radcliffe's home phone number. The phone rang once and then twice. He almost decided to abort the call, when he heard Rachel's voice.

"Hello," she sang out in her usual upbeat manner. Corey hesitated and then heard her say it again.

"Hello, Rachel," he said softly.

"Corey, is that you?" she responded.

"Yes, it is, Rachel. Forgive me if this call is an interruption to something you were doing," he said apologetically.

"It's all right, Corey. I wasn't doing anything except catching up on some much needed paperwork," she said. He was pleasantly surprised and greatly relieved that she sounded so well and most of all, that she didn't just hang up when she heard him.

"How are you, Rachel?" he asked. "I've been thinking about you, and, uh, Blaise and just thought I'd touch base to see what's going on in your lives." He sighed and waited for her response.

"Well, Corey, I've been doing just fine, thank you, and Blaise is getting better by the moment," she said. "I am a little surprised to hear from you, though. I just figured that after our last encounter at the police station, you wouldn't ever want to talk to me again, and I can't say I'd blame you, Corey."

There she went again, always blaming herself for the things others had done.

"Rachel, how you can even consider my feelings after what I put you and Blaise through is almost beyond my comprehension. However, it's not out of character for you who been one of the most forgiving people I've ever known." He stopped and swallowed as though to hold back some of the emotional feelings that were erupting quickly.

Rachel's sensitivity to Corey had been altered since the incident with Blaise, but she was still concerned about the man with whom she shared an intimate relationship for a good many years.

"Corey," she said quietly, "I believe we've said everything that had to be said in that regard, and I'm perfectly willing to let bygones be bygones." She hesitated and then continued. "However, I don't believe that you and I could ever coexist as just friends. Do you? Honestly, Corey?"

Corey was accused of a lot of things that weren't exactly complimentary in his life, but no one could say he was a fool. And Rachel, his precious kitten, wouldn't be able to say it either.

"No, Rachel, I guess I couldn't. Having had the privilege of intimacy you allowed and were so willing to share during our relationship, I truly, in good conscience, could never settle for something less and be happy." He thought for a second and spoke again. "Sad isn't it, kitten, that when a relationship like ours dies, we can't even muster enough understanding and support to be kind to one another at some new level."

Rachel was already teary-eyed before Corey finally arrived at the inevitable conclusion.

"Endings have always been my undoing, and I pray Corey that this will not be your undoing, but rather, a new lease on life. Another open door through which you'll embark on a new and fulfilling life." She sighed deeply and waited for Corey's response.

"Well, if I ever do get beyond this point and am fortunate to get another chance at a meaningful relationship, believe me, kitten, I won't make the same mistakes I did with us, and, Rachel, I want you to know that you will always hold a special part in this ofttimes fickle heart."

Rachel thanked Corey for his consideration and thoughtfulness concerning Blaise and herself and asked him to keep in touch from time to tine.

Corey uttered his final good-bye, and when they each put down the receivers, tears flowed down both their faces, once and for all releasing the emotional drain that each had fought for a very long time. Rachel lowered her head and put her face into both hands. "Oh Corey," she sobbed, "I'm sorry, I'm sorry, I'm sorry," and cried without inhibition. Before she could get back her composure, the telephone rang again. She blew her nose and then wiped away the last traces of tears from her face and picked up the receiver.

"Hello," she sang out.

"Hello, my beautiful Rachel, it's Christian." She was surprised even though she anticipated his call, and her voice echoed the happiness emanating for her heart.

"Christian," she exclaimed, almost gasping with joy. "Christian, darling, how are you?" she asked excitedly.

"I'm fantastic now that I've heard your voice, my dearest. Are you well, and am I disturbing anything?" he asked in his inimitable manner.

"No, no," Rachel exclaimed quickly. "I was just tidying up a little and trying to decide about a snack."

"Well," he responded, "a snack sounds like a great idea to me. How about the Grosse Pointe Yacht Club?" he grinned slyly.

Since she wasn't supposed to know about his trip, she played along.

"Sure," she said, "I'd love that! Where will you be going for yours, the

Club Intrepid?" She chuckled.

"No," he responded. "the Grosse Pointe Yacht Club sounds fine with me, particularly since I'm calling you from Estelle's house." He waited for her response.

"Oh, Christian, are you really in town?" she asked anxiously. "When did you arrive? You didn't tell me you were coming," she went on and on.

"Well, surprises generally don't lend themselves to all those factual items," he said and smiled.

His voice and his caring manner quickly embraced Rachel's thoughts and recollections of that magical time in New York. She could feel her pulse race and her face radiate as she recalled the excitement and thrill of their first kiss in the underground parking lot of the World Trade Center. Suddenly, she could hear Christian's voice.

"Rachel, oh, Rachel, are you there?"

"Yes, oh, yes, Christian, I'm here. Forgive me; my mind was wondering for a split second—I can't imagine how this happened, I'm sorry!" she said pleadingly.

"It's all right, my darling, and I guess this surprise is a little more of a shock than I had anticipated." Christian could tell now that the best way to rectify this was to go to her immediately so that his visit would be as real for her as it was for him. "Rachel, I think rather than wait to meet you at some way too public place, I should come over now and continue this whole meeting again process." He laughed as he tried to add some calm to an already anxious beginning.

"Here? Oh, my, Christian, not here," she stammered. "This place is a wreck, and I couldn't allow you to see this messy, disorganized side of me just yet." She was quite nervous about the prospect of Christian meeting Blaise without her ability to lay some much needed groundwork. "Do you mind, Christian, if we just meet at the Yacht Club as planned, and then we can talk about your visit and make some plans, as well." She sighed deeply as she waited for Christian's response.

"Well, okay," he hesitatingly answered, "I guess that will work." He stopped for a moment, trying to rearrange his thoughts, and then he said, "That's fine, my darling, and I do apologize for upsetting you like this. Unfortunately, one never considers the other side of a surprise of this magnitude, and I guess the director in me is always trying to imagine both parts of a scenario. This is not an act in one of my productions, and I implore your forgiveness, dear, cool lady."

Rachel smiled and breathed a sigh of relief.

"You're wonderful Christian, and I'm so happy you understand my concerns right at this moment. I do so want you to be amply impressed when you see my humble but organized and clean dwelling."

Christian smiled as he thought about anything in Rachel's life that could be disorderly, messy, or disorganized, but he was perfectly content to defer to his lady's wishes.

"Your 'dwelling'—my, my, your choice of words is also a refreshing part of your unfettered and distinctive approach and description of your past, present, and future." He quickly offered what he hoped would be a more successful Plan B. "So my lady, how about if I meet you at the Grosse Pointe Yacht Club at 9:00 P.M.? Does that give you enough time to do whatever you have to before meeting me later on tonight?" He waited anxiously for her response, and when she agreed to his alternative plan, he smiled broadly, and they said their good-byes and see-you-laters, and went about their respective business until later.

Christian thought a nice shower and change of clothes into something a bit more classically casual would be appropriate to the club's dress code and his need to stay away from the formal lifestyle that was his everyday attire.

On the other side of the city, Rachel thought she'd let Blaise know that Christian was in town and that she would be meeting him later on this evening. She rapped gently on Blaise's back door, and as usually was the case, he called out.

"Hi, Ray, I'll be right there." No one else had access to his back door except Rachel or any other tenant who might occupy the adjoining duplex. Blaise, clad in a terry cloth robe, opened the door, and was looking extremely refreshed and without any trace of bandages.

"Blaise," exclaimed Rachel, "where are your bandages?" She was astounded to see him without any on his head.

"All done," he exclaimed, with a big smile. "See, no more scabbing, and the redness has diminished more quickly than I could have imagined." He turned his head toward Rachel so she could see that what he said was true. Then, in the very same motion, he bent down and kissed her as if it were the natural thing to do. "You've made my recovery and this whole situation so easy for me, Ray." He put his arms around her small frame and hugged her. Rachel was touched by Blaise's comments and his open expressions of love and gratitude.

"Easy?" she exclaimed as she looked up at him smiling. "Only easy thing about any of this has been your marvelous attitude and your almost magnanimous manner of making me feel as though I were just some interested party who happened to be there and sympathized enough to take care of you."

The same confusing feelings crept into Rachel's mind, and no matter how much she tried to deny her emotional involvement with Blaise, it was as real and as moving as her feelings for Christian. And to add to this uneasy triumvirate mishmash, her usual ability to decide and determine what to do in such instances had gotten railroaded somewhere between her brain and her much too overacting heart.

A good part of Rachel's problems in life, she thought, included self-examination and downright soul-searching and now she had traced the root of her problem to the same cause; that is, whenever her heart was the dominating force, her common sense and logic were nowhere to be found. Her usual calm and quiet nature, which allowed her to handle her chosen career so efficiently and effectively, was so overwhelmed by the emotional roller coaster she rode whenever she was in love. Now, the true meaning of adding insult to injury; she was incredibly and absolutely in love with two men.

Her head was resting comfortably on Blaise's chest and she could hear his heart beating furiously. She moved away from him slowly and looked up at him. His eyes and his face were radiant. He smiled ever so softly as he looked at the face only God could have crafted.

"Uhhh, hmmmm," she uttered, trying to garner enough strength to interrupt this precious moment and, more seriously, to tell Blaise about her arrangements to meet Christian. "Blaise?" she started. "I came over to let you know that I would be going out for awhile this evening." She hesitated and then came right to the point of her visit. "Christian is here in Grosse Pointe, Blaise, and he's asked me to meet him at the Grosse Pointe Yacht Club for dinner." She could feel his body wilt and his breathing change. "I hope you understand that I feel some sense of obligation—"

"—and a sense of longing as well?" he interrupted and sighed deeply. Rachel's eyes brimmed with tears, and while she would have given anything to be able to lie and say no, she couldn't, she wouldn't ever lie to Blaise.

"Yes, yes, that's partially true, Blaise. I—I—" Suddenly without any intention to do so, she began to cry. The tears were streaming down her cheeks, and she couldn't speak because the words were getting stuck in her throat, and she began to shake almost uncontrollably.

Blaise couldn't stand to see her cry, and he held her and caressed her, stroking her hair and trying to hide his own disappointments and hurting.

"I know, sweetie, I know you have to do this. I would be a fool to believe that this moment was never going to happen. But I've been in this place before, and I can handle it, Ray, honest."

Rachel was astounded at this response, and yet it wasn't any different than any other time in their past. Blaise was always there for her. The only difference now was that two very impacting and influential things had changed. He wasn't a homosexual, and he had confessed a very deep and long-standing love for her. She reached searching for a Kleenex in the pocket of her sweater, not finding one, Blaise offered her his handkerchief and she dried her eyes and face and blew her nose. After swallowing several times, trying to discourage the overwhelming urge to start the whole crying process again, she spoke quietly.

"I know you understand, Blaise, and I'm touched that you see the need for me to do this." She swallowed yet again and whispered, "What you don't know is that this burst of emotion is due to the confusion I can't resolve." She was whimpering and trying to talk as clearly as possible. "I'm absolutely divided here." Blaise looked at her quizzically.

"Divided? How so?"

She could no longer deny or hide this from him.

"I do love Christian. I do." The tears came again as she looked deep into Blaise's eyes. "And, I love you, Blaise." Her chin quivered and her expression was one of pain and fear. "What am I going to do?" she implored. "Oh, Blaise, how can this be happening? I can't deal with this. I don't know how."

Blaise's own mixed emotions were hard enough to handle, but his overwhelming need to make Rachel happy came to the fore.

"Look, sweetie, first of all, ain't none of this going to be settled in the next five minutes. You've obviously said the words that have made my world complete, but in the same moment, brought my elation to a screeching halt." Blaise stopped for a moment, trying to cope with his own anxieties. He dug deep for the strength it would take to express what he knew in his heart was complete honesty, what he owed his friend and the love of his life, the truth.

"Ray, babe, look at me." He put his hand under Rachel's still quivering chin and gently lifted her head so that she could look into his eyes. As he looked into her teary and now bloodshot eyes, Blaise clenched his teeth, swallowed, and breathed deeply. "You and I have known that this moment was coming. We may have danced around it for our own respective reasons, but somehow, we knew this was inevitable. Perhaps if I were true to myself and looking out only for what I felt would be best for you and for me, I wouldn't be telling you what I'm about to."

Rachel listened intently to Blaise's words, their eyes almost locked in each other's.

"Things happen in our lives. Some are planned, while others are unexpected. If we're real lucky, once in a lifetime the things we plan that coincide with the unexpected are one and the same. Against all odds, and no matter what anyone says or does, something comes along that, excuse the cliché, was written in the stars or destined by the same master plan. When I saw you in that cocktail lounge eight years ago, something wonderful changed the course of my life and during our relationship, even though you'd class it as deceptive, I was able to befriend and eventually fall in love with a pretty special lady." Rachel listened and smiled as she once again wiped her eyes and blew her nose. "Little did I know then or at any time that I would ever meet what fate had destined for you and me in such a dramatic and life-threatening turn of events." Blaise sat down and sipped on a glass of ice water from one of the coffee tables.

"Almost losing my life made me realize that seizing the moment is what's critical. Procrastinating in facing the truth, and then trying to cover the truth with excuses of preventing hurt and sadness, never worked. Certainly, skirting issues because they're too painful never corrected any situation either. My deluding you by letting you assume my homosexuality was a game I was destined to lose. But I couldn't or wouldn't see any dangers. I only saw what I wanted to, that being a safe haven for me to hide while I waited for the 'perfect' opportunity to let you know the truth about me and my love for you.

"It took Corey Davidson's jealousy to bring all of us to our senses and to face the reality of what life is all about and that we should never take it for granted. Imagine, learning a good lesson from Corey Davidson! Life is strange!" He sighed and stood up and walked over to where Rachel was still standing, almost spellbound.

"I'm lecturing, sweetie, and I apologize for rambling on. Really what I'm trying to say is, you know I love you, Rachel. I shall always love you. When you told me you loved me too, I was flying higher than I ever imagined. But then the reality of it all became clearer, and the picture I imagined changed when I realized your obvious dilemma. I can only wait now to see where your heart is Rachel. You must go to Christian! You must find what's in your heart, and, more specifically, with whom you will share your heart."

Rachel's understanding of the words was no problem, but her thoughts continued to spin like a top. Her perceptions were fragmented and she winced as she struggled to keep everything in its proper perspective. Blaise would always be here. That's what he said. Christian came to Grosse Pointe to assure her that he'd be there. The overwhelming question was, where was Rachel? Beads of perspiration were on her forehead and upper lip. She couldn't believe how suddenly tired she became. She breathed deeply one or two times, and finally, she looked at Blaise.

"I don't know—I don't know if I'll ever be able to decide what's in my heart, and I'm extremely tired right now, Blaise. Do you mind if I just lie down for a few minutes?" She stood almost motionless with her hand on her head.

"What about Christian? Isn't he waiting at the club for you?"

Rachel was so tired, she just barely heard Blaise. Her vision was becoming blurred, and her breathing gasplike. As he looked at her more intently, Blaise could tell that something was going on with Rachel, and it wasn't good. She walked toward his sofa, and in a swooning motion, fell on the cushions and appeared to sleep.

Blaise sat down beside her. He touched her forehead and the side of her face. She was clammy and cool. He then put his arm around the back of her head and pulled her forward calling her name.

"Rachel!" Rachel!" She was still limp, and her breathing shallow. Blaise then took her wrist in his hand and searched frantically for her pulse. He was getting more upset by the minute, and finally, when he couldn't arouse her, he went to the phone and dialed 911.

It didn't take long before Blaise could hear sirens, initially in the distance and then getting closer. When the rescue squad unit pulled into their Bedford driveway, a couple of neighbors came out to see what was going on. Their immediate next door neighbor told his wife he thought it was about his fight and surgery as a result of his injuries.

The paramedics, one man and one woman, knocked on Blaise's front door and asked where the victim was. Blaise led them to Rachel, who was still unconscious, but by now had developed a raging fever. The two trained medics proceeded to check Rachel's vital signs and as they communicated back and forth, Blaise was asking over and over what they thought was the problem.

"What's her name?" they asked.

"What was she doing before she fainted?" the lady asked.

Blaise explained that her name was Rachel Radcliffe and that they were just talking about her visit with a friend from New York.

"Was she upset, or had she ingested anything while this discussion was going on?" Blaise explained the emotional nature of their conversation and advised that she had not taken anything by mouth since she arrived.

"Rachel! Rachel," the male attendant called, but she did not respond. "She's in shock," advised the male paramedic. "Vitals are okay, but she appears to be terribly dehydrated, and the fever would indicate some virus or food poisoning is causing the fever. She's at 103.5 and rising."

"Let's get her to Saint John's," said the female. "I'll call ahead and advise emergency we're coming in stat. I'm putting her on a saline intravenous and asking if there's anything else we can do during transport."

Blaise was upset and shocked by these surprising events and couldn't imagine what or how this state of affairs happened.

"Will you be going along with her?" the female medic asked.

"Yes," he said. "I have to make one phone call, and I'll be right with you."

While Blaise went into his bedroom to make the call, the two paramedics put Rachel on the gurney and wrapped her in a red blanket and strapped her tightly to the frame so she would not slip during transport.

In the other room, Blaise called information and asked for the phone number for the Grosse Pointe Yacht Club. He had that number in his address book, but it was in the other room, and time was of the essence. He punched in the number quickly, and the receptionist for the club answered.

"Good evening, Grosse Pointe Yacht Club. How may I help you?"

Blaise explained that he wanted to leave an urgent message for Mr. Christian Avian, who was supposed to meet Ms. Rachel Radcliffe there at 9:00 P.M. She made certain that she had the names of the people spelled correctly and said she would start to page Mr. Avian right at 9:00 P.M. He left the message for Christian to meet him in the emergency room at Saint John's and that he would explain later. After the receptionist assured him that she would take care of this situation, Blaise hung up, quickly donned a pair of slacks and a sweater, and returned to the living room where Rachel, now looking more critical than before, was still unconscious.

"We're ready to transport. Let's go!" said the male medic.

Blaise opened the front door, and by this time, half the neighborhood was on the street and sidewalk wondering who was in trouble. A couple of the women gasped as they recognized Rachel on the stretcher. One of the elderly ladies, whom Rachel had always looked after during rough times in her life, began to cry. Blaise was following behind and tried to answer the questions of inquisitive neighbors standing by.

"She'll be all right," he responded as assuredly as he could. "She'll be okay. I'll let you know later on. " He tried desperately not to alarm everyone prematurely.

When the door closed and the ambulance started up Bedford, Blaise was sitting next to Rachel, who still lay unconscious on the stretcher while the female paramedic checked her vital signs and wrote down the information gathered from the variety of indicators and equipment attached to her. They advised Blaise when they were putting Rachel into the ambulance that a siren would not be necessary since in their opinion, this was not a life-threatening situation.

Rachel's expression was almost stark, but in her unconscious state, she was walking on the same familiar street that haunted her in nightmares too numerous to count. The only difference this time was that she seemed to be moving in slow motion. Her feet felt heavy, and it took an enormous amount of energy to pick them up one after the other in her struggle to get away from this all too familiar and frightening place. She could feel droplets of water on her face that ran down her cheeks and nose, the raindrops moving in slow motion, as well. Her view was obscured by the rain, and once again, black umbrellas moved toward her. As she tried to look behind them, faceless people poked their heads out and moved right through her just as though she were invisible. She tried to cry out, but the sounds were muffled and distorted.

Her mouth could hardly move to speak. Then, as in her last episode with this recurring nightmare, a man carrying a black umbrella approached her slowly. He picked up the umbrella to reveal his identity. This time it was Blaise's face that turned into Christian's face. She threw out her arms to embrace him. He just barely called her name, "Ra-a-chel!" It echoed resonantly in her ears and in her heart. When her arms reached him, she embraced only air. He was only a vision. An image. A figment of her imagination.

"Christian!" she cried as she awakened. It startled both the paramedic and Blaise. The sudden jerky motions of her arousing from this strange unconsciousness caused the intravenous needle to disconnect from her arm, and she became extremely frightened as she focused on the paramedic standing over her.

"Who are you? Where am I?"

The paramedic responded to both of her questions and advised that she had collapsed at her friend's house and that he was in the ambulance with her. It was then that Rachel realized that Blaise was the other person in her blurry state and that it was he holding her hand and stroking it gently as the ambulance proceeded on its way to the hospital.

"Blaise," she whispered, "is that you?" she queried. She tried to pick up her head, but it felt as if she had a few hundred-pound weights lodged at each side that were preventing her from too much mobility.

"It's me, darlin'," replied Blaise. "It's all right, Ray. You're just extremely tired, and you passed out in my studio." Blaise tried to be as calm as possible, but it still didn't dispel the fear expressed on his precious Rachel's beautiful face.

"Christian?" She quivered. "Blaise, where's Christian?" Her eyes were blinking frantically, trying to focus on Blaise's face so she could hear his response.

"I've left Christian a message at the Grosse Pointe Yacht Club. I've asked him to meet us at Saint John's." Blaise stroked Rachel's hand and repeated over and over. "It's going to be all right, Ray, you're going to be all right." Blaise spoke softly as he held Rachel's hand and looked at her lovely face. He hoped she could not see the fear and anguish that were ravaging within him.

The emergency room at Saint John's was all too noisy and technical. Medics were scurrying about, and questions were darted like arrows splitting the air in their search for a target. Finally, Rachel opened her eyes and was looking at a man who was now almost face to face with her. He examined carefully her eyes, flashing that painfully bright light that left black spots dancing about as she tried to focus on his face.

"Rachel," he said in a very deep and resonant voice. "Rachel, are you in pain?" Rachel's frame of mind was still one of confusion, but she responded negatively. "Did you eat or drink anything that may have made you ill or eventually faint?" She tried to remember what happened at Blaise's house, but she could not.

"I don't think I did. I don't remember." She sighed and continued. "I do remember becoming extremely tired and wanting to lie down."

The doctor proceeded to examine her. Stethoscope, pressure being applied to her abdomen, and finally she could feel his fingers behind her head and neck. Searching—searching!

It felt good when the examination was over, and she closed her eyes once again trying to rest. But to no avail. A nurse put a thermometer in her mouth and took her wrist to get a pulse rate. How long would this incessant probing go on? All she really wanted to do was sleep. All the stories Rachel had heard about no one ever getting any rest in a hospital were slowly being confirmed one at a time. The odor of medicinal products kept her awake now. They were too pungent, and as she looked up and backward to observe her surroundings, she was somewhat startled by all the equipment attached everywhere. She could feel her heartbeat increase. Finally, the nurse took the thermometer out of Rachel's mouth and looked at it with a serious expression.

"One zero three point one," she said, and "pulse rate one hundred."

Rachel knew enough about fevers to understand that 103 was too high for anyone. Yet, she didn't feel that hot. She was finding it more difficult to focus and concentrate, and perhaps this was caused by a state of delirium.

"What's wrong with me?" she asked.

No one responded, but the nurse came over to her bed.

"We're trying to determine that, Ms. Radcliffe. For now why don't you just close your eyes and rest!" Rachel, even in her delirium, smiled and thought, *That's what I've been trying to do, silly.*

The waiting seemed interminable, and Rachel couldn't stand looking up at those metal rings that kept that white curtain separating her from other patients, medical people and possibly, from the world outside that had become such a maze, such a struggle. She found a certain peace in keeping her eyes closed. She would let her other senses take command. The mixed voices of people chattering; some more loudly than others, some less definite, became the guidelines by which she would cope and determine her way out of this place where only the sick and the dying dwelled. She could feel herself become calm. Her heart rate slowed, and the spinning that kept her so confused subsided. *Yes*, she thought, *this will work. I don't have to open my eyes. I will respond to their questions as I hear them and not be fooled by expressions I can't figure out and equipment I am afraid to see.*

The next voice she heard was, indeed, much more appealing than any other thus far.

"Rachel," he spoke, "Rachel can you hear me?"

"Yes," she responded.

"Can you open your eyes?" he asked.

"Yes," she said, "but I won't," and a smile bloomed ever so lightly on her lips.

"Why not?" he asked.

Rachel sighed and responded quietly.

"It's easier this way!" She was direct and succinct in her answers. She waited and anticipated the next question.

"Easier? Are you hiding from someone, Rachel?" he queried.

"Hmmm," she mused, "could be." she answered.

"Your fever stems from a virus you recently contracted, and your body dehydration led you to 'blow a circuit,' if you'll permit the metaphor."

Rachel smiled again and sighed. She thought about this evaluation of her malady, and because of his deep and authoritative manner, decided she should trust his assessment.

"Okay," she responded, "now what?"

The doctor now looked at his other colleagues, smiled, and responded.

"Now we get about the business of getting you well and out of here."

Rachel knew she was right about her assessment of this man, and she simply tightened her eyelids and giggled.

"Lead on, Macduff!" and everyone in that small area laughed.

Upon giving such rash permission to this guardian of her recovery, she felt someone grab her arm strongly.

"This will hurt a little Ms. Radcliffe, but it will make you get some much needed rest."

Before Rachel could even consider giving permission, the sting of the needle penetrated her upper arm, and she winced as the medicinal elixir entered her body.

"Ohh, you were right about that. It did sting." She breathed deeply and fought the urge to put her hand on the spot where the pain persisted. She waited for whatever effects she'd experience as a result of this shot, and once again she heard the voice of her guardian.

"Rachel, my name is Dr. Mannix, and I'll be your doctor during your stay at Saint John's. Just rest now and I'll come to see you later on."

She tried to respond, but her tongue seemed to thicken, and it was hard for her to concentrate as the drug began to accomplish its mission. Tissue paper, the rustling of tissue paper echoed in her ears. Muffled and distorted voices became softer and further away. Soon, she was drifting off, weightlessly in the arms of Morpheus, in the land of sleepers.

Fifteen

The telephone ring pierced the silence at the Domani residence, and Amber jerked slightly as she awakened from some cable TV news show.

"Hellow!" she sung out. "Domani residence." Blaise answered quickly.

"Hi, Amber, this is Blaise, Blaise Kinley, Rachel's friend and neighbor."

"Yes," responded Amber. "How are you feeling, Blaise?" Amber asked in her usual friendly manner.

"I'm well, thank you, but that's not why I'm calling," he said, almost not making any sense.

Amber thought about his response and then it hit.

"Rachel, how's Rachel, Blaise? Is something wrong with Rachel?" She was breathing excitedly waiting for Blaise to respond.

"I'm afraid she's not very well at the moment, Amber. She's in Saint John's right now!" Before Blaise could continue to explain what had happened, Amber blurted out.

"I'm coming, Blaise. I'll catch the first plane to Detroit. Can you let Rachel know I'm coming?" she asked. Amber hung up before Blaise could give her any details about Rachel's prognosis, but he decided to leave well enough alone and let Amber follow her instincts and come to her friend's side.

Blaise no sooner hung up the telephone, when he heard a man's voice.

"I'm Christian Avian, a friend of Ms. Rachel Radcliffe, who I believe was brought into your emergency room earlier this evening. Can you please tell me how to get to the emergency waiting room? I'm supposed to meet someone there by the name of Blaise Kinley." Christian was waiting for directions from the receptionist.

Blaise walked over to Christian.

"I'm Blaise Kinley, Mr. Avian. I called you about Rachel's sudden illness this evening."

Each sized the other up, and Christian, not usually having to look up at most of the people in his world, found it a bit uncomfortable to almost have to tilt up his head in order to get eye contact with Rachel's next-door neighbor and friend of many years.

"Thank you for calling me at the Yacht Club, Mr. Kinley." Christian in his usual polite manner offered his hand to Blaise. "Do you know what happened, and would you be so kind as to fill me in?" Blaise shook Christian's hand and was taken with his easy manner and concerned thoughts about Rachel.

"I'm afraid I don't know much more than I did when we first got here. You know, I'm sure, the incessant forms that need to be filled out, along with the inane questions about communicable diseases and how many warts one had as a child." Christian smiled at Blaise's humor.

"Why don't we sit down for a while, and I'll try to explain the events leading to Rachel's collapse," Blaise said as he ushered the way to an empty two-seater sofa in the back of the huge reception area.

"Collapse?" said Christian. "Good Lord, whatever happened between seven-thirty and nine o'clock tonight that could cause her to collapse? Had she been ill?" Blaise could tell from the tone of Christian's voice and the concern on his face that these questions would be the first of many once he began to relate what happened then and earlier.

"Bad choice of words. I'm sorry, Mr. Avian."

"Uh, can we please proceed as Christian and Blaise? I already feel as though I know you given what Rachel has shared with me thus far."

Blaise liked that. He smiled and apologized again for the bad choice of words.

"I truly didn't know what was going on until she fainted onto my sofa, and when I couldn't arouse her, I called 911." Blaise hesitated and Christian came right back.

"Please, Blaise, can you start from the beginning?"

Blaise heard the words and mulled them over in his mind. "Start from the beginning." Which beginning? Tonight? Eight years ago? the Revelation of his admission of loving Rachel? None of this was going to be easy, but Blaise owed it to Rachel to be kind to Christian. After all, Christian didn't know that they were rivals.

More than an hour passed since Blaise related the sequence of events that led Rachel to Saint John's this night. He was right about the questions that Christian would ask and expect answers to. Waiting for an update on Rachel gave Blaise time to spend with the man who may ultimately end up with his beautiful Rachel. Never once did Christian show any cognizance of Blaise's deeper involvement with Rachel.

They really got along quite well during this unexpected meeting. Perhaps a lot better than if it would have somehow been designed by Rachel.

Somehow, fate played a softer hand in all of this, and at least for the moment, Blaise and Christian were allied toward the common cause of getting Rachel back on the road to recovery and good health.

Christian excused himself for a moment and called Estelle.

"She's all right, Stellar, honest! I've been sitting here in the lobby with Rachel's neighbor, Blaise Kinley, and I think everything's going to be all right, at least according to what Blaise has told me."

Estelle was happy to hear the good news. More particularly, since Master Randy had been driving her crazy with questions ever since he found out what happened to his cool lady. Estelle thanked her brother for calling and reiterated her support and assistance if needed. When she hung up, Dr. Markham approached her and asked if everything was all right.

"I think so," responded Estelle as she walked toward him and laid her head on his shoulder. He put his arms around her and held her close to him. They stood there, embracing each other for quite a while. Finally, Estelle raised her head and looked up at Randall. There were tears in her eyes, and he took her face in his hands.

"What's the matter, darling? Is there something wrong with Rachel that we didn't know?" He waited patiently for her to respond.

"No . . . uhh . . . it's not about Rachel," she stammered. "I'm afraid for Christian. I can't shake this uneasiness I've felt ever since he met Rachel." Estelle took a Kleenex from her dress pocket and wiped away the tears from her cheeks. Then she blew her nose and continued to explain. "You know," she sighed, "you know how lost Christian was when Tia died. He was literally devastated. We were all devastated, and I prayed to God for His direction and guidance to help us cope and sustain that horrendous and untimely loss." They walked over to the loveseat in the nearby living room and sat down. Randall listened intently as he always did to Estelle as she struggled with her anxiety.

"I prayed that someday, somewhere, someone would come along for Christian to love and share the rest of his life. And like everything else in life, sometimes our prayers are answered, but not quite as specifically and acceptable as we'd like. I realize I don't have any right to judge Rachel, or anyone for that matter, when it comes to Christian, but I'm terribly afraid that she has much too much on her plate at this stage of her life and that Christian may not be her first priority." Estelle swallowed hard and sighed deeply as she turned again now to look at Randall. "Am I overreacting here, Dr. Markham?" she queried with a little laugh and smile.

"I love you, you know that?" Randall leaned forward and kissed

Estelle on the forehead. "You've always been such a caring and loving sister, and Tia was your friend as well as your sister-in-law. And," he continued, "I think you still feel a sense of loyalty to her since she's no longer here. But my darling, you know as well as I do that we cannot live the lives of those we love. We can only stand by if they need us, and support and endure whenever and wherever we can." With his arm around her, he put her head on his shoulder and caressed and stroked her gently. "I don't buy problems and anxieties. Let Christian work this out with Rachel. If it's meant to be or not will be determined with or without your participation. We're none of us getting any younger, and God only knows we're far better off with love in our lives than without it. Love does exact a certain risk and a price, but it falls very short of the possibility of never loving at all."

Estelle loved Randall deeply and passionately and each day they lived together only confirmed the reasons why.

"You are my rock and my life," she said as she looked into his adoring eyes. "I hope and pray that Christian will find in Rachel the very same wonderment and contentment I've found in you, my darling."

Randall smiled and bent over to kiss his precious Estelle. She pressed her lips to his and still felt the tingling sensation she had experienced the very first time they kissed. They were still kissing when Master Randy walked into the living room.

"Oh, oh," he uttered, "Excuse me, Mother. Excuse me, Dad." Twelve was such an awkward age when it came to things like this. Randall and Estelle separated upon hearing their son's voice, and they smiled as he walked toward them. "Anything new about my friend, Rachel?" he asked with concern on his face and in his voice. Not something too common for this young and vibrant young man.

Estelle walked over to her son and embraced him.

"It looks like everything is going to be all right, Randy. Rachel has to undergo some further testing in order to determine what caused her collapse, but when Uncle Christian finds out more details, he'll call us back."

"Can I go to visit her?" he asked excitedly. "Or can I call her?" he persisted.

Dr. Markham got up from the loveseat and joined his wife and son.

"You know, Randy," Dr. Markham said softly. "I think until all of the medical information is obtained, it's probably better for Rachel if we just wait a while before we start visiting or calling. I'm certain she wouldn't want you to see her until she can look at you with that usual beautiful smile on her face."

Randy moved closer to his father, and in a voice just short of emotion, he thanked him and said he was happy that he, too, noticed the cool lady's dynamite smile.

Estelle suggested that they all turn in for the night. She looked at Randy's still forlorn face.

"Some prayers would certainly be the nicest gift you could give your friend right now, Randy. In the morning, your father will check on her condition when he makes his rounds, and perhaps by that time, everyone will have a better idea about Rachel's condition. Okay?"

In his usual all-too-gentlemanly fashion for such a youngster, he thanked his mother and then scaled the stairway two steps at a time!

"If this is the greatest hurdle he must overcome in his young life, we will be most grateful," she said, with a nod of approval.

"Well," said the senior Randall, "if he can accept sadness, disappointments, and hardship and still exude that survivor mentality, he'll do just fine."

They walked slowly upstairs, and just as they reached the top step, Randall put his arm around his dear Estelle once again, and they hugged one another as they walked toward their bedroom for the evening.

Sixteen

For Rachel, that Saturday was probably the longest day of her life, and as she lay in her hospital bed trying to sort out the events that got her here, she felt exhausted even having to think about it. She put her hand on her forehead. and she felt warm. As she self-examined her physical situation, she didn't feel sick. No nausea, no headache, but, if that were true, why this fever, if it were one?

Daylight. The hospital nurses arrived about the same time. Soon there would be doctors, nurses, and technicians everywhere. What happened to Blaise? And did he ever reach Christian at the Grosse Pointe Yacht Club? Questions, questions. She was tired, too tired. If she could only rest. Get some sleep, she would be fine. She kept her eyes closed and tried desperately to make her mind a complete blank, but to no avail. With that last attempt for peace and quiet in her turmoil-filled head, the door opened, and she heard Dr. Mannix's voice.

"Good morning, Rachel. Looks like a wonderful day. How do you feel?" He came directly over to her bedside and placed his hand on her forehead. Then he picked up her hand and felt her wrist for a pulse. Rachel's decision to keep her eyes closed seemed like a good one, so she continued to do so. It was one less sense she had to concern herself with. Dr. Mannix smelled almost antiseptic and squeaky clean. *Why shouldn't he, he's a doctor, isn't he?* she thought. With this little humor, she smiled, and Dr Mannix reacted to it quickly.

"Aha, she lives!" And with that, Rachel smiled even more broadly. "Why don't you open your eyes and drink in some of this magnificent sunshine?" he cajoled

Rachel sighed deeply, wanting to obey, but it felt so comforting to just shut out the world, at least to this extent and at this time.

"It's too much for me right now," she uttered, almost in a whisper.

"The sunshine or the world?" he asked perceptively.

Rachel really liked his voice and his manner of trying to examine all aspects of her condition.

"Both, I guess, both." And with that, she once again brought her hand to her forehead. He immediately asked if she was experiencing any dizziness or a headache.

"Uh, uh," she said. "My hand is cooler than my head, and it feels great. Do I have a fever?" she asked.

"Well, I don't know. I don't think so, but let's find out." And with that, she heard glass tinkling on glass. He asked her to open her mouth, then slipped the thermometer between her lips and under her tongue. "Three minutes. Can you keep your mouth closed tightly for three minutes?" He laughed. "Most of my women patients find that extremely difficult to do."

The grin on her face did not violate the position of her lips nor disrupt the placement of the thermometer. Dr Mannix observed Rachel's natural beauty, and even though her makeup was less than perfect since the events of last night, her beautiful facial structure and that magnificent head of hair were definitely appealing. It's good he wasn't taking his own pulse right then, because the count would absolutely be elevated. His next thoughts naturally went to the cause of her collapse. What could this beautiful lady be contending with that caused her to collapse?

"Okay," he spoke loudly now, "let's see . . . ahhhh . . . Yes, you do have a fever. Not a big one, but one, nonetheless; 99.5 isn't anything we should be very alarmed about. Perhaps a low-grade infection, or possibly your menstrual cycle?" he inquired.

"No, that's not it," she responded quickly. "But," she continued, "I have been doing a lot of running around recently. Staying up late, and I'm afraid not getting too much sleep." She waited for some quick response, and it seemed like a long time before he said anything.

"Something bothering you, Rachel?" was his next question.

Wow, she thought. *In what order do you want that list?* Where was her life going at this very moment and how did it get so out of control that she found herself here?

"Questions, more questions," she blurted out. "Questions, questions, everyone has questions! Fine, but am I supposed to know *all* the answers? Did God give me the only answer book and everyone else the questions?"

It was an outburst that really didn't surprise Dr. Mannix, and he reacted quite calmly and in his usual compassionate manner.

"I guess we'll have to help you find out, Rachel. Although I'm certain, you, too, have many questions that you can't answer. Like, how did you get here?" He looked at her expression changing by the second from confusion, sadness, fear, and almost sheer desperation.

"Help me," she gasped. "Please help me," and tears came streaming down her face and onto the pillow.

Dr. Mannix had been a physician for many years, and cries for help were not new to him. But there was something different about Rachel Radcliffe, and he was going to find out just what.

"Of course, I'll help you, Rachel, but it's a two-way street, and you may have to help me to find a way to resolve some of your dilemma. What do ya say? Will you?" Suddenly, he laughed and said, "I know, Rachel, one more question, right? Oh, well, let's see if we can get you some rest right now." Rachel was still crying when she felt a wet cold swab on her upper arm. Then a prick of a needle and a little stinging sensation that made her wince.

"This will help you to get some much needed sleep, Rachel, and when you awaken, we'll embark on that road to recovery, the road leading to the answers."

Rachel then heard the door of her room open and close. The effects of the drug he gave her were working quickly. She didn't fight it, and soon she drifted off to sleep.

Possessed of only one very tightly packed overnighter and a makeup case, Amber stood patiently at Gate 27 of the American Airlines terminal at JFK Airport. She was categorically running through the list of things that had to be done before she left her New York home. It's not like the children were a big problem at their responsible ages, but being the wonderful mom she was, she had to make certain that they had enough money to get around for a few days, telephone numbers in Detroit where she could be reached in case of an emergency—heaven forbid! And a well-stocked refrigerator so that they wouldn't starve. She grinned at that remote possibility. As for Tony. Oh, thank God for Tony. The only thing Tony needed was Amber's happiness, and maybe pasta once a week, but he would be just fine.

She sighed deeply and began to think about how she'd get to Saint John's Hospital from the airport. Having only been back home once or twice in the last few years, she hoped that the route had not changed too dramatically. She did have a key to Rachel's house, and she could always go there first. Her thoughts were interrupted by Tony's voice.

"Here, sweetheart, I bought you a couple of magazines and a book on your horoscope for the last quarter of this year. If these don't get your mind off Rachel for at least one-half hour, the bookstore attendant guaranteed my money back!" Amber hugged Tony quite spontaneously and then kissed him lovingly.

"I love you, my darling, I love you," she whispered in his ear. Tony uttered the same words to his precious Amber and gave her a few last-minute instructions about how to pick up the rental car at the airport, find 1-94, and so on.

The flight attendant announced the boarding sequence for American Airlines flight 824 leaving for Detroit at 11:30 P.M. and Amber was one of the first to go, since Tony had a purchased her a first-class ticket.

"So long, my darling," Amber called to Tony, "I'll call you first chance I get."

"Love you," responded Tony. "Take care and give our love to Rachel. Everything's going to be all right. I know it." With their farewell exchanges and the final waving, Tony watched Amber as she disappeared down the connector tunnel that led to the 767 parked at its door.

Amber smiled, as she always did, at the flight attendant greeting the oncoming passengers, and as she turned and looked immediately for her seat number, 2A, she placed her overnighter and makeup case in the compartment overhead and slid into her seat and fastened her seat belt. This was truly a "red-eye" flight, and one and a half hours' sleep sounded wonderful right now! The plane wasn't as empty as Amber supposed it would be and she kind of hoped that no one would sit next to her on the aisle seat. Many passengers walked past her single file, and no one even appeared to be looking for a seat next to hers. Her wish was granted, and when she saw the flight attendant close the door and lock it, she breathed a sigh of relief. This was the first opportunity she had to look at the magazines that Tony bought for her and as the plane began to move away from the gate, the terminal became smaller as the distance away became greater.

Being a Gemini, one of the zodiac's air signs, she loved to fly and so she did not experience one moment of anxiety as the plane approached the runway. The surge of energy and the force that it would take to get this enormous piece of aircraft airborne was almost exhilarating to Amber as she watched that magnificent city below become miniature through her window.

It was always exciting to see New York City from any angle, and from the sky, it looked like a million sparkling diamonds in the black of night. Amber was on her way to be with her childhood friend. A friend in need—indeed. After the attendants had asked if anyone would like coffee or tea or a drink, they passed out pillows and suggested that everyone take a brief nap given the lateness of the hour.

Amber didn't require much coaxing. She placed the magazines on her purse, reclined her seat to a more comfortable position, and put the pillow to the right of her head, and her eyes closed on contact. The skies were about as clear as could be, and since it was late summer, the winds were calm, and fortunately, no rain had been forecast anywhere in this quadrant of the United States. "Smooth as silk" would fit the description of the entire flight so far, and even if that were not the case, Amber was sleeping so comfortably, she would not have noticed.

The time passed very slowly as Christian and Blaise spent another entire day in the waiting room. Still talking. Still waiting. And still hoping.
"I don't think we're going to find out anything more here, and I'm going to believe that no news is good news is the case," said Christian.
I think you're right," agreed Blaise. "Why don't we go home and check back here tomorrow morning. Perhaps by that time, we'll get some good news about our mutual friend." He suggested they call a cab and have the driver take Christian home first and then himself.
Grosse Pointe was a beautiful community and no less so during the middle of the night. Twinkling lights gleamed through panes of French windows and doors, and quaint street lights lined the empty streets. The Markham mansion was better lit than most in that area, and the circular driveway had implanted lights lining the rim of the curb that framed it.
Christian thanked Blaise for being so considerate and hospitable. They reiterated their plans to meet later on the following morning at Saint John's and as Christian entered the front of his residence, the cab continued on its way to Bedford Avenue.
Blaise arrived home about fifteen minutes later and paid the cab driver an extra ten dollars for picking them up so promptly. As he opened the door and walked into his living room once again, the memory of events that took place there only hours ago came rushing back at him. He sat down in one of his opulent chairs and stretched his long, languid body. Tiredness was creeping in slowly, and his mind and body were poised and ready for some badly needed sleep. He yawned deeply and forced himself to get up from that comfortable position. His head was hurting now, and as he placed his hand over the area where the incision was still a little tender, he winced at the pain of his touch and was reminded that he wasn't as free of his own recovery as he imagined. Thinking about Rachel's well-being caused him to forget his own tenuous situation.
The bed looked extremely inviting, and after he removed his shirt and trousers, he lay across his king-sized bed and placed his head on the down pillows. With his eyes now closed, he thought about what the future was going to hold for him, for Rachel, and for Christian. His first concern was

Rachel and her recovery to good health. Everything else, including his own part in Rachel's life, would have to take second place; however, he couldn't help but wonder how this situation was going to play out.

Christian was able to go directly to his room, since he found a note from Estelle, saying that they had retired and, pending any emergencies during the night, they'd see him at breakfast in the morning.

As he lay in bed trying to process all of the events since he left New York not twenty-four hours ago, and although he didn't know about the relationship that had been developing between Rachel and Blaise, he was perceptive enough to know it wasn't as platonic as he'd like. The next couple of days were going to be interesting ones, and in order for him to be up for whatever happened, he decided some sleep couldn't hurt.

The only person in this entire circle of friends and family who was not asleep now was Amber. Her arrival at Detroit Metropolitan Airport was uneventful, and picking up the rental car and finding I-94 East turned out to be a piece of cake. Driving at night was not an uncommon experience for Amber, but it had been years since she had to do so back home in Grosse Pointe. Fortunately, the traffic was light and the street names at the exits became more and more familiar as she got further east.

The decision to go directly to Rachel's house turned out to be a good choice, since it was now almost 2:30 A.M. and she was certain the hospital wouldn't be able to tell her anything at this hour. As she turned off Jefferson onto Bedford, she breathed a sigh of relief and, in fact, smiled almost triumphantly at accomplishing this unplanned trip to see her sick friend. The driveway along Rachel's duplex was convenient. Amber pulled into the driveway, turned off the motor, and took the two pieces of luggage from the trunk without any difficulty. She walked up the couple of steps and reached in her purse for the key that Rachel had sent to her ages ago.

It fit! She opened the door slowly and was not surprised to find the lights still on. Given the manner in which Rachel was rushed to Saint John's yesterday, Rachel didn't have time to turn anything off. After walking around and checking out the rest of the house, Amber settled in the guest bedroom that Rachel always kept for visiting friends and family. Amber's last remembrance of time as she drifted off was 3:20 A.M. She set the alarm for 7:00 A.M. and hoped she'd hear it.

Rachel awakened with a start upon hearing all the noises that were so identifiable with hospitals. The clanging of bed pans, the hustle and bustling of people changing shifts, and finally, her own door opening as a nurse entered and, in a voice much too loud for Rachel's ears, bellowed.

"Good morning, Ms. Radcliffe, time for temperature and blood pressure check. And then, how about some breakfast?" Rachel was trying desperately to put her thoughts in order, and breakfast didn't quite fit. Before she knew it, the thermometer was in her mouth and the pressure band was around her upper arm and the nurse was pumping the machine to the max, squeezing Rachel's arm until it almost hurt. When the nurse released the pressure and began to read the indicator Rachel was curious about the reading, but she couldn't ask because she had a thermometer under her tongue. Rachel's focus was clearing as Dr. Mannix came into her room. She still chose to keep her eyes closed, but she recognized his voice and smiled.

"Good morning, Rachel. Feeling better this morning, I hope?"

Rachel sighed and pointed at the thermometer still protruding from her mouth. The nurse removed it and wrote down something on the clipboard she was holding.

"Good morning, Dr. Mannix," the nurse greeted. "Her fever's gone, and her pressure is 110 over 60. Not bad, huh?"

"That's good news, Rachel. Now, all we have to do is find out how you're feeling." There was silence as the nurse and Dr. Mannix awaited her response.

"I guess I'm better," Rachel said, a little shakily. "I don't have a headache any longer, and I'm not in pain, but I'm still pretty tired." She lifted her hand to push the hair off from her face. After the nurse left, Dr. Mannix grabbed a chair and sat down beside her bed.

"Well, Rachel, I think I have some good news for you," he said as he took her hand and held it in his. He was waiting for her to open her eyes, but she didn't. Rachel heaved a sigh of relief and hearing the phrase "good news" brought yet another smile to her face. "Well, I think I pushed the right button this morning. Two smiles. I must be doing something right!" And with that, he became a bit more serious. "After examining both your physical and mental test results, I believe the real problem here is more of mental fatigue, which led to your physical collapse."

This couldn't possibly be the good news, thought Rachel, but she waited for him to finish.

"Because we were fortunate enough to catch this condition in its early stages, I think the recovery will be just as swift."

Sighing had almost become a pastime for Rachel, and it truly did make her feel better. She was more than a little tempted to open her eyes, when Dr. Mannix spoke again.

"Dr. Jack October is perhaps the best psychiatrist in the medical profession today, and he just so happens to be a good friend of mine and on staff here at Saint John's." Rachel listened more intently after hearing the word "psychiatrist."

What on earth did she need a psychiatrist for? The only thing that kept her listening and considering was her staunch and unshakable faith in Dr. Mannix's prognosis and evaluation.

"What a nice name," replied Rachel. "Is he from around here?" she inquired.

"As a matter of fact, no, he's not," Dr. Mannix responded. "He's a Latin American." Rachel's quizzical expression amused Dr Mannix. "What's the matter, Rachel, don't you believe me?" he said, smiling.

"Well," she returned, "you've got to admit, his name certainly doesn't sound Latin American." She thought for a moment then added "Unless it's the English translation." She appeared quite pleased with this deduction and waited for Dr. Mannix's response.

"Yes. Yes, you're absolutely right, but I wouldn't begin to try to pronounce it in Portuguese, so please don't ask me. But," he continued, "you will have the opportunity to ask him yourself, since I've asked him to drop in to see you later on this morning. I hope you like him, Rachel. He's really a great psychiatrist and a very nice guy."

Rachel cleared her throat, and in her own inimitable way, retorted.

"I guess I'm captive here at the moment, so I don't know how I could possibly avoid this visit, even if I wanted to."

Dr. Mannix didn't know her well enough to tease her about the truth in her assumption, and he most certainly didn't wish to risk any possibility of her trying to get out of it.

"You must remember, Rachel, that you were brought to us unconscious and not really doing too well. As doctors, we must try to diagnose, treat, and hopefully to cure or alleviate whatever the determined cause happens to be." Without watching her eyes and seeing their reaction to any of this, Dr. Mannix was basing his mode of treatment and continuance of diagnosis merely on the results of tests and the limited information he'd received upon her arrival. "Are you all right with my professional opinions so far, Rachel?" He waited for her response.

She knew the answer was yes, because from the first moment she heard his voice, she experienced a sense of calm and trust and those feelings had not changed.

"It's quite all right, Dr. Mannix, and I apologize if I appear to be giving you a difficult time. I guess I really don't think I should be here, particularly since I'm certain there have to be many, many patients who need your services more than I. Of course I trust you, and I understand your commitment to healing the sick, even though I feel I don't qualify."

He smiled and thought how wonderful his profession would be if all his patients were this understanding and this trusting.

"Thank you, Rachel, and believe me, at this moment, you are the most important patient I'm treating. Granted, when I walk out of this room, that priority may change, but I can guarantee that your care would still be handled as though you were my only patient."

Rachel liked this man. She liked him a lot.

"You're wonderful, you know that." She giggled. "I hope Dr. October is as diplomatic and charming as you." And she moved her head to the side of the pillow, looking for a cooler spot to lay her very warm head against.

"Here," said Dr. Mannix, coming up to the bed and adjusting the pillow for her. "Is this better?" he asked as he elevated the head portion of the bed and leaned her up against the fluffed pillows.

"That's great. Thank you very much."

"Just get some rest now, Rachel, and breakfast should be here in about a half-hour." There was a slight hesitation, and then he added, "You might find it easier to eat with your eyes open, unless you'd like the nurse to feed you. Either way, Rachel, ask the nurse to help you if you so choose."

He then left and she heard his footsteps as he walked away and down the hall. She opened her eyes just briefly and caught a glimpse of the beautiful day that was happening outside her hospital window. This Dr. Mannix was, in Master Randy's parlance, a cool guy. He didn't ask or demand anything. Just subtle suggestions. Rachel thought how wonderful it was not to have to deal with demands and directives. All she really felt like doing right now was resting. As the clanging of dishes and squeaky cart wheels approached her door, she knew this was not going to be a time for rest. The kitchen helper came through her door toting a tray in one hand so she could pull out the table at the foot of Rachel's bed with the other.

"Good morning, Miss. Here's your breakfast and a menu for tomorrow. On your first day, your doctor usually picks out what he feels you can have for breakfast depending on your condition and nutrition restrictions, if any." Rachel thanked her, still with her eyes closed, and the aide, upon seeing that Rachel hadn't looked at the tray, inquired. "Miss, if you can't see, I can have someone come in and feed you."

"Uh, no, it's all right. I can see. The light is a little bright for me this morning, and it just felt good to keep my eyes closed." She opened her eyes slightly and looked at the tray and then pushed the table back to its original location at the end of the bed.

When the aide was gone and things seemed to quiet down, Rachel sat up in bed, which was a lot easier to do since Dr. Mannix had adjusted it for her. There were a lot of question marks floating around in her very tired brain, but one thing was very certain, she had to go to the bathroom, and she absolutely knew the only way that that was going to happen was to get up and go—or ask for a bed pan. The former was much more acceptable to Rachel in spite of the risk that she may be caught with her eyes open.

Oh well, she thought, *enough of this,* and in a direct approach, she swung both legs over the side of the bed, and for the first time since she was brought there, she was able to see the distance from the floor to the bed. It was higher than she thought, and even though she was blessed with those beautiful long legs, it was going to take some maneuvering to get down. So, she turned her body completely around and proceeded to slide on her stomach with her toes pointed toward the floor. The floor was cold, but she managed to stand up, and suddenly, her knees began to weaken. "Ohhhh," she cried out, "I think I'm going to fall." She grabbed at the bedding, trying to prevent herself from falling to the floor. Her legs felt like disassociated parts of her body. Heavy and unwilling to move. Finally, with all the energy she could bring to bear from her upper body, she pulled herself up on the bed and was trying to move her legs back onto the end of the bed, when the door opened.

"Ms. Radcliffe?" the deep resonant voice spoke out. "Ms. Radcliffe, let me help you, but first, please tell me what it is you're trying to accomplish?"

Rachel struggled and allowed this stranger to assist her. She adjusted herself on her back and laid her head back on the pillow. She was exhausted and now very upset about this latest physical discovery. She brought both hands up to cover her face and suddenly began to cry.

"I was trying to get up so that I could go to the bathroom. Is that a crime in this God-forsaken place?" she lashed out.

"Not at all, Ms. Radcliffe, I would challenge just one part of your description of this place. I don't believe that it's 'God-forsaken,' otherwise, I surely would not be here, and from what little I know about you, I don't think you believe that!"

Rachel was still sobbing and now was sniffling and wondering desperately where her box of Kleenex had ended up in this incredible mess.

"Whoever are you," she said, "Whoever you—you don't know zilch about me, and as for this place, I don't belong here, and I want to go home. I want to go home. Do you hear me." She was groping around and still looking for something to wipe her tears and blow her nose.

"Here," the voice said, "here's my handkerchief. Please calm down and let me explain a few things to you." Rachel could discern a slight accent in his voice, and he evidenced some concern about her wellbeing, so she listened. "I understand your frustration and confusion and your eagerness to go home. Believe me, I probably want that for you as badly as you do."

Rachel took the handkerchief, and after she had the opportunity to compose herself slightly, she began to open her eyes. The tears were still streaming down her cheeks, but she could see a very tanned and pleasantly smiling face looking back at her. She kept rubbing her nose and sniffling, trying to get hold of herself, and finally, after a few more sighs, and a final wiping of her face, she asked.

"Who are you, please? Is anyone in this place supposed to rest, or is it only a pipe dream?" He laughed and she, upon seeing his pleasure at her statement, began to laugh, as well.

"Jack October is my name. And I hope you and I can find the quickest and best way to get you out of this place." He rolled a stool close to her bed and sat down next to her. "First things, first, okay? Rachel? May I call you Rachel?" he asked.

"Yes, you may call me Rachel and yes, let's get to first things first. What's first?" she asked.

"Well, I think if I were you, I'd probably want very much to find out what got you into this most recent situation. The bathroom, yes?"

With everything else that happened, she had almost forgotten about that very necessary bodily function. The power of suggestion began to work quickly, and Rachel agreed that that definitely should be item number one—for the play on words.

"You're absolutely right, and how do we accomplish that? Bedpan, right?" she queried.

"I think for right now it's the better option, and I will call a nurse." He pressed the monitor on the side of Rachel's bed, and within a few seconds, a nurse came walking in the room.

"Good morning, Dr. October," the nurse greeted him with a smile. Dr. October acknowledged her and then asked her to get the bedpan for Rachel and then instructed her to assist her with some breakfast, even if she only got down some juice and toast. A light sponge bath was next on the list and perhaps a change of bedding, and then she was told to get him immediately thereafter.

"Does that sound okay to you, Rachel?" he asked gently. Rachel was always secretly attracted to men who had foreign accents and who were so in control of themselves and their surroundings.

"Hmmm," she replied. "I will see you later won't I?" she asked.

"Most definitely," he responded. As he stepped off the stool, Rachel was again stunned. This time by the rather small frame of this man possessed of such a powerful voice and demeanor. As a matter of fact, he reminded her very much of Papa DeRoca.

How strange, she hadn't thought about Papa for a very long time. Losing him was like surviving a stake through her heart. The loving memories of her father were still oftentimes painful. Losing her mother was extremely hard for her, but for different reasons. Papa was her haven. He cushioned her from the cruel realities of life and allowed her to be a child, free from worry and always free to play, to laugh, and to pretend. Time with Papa was like a day at the circus, sadly over much too abruptly. Somehow she knew she would never find such a peaceful place again. Now, meeting Dr. October had somehow unleashed all those memories that she thought were locked away safely in her heart and mind forever.

The bedpan experience was not the worst she had to endure, but it was certainly one of the most humiliating. The inventor of this awkward, oddly shaped and always cold metal object obviously believed he would never have to use it!

Later on, after that ordeal, the freshly squeezed orange juice and half a slice of toast was about all Rachel could handle, and when the nurse brought the pan of warm water over to her bed and asked her to remove her gown, Rachel was more than ready to go along with this next step in Dr. October's list of things to do for her this morning. The sponge bath seemed to wash away some of Rachel's tiredness, and the lotion that the nurse used to massage her arms, legs, and back seemed to penetrate and soothe her aching bones.

"That felt wonderful," Rachel exclaimed as the nurse gathered all the paraphernalia off the bed. "Thank you very much. I almost feel like a new person."

"You're welcome, Ms. Radcliffe," responded the nurse, "I hope you'll be able to get a little rest before Dr. October returns."

Rachel smiled again—"rest" was something everyone in the hospital asked you to get but no one allowed you to pursue. But, it wasn't this nurse or anyone else's fault that it never happened. In their common quest to get all patients better and out of there, rest was usually something you did in brief intervals between activities that were administered to make you feel better. As she lay and looked out the hospital window once again, her thoughts went to Christian and Blaise. She hadn't heard or seen either of them since her admission, and she was more than a little curious about their meeting under such strange circumstances. What would happen as a result of this interruption in her life? She had always believed that everything happened for a reason and that God was the master of our destiny here on earth. What purpose would all of this serve? Who was going to gain from this? And, more frighteningly, who was going to lose?

Seventeen

Amber awakened to a new sound—silence. It was unusual not to hear the hustle and bustle of Westbury. Suburban New York was almost as noisy as Manhattan, and Amber wondered if she'd ever be able to get used to this seemingly slower pace. As close as she and Rachel were as children and young girls, it was strange to walk around Rachel's house and see all the things she had acquired over the years. The framed photographs that lined the hallway brought back memories of those fun years in Grosse Pointe. Mama and Papa DeRoca's photo brought tears to Amber's eyes, since they were second parents to her. She wasn't surprised to see the yearly photos of Carlo and Marisa and her and Tony, but she didn't expect to see a great photo of Neil taken before Rachel married him. The more Amber looked around, the more she was aware of the tender and caring and sentimental heart of her friend. And now, she may be facing a situation in life brought on by the constant underlying conflict within herself. What could she, Amber, do to help her distraught friend?

After showering and getting dressed, she was startled by a knock on the door. Who could that be? Amber walked over to the door and looked through the peephole. It was Blaise. My goodness, he looked marvelous. She quickly unlocked and opened the door.

"Hello, Blaise," she blurted out, "How are you?" Amber was an extremely physical person, and before Blaise knew it, she was hugging him.

"Hi, Amber," he responded, "It's been a long time since I've seen you. You look fabulous!" he said, with a big smile. "I didn't recognize the car in the driveway, and I wondered who was here!"

"Sorry I didn't let you know that I was coming, Blaise, but when Christian called me about Rachel's collapse, I decided on the spur of the moment to be with Rachel, and here I am only hours later. Rachel had given me a key to this place ages ago, and the early hours of the morning didn't allow for too many options of places to stay close by."

Blaise was happy to see Amber because he knew she would be great for Rachel and could also give him some insights about Christian.

"I'm getting ready to pick up Christian before going over to Saint John's. Want to join us?" he asked.

"Sure," said Amber. "Let me grab my purse and check my hair and we can go." She scurried into the guest room and picked up her purse, looked in the mirror, and decided she looked all right. "Okay, I'm ready," she said and then offered to drive since her car was blocking Blaise's. "If you tell me how to get to Christian's, we should do all right with me driving," she said coyly. "It's been a few years since I've driven around Grosse Pointe, but I'm certain I'll remember some of the streets."

After driving a couple of miles, Amber gained some confidence, and just about the time she thought she could find Christian's place on her own, they were there.

"Boy!" she exclaimed. "I remember this place. It belonged to an architect when we were kids." She was astounded by the size and apparent opulence of Christian's sister and family's home.

The door opened without a knock or a ringing of a doorbell. It was Master Randy, and he quickly recognized Amber.

"Hello, Mrs. Domani, remember me?" He laughed.

"Of course I do, Randy. My friend Rachel is your cool lady, right?"

"Yes, ma'am. I do so wish I'll be able to visit her. Mom and Dad are reluctant for me to see her until we know precisely what's wrong. Are you going to the hospital now?" he asked.

"Yes, we are, dear, and Blaise and I stopped by to pick up your Uncle Christian. Is he ready?" Amber asked.

"Yes, he is, and I'll let him know you're both waiting." As he turned to go and get his Uncle Christian, Christian came outside.

"Hello, Amber. Blaise. Nice morning, huh?" he said. "How was your trip, Amber?"

"Pretty uneventful and quick," she responded. They stood and exchanged pleasantries for a few minutes when Christian spoke up.

"My goodness, please excuse my poor manners. Please come in and say hello to my sister, Estelle, and her husband, Randall. I can't believe I just stood here like a lump without inviting you in."

Both Amber and Blaise followed Christian through the magnificent portals and into a foyer that was beyond description. Amber had seen a lot of exquisite homes in her life, but this one had to be at the top of any list. Estelle Markham was descending the stairs and, with arms extended, approached Amber and embraced her.

"How are Carlo and Marisa, and, of course, Tony?"

Amber was pleased with the very friendly welcome and responded that they were all well.

"This is a beautiful house, Estelle. I'm awestruck by this foyer," Amber said. "It's decorated magnificently."

Estelle smiled and thanked Amber for her praise and compliments. Blaise was still looking up at the cathedral ceilings and stained glass sections above them.

"This place is a work of art," interjected Blaise.

Dr. Markham made his way to the entrance hall from the breakfast nook and greeted all the familiar faces.

"I certainly hope we'll all be together here real soon," said Estelle, "when Rachel is released." Everyone sort of stopped and agreed with Estelle.

"We best be leaving so we can get to talk to some of the doctors who are taking care of Rachel," said Christian.

"Yes, I agree," tuned in Blaise, and with that, everyone agreed to meet back there later to talk about Rachel's condition and their next steps. Master Randy came running from the back of the house.

"How about me? Can I go, please?"

Estelle and Randall looked at each other, and Dr. Markham responded.

"You know, son, you may have to wait a considerable time in the lobby until we find out how Rachel is doing and what, if anything, is being prescribed for her recovery." Master Randy smiled, since that certainly sounded like a qualified yes.

"Thanks, Dad."

Dr. Markham and Estelle led the way to Saint John's. Master Randy was happy he got permission to ride along with Amber, Blaise and his favorite and only uncle, Christian.

"You drive around here like you know where you're going Mrs. Domani," said young Randy. A statement that made everyone chuckle, particularly since she was following Dr. Markham's car pretty closely.

"Well, thank you, Randy. You do know that I once lived in Grosse Pointe, don't you?" she responded quickly.

"Astonishing!" Randy stated, quite surprisingly. "It's incredible that every one of us has somehow been destined to meet, and isn't it ironic that we've all come from Grosse Pointe. If I weren't so logically disposed, I'd almost admit that this whole gathering were somehow directed by an alien intelligence."

"Coincidence suits this situation just fine, Randy," interjected Christian. "Since I can't imagine that any 'alien intelligence' would even bother with such an insignificant assignment, can you?" Christian smiled at his very bright and inquisitive nephew.

"All things considered in this day of universal exploration and man's quest for other galaxies, I guess a preponderance of evidence would suggest your theory to hold more veracity than mine, Uncle Christian."

"Uh . . . uh," interrupted Blaise, "would you care to repeat that, Randy, only this time in English," he laughed. "Wherever did you possibly gain such a confident use of our language? Did you read the encyclopedia at day care?" Blaise kidded Randy.

"While that was an option, Mr. Kinley, I did not partake of that venture then, but by the second grade, I was well into several books of the Britannica," Randy responded quickly but not the least bit bratty.

The youngster was extremely intelligent for his years, and the rather attractive thing about him was his gentle manner in making it known. However, there wasn't an adult who'd ever been exposed to young Randy who wasn't at some point in their relationship in awe of his language expertise.

The parking lot of Saint John's visitors' section was filling up rapidly, and Dr. Markham drove directly to the staff parking structure. Estelle would meet them in the lobby after accompanying her husband to his office, something she didn't do too frequently.

Amber looked around curiously as they approached the very large entrance to the hospital. She was amazed at the expansion since her long absence.

"My God, this looks like a city. I can't believe how enormous it's grown. Must be a lot of sick people in these parts," she said, half-jokingly and half in truth.

Master Randy was already ahead of the group, and Blaise led them through the corridors and into the lobby as though he made that trip every day. They found a couple of sofas in the visitors' waiting area. Blaise and Christian suggested that Amber and young Randy wait there while they went to the desk to inquire about Rachel's condition. Estelle rode down the elevator to the ground floor and walked directly to the area where Amber and Randy were sitting.

"Where are Christian and Blaise?" Estelle inquired.

"Up at the desk, Mom," responded Randy. "They're trying to find out Rachel's condition. I hope she's up for some heavy visiting. I have so much to tell her about my new semester and our class's outing next spring in New York." Estelle smiled at his exuberance and hugged him for his caring manner.

Christian and Blaise returned to the visitors' area and were advised that a Dr. Mannix would be down to see them in about half an hour.

"Dr. Mannix?" questioned Estelle. "I think I've met him at one of the staff parties. If memory serves me correctly, he's got an impeccable reputation in clinical medicine."

"Well," interjected Blaise, "we won't know if he's right for Rachel until we know what caused her collapse and what the treatment or therapy will be."

"All I want to do is see her and make sure she's all right," said Christian.

Amber was just sitting back and waiting, although she was unconsciously twisting a Kleenex in her hand. The group had settled back and was quiet when Dr. Mannix approached them from the elevators and inquired as to their knowledge or relationship to Rachel Radcliffe.

"I'm her next-door neighbor. I brought her in. My name is Blaise Kinley."

"Christian Avian, Dr. Mannix. I'm a friend from New York."

"Me, too," echoed Amber.

"I know you, don't I? You're Mrs. Markham, right?" asked Dr. Mannix upon seeing Estelle Markham.

"Yes," Estelle responded. "Nice to see you again, doctor. This is our son, Randall, Jr."

Dr. Mannix remarked on how much young Randall had grown and then sat down where he could see all of them. He began his explanation about Rachel's condition.

"While her vital signs, temperature, blood pressure, and urine samples are all right now, we are concerned about what provoked her collapse. Were you with her, Blaise?" he asked. "We understand it was you who called 911. Would you please tell me everything that transpired immediately before Rachel's collapse."

Everyone looked at Blaise and waited for him to respond, but his answer and the truth would have to somehow be the same. Blaise related as much of the scenario as he could, only leaving out anything that might be insensitive and slightly inflammatory at this very moment.

Dr. Mannix was jotting down a few notes as Blaise spoke. Then he turned to Christian and asked him about his last communication with her that day. Each of them had an opportunity to add one more piece to this puzzle that led to Rachel's collapse.

Dr. Mannix heaved a great sigh after listening to everyone who had any possible information about Rachel's sudden onslaught of this unexplained fatigue.

"I'm going to recommend that Rachel stay here at Saint John's and undergo a few more tests before I conclusively determine not only what caused her sudden illness, but also what treatment may be necessary to get her back to good health."

Amber was taken completely off guard by Dr. Mannix's assessment and began to cry.

"She's really more sick than you're telling us, isn't she?" Amber sobbed. "You're hiding something, I can feel it," she stammered as she took a Kleenex from her pocket and put it over her nose and mouth.

"No, I'm not hiding anything from any of you. I really believe that there is something more here than any of us can see, and my first concern is for my patient. That doesn't mean it's more serious; it only means I need more time to be certain of what we're dealing with here." Dr. Mannix knew his decision to keep Rachel hospitalized was not going to be a popular one, but he had hoped Rachel's family and friends would agree with his decision.

Christian was almost as shocked as Amber. Everything seemed to be so wonderful. How could this situation change so dramatically, so quickly?

"Can we see her?" Christian asked, almost hesitatingly. "How long do you think you'll keep her here?"

Dr. Mannix was trying desperately to calm all the fear and apprehensions he could see and sense, and then decided to let them know about the other doctor on the case.

"Yes, you'll be able to see her, but only briefly, and only two at a time, please. I should also tell you that after speaking at length with Rachel, we decided to bring in a staff psychiatrist, Dr. Jack October." No matter what Dr. Mannix said, his explanation went from bad to worse.

"Psychiatrist?" shrieked Blaise. "What on earth for? Rachel's not crazy, for goodness sake, she's tired."

Master Randy was sitting silently through all this, and the only way that Estelle could tell that he was upset was his hand holding her arm as though he were somehow attached to it. The pressure was so tight, she had to put her hand over his and whisper that everything was going to be all right.

No amount of assuaging was going to turn this situation around, and finally, Dr. Mannix stood up.

"Look, I realize this probably isn't what you expected to hear and certainly not what you wanted to hear. But all of you must care for Rachel very much or you wouldn't be here." Their eyes were locked into his and he continued. "The last thing, and I'm going to emphasize this, the last thing she needs right now is to see any of you looking like whipped dogs. She will need your support and your encouragement, and if you feel you're not up to giving her that, then I'm going to suggest that you not visit with her until you can. Is that clear?" Dr. Mannix said sternly but with definite caring.

There was a moment of silence, and then Blaise offered his apologies to Dr. Mannix for his outburst. Amber followed with some words of humility and apologies for her mistrust. Christian added his hopes and wishes that they could all put their own selfish feelings aside and think strictly of Rachel's well-being and speedy recovery. Master Randy was still hanging onto his mother's arm in almost total disbelief at the scenario just presented by Dr. Mannix.

As the acceptance of Dr. Mannix's suggested treatment settled in, everyone seemed more amenable to helping in whatever manner each could. When he could see that the stress was gone from their collective faces, Dr. Mannix offered to take two of the five of them up to see Rachel. After a little conversation between them, it was decided that Amber and Blaise would go first. Christian sat down with his sister and nephew and watched the others walk toward the elevator that would take them up to Rachel.

Rachel was dozing when Amber and Blaise walked slowly into her room. They stopped just short of her bed and observed their friend looking so frail and so lonely. Amber whispered to Blaise that perhaps they should let her rest and return later in the morning. Blaise nodded his agreement, and they were turned around to leave when Rachel opened her eyes.

"Amber? Is that you?" Rachel asked almost in a whisper. Amber turned quickly and rushed to her friend's side.

"Yes, doll, it's me. It's me." She couldn't hold back the tears as she embraced Rachel. "Sorry, doll, getting you all messed up. I thought I was in better control, but seeing you in here just got the floodgates moving." Amber reached for a Kleenex and Rachel patted her friend on the side of the face.

"Oh, my dear Amber, please don't ever be anyone but you. It's wonderful to see you. But I don't think this trip was really necessary. I just got a little tired, that's all." Rachel smiled in an attempt to ease the fear and pain that she saw in Amber's face. "My goodness," Rachel continued, "all this fuss over a little fatigue." Amber smiled; these comments were vintage Rachel. The rock.

"Baby," Amber continued, "you're here for some much needed rest, and I am here because I wanna be. Tony couldn't stand having his two girls in distress without one of us nearby." Amber sighed and brushed Rachel's hair from her forehead. As she did so, Rachel got a better view of Blaise who was standing at the foot of her bed silently taking this all in.

"Hello, Blaise," greeted Rachel. "How are you feeling?" she asked. Both Blaise and Amber laughed, and Blaise, not surprised by Rachel's concern about him, responded.

"Obviously a lot better than you." They all smiled. Rachel raised the head portion of her bed so she could see both her visitors.

"Thank you for coming by. It's taken a while to put all my ducks in a row, but I'm feeling a lot better, honest." Rachel could tell that her expression of well-being wasn't bought by either Amber or Blaise, but she continued. "I should be out of this place by this afternoon, and then we can all have a good visit." Rachel could hear her words, and oddly enough, it was as though she was somehow programmed to repeat them. She knew she wasn't going home today. Both Dr. Mannix and subsequently, Dr. October told her she needed rest and some counseling. Yet, she played her usual game of "I'm okay," and the only problem was, nobody was buying it.

Blaise tilted his head to one side and smiled.

"You know Ray babe, I've been concerned about you for quite some time, and I think you owe it to yourself and to all of us who love you to take care of this problem as quickly as possible. Don'tcha think?"

"Well, I guess a rest for a few hours couldn't hurt, could it?" She laughed.

Amber sat down in one of the chairs and explained that their visit wouldn't be too lengthy for a couple of reasons. One, the doctors wanted her to get some rest, and two, Christian, Estelle and Randy Jr. were waiting to see her, as well. Rachel's eyes opened widely when she heard Christian's name.

"Is Christian here now?" she asked nervously. "He mustn't see me like this?" she said. "I don't want him to see me like this, do you hear me," she repeated.

Blaise drew closer to her bedside and tried to calm her down.

"Wow, Ray, Christian's been going through this agony with all of us. Why don't you want to see him?" he asked.

Rachel's attitude had changed from a reassuring one to one of fear.

"I can't let him see me like this," she said again.

Amber was holding Rachel's hand and patting her arm, trying to calm her down.

"Hey, doll, do you think you look bad? Nah! you couldn't think that. You've been gorgeous since the day you were born. So what's the problem, sweetie?" Amber waited for Rachel to get her composure once again, wiping the tears from her face and getting her some water to drink.

Rachel sipped slowly from the cup of ice water and sighed deeply. The taste in her mouth was wretched. The medications may have been taking care of some of her physiological problems, but she couldn't vouch for it by the nasty, almost cottonlike, feel of her mouth.

"You've got to admit, Amber, this isn't exactly the place to entertain visiting guests and for someone who's been named 'beautiful' and 'cool lady' recently, it doesn't do zilch for maintaining that image." Rachel sipped more water from the cup and leaned her head back on the pillow. "I don't know," she sighed, "I so dislike having anyone see me at my possible worst, much less someone whom I recently met and have become romantically involved with." She swallowed hard and moved her head from side to side. "What do you think, Blaise? You've always been my voice of reason and sound judgment?"

"Hmmm," uttered Blaise. "You know me, Ray, that's enough intro for at least a half-hour response; however, given the time constraints we've been handed, here's what I think." He was now leaning on the edge of the footboard of Rachel's bed. "First of all, babe, you're here because you need to be, not because you want to be. Secondly, we're here because we care about you, and you can't direct everyone's reason for being." His jaw was set and his eyebrows raised as he continued.

"If Christian is here because he, too, cares about you, and from what you've told us and what I've heard directly from him, I know that's a fact, that puts him in the same category with me and Amber, and I think you know, sweetie, we all love you not because of your outer beauty, but your overall beauty. I'm not going to be the first or the last person to remind you that beauty in the eye of the beholder, and that's probably the last thing he's thinking about at this minute. Finally, if your relationship with him is based solely on how wonderful you always look, then it's better that it hit the skids *now* rather than later." He swallowed and continued. "I've only known Christian for a very short time, Ray, but I believe he is a man of substance and that his concerns for you go way beyond your physical appearance. You asked, sweetie, and that's how I feel."

Amber took his arm and hugged it.

"You're a pretty special guy, Blaise. It takes a man of stature and substance to recognize another one."

Rachel teared up as she looked and listened to this man whom she'd also come to trust and love. She extended her hand to Blaise, who quickly walked around the other side of the bed and took her hand in his. He kissed it and then gently bent over to kiss her on her forehead.

"I love you, sweetie," he whispered as he raised his head from hers. And with that, he backed away and returned to his place next to Amber.

"I guess I've got my answer, huh?" said Rachel. "You're both so wonderful for being here for me, and I'll never be able to thank you enough for all your concerns on my behalf. Friends like you are treasures, and I hope you both know that I hold both of you in the deep recesses of my heart and soul." She sighed again and then she suddenly thought about Randy. "Oh, my goodness, what about Master Randy? I don't think I can handle seeing him, as well. He's so impressionable and much too intelligent to believe any act I might put on to make him believe I feel better than I am."

Amber spoke up quickly.

"You know, doll, he is a pretty perceptive young man and quite smitten with you as well. His friendship is as critical as all of ours, and you don't want to short-change this little guy who is really responsible for your meeting Christian in the first place." Amber looked assuringly at Rachel and saw the smile on Rachel's lips begin.

"You're right. You're both absolutely right. This is not the time to try to direct anyone's feelings. I can hardly gauge my own. I should be so grateful to all of you for being here with me, and I apologize for my somewhat selfish attitude about how and when this should all take place. If it were I, visiting one of you, none of the gobblelygook I just ran by you would have mattered to me. So let's get on with it. I'm ready for their visits, and again, to the both of you, thank you," she whispered, "thank you for the honesty and love you've shown for my well-being. I love you both very much." Rachel once again extended her arms to her friends who answered their beckoning with an embrace and a kiss.

Christian sat almost in a state of inertia as his thoughts began to wander. This lobby, this hospital began to open doors in his memory long since closed. The pain and the agony and the uselessness began to sneak into his mind, and the flashes of memory concerning the loss of his precious Tia returned. He could see her beautiful face looking up at him from her death bed. The smile that was always there for him was fading as were here eyes that strained to focus on the man whom she loved so deeply, so totally. Christian could feel the strength of her hand in his weaken, and suddenly she was gone. Her hand no longer grasping his, her voice, so sweet, so gentle, now silenced forever. "Tia, don't leave me." He writhed in indescribable agony. "Don't leave me, my darling!" His tears seemed unending and he felt that the source of those tears would never be depleted. His cheeks burned with each new stream, as though to etch the pain on his face forever.

"Christian, Christian," he could hear being called from a distance.

"Is that you, Tia?" he whispered.

Estelle was surprised at her brother's response as she tried to arouse him from a brief nap.

"Christian," she called, again, "it's me, Estelle. Amber and Blaise are coming back from seeing Rachel."

Christian sat up and brought his hands to his face and rubbed his eyes in order to get more focus on the present.

"Sorry, Stellar. I guess I must have nodded off briefly." He felt as though he'd been crying and took his handkerchief from his pocket and over his face, exclaiming that it had gotten warm in the lobby. "Must be that unpredictable Michigan sun beaming its hot rays on us just before autumn arrives."

Estelle and Randy waited anxiously to hear from Amber and Blaise about Rachel's condition. Blaise was the first to speak and he smiled graciously at all of Rachel's waiting friends.

"She looks beautiful, as always," he exclaimed. "Just very tired and a little anxious to get out of this place, as you might imagine. I think she'd like to see you alone, Christian, if that's all right with you, Estelle, and you, Randy?" he queried very diplomatically.

"Fine," responded Christian. "Is that all right with you and Randy, Estelle?"

Estelle nodded in agreement, and Master Randy had sort of lost his zeal for seeing his cool lady. He was a bit frightened by all the conversation about his friend, and waiting a little longer to see her seemed like a good idea. Estelle urged her brother to go ahead and assured him that she and Randy would be just fine.

Blaise told Christian which elevator to take and how to get to Rachel's room once he left the elevator. Christian thanked Blaise and went to the indicated elevator. No one was in it when he got there. He remembered the elevator ride with Rachel in the World Trade Center not very long ago. He breathed deeply as he left the elevator and walked toward Rachel's room. His heart began to beat faster, and beads of perspiration developed on his upper lip and along the sides of his face. Once again, he took out his handkerchief and wiped his face. He also pulled out his comb and ran it through his hair. He didn't want to look upset when Rachel saw him. As he approached the door he sighed and, with a smile on his face, opened it and walked in.

Rachel was sitting up, looking as beautiful as ever. She smiled when she saw him.

"Welcome to Grosse Pointe, my darling." Christian rushed to her bedside and embraced her gently and lovingly.

"Oh, Rachel, my darling Rachel, I've been so worried about you. This is the last place I wanted us to meet." He laughed. "But fate has been kind; at least we've managed to find our way back to each other." He looked deep into her glowing brown eyes and then kissed her softly. Rachel moved her lips gently to respond to his kiss, and as she moved her head in order to speak, she smiled.

"You have definitely caused both my heart rate and my temperature to rise, my love, and just seeing you and feeling you in my arms makes me feel better already." He smiled as he moved away from her. *My God,* he thought, *she's beautiful.*

"Amber and Blaise have filled me in a little bit on your condition, and Dr. Mannix has been wonderful. But now, my dear Rachel, what brought you to this place?" Christian asked simply.

Rachel breathed deeply and looked lovingly into Christian's inquisitive eyes.

"I—uh—I guess I bit off more than I could chew, metaphorically speaking," Rachel responded with a little smile. "I have been extremely busy for quite some time, and I haven't done a very good job of eating and sleeping. Two things I'm told humans require to keep up their strength and stamina." Rachel hoped that Christian wouldn't probe any deeper than that, but she wasn't going to get her wish.

Christian then asked what led up to the collapse and how it happened that she was with Blaise when it occurred.

Rachel sat up quietly, her head resting comfortably on her pillow. She thought about some clinical response that would tie in with her asking Blaise for his assistance. That would explain her being with Blaise at that moment. But then, she quickly thought about how important honesty was in any relationship. How could she demand it from everyone else and not from herself as well? Trust was so important for her and something she'd have to build with any future relationship.

"I had been out with Master Randy most of the day, and realizing I had become quite far behind in my clients' wardrobes, I tried to get a few things done before I picked up Randy and afterward as well." Rachel sipped from her cup of ice water and continued.

"Keeping up with your nephew, both mentally and physically, is no small task. I'm sure you know. Plus eating things I'm not accustomed to, like tacos and chocolate shakes, I'm sure each of these things compounded the events that led to my collapse." Rachel rested for a moment and Christian observed how quickly she tired after speaking for a while. He moved toward her and took her hand in his.

"You don't have to chapter and verse everything for me now. I can tell you're weak, and talking appears to make you more so. We can finish this conversation at some later time." He raised her hand to his lips and kissed it.

Rachel was both happy and relieved at Christian's sensitivity to her feelings and her current situation.

"How are Estelle and Randall and my favorite young man, Randy?" she asked.

Christian smiled. As long as he had known her, Rachel was always concerned more about the well-being of others than herself.

"They're all well," he said nodding his head positively, "and a matter of fact, Estelle and Randy Jr. are downstairs in the lobby waiting to see you, if you're up to it."

"That's right," exclaimed Rachel, "Amber and Blaise did mention that they were here. Do you think Master Randy will be upset seeing me in these surroundings?" she asked in a very concerned manner.

"Well, I guess he's no different than the rest of us who love you, sweetie. He'll not be that happy, but he'll feel important to be included among those of us who Dr. Mannix permitted to see you."

After Rachel thought about her next visitors for a brief time, she remembered Christian's new show.

"Sorry, Christian, for not asking about 'Cinema.' How's it coming along?" she asked apologetically.

"No need to apologize for not asking about my work, darling. It's doing well, I suppose," he responded humbly and smiled broadly.

Rachel loved that humility that was such a major part of Christian. She couldn't remember a time in their relationship when Christian bragged about anything, except his sister, Estelle, and his nephew, Randy.

"Just well?" Rachel asked coyly. "From what I hear from Amber, it's quite exciting. Maybe because Carlo and Marisa are a part of the opening cast."

Christian remembered those times in his life when he was just starting out. He and Tia were just newly married when he directed his first musical on Broadway. Times were tough thirty years ago, and the only exciting thing about show business back then was knowing where your next meal was coming from. Many sacrifices added to hours and hours of working through the night and on weekends. Missing holiday dinners and never having the time to get away for a vacation or any other kind of R and R. In so many ways Rachel reminded him of Tia. So selfless and understanding. So vital and beautiful. He was having difficulty keeping his focus on Rachel and his world today.

"They're quite exciting." Christian finally spoke. "I guess the best part of this entertainment industry is being able to see the constant emergence of new talent. Seeing glimpses of another Fred Astaire and Ginger Rogers was the thing that attracted me to Carlo and Marisa. It gave me chills to be a part of the cycle that could possibly bring the world such joy. I guess that's why 'Cinema' represents kind of the hallmark of all my work up until now." He cleared his throat and then stood up and approached Rachel's bed. "I think I'll leave you now, my dear cool lady. I think it would be comforting and assuring if Randy and Estelle could see you even for a few brief minutes."

"Thank you, my darling, for coming to see me and for being so wonderfully sensitive to my needs at this time," and Rachel smiled and extended her arms to Christian.

He leaned over into the reach of her waiting arms, and she raised her head and positioned her lips for a kiss she loved. His lips were warm and soft as he pressed them on hers. Rachel's emotions during these kisses had not changed. She was still thrilled and moved by them. She placed her hands on both sides of his face and drew away from him.

"Thank you," she whispered, "thank you for loving me."

"My pleasure, beautiful lady. My pleasure," Christian chuckled and after lightly kissing the tip of her nose. Christian was moving away from Rachel's embrace as the door opened.

"Ooops, excuse me," exclaimed the male voice.

Christian turned around to see who it was. He didn't recognize the man and moved to the side to allow Rachel to see who it was.

"Dr. October," she exclaimed, "it's all right, please come in." Dr. October responded to Rachel's invitation and introduced himself to Christian as he neared her bed.

"Dr. Jack October," he said crisply, extending his hand to Christian.

"How do you do, Dr. October. I'm Christian Avian, a friend of Rachel's from New York."

"Well, well, Ms. Radcliffe, you do appear to be special to quite a few people." Dr. October said with the smile that was becoming familiar and welcomed by Rachel. It was a smile that brought comfort and reassurance, and she smiled in return.

"It appears so," Rachel agreed.

"How much longer do you plan on visiting, Mr. Avian?" Dr. October asked quite politely and considerately.

"Actually," responded Christian, "I was just about to leave; uh, however, my sister and nephew were waiting to see Rachel for just a very brief time, if that's all right."

"Certainly, certainly," Dr. October said, nodding his head. "I was merely inquiring so I could gauge my schedule with Rachel this morning." He then walked over to Rachel's bedside and put his full hand on her forehead. His hand was cool and soft, and she looked up at him as though to seek an answer about this puzzling gesture.

"Hmmm," he said with a little lilt in his voice, "no fever! That's wonderful." He then took Rachel's wrist and felt for a pulse. Looking down at his watch, he counted the pulsations for fifteen seconds and grinned and nodded as he spoke. "The good news is your pulse is quite normal this morning. The bad news, for me, is that I didn't cause it to elevate."

Dr. October's sense of humor and relaxed manner put both Rachel and Christian at ease. Rachel's eyes were sparkling at hearing these positive statements and she heaved a sigh of relief. Dr. October walked away from her bed.

"I'll be back later on, Rachel, so we can continue with our previous discussion and see how quickly we can get you out of this place." He nodded at Christian and acknowledged his pleasure in meeting him and then left the room.

Rachel was elated by the last part of Dr. October's statement, and she smiled as broadly as she could.

"Maybe, just maybe," she said, "I might be out of here today or certainly by tomorrow." Christian moved toward her and took her hands in his.

"That would be wonderful, my darling, but let's not get too overenthused until we know for certain what the good doctor determines to be the cause and the cure for this episode."

Rachel looked at his marvelous face and depth of his piercing blue eyes. *He loves me,* she thought to herself. *He really, truly loves me.*

"I suppose you're right, Christian, but I can't help but feel a little more optimistic than I did earlier." She sighed again and could notice that her energy level was waning once again. "Whew!" she exclaimed. "I do believe this excitement can be a little tiring." Christian leaned forward and kissed her lightly on her forehead.

"What do you say, I go downstairs and get Estelle and young Randy. They must be getting pretty anxious to see you."

Rachel smiled and acknowledged that that sounded like a great idea.

"Will you come back later on, Christian?" she asked, almost hesitantly.

"Wild horses couldn't keep me away, darling," he responded, then humorously added, "I always secretly wanted to say that to someone I loved, and I thank you for the opportunity."

Rachel laughed and thought what a great morning this had been so far.

"I love you, Christian Avian," she said firmly and with certainty. "You'd better go and get Estelle and Randy before they think you've abandoned them."

Christian bent to kiss Rachel again, only this time, he kissed her lips in a manner that held much more of a promise of things to come.

"I love you," she again whispered, against his soft and urging mouth, and stroked the side of his face.

"Hmmm," Christian sighed, then quickly raised his head and kissed the tip of her nose. "That, my dear lady, was a rain-check kiss. Very soon we'll have a chance for a makeup day, and believe me, no one will call time on that day." As he moved away from her, Rachel's body tingled with excitement at the prospect of getting to that special place in the future.

"I can hardly wait," she answered. He blew her a kiss and was gone.

Soon, the room was quiet, and Rachel had an opportunity to sit and think about her feelings for Christian and how they might be affected by this temporary setback. Her thoughts bounced like rubber balls between Christian and Blaise. The confusion seeped slowly back into her head, and she felt weary thinking of the consequences of her actions no matter how she finally decided between the two of them. Her breathing became more shallow. She closed her eyes and once again gave in to the thoughts that filled her mind. How peaceful it was right now, and how serene the rest of the world appeared from this protected and secure place. She was almost dozing when the door of her room opened once again.

"Hello, cool lady!" Rachel heard Master Randy's salutation. "What's happening?"

Rachel smiled broadly as she opened her eyes to see young Randy and his mother, Estelle, peering at her from the door.

"Hi, Randy!" Rachel responded in a tone not known to him. Her voice was softer and not as dynamic as usual. "Nothing's happening that I'd like to write home about, but your visit is certainly making my day," she said laughing. "Hello, Estelle," Rachel continued. "How sweet of you to come to see me," she said humbly.

Estelle walked over to Rachel's bed and took her extended hand in hers. Young Randy was right next to her, and he was surprised to see how pale his cool lady looked.

"We're not going to stay very long, Rachel, but Randy was almost insistent on seeing for himself just how you're doing. I must admit, you look a lot better than I had imagined." Estelle patted Rachel's hand and asked how she was doing.

Rachel was pleased to see both of them, and she responded quickly to Estelle.

"I'm feeling much better. thank you. I'm still trying to piece together just how I got to this place." Rachel pushed herself forward and sat up a little straighter to get a better visual vantage point of her two visitors. "I'm hoping that after the results come in from all the tests they took that I'll be able to get out of here soon."

Randy observed his friend closely and was more than a little uneasy about his friend's sickly appearance. In the very short period of time that he had known her, she never was anything other than enthusiastic and eager to move. Their conversation on the airplane when they met was being rerun in his head, and he smiled at the recollection.

"What's so funny, Master Randy?" Rachel asked.

He was almost embarrassed that he had smiled, and more particularly, that she saw him.

"I was thinking about how we met and the fun we've had since. I sure hope you're going to get well soon so we can continue doing that." Randy looked down as though almost afraid of Rachel's response.

"Listen, pal," she said with a little more vigor, "we're going to have a lot more fun. Just wait and see. This malady is not going to be long-lived, and we'll be back in business before you know it." Rachel was straining now, trying to put Master Randy at ease. It didn't take much for Estelle to notice what was going on.

"Sweetie," Estelle called to young Randall, "we mustn't tire Rachel out by staying too long. And you know that Uncle Christian and Dad will keep us updated about Rachel's recovery." Estelle put her arm around Randy's shoulder and hugged him briefly. Rachel swallowed hard, trying not to shed any tears as she looked at her young friend's sad face.

"I'll tell you what, Master Randy, let's make a promise to do a duplication of our last date as soon as I'm released. What do you say?" she asked.

Master Randy smiled as he heard exactly what he had hoped for coming from his cool lady.

"Cool!" he responded. "I'll pick out another good movie, and this time, you can pick out the eating place." Rachel blinked, positively acknowledging Randy's suggestion and then took the cup of ice water sitting on her night table and sipped from it. Estelle exchanged a few more amenities with Rachel and then suggested that she and young Randall leave so that Rachel could get some rest.

"Please get well, quickly, Rachel," Estelle said, and then young Randy offered his few words of encouragement and winked.

"Uncle Christian said he's going to stay here until you're well enough to come home." Estelle pulled on young Randy's sleeve, and Rachel smiled and winked back at her young friend.

"I hope I'm out of here real, real soon!" Estelle and Randy then left, and Rachel grinned at her pleasure to have found such a neat friend and his family. She lay back on the pillow and closed her eyes. Her eyelids were heavy, and it didn't take long for sleep to come.

Eighteen

No sooner had she finally drifted off than the black umbrellas began to appear. She moved her head as though trying to dismiss their presence, but to no avail. The next sequences of her recurring nightmare began. Faceless people were running toward her and through her. She strained to hear the voices calling to her. Beads of perspiration began to form on her forehead, and her breathing became irregular. She moaned as she strained to hear the voices to determine what they were saying. But the words were garbled, and the shapes and forms of shadows in her nightmare were distorted and blurred. She strained to see through the fog and rain. A small ray of light pierced the darkness and shone on the figure closest to her. It was a man. His features became clearer. It was Blaise—no, it was Christian. She moved her head back and forth and frowned as she tried desperately to see who it was. Finally, she called out, "Christian, is that you?" The silence remained, and she called out again, "Blaise, is that you?" No one responded, and as she focused on the faceless figures, some features appeared. Some were smiling and some were crying. She could feel the rain on her face, lightly pelting her face and running down her cheeks. Was it rain? Or was she crying? She began to tire of the struggle. "Where am I?" she thought. "Help me!" she called out.

Suddenly she felt a cool hand stroking her forehead.

"You're all right, Rachel. It's okay." The voice was familiar, but it wasn't coining from her dream. It was far away. Yet so close. "Rachel! Can you hear me?" the voice asked.

"Hmmm," she moaned as she tried to recognize who was talking. She tried to open her eyes, but her lids were too heavy. Finally, the coolness of the hand on her head aroused her and she opened her eyes to see Dr. October's smiling face looking down at her.

"What happened?" she said, trying to sit up.

"Now, now, it's all right, Rachel. I think you were having a nightmare," he said quietly.

"Oh, no," she murmured. "Oh, no," and tears came to her eyes.

Dr. October sat there and allowed Rachel to calm down before he asked any further questions. He observed the various expressions on her face as she tried desperately to compose herself. He wondered if this nightmare could somehow be a part of the apparent internal struggle within his new patient's mind.

"I'm sorry," Rachel apologized. "I'm sorry," she repeated.

"No need to apologize, Rachel. Generally speaking, bad dreams and nightmares are beyond anyone's control." He smiled at her, and Rachel could feel a sense of comfort and security. "Just how long have you been having this bad dream?" he asked.

As Rachel thought about that question, it became frightening, as she couldn't remember when it began. It seemed like a lifetime. Her recollection became a maze of thoughts interjecting themselves in and out of her mind like flashes of lightning sometimes brightening the deep recesses of her mind and then resounding noisily as they clashed against one another. She struggled to put them in proper perspective and order, but to no avail.

"I don't remember when it started. It feels as though I've always been plagued with it." Rachel sighed deeply and wiped her hand along the side of her face. Her hand was damp from perspiration, and she could feel the quivering throughout her body. The results of the dream were almost always the same.

Dr. October sat quietly allowing Rachel some time for composure and relaxation. It was obvious that these dream episodes were both mentally and physically exhausting.

"Do you think the dream could somehow be the cause of my collapse?" she asked hesitantly.

"It's possible." Dr. October shook his head positively. "It's also possible it may be one of several reasons which led to your collapse. That's why I'm here," he said in a rather certain and assured manner. "You and I will try to find out the answer to those questions together. Are you game, Rachel?" he asked.

As she looked at him, she could see the resolve in his eyes and a certain glow that made her feel comfortable with the suggestion.

"I don't know you very well, Dr. October, but somehow I believe if anyone can help me, it will be you." They both sat for a moment, almost giving each other time to think about their next step. Rachel broke the silence with a question, although the answer was already determined in the past five minutes. "I suppose this means I won't be going home anytime soon. Right?" She knew the answer but still hoped she was wrong.

"Your willingness to stay in the hospital for a while longer could certainly expedite the healing process. And the rest you so desperately need could be provided much better for you here than at your home. Right?" Rachel's logical mind knew he was right, and her very tired body confirmed it!

"Then, Dr. October, let's get on with it. I've got a lot of living to do, and I can't tell you how happy I would be to be rid of that dream and the fear of future ill health. I will, however, have to notify certain of my clients about this brief leave of absence. I do have responsibilities to these people, and it is, after all, my livelihood that's at stake here."

"By all means, Rachel," he responded, "I'm certain when they hear about your problem and its apparent resolution, they'll be agreeable to this brief absence. Better to lose you for a little while than for good."

Rachel shivered as he finished that sentence. Suddenly, for the first time, she was frightened at the prospect of not ever recovering from whatever was causing this condition. She'd lived with it for so long on her own, she never thought about the possibility of it reaching a point of no return. Again, she sighed deeply, and her eyes welled up with tears.

She swallowed, then said in almost a whisper, "I'm going to be all right, aren't I?" The tears streamed down her cheeks, and she reached for yet another Kleenex.

Dr. October stood up and approached her.

"I'm sorry if I alarmed you, Rachel. I didn't mean to sound so ominous. Of course you're going to be all right. I have a sterling record as a psychiatrist, and I'd stake my reputation on your odds for beating this dilemma. You'll have to bear with me when I try to put things in perspective. I don't always match what my patient's understanding or evaluation may be. When I said that your clients should be satisfied with being without you for a brief time rather than not at all, it was too strong a comparison, and I apologize. I may be a good psychiatrist, but I'm not perfect. Forgive me for upsetting you, Rachel."

Even if those were the words he used on all of his patients, Rachel, wanted to hear and believe them. She had always valued the gift of life and prided herself on not wasting it or taking it for granted, but suddenly, she was faced with a possibility of a diminished quality of life, and it was a frightening prospect. This gift demands responsibility and care, and Rachel's faith in herself. This doctor and God would get her through. She was a survivor, and survive she would!

She straightened the sheets around her and sat up just a little bit straighter than before. She then took some Kleenex and blew her nose. Placing the back of her hand on her nose, she looked directly at Dr. October.

"It's your move, doctor. When do we begin?"

Dr. October smiled and patted Rachel's hand.

"We just did! You've just taken the first step to recovery. Acceptance of assistance is a step in the right direction, Rachel."

Amber and Blaise got back to Rachel's house and sat down in her living room. Amber looked around and turned to Blaise.

"I can't believe how worn out I am. I feel like I walked here from New York. What's making me so tired?" she asked.

Blaise straightened out some throw pillows on one of the love seats and sat down.

"The unknown," he said. "Nothing more tiring than not knowing, particularly when it concerns someone you care about. We're all worried about Rachel, and none of us knows how to help her." He was as frustrated as Amber. "I really don't believe that she'll be out of the hospital right away. And, I know Rachel, she'll be worried about me, you, Christian, Master Randy, her clients, and everyone else before she realizes that she needs help. So what can we do to make this easier on her?" he asked.

"Beats me," Amber replied. "I feel so useless. Uh, oh, my goodness, I have to call Tony and the children. They must be worried sick." Amber reached for the telephone and dialed her home number.

Blaise got up and started to walk from room to room. Rachel was always there for him. What could he do to make Rachel know that he was there for her? He walked into the kitchen and looked at all the knickknacks and items that were always there. Only now, they seemed to be so much more precious. The only thing Blaise wanted to think about was Rachel and her ability to get better as soon as possible. He placed both hands on the counter where they both had sat so often and closed his eyes. "Please let her be well, dear Lord. Let her overcome this condition and get on with her life. Guide me. Direct me to do whatever I can to help her in her hour of need. I love her. You know that. Watch over her and care for her until she's well enough to come home again." His head was still bowed when Amber walked into the kitchen.

She could see how deeply the strain of it all had affected Blaise, and she felt she had to share what Rachel confided in her about their feelings for one another.

"It's a bummer, isn't it Blaise? Just thinking about Rachel in that hospital, not really knowing what's causing her situation, and being here, so close and unable to help is frustrating and wearisome." Blaise looked up and turned to Amber. The expression on his face was answer enough for Amber. He looked so desolate, so pained, so helpless. Amber walked toward him and sat down on the breakfast bar stool right next to him.

"Blaise," she whispered, "Rachel told me about your feelings for her and the pretense you've lived with for so long." His expression of surprise upon hearing Amber's words caused her to continue quickly. "Please, please, don't be upset with me or with Rachel, dear heart. That poor girl has been through so much, emotionally, over the years; she's had to have someone in whom to confide, and I'm just grateful I could be that person." They looked at each other, waiting for the other to say something, anything.

Blaise's face was as easy to read as anyone Amber ever knew. No games here. His expression displayed his inner feelings. So when he suddenly smiled, Amber was elated that something she had said caused it.

"I'm glad the secret's out," he said clearly. He breathed deeply and went on. "We've all shared, somehow, in Rachel's hospitalization, but in retrospect, I don't really think any one of us could have prevented it. It's not as though you lived all that time knowing what the outcome would be, because I believe in my heart that to know Rachel is to love her. She's just so wonderful to everyone, so giving and so caring. And as I look back now, there were signs and indications that this breakdown was imminent, but I always felt I could help her past one more day, one more bottleneck." Amber listened intently to Blaise's words. She couldn't agree with him more.

"How much can we really do to keep someone we love out of harm's way? We can't stifle them. We can't possess them. True love is founded on trust and respect. It should be binding, but not enslaving. It should allow you and your lover to be the best they can be, in the relationship and outside of it. Love is blind sometimes and as ominous as Mount Everest. You can't put a harness on it; it must be free to stay or go."

Amber knew Blaise only through Rachel. But listening to him now certainly made her see how Rachel came to love this man, who was such an enigma for so long.

"I waited so long to tell Rachel that I was a fraud, that I had secretly loved and longed for her since I first saw her. Now it's all out in the open, and I may have to give her up to show her how much I truly love her." Blaise smiled and shook his head. "Timing is everything in life. How many times have we heard that? And how many times were we certain that it referred to someone else other than ourselves?"

Amber caught a second wind and spoke a little more loudly.

"Now, just a minute here," she exclaimed, "Let's not write the final chapter before we find out a little more about what's going on." Amber wiggled around on the bar stool and put her feet on the wooden bar below the seat. "I'm no psychiatrist, and I certainly would never try to counsel anyone in matters of the heart, but it seems to me that you're overlooking something pretty important here." She hesitated, and Blaise waited as she continued. "Rachel. We must put Rachel first. And it's not her love life that's in trouble at the moment, although it could very well be affected by it. It's her mental and physical health that are at stake. First things first, okay?" she swallowed hard and nodded her head for affirmation.

"You're right, Amber," agreed Blaise, "but doesn't that bring us full circle to where we were when we walked in here?"

"Sort of, Blaise. However, all I know is that we can't rush this situation or try to correct it. We're not physicians, and so we have to do the only thing we can do on the sidelines. Wait, hope, and pray."

Blaise embraced Amber, and she realized quickly how very tall this man was, tall in height and in stature.

Christian, Estelle, and Randy Jr. left Saint John's together, and Christian offered to take them to the Yacht Club for lunch. while the responses didn't evoke any kind of enthusiasm, Christian thought a change of scenery and other people might help all of them get through this day. The silence in the car emphasized the sadness that had overcome them. Rachel's situation had somehow ended a period of happiness for all of them. Since their first encounter in New York, each of them had been so positively impacted by her loving and caring nature, only to have it somehow snatched from under them.

"Some surprise visit, huh?" said Christian. "I really thought this was such a great idea a few days ago. Well, I guess the surprise is on us." He tried to erase negative thoughts from his mind, and the more he tried, the more the memories of Tia returned.

"Darn!" he exclaimed. "I wish bad things didn't happen to nice people. He smiled and continued. "And I wish money grew on those trees that line every street and fill every forest." At that, they all chuckled. "Let's try to keep our spirits up, okay? We've got to believe that Rachel will be fine and that we can all get on with our lives."

Although Estelle and Randy Jr. remained silent, the smiles on their faces evidenced their total agreement with Christian.

Time always passed so quickly for Rachel. She was upset at how slowly time passed since she arrived at this hospital. Each time someone came into her room to take blood, her temperature, or bring her daily meals, she would ask what time it was. The hours that seemed to whisk away when she was trying desperately to meet deadlines and other demands in her life, had become sedentary; time just seemed to sit around. The only thing that helped at all was her ability to fall asleep quickly. The tiredness that had taken over her body and mind demanded payment. As she rested and looked out the window at the changing sky, she wondered how long it would be before she'd once again get back to the busy lifestyle to which she was so accustomed.

Wishing for the opposite situation of the present was not uncommon, and the old saying about being careful about things you wished for was coming true for Rachel. If only she had something to do. Something to help pass the hours, it would help. But what? What could she do that would keep her interested and yet allow her to catch up on her much needed rest? That dilemma was short-lived, as the door opened and Dr. Mannix entered. He smiled and expressed his pleasure at seeing Rachel sitting up and with her eyes wide open.

"Well, well, Rachel, have you found that the world you tried so desperately to hide from earlier isn't really that terrible or that displeasing?" His voice and his smile combined brought a similar smile to her face. He truly seemed to care. It wasn't just his job, he loved it, and she reacted.

"I'm better than I was earlier, and, no, it's not as awful as I thought." She reached for her glass of water and took a couple of sips. The effort it took for even such simple movements was of concern, but she tried to maintain a positive attitude in the belief that this, too, would pass.

Dr. Mannix approached her bed and asked if there was anything she needed. A magazine? The daily paper? Playing cards?

Rachel smiled again and placed her hand on her forehead, rubbing it back and forth.

"It's nice of you to ask, and particularly since I was thinking about how slowly time has passed since I've been here and I'd like something to do." She swallowed and put her hand down and sighed as though trying to prepare for his response. "I don't suppose I could sketch, could I?" she asked, with her eyebrows raised and a sheepish grin.

"Sketch?" he asked. "My goodness, Rachel, are you an artist? I don't believe we ever asked about your profession or career."

"Hmmm," she mused, "I guess you could say I'm an artist of sorts, but sketching is only one part of my work. I'm a wardrobe coordinator. Most of my clients are local, many from Grosse Pointe. Believe it or not, there are some women who have the wherewithal to shop, but when it comes to coordinating and developing an appropriate wardrobe for any occasion, their taste is strictly in their mouth."

Dr. Mannix laughed and thought about some of the women he'd seen recently who could certainly use Rachel's assistance.

"That's a pretty exciting profession, and I bet it involves a lot of research. Not only about your clients, but about what's available and where. I'd imagine you must travel some in your pursuit for just the right outfit or accessory, don't you?"

Rachel was amazed at how quickly he had picked up on the essence of her work and could see the excitement in it, for that was always the key factor for Rachel. It was exciting and challenging to engage in recreating a person's image. Helping someone to look and feel good about themselves. Opening up new vistas in fashion that were unknown to many of her clients. The results of some of her efforts were extremely gratifying. Pleasing her clients was always her number-one goal. Improving their self-image prodded her to make each client look better than they ever believed possible.

"You've hit the nail on the head, Dr Mannix, and how quickly you've arrived at the very essence of my work." She sighed and waited for him to respond.

"I guess most doctors only concern themselves with symptoms and conditions. I'm guilty of the same. What, if anything, could you do for me?" He chuckled. "Two colors to be concerned about, white and surgical green. Ugh, not exactly a palette range for a man marked for success!" Now they both laughed. Rachel could almost imagine a finely cut suit of the best worsted in surgical green with white lapels. The vision only made her laugh harder.

"You have a wonderful laugh, Rachel," Dr. Mannix remarked, "and your eyes sparkle to make it even lovelier!"

As worldly and exposed to the many charming and wily ways of males in her life, she discerned a sincerity in Dr. Mannix's comments that made her blush. She put her hands up to her cheeks and was amazed at the heat radiating from them.

"A school girl's reaction," she said. "Highly unlikely from someone as seasoned as myself." The grin remained on her face, and it felt good to laugh and to enjoy the humor she'd just experienced.

"Aha, aha," Dr. Mannix cleared his throat, "you sound like you're approaching ninety, Rachel. I happen to believe we're as young or as old as we feel. And blushing isn't a sign of youth, it's a sign of shyness, humility, and probable embarrassment, all of which are attractive and endearing traits." He clasped her chart firmly to his chest and tilted his head ever so slightly. "I like you, Rachel Radcliffe. And when all of this medical business is past tense for us, I'd like you to coordinate a new wardrobe for me, whattaya say?"

Rachel was stunned by his comments but pleased that she may be embarking on a new friendship. She sighed deeply and still smiling, she responded excitedly.

"Deal!" she said. "I hope my recovery is fast enough so that we won't be too much older than we are now. Although I admit that appreciation for finer things and image improvement are acceptable at any age. Changing, modifying, or enhancing one's appearance is a great way to bolster one's inner spirit and elevate one's self-worth. I think, for you, Dr. Mannix, it would just be pure fun."

He agreed to allow Rachel to have a sketching pad and writing implements, but made her promise that it would only be diversionary and not an all-day work process. She agreed wholeheartedly and thanked him for understanding and approving her request.

"I'll be good, I promise," she assured him. "If it's all right, may I call my friend, Amber, who's staying at my home and ask her to bring them to me today?"

"Of course," he said quickly. "You have a telephone, and we have your credit card number, so help yourself." Rachel liked his sense of humor, and she felt elated at having an opportunity to assist in her healing process. "We'll talk more later, Rachel. Right now, after you make your phone call, why don't you try to sleep for a while. I'll see what I can do to make certain you're not disturbed." Dr. Mannix put her chart under his arm and walked to the door.

"Thanks very much, Dr. Mannix," she said quickly. "Bless you for your kindness to me." He was taken with her caring and gentle manner.

"My pleasure, ma'am, my pleasure." He nodded his head and left the room.

For a brief moment, Rachel thought she was going to cry. Such mixed emotions. She bit her bottom lip and tried to contain herself. *No tears,* she thought. *Think positive.* Then quietly, she whispered, "You're going to be all right, Rachel Radcliffe. Everything is going to be just fine." She hesitated and then added, "Please, God—"

Then, almost automatically she leaned over to pick up the telephone.

The dial tone was there. Now, if only she could remember her telephone number. She pushed on the corresponding numbers and smiled when the phone began to ring. It rang twice, and on the third ring, Rachel heard that familiar voice.

"Radcliffe residence, this is Amber Domani."

"Hello, Amber. I like the way you answer my phone. Any chance you might like a permanent job?"

Amber was so excited upon hearing her voice, she yelled.

"Rachel, sweetie, it's you! How are you! Is everything okay?"

"I'm all right, Amber, honest. How are you doing?" Rachel asked.

"Who me?" Amber stammered. "I'm fine, honey, just darned concerned about you."

Rachel was so happy to hear her voice and could hardly wait to let Amber know the reason for her call. Amber was almost hyperventilating with excitement.

"My goodness," she said, "I'd better calm down here, or they'll have to add another bed in that room of yours."

Today was turning into a smiling day for Rachel, as she could just imagine her friend in somewhat of an excited frenzy.

"Listen, Amber, Dr. Mannix has given me permission to do some sketching while I'm in here, and since you're right there, would you mind awfully, putting together a couple of things and bringing them to me later on?"

Amber was most willing to do whatever her dear friend asked and said she would get about doing so as soon as Rachel told her specifically what to bring. Amber reached for a scratch pad and pen which lay conveniently at each telephone site. Her totally organized friend, Rachel, made certain that even visiting guests could find whatever they needed.

"Okay, shoot," said Amber.

Rachel told Amber where to go in her little office to find the tools of her trade, and then which sketch pad and drawing items she'd like.

"There's a small portfolio at the base of the shelves to the right of my drawing table, sweetie. If you put everything I've asked for in there, you should be able to handle it without a problem." Rachel was truly sticking to the promise she'd made Dr. Mannix.

Amber repeated everything to Rachel to make certain that she didn't bring the wrong items.

"Great! Now, Amber, I don't expect you to come rushing over here. Maybe sometime after dinner would be just fine." Rachel suddenly thought about what she just said. "Dinner? Oh, sweetie, will you be all right there? What are you planning to do for dinner?"

Amber wasn't surprised that even during difficult times in Rachel's life, she was so concerned about others she loved.

"Well, babe, I know you're worried about me, but I'll be just fine. Blaise has been kind enough to offer to take me out later on, and I think we'll stop by the hospital afterwards and see our sweetheart. How does that sound?"

"Perfect!" Rachel responded. "I'm so very blessed to have such wonderful friends."

"You must be a friend to have a friend, and you, sweetie, are the best there is." Amber responded quickly.

Rachel swallowed hard and could feel a tear rush down her cheek. She laid her head back after hanging up the receiver and closed her eyes. She was tired and the thought of a nice nap appealed to her. It wasn't long before she dozed off and drifted into the mysterious world of sleep.

Dr. Mannix must have done a superb job of notifying everyone on the floor to let Rachel alone. The next few hours slipped by quickly, and Rachel had some of the best rest she'd had in months. No dreams, no nightmares, just deep undisturbed sleep.

As she opened her eyes, she noticed the sun was still shining through the blinds, and as she looked at her watch that had been placed on her nightstand, 5:00 seemed like the wrong time. She blinked to adjust her vision and to make sure that that was the correct time. It was. And she no sooner began to sit up when the door opened and the pretty young kitchen helper walked in with her dinner. Rachel hadn't filled out any menus for herself, but whatever was on that tray smelled great. A small piece of chicken, half of a baked potato, and some glazed carrots looked as appetizing as anything Rachel had ever eaten. She must have been hungry.

The taste matched the aroma, and she savored every bite. Rachel had never been a big eater, but no one could ever say she didn't have a healthy appetite. How peaceful and relaxing, she thought. There hadn't been too many moments in her life recently when she could sit down and enjoy a meal. Rushing had been the order of the day for months, and perhaps all this business about her having some rest was not a bad idea after all. When the kitchen helper returned to pick up the tray, she smiled as she looked at the empty dishes.

"You must have been hungry," she commented, and Rachel responded that her hunger was wonderfully satisfied with that selection.

"Will I be able to select my own menus for tomorrow?" Rachel asked. The aide answered that it wasn't up to the kitchen, but rather her doctor who would have to make that decision.

"Just ask your doctor the next time you see him, and whatever he decides, we follow." She smiled again and took the tray and left the room.

Rachel didn't feel sick, and she was certain that either Dr. October or Dr. Mannix would allow her to make her own choices.

The Markham household was unusually quiet, and Christian found himself a little at odds, not having to deal with his usually busy schedule. He thought about the rehearsal schedule going on right now and his production of "Cinema" brought his responsibilities into clear focus. "I'll call Sid and find out what's going on!" he uttered. The phone location at the back stage of the theater rang and rang. He was just about ready to hang up when someone answered.

"Hello," the male voice answered.

"Hello, this is Christian Avian, is Sid Goldman there?"

The young man almost stood at attention after hearing who was calling.

"Yes sir, Mr. Avian, Mr. Goldman is here. I'll get him for you."

He must have left the receiver dangling off the hook, because Christian could hear the music and sounds of dancers quite clearly. *Well, at least they're busy and obviously not needing me at this time,* he mused. Suddenly, Christian heard the familiar voice of his partner.

"Christian, it's Sid! How are you? More importantly, how's Rachel?" Sid blocked his other ear with his hand in order to hear Christian's response.

"Fine, Sid. Rachel is doing all right, and so am I. I was just between family functions and I couldn't help but wonder how rehearsals are going."

Sid was the best manager of people in this business, and Christian always felt quite comfortable with having him take charge in his absence.

"So far, so good," he responded. "We're trying to trim a couple of the arrangements in order to meet the three-hour show time, and I think we're just about there."

"Aha, that's a good sign, Sid. At least we don't have to use fillers. Must be enough good numbers to allow us to trim some."

"You've got another winner, my friend," answered Sid. "This show doesn't need any fluff, Christian. It will sell itself."

"We've got another winner, Sid. Can't remember a time that I won anything without your experience and eye for talent." While Christian felt pretty secure that "Cinema" would be a success, anyone who had been in show business for a long time, as he had, knew that it was always healthy to have a few butterflies. It kept you on the cutting edge of your experience and never allowed you to rest on laurels already achieved.

"These kids are wonderful, Christian. I think that's the addiction in this business. They keep comin', and we've got to ensure that there'll always be a place for them to perform and grow."

"Of course, you're right, Sid, and the perpetuation of this medium is what we're all about—you and I. I don't know how long I will stay here, Sid, but you can reach me at my sister's home if you need me." Christian smiled and then, in jest, said, "Or more probably, if you just want to call and say hi."

They both laughed. When partners were as interchangeably talented, the need for one another was really only courtesy. Christian always felt that Sid Goldman, on his own, was an award-winning producer and director.

Nineteen

Rachel felt quite satisfied after that delicious dinner as she lay there quietly in this room that had become almost homelike, she began to think about the past few months and wondered what, if anything, would have prevented her current situation. Perhaps the one thing that was truly out of character in her recent behavior was leaving the set of circumstances brought about by the separation of her and Corey.

But, how could she punish herself for something that happened during that trip—meeting Christian. Rachel had always been a person who dealt with day-to-day problems head-on; it wasn't any different in her personal life. Why, then, was she so compelled to flee? The days leading up to her trip and her return, culminating in Blaise and Corey's fateful confrontation played in her mind like one giant video tape. She felt responsible for all of it. How could she shirk any participation when it was obvious that she was the center of the problem? She uttered a sigh of frustration and wished that this all would somehow go away. Of course, it wouldn't, but where would she find the strength to resolve it. Just thinking about it made her even more tired and weary. Her thoughts were interrupted by a voice she recognized quickly and loved dearly.

"Helloooo," said Amber, as she peeked inside Rachel's door. "How's my beautiful doll doin' this evening?" Amber entered Rachel's room in the same manner she did everything else, bounding enthusiastically toward her friend's bed.

Rachel smiled and couldn't stop the tears of joy upon seeing her best friend.

"Amber," she uttered, "that was quick. It seems like I just called you a few minutes ago." They embraced and Amber shed a few tears, as well.

"Hey, look at us. We must look like a couple of overemotional dames." Amber laughed.

"Well," replied Rachel, "I think right now that's a pretty good description." They both sniffled and reached for the box of Kleenex on Rachel's nightstand.

"So," Amber said, "what exotic cuisine did m'lady enjoy this evening?"

Amber kept rubbing her nose and drying the tears that somehow wouldn't stop.

"Ah, 'twas a feast for a princess. With pheasant and truffles and flowers and herbs."

"Ugh!" retorted Amber. "That sounds like they confused your serving with that of your horse, m'lady." They laughed again, and Kleenex was being used at a much greater rate, since their laughter brought a few more tears.

"Oh, my goodness," uttered Amber, quite out of breath. "Here I am, visiting my best friend who's in the hospital, and I'm probably getting her more upset than I should be." She shook her head back and forth and enveloped Rachel's hand between hers.

"Nonsense." You're the absolute best medicine for this best friend." Rachel swallowed hard and tried to compose herself. She brushed away another tear and patted Amber's hand. "I was lying here trying desperately to figure out what I could have done differently to avert this hospitalization, and as I review each day, I don't know how I could fault myself for running to the very person who's always been there for me during my whole life, Amber—you." Amber got up and hugged Rachel once again.

"Listen, sweetie," she whispered, "nothing or no one is going to hurt my Rachel without coming to terms with me." Amber raised her head and looked at a weeping Rachel. "We've conquered bigger problems than this, and by golly, we'll put this in the past, too. Do you hear me, sweetie? You're not going through this alone, either."

Rachel was now crying both from joy and an enormous sense of relief and gratitude. With the Kleenex box now empty, and the settling of this revisitation, Rachel and Amber were happy when one of the nurses walked in the room. Observance was certainly one of the skills that this somewhat seasoned nurse had honed to perfection.

"My, my," she said, "What do we have here? Looks like an audience for some of the daytime soaps." She grinned, as did Rachel and Amber.

"I guess you could say that," answered Rachel. "My life recently could provide a good story for a soap opera."

The nurse asked Amber if she could move in order to allow her to take Rachel's temperature and blood pressure.

"I would imagine that most of those stories are products of someone's maladjusted life." After she said it, she knew it was wrong. "Sorry, I didn't mean that as a criticism of your life, Ms. Radcliffe."

Amber was already frowning, but Rachel excused the nurse and said it was all right. As Rachel grinned at her best friend's disapproving expression, she chuckled aloud.

"What's so funny, bella?" asked Amber. "That was sort of a hit below the belt." Amber shrugged her shoulders and decided to change the subject before she upset Rachel. Amber reached for the package of art materials that Rachel had asked her to bring over.

"Here's your sketching stuff, sweetie." Amber handed the portfolio to Rachel to see if she had brought everything that her friend requested.

Rachel felt a certain excitement as she opened the portfolio filled with the tools of her trade. The sketching pad, charcoals, and sets of pastels brought a smile to her face.

"Bingo!" exclaimed Amber. "Looks like I did a good job."

"I don't know if I'm acting a little premature in asking for these things, Amber. But I have a pretty good feeling that I may be here for a while, and I will go stir crazy if I don't have something to do. Not only that, but this is a part of my work, and it will keep me focused on what I do for a living and increase my desire to get out of here ASAP."

"Listen, Rachel," Amber responded, "it took a while to get you here, and if we want to be real honest with one another, I think it will take a while to get you back on track." Amber hesitated for a moment because she didn't want to either add or subtract from a situation she knew nothing about, and so she reverted to the one thing that always worked, her innate ability to make her friend laugh. "You know that those two doctors are already smitten with you, sweetie, so just be careful that their motives for keeping you here aren't somehow self-serving."

Amber succeeded in making her friend laugh. Rachel chuckled and shook her head fiercely.

"Sure," she said, "they'd have to be crazy not to become instantly infatuated with this washed out, wiped out forty-year old. They'd also have to be blind and suffering from dementia." Her mouth kept getting dry from whatever medication they had prescribed, so she took her cup of ice water and sipped on it, still smiling at her friend's attempt to make her feel better about this hospital stay.

"Washed out? Wiped out? Whoa, get a grip on it, sweetie. Perhaps a little rest and quiet surroundings will wash out some of the cobwebs that have developed in your head. If there's a couple of things that Rachel Radcliffe will never be, its 'washed out and wiped out'. Whew, doll, at eighty, you'll be a catch for someone and still a beauty." Amber was great for Rachel's ego, and she needed some encouragement in order to get past the underlying fear that may have been the basis for her collapse after all.

"I love you Amber, you know that. You haven't changed the way you've treated me since the day we met when we were six years old. And if I've learned anything for certain in this topsy-turvy life of mine, it's the value of the things in your life that get you through the tough times and keep you grateful for the good ones." She brought her hand to her head and rubbed it. "You and Blaise have been the stalwarts of my life for quite some time," she sighed.

"Well, sweetie," Amber interjected, "until Blaise came along and sort of became my Michigan eyes and ears, I worried and sweated out a lot of nights, concerned about you, and we've come past too many rough edges to give up now." Rachel's sensitivity was still fragile, and the tears welled up in her eyes, once again.

"My God, Amber, what am I going to do to get myself back to some place of normalcy? Will I ever know my heart and mind again?" She was crying and sobbing now. Amber went over to comfort her.

"Hey!" she said. "This is no time for questioning. Of course you're going to get better, and of course you will once again get back to your life and your career." Amber was hugging Rachel and getting her some Kleenex, when the door of her room opened.

"Room for one more visitor?" Blaise said, as he peeked around the door.

Rachel and Amber, with teary eyes and running noses, commenced to sputter and compose themselves.

"Great timing, my friend," said Amber.

"You couldn't have picked a better moment, Blaise. We were just commiserating our fate, and you saved us both."

Blaise was as handsome as ever as he walked toward his two friends. He looked first at Rachel and couldn't remember a time when she looked so forlorn and depressed. It could not detract from her inner and outer beauty, though, for when she smiled at him, it was like seeing a rainbow after a storm.

"Look at you, beautiful lady, all dressed up and nowhere to go," he said comically.

Rachel and Amber laughed aloud, and Amber picked up on that remark.

"Gee, Blaise, thanks for the compliment, but I do have someplace to go, probably home!" Levity may not be the only catharsis in some difficult situations, but it was certainly a good part of it.

Blaise walked to the opposite side of Rachel's bed and bent down to kiss her on the forehead.

"It's a pleasure to see that smiling face, Ray. As for you, Amber, you'll probably always run a good second in my book of beauties, but hey, you're well ahead of Demi Moore and Melanie Griffith." He chuckled and stepped back to observe his precious Rachel. "I debated about coming over tonight because I didn't want to wear you out or be one too many people in line to see you." Rachel cleared her throat and reached for Blaise's hand.

"I guess I must be worn out, since that seems to be one of the reasons I'm here and what everyone, both medical and lay, believe to be the case." She swallowed and took a deep breath. "That somehow doesn't affect how I feel about all of you and how much I love and appreciate all your concern for me."

Blaise loved her so deeply, and since his recent revelation, he found it difficult to hide his feelings or even temper them. However, now was not the time to emote, and certainly not with Amber sitting here; the suppression of his feelings was eminently clear.

"Any news since I saw you earlier today?" Blaise asked, as he grabbed a chair from the window side of the room and sat down next to Rachel's side.

"Afraid not," responded Rachel. "I really think they're just trying to give me an opportunity to rest, or they're figuring out what caused my condition and what they're going to do about it."

Blaise nodded in agreement and then, in quite the same manner as he usually kidded Rachel, he got the silly grin on his face that Rachel had come to know and love.

"So," he continued, "if they're not back here in fifteen minutes, whattaya say the three of us blow this pop stand and head out for some vittles and vino?" With his eyebrows almost raised to his hairline and his limpid blue eyes shining, Rachel and Amber burst out laughing.

Rachel shook her head at her visitors' attempts to add some humor to her somewhat uneasy situation. She thought about how wonderful that each of them had sort of similar lifestyles and how comforting it was to be herself no matter what the situation or place.

"Well," responded Rachel, "this white evening gown should pop the eyes of any patron at Da Eduardo's."

Amber continued the charade by standing up, and in a manner only she could portray, raised her left hand over her head, and with her right hand on her hip and her chin raised so high, her head could lean no further and she uttered in a throaty voice. "And I, dear sir, would stop them dead in their tracks in this ensemble of denim, dirndl, and dress-down clogs." Amber's animated facial expressions and haughty demeanor were more than Rachel and Blaise could stand, and now they all laughed freely. The next voice they heard was not one of theirs.

"Sounds like a party," exclaimed Dr. Mannix as he came into Rachel's room to check on his new patient.

"Oh, oh," uttered Blaise, "caught."

Amber quickly lowered her arms and straightened out her somewhat rumpled clothes and smiled slyly as she turned to meet Dr. Mannix eye to eye. He smiled broadly and quickly put them all at ease.

"A little laughter and some well-intentioned humor has always been one of the treatments I've prescribed over the years. And I must admit that in this instance it appears to have the curative effect that I'd hope it to have."

Blaise stood up and began to back away from Rachel's bedside, and Amber followed his lead.

"Please, please," continued Dr. Mannix, "stay seated. It's still visiting hours, and I merely stopped in to see how Rachel was doing. Having done that, I would only wish that you try to meter your visits along with others so that Rachel doesn't become overtired. Enjoy your visit, and Rachel, I'll stop in to see you later on before I leave for the night!" That dynamic smile beamed, and he nodded good night to Blaise and Amber and left the room. Blaise felt a twinge of jealousy as he watched the unspoken admiration that showed in his Rachel's eyes.

"Nice guy," said Blaise. "I've just met him a couple of times today, and I feel a certain comfort having him in charge of your treatment, Ray babe!" Blaise swallowed and hoped that Rachel didn't detect any sign of rivalry in Blaise's tone or inflection.

"He's been just great," exclaimed Rachel, sighing and trying to settle down after the excitement of this evening. "But he's not in charge of my case, Dr. October is, and I consider myself extremely fortunate to have such qualified and sensitive physicians assisting in my quick recovery."

Blaise was a little relieved at Rachel's somewhat unaffected response to these two doctors, and he sighed deeply and sat down again. Amber appeared to be following Blaise's lead, as she sat down, too. There were a few seconds of silence, when Amber spoke up.

"Good looking devil, isn't he? Is he married?"

That's all Blaise needed.

"He must be," he interjected and almost sputtered. "You know that someone with a medical degree, good looks, charm, and money wouldn't be wandering around unattached very long." He could almost detect the nervousness in his own voice, and then he jokingly added, "Should I be interested?"

"Oh, stop, Blaise," Rachel grinned and responded. "You may have gotten away with that a few days ago, but not now. Besides, he is married. Dr. and Mrs. Markham know him socially, and they've met Mrs. Mannix, so let's settle that inquiry. Blaise, I've got quite enough charming, good looking, financially stable men in my life, God knows, I don't need another." Rachel began to feel her energy wane and she laid her head back on her pillow and brought her hand to her head once again. Amber noticed this and realized that Rachel had done this a couple of times during her visit.

"Do you have a headache, sweetie?" she asked.

Rachel opened her eyes widely and swallowed.

"Uh, no, it's just that I seem to get really tired after a short visit or even one-on-one communication lately."

"Hey, Ray, perhaps I should make like a tree and leave. Huh, what do you think?" Blaise was really becoming uneasy, and he certainly didn't want to contribute to Rachel's fatigue.

"No, No," Rachel responded quickly, "please don't go, Blaise." She turned to Amber and continued, "Please stay, Amber." Blaise looked at Amber, and Amber returned the look.

"Okay, bella, for a little longer, but Dr. Mannix is right, we're going to have to set up a visitation schedule with you so you only have one visitor at a time."

"Capital," retorted Blaise, "I'll stay for a little while more, as well, but from now on, Amber and I, along with Christian, Estelle, and Master Randy will develop a visitation schedule to allow you to get the rest you need to get better!"

"I love you, Blaise," whispered Rachel. Blaise's knees weakened and his heart raced as he listened to the words that he so longed to hear. Rachel continued. "I love Amber and Christian and Master Randy and, yes, even Estelle Markham, for all your combined expressions of concern in my behalf."

Oh well, Blaise thought, *so much for that encouragement. She loves the world in general, and I'm happy to be in the general world—for now.*

The next few days came and went, contrary to Rachel's belief that time would drag. One last visit from Christian before he had to return to New York to finish up the rehearsals and all else necessary for a holiday premiere still left Rachel with some disturbing decisions to make and unresolved situations.

The transfer to a less restrictive area of the hospital and the permission to dress in casual street clothes during the day helped Rachel to feel that some progress was being made. Her appetite and rest periods had been more regulated than she could recall in recent memory. Three squares, a nap in the early afternoon, and a choice to read, sketch, or visit with other patients had brought Rachel to a place in her life she'd not experienced—peace.

Dr. October was as gentle and caring and certainly as skilled at his profession as she had thought. Scheduled daily sessions on a one-to-one basis with him had helped her to look at herself and those people close to her in a different light. Once her condition had been diagnosed and labeled as "extreme and threatening fatigue" caused by an inexhaustible lifestyle routine, the fear of the unknown began to give way to clearer thinking and a sense of well-being.

Dr. October, whose I.Q. could have probably matched that of any genius she could imagine, began to draw a clear picture of her and her life. His incessant inquiry about her past could almost certainly determine everything about her from infancy up until now.

"Imagine," he said in one of his sessions, "that you are a priceless, very beautiful vase. Complete in your makeup, revered by all who observed or even owned you," he continued and, with the expressions and movements of his hands as he spoke, held Rachel captive. "Suddenly one day someone nudges the vase, perhaps unintentionally, and it falls to the floor and shatters into a million tiny pieces." Rachel swallowed hard as she concentrated on the scenario that Dr. October was creating. "The disturbance of the very structure of molecular makeup is vast and almost irreparable." He sighed deeply and kept Rachel's eyes locked into his. "Such is the case with our minds and our mental stability." He raised his eyebrows as though to query Rachel's comprehension of where he was leading her.

"Someone or something nudged you enough to cause your mind, in this analogy, the vase, to tumble and shatter. It's up to me to determine how bad the break is, and then how much time and determination it will take to fix it." He reached for a carafe of ice water on the credenza directly behind him. He poured some water in two of the four glasses sitting next to the carafe, and they each enjoyed the refreshing respite as they both sat quietly for a minute or two. Rachel remained silent and anticipating as she waited for him to continue.

"When I initially asked you about your mother and father and your relationship with each of them individually and collectively, you winced, and I thought that I may have hit the right road in discovering the root cause of your problem However, when you explained that they were killed in an auto accident several years ago, I realized that this incident alone could have slowly and certainly led to this breakdown." He paused for a second, and as he looked at Rachel's face, he saw a tear going down her cheek. He sat back in his chair and spoke quietly. "Forgive me, Rachel. I know that as we put this puzzle together there will be times when you will experience feelings of sadness, like now, also happiness, excitement, disappointment, joy and rejection. I don't intend to upset you, but my job right now is to get to the cause of your current situation, and unfortunately, that may mean traversing over your life's past experiences, good and bad, in order to come full circle to the present."

"It's all right," Rachel whispered, as she wiped away the tears and proceeded to listen intently to Dr. October's words. "It wasn't so much that painful memory as your expressing that perhaps it is why I may be suffering a breakdown." She sniffled and rubbed her nose and shifted in her chair as she tried to compose herself.

"Is there something about that term that bothers you, Rachel?" he asked. "While in this instance, I only meant it as a description of your physical undoing; let's talk about this word for a moment, okay?"

Rachel, still recalling his past session, smiled quietly to herself and continued to recall Dr. October's fascinating and therapeutic treatment.

"Breakdown, or nervous breakdown, as it's been called, is one of the medical profession's, primarily psychiatric, misnomers brought about by its inability to come up with a better term to allow lay people to understand the condition. Certainly, realistically speaking, if your central nervous system did break down, you could be rendered totally disabled or, even worse, dead!"

Rachel's ability to listen and concentrate was in high gear now as she waited anxiously for Dr. October to continue.

"I won't bore you with medical terms that more correctly zero in on that term, but I can tell you that if you were to tell anyone outside of our profession about your collapse and the events leading up to it, most lay people would say you had experienced a nervous breakdown." He sighed and sipped some water and cleared his throat.

"While I might concede that your condition could be classed as a breakdown, in that description, I'm not going to allow you to be hung up or concerned about that possibility right now." Rachel quietly sighed upon hearing Dr. October dispel any thought or fear of this happening.

"Battle fatigue, more properly describes what you're suffering from, Rachel. It's caused by men and women following orders and pushing themselves constantly. First, to follow, next to perhaps lack food and drink caused by war conditions, and lastly, to either deprive or be deprived of regular sleep. Add to that the stress of not knowing if you will live or die, and it's symptoms like these that lead to that extreme tiredness or burn out." Dr. October looked at his watch and then at Rachel. He smiled and said, "Time flies when you're having fun."

Rachel blinked her eyes and came back to the present; she was scheduled to see Dr. October in a couple of hours. She walked down the hall to go to breakfast. As she entered the patient cafeteria, she noticed Zena Porter sitting alone at one of the large tables in the center of the room. She waved, and Rachel continued toward the counters where the breakfast choices were waiting. She placed a dish of fresh fruit and a glass of orange juice on her tray. She then asked for an order of rye toast and hot tea, then went past the entire selection and directly to the table where Zena was sitting.

"Good morning, Zena," Rachel said as she pulled out the chair to join her new friend.

"Mornin'," responded Zena. "How are ya, girl? It's gonna be a good day. Ya know that dontcha?" she smiled.

Rachel looked at Zena's empty dishes and knew she had the same breakfast again today. A bowl of oatmeal with skin milk and a little brown sugar, fresh orange juice and a cup of decaf coffee.

"It looks beautiful outside, with the sun shining and the leaves aflame in their autumn best." Rachel finished her dish of fruit and orange juice as one of the cafeteria's aides brought over her rye toast and tea.

Zena asked about the time of Rachel's session today, and when she found out it was 10:30 A.M. she nodded.

"Good show." Zena responded.

"Me, too! Maybe you and I can sit and rap for a spell. What do you think?"

Rachel had met Zena one morning as they both waited to have a series of X-rays taken in the downstairs laboratory section of the hospital. As Rachel came to find out, no one in that hospital was there for fun or because they had nothing better to do.

Zena had been involved in a swimming accident some ten years ago in which her younger sister drowned. She took full blame for the loss and was never able to get over it. She couldn't believe that her swimming skills had failed so horribly, and no matter how hard her mother and father and other family members tried to assure her that it couldn't be helped, Zena's mind could never quite shed the overriding guilt. Now, some ten years later, the "ifs" still echoed in her thoughts: *If I said no, you can't come with me because the water's too deep and I'm not good at rowing a boat. If she stayed home with Mom and Dad instead of saying yes when I asked her to come along.* The unsettling and unresolved answers to all of these questions would haunt Zena forever. And while her life appeared to be normal, from time to time the guilt would take over and Zena would find herself back at Saint John's for therapeutic psychiatric treatment.

Rachel was devastated upon hearing Zena's tragic story and her heart immediately went out to her. Zena was easy to talk to, and Rachel loved her quick wit and caring nature. They discussed the men in their lives and it was obvious to Rachel that Zena had dealt with a couple of Corey Davidsons in her life, so male-bashing was a fun topic which kept their minds off more current problems.

"Girl," Zena would say upon listening to Rachel lament her lifelong unsuccessful relationships with the men she had known, "consider yourself lucky." She'd grin, and Zena's eyes would sparkle. "Some of us never had such a selection. How about people like your mama and mine who got one shot at a male relationship, and because they loved hard, had faith in the Lord, and nurtured and cared for their families, never had a choice." Zena would shake her head and purse her lips. "Hmm hmm. These ladies took life as it was given to them, or thrown at 'em, and they believed in their hearts that it was what was meant. It wasn't until the NOW generation that people came along and convinced us we had a choice and an option to fight back or say no to abuse, inconsideration, and just plain mistreatment."

Zena was on a roll.

"Before, any lady who was unsatisfied sexually by her partner was considered 'frigid' or called an 'ice princess.' At least today we have a forum, where we can speak up and someone listens. I know the good Lord in all His wisdom didn't intend to have us live our lives less fulfilled than our male counterparts. He gave us all a free mind and a free will, and when He said, 'seek and you shall find,' He wasn't talking only to the males."

Rachel loved Zena's simple and untethered approach to life. It was too bad that she couldn't approach her sister's drowning as clearly and rationally as everything else in her life.

"My problem, baby," Zena continued, "my problem with men was that

I always felt sorry for the men I fell for." She sighed deeply and continued to shake her head. "There was Ted Washington, my first so-called love. He was the class reject. Not real good looking but smart as a whip. I picked up his banner and for three long, uphill years, tried to convince him, my family, friends, and me, that he was wonderful and that I loved him, just like I love this hospital food!"

Rachel had finished her breakfast, and they both brought their trays to the clean-up section of the cafeteria and left.

There were visiting areas throughout the hospital where visitors and patients alike could gather and talk. Zena and Rachel found a comfortable spot in an area not yet invaded by anyone, and Zena continued.

"To add insult to injury, after we graduated from high school, Ted asked me to marry him, and I accepted, and we did—mistake number one. Ted was always kind to me and very loving, I found out quickly that I wasn't in love with him, and now, I was going to have to tell him that and try to initiate some damage control and get out."

Rachel could empathize totally with Zena's feelings for Ted, for they matched almost exactly those feelings she had felt for Neil.

"Thank the good Lord we didn't have any children and Ted was possessed of the good common sense to see the mistake, too. So, here I was, twenty years old, married and divorced and out on my own." She hesitated and then went on. "The double standard that everyone says doesn't exist in this world, kicked into high gear. Ted was able to get on with his life. He took the SAT and was accepted at U of M in a proverbial heartbeat, while I, who didn't have any aspirations to go college, was left now to pick up the pieces and carry on."

Rachel sat spellbound as she listened to Zena's life story.

"My mom and dad said I could come back home, but I knew I'd hear 'I told you so' forever if I did. So I increased my hours at work whenever I could and resolved that the next man in my life would be the last one." Zena rubbed her eyes as though to stop some tears that came unexpectedly to the rims of her eyes. She sniffled and took a Kleenex from her cardigan pocket and blew her nose. "Wow," she exclaimed, "you'd think I could tell this story without all the emotional effects wouldn't ya?"

Rachel put her hand on Zena's shoulder to comfort her.

"I guess you and I are suffering from the same kind of malady with symptoms equally as blubbery."

Zena liked Rachel's choice of words, and she smiled as she continued her story.

"Well, a good many years passed before Mr. Right came along, and that left me more than just a little bitter. Struggling to get by on a salary that maxed out at what some kids get today at entry level didn't help. But something inside of me kept gnawin' at my innards." Zena sighed and asked if Rachel was becoming bored with this seemingly unending melodrama of hers.

"No, I'm not bored, Zena. Please continue. I want to hear the rest of what events led you to this time and place."

Zena settled back in the soft wing chair directly next to Rachel's and went on with her story.

"Against all odds, I kept a goal in my mind and heart that my 'one and only' was as close as tomorrow! I know," she chuckled, "tomorrow supposedly never comes, but it was the one thing that kept motivating me to get up every mornin' and face another day."

Rachel was amazed at the emotion that came over Zena. While she had only known her a few short days, Rachel had seen this new friend come from the very depths of despair and sadness to a place of resolve and determination. Rachel sighed as she stared at Zena's face. So inspired and resolute, and yet in such pain. What was it about love and the search for it that drove people to reach such incredible lows and such exhilarating highs? What other emotion could motivate you to forgive one moment and kill the next? Rachel sighed again and listened intently as Zena continued.

"Then it happened!" She smiled. "On a day that seemed just like every other, he just walked in the front door of the bank, and when I saw him, I knew he was it." Zena swallowed, and a look of peace and contentment came over her face. Her eyes shone and her demeanor was quiet and in control. "He was an English teacher at Central High School. Articulate, impeccably dressed, and apparently as attracted to me as I was to him. The only normal thing about the next few minutes was a brief introduction by my supervisor. 'Ms. Porter, this is Jerry Quilter. Mr. Quilter is interested in obtaining a car loan. Can you help him, please?'"

Zena smiled and so did Rachel. There was something so special about meeting someone new, someone exciting and someone you knew would never quite leave you the same way he found you. It was a connection or a fusing of spirits that made you feel glad to be alive. Each of them had been there. So they related physically and spiritually to the encounter.

"The car loan was a shoo-in." Zena laughed. "I remember looking at that application as though it were written by God Almighty Himself. Each square more interesting than the next! 'Single, thirty-five years old, Owned own home. No dependents. I kept thinking, I'd stumbled on something negative, like draft status 4F, but he had served two years in the army and was still in the active reserves." Zena sighed, and with a twinkle in her eye, pursed her lips, she whispered, "This was too good to be true. Where's the rub? Well, if there was one, it wasn't on that loan application, and the next few days and weeks were the most wonderful of my life."

Rachel was beginning to enjoy Zena's story but she had become aware that her session with Dr. October was only fifteen minutes away, and she wanted to check her makeup, comb her hair, and make certain that she was on time.

"Sorry, Zena, but I'm going to have to run. I don't want to be late for my session with Dr. October, and I must go to my room first." Rachel rose quickly from her chair and Zena got up, as well."

"It's okay, Rachel, this story can wait." Zena smiled and agreed to meet later on sometime after lunch.

Twenty

There wasn't anything different in Dr. October's office as Rachel walked in, but for some strange reason, she felt differently. He greeted her in much the same manner, and his opening questions were pretty much the same.

"How are you feeling today, Rachel? Have you thought about our previous session? And are you prepared to continue your and my journey into the land of discovery?"

"Discovery," she mused, "an interesting word and certainly an exciting place."

As she began to think about their last session and the preparation for this one, a bell rang suddenly. Dr. October had asked her to go back in her past and try to remember the emotions and feelings that led to her love relationships. He claimed a common denominator should be in evidence if her relationships were like most everyone else's.

"Common denominator" was not a term that set well with Rachel. She had always been treated as an exception ever since her earliest recollection and, consequently, always felt, and still did, that she was, indeed, an exception. However, in order to abide by Dr. October's wishes and thereby cooperate with his treatment, Rachel dug deeply into the recesses of her memory to see if she could recall and relate the emotions that led her to fall in love with Neil, Corey, Blaise, and Christian. She would have to discount her feeling for Donald Ramchek, for certainly Dr. October would consider her to be infatuated and not in love at such an early age.

Even as Rachel concentrated on her past relationships, Zena Porter's experiences came to mind. Rachel kept remembering Zena's regrets that she had almost always fallen in love with men for whom she felt sorry.

Rachel sighed and immediately could see where she might have fallen in love with Neil out of some sense of pity. He was weak, and when he professed his love for her, she recalled thinking how devastating it would be for Neil if she did not return his love. She remembered trying to convince herself that she would eventually learn to love him. Not only did this lie hurt her, it ultimately led to the destruction of their marriage and the mental health of both of them. As Rachel rambled on, Dr. October listened and took notes. There were times when he would stop her to ask a question or two beyond what she related.

Corey Davidson, she thought to herself, *now he was a case!* Rachel began to think back to when they first met, she recalled early in their relationship, it wasn't as upsetting and disturbing. As a matter of fact, there were times when she was suffering and struggling with the hardships brought about after divorcing Neil that could have sent her stark raving mad had it not been for the support and friendship of Corey Davidson. He was so kind and understanding. Available day or night, and God only knows, there were many nights when she found herself at his door, seeking solace, refuge, and peace. Not once, back then, did she ever believe that caring and eventually loving this man would evoke such turmoil and violence in her life.

Dr. October finished writing his notes and looked up at Rachel. She appeared to be deep in thought, the expression on her face one of pain and sadness.

"Rachel?" Dr. October called her name, trying to get her attention. "Hello! Are you with me?" He smiled.

Rachel became aware that Dr. October was staring at her. She shook her head in an attempt to bring herself back to the present.

"Sorry, uh I guess I was wrapped up in my thoughts about past incidents. Were you asking me something, Dr. October? I'm sorry I was so distracted." Rachel blushed slightly as she always did when she was embarrassed.

"It's all right, Rachel," Dr. October responded. "I did observe that you had done exactly what I had asked you to do, and that was to recall some events of your past relationships so that you could try to feel some of your emotions during those times. So how can I forgive what I provoked in the first place?"

Rachel sighed and smiled at him. He certainly was able to put her at ease and make her feel like everything was going to be all right. She swallowed and adjusted her position in the chair.

"I guess I'm not alone when it comes to having the luxury of time to reflect and review one's life. I can assure you that, of late, I couldn't seem to find the time to eat or anything else that normal human beings did every day!" She hesitated long enough to notice that Dr. October's eyes were locked into hers. This was a no-nonsense kind of doctor. She felt as though he could see her inner thoughts and, scarier than that, that he could see the very essence of her soul. She shivered for a moment, and even though she knew there could be no turning back, she felt she must allow him to delve, to search, and ultimately to discover the very core of Rachel Radcliffe. She shook her head and continued.

"I always felt as though I was somehow charmed or blessed. Does that sound weird?" she asked.

"No," he responded. "So please continue, Rachel, and don't analyze what you're saying; just say it as it comes to you."

"Among my earliest recollections are overhearing family members, teachers, and friends express their high esteem of my character and my intellect. Being told you're a genius at age seven is an awesome thing to deal with. I'm not even sure I understood what the word meant when I first heard it. All I did know was that it set me apart from all of my friends and classmates. It even made me a few enemies. Even during those young years, I remember being treated so lovingly. In fact, I can recall a time when I had been honored for my scholastic achievements in front of the entire school assemblage, parents, and friends.

"At first, I was embarrassed, and then I thought to myself, 'I must be special! No one else is up here doing this. No one but me!' It was a feeling I would come to know again and again in my life. It wasn't always pleasant, for being so singled out exacted its price. Being dubbed 'beauty with brains' brought a lot of sadness along with its glory. Envy and jealousy were characteristics I learned early in my life, for they were the reasons I ended up without close friends.

"Even though this was true, I felt a certain sense of inner strength that seemed to get me away from negative feelings and propel me toward a more positive mode of life. Mama and Papa DeRoca could not have given me much more in the way of love and counsel. Because of them, I always felt as though no matter what I tried, I could succeed. They were my source of love and encouragement until the day they died." Tears came quickly to Rachel's eyes as she said those words, and Dr. October could see the obvious sadness that was still, some ten years later, as agonizing and painful for her.

"It's all right, Rachel. We will talk about this again, some other time. Perhaps it would be best to end this session at this point."

Rachel sighed and wiped the tears from her cheeks. She blew her nose and sniffled, still trying to hold back further tears.

"Thank you," she managed to say. Then with a little chuckle, she looked at him and continued. "I hope you're prepared for these kinds of reactions, since I seem to cry at the drop of hat lately."

Dr. October rose from his chair and walked around his desk. He was almost standing in front of Rachel, when he leaned back up against the desk.

"We are human, before anything else, Rachel, and human beings cry when they are sad, in pain, or, yes, happy. Your tears are a genuine reaction to what's troubling you. Crying is about as therapeutic as any prescribed medication. It is man's release mechanism brought about by the strong emotions we just talked about." He sighed and then continued. "If you will remember, when we started our sessions, I told you that the road to discovering the cause of your problem would put you on an emotional roller coaster, and . . . here we are." He then extended his hand to Rachel, and she put her hand in his. He helped her as she rose from her chair and then in a natural and compassionate manner, he put his arm around her as they walked toward the door of his office.

"Try to concentrate on different things for a while, Rachel. Have some lunch. Perhaps visit with family and friends and, most of all, keep a positive attitude. Smiling is a great healer. It not only makes those looking at us believe everything is all right, it also convinces us that it's true."

Rachel did smile and thanked Dr. October for being so understanding and patient. He confirmed that he'd see her the following day at the same time. Rachel walked down the hall to the elevator that would take her back to her floor. When the elevator door opened, Rachel was happy to see Zena standing there.

"Are you going up or down?" Rachel asked.

"Up, for a few minutes," Zena replied. "I'm going to squeeze in some much needed exercise before lunch. Got to keep in shape, right?"

Rachel laughed, for Zena was about as close to being runner-up to a bean pole as anyone she'd ever known. But she also knew that exercise was as much for the cardiovascular system as it was for the physical shape.

"Yeah, right," Rachel responded. "Keep in shape. We're not going to be here forever, and the world out there demands a healthy mind . . . and body." With that, Zena walked into the elevator and said she'd stop by to see Rachel after her exercises were over.

Having some time for herself sounded like a great idea, and maybe she'd call Amber to find out when she'd be stopping by for a visit. Her new room wasn't as hospital-like as the first. There was a grouping of chairs and a table to one side. A lamp and recliner were situated just near the entrance to her bathroom, on the other side of the room. All in all, it was kind of cozy.

Being ten floors up gave her a beautiful view of the outdoors, and today was a great day to be looking out and enjoying the view of the city she loved so dearly. She sat down on one of the wing chairs and reached for the telephone. She dialed her phone number, and Amber picked up on the second ring.

"Hello, Radcliffe residence." Amber sang out in her usual melodic voice.

"Hi, Amber, it's me."

"Oh, sweetie! I was just talking about you. Blaise came over, and we talked about coming to see you later on. How are you doing, doll?" Amber asked.

"Well," Rachel sighed, "I think I'm making some progress. My sessions with Dr. October are really thought-provoking and I think if anyone can get to the cause of my problems, it's he."

They exchanged the usual amenities, and then Amber told Rachel that Christian had called a couple of times. Amber said he didn't want to risk awakening Rachel at the hospital, so he decided to keep track of any improvement through Amber.

"That's nice. In fact, I thought about calling him, but I guess my fears were the same. I didn't want to disturb him at the theater, particularly since the regularity and intensity of rehearsals has kept him there almost around the clock."

"My, my, aren't you two on the same wave length? But listen, doll, he did mention that they usually take a dinner break around 7:00 P.M. So why don't you try calling him this evening?" Amber was certain that this suggestion would be successful. Rachel was excited about the possibility of talking to him in just a few hours.

"Great idea, Amber, and I can take a whole half hour if he can." Rachel breathed in deeply and thanked her friend for being the messenger of such good news.

"Hey," responded Amber, "what are good friends for? But listen, sweetie. There's something else I have to tell you." Rachel could sense that this news would not be as exhilarating; she held her breath momentarily as she waited to hear further from Amber. "I'm going home day after tomorrow, sweetie."

Rachel could feel an instant let-down, and while she knew this news was forthcoming, it still left her sad and a little shaky.

"Listen, doll, I know you understand that I must get home. Even though Carlo and Marisa are old enough to take care of themselves and Tony is absolutely as self-sufficient as any husband can be, they do need me for something, even if it's only to remind them that I love them." Amber smiled and Rachel answered immediately.

"And they love you, too, Amber. My God, I can't believe how selfish I am to even feel the least bit slighted when you've been so generous and supportive on my behalf and at the expense of your own family."

Amber tried desperately to assure Rachel that she would be in touch daily and that Blaise promised to visit every day and keep Amber updated regularly.

"Besides," Rachel continued, "I'm feeling much better, and I know I will be going home very soon." It was difficult for Amber to believe that Rachel may have said this to convince herself, as well.

"Okay," said Amber, "I'll be there at visiting time tonight, and Blaise and Master Randy are coming, too."

"Wonderful!" responded Rachel. "We'll have a good chitchat, and it will be nice to see Master Randy. I have been worried about how he's handling my hospitalization, and I think he'll feel better once he sees how well I'm doing."

"And Blaise?" Amber asked. "What about Blaise? Are you looking forward to seeing him, too?" Amber was a devil when it came to stirring the pot, and it wasn't only idle curiosity. She had been visiting now for a while, which gave her some one-on-one time with Blaise, who took the opportunity to make certain that Amber knew how serious he was about Rachel. There wasn't any doubt in Amber's mind. Blaise loved Rachel deeply and passionately, and he wasn't going to give her up easily. Particularly now, after having revealed the whole deception about his not being homosexual. Add to that, almost losing his life as a result of the confrontation with Corey, and he was a man committed to winning Rachel's heart and her love. Even though he liked Christian and could see why Rachel fell in love with him so quickly, Blaise would do whatever he could to win Rachel.

"Of course I'm anxious to see Blaise, silly," responded Rachel. "What kind of inquiry game is this?" she chuckled. Rachel knew her friend all too well and had an idea that she was up to something. "Amber, you know how important Blaise is to me. And I'm not overlooking him. That just happened to be the order of questions for today."

Amber detected a little anger in her voice and bit of disappointment in Rachel's tone.

"Okay, doll, you're right. I guess I was pushing a button I should have avoided. But you know I wouldn't play games with you. In the first place, it's not the time or the place for games, and I certainly wouldn't knowingly add to your current dilemma. Forgive me, sweetie? Hope I haven't upset you."

Rachel felt badly that she had even intimated that Amber was anything less than genuine in her concerns for Blaise.

"Oh, I know, Amber. I know. I guess I'm so God-awful touchy about everything that nothing seems to get past me without some quick judgment as to whether I feel it's acceptable or not. Let's forget it. Okay? I'm much too anxious to see you all tonight and look forward to hearing Christian's voice, as well. Have you bought out all the shops in the Village and on the Hill as yet?" Rachel hoped that changing the subject would help to get past this awkward episode.

"Sure thing!" Amber smiled. "I have enough mementos in pink and green for each of my three sweethearts to make them think they're the only two colors that Grosse Pointers wear." Amber's infectious chuckle made Rachel laugh, as well, and she felt better already.

"Ciao for now, bella." Amber bade her friend good-bye.

"Until later, dear heart," responded Rachel.

Rachel stood up to go and get her sketch pad, when there was a knock on her door. She went over to open it and was surprised to find Zena standing there, holding two very large glasses of orange juice.

"*Wow!*" exclaimed Rachel. "Has it been twenty minutes already?"

Zena came walking in the door as effervescently as always and placed the two glasses on Rachel's reading table.

"Yes, ma'am," responded Zena. "Remember, girl, when you were complainin' about how slowly time was passin'? Well, the reverse situation has arrived." Zena was extremely upbeat and good for Rachel.

"It's funny," Rachel commented, "but no matter what you do in life, either enjoyable or not, at some point, you're right. Time takes off like a supersonic jet. I certainly have never been too successful in slowing down the process, so I should be grateful when it lags."

Zena had drunk about a half of her juice and sat down at the table closest to the outside windows.

"We both know that that's easier said than done. But what the heck, I don't see anyone else in here to refute it."

Rachel was enjoying the cool and refreshing juice and commenced to tell Zena about her visitors and the upcoming phone call.

"That's wonderful, Rachel. Your friend, Amber, is a rare treasure. Friends like that only happen once, if at all, in one lifetime."

Rachel breathed a sigh of contentment.

"I'm so blessed in so many ways, Zena. Why am I here in this place and so messed up?" Zena shook her head and grinned.

"If I knew the answer to that question, I'd be on the other side of the session table." It was that kind of humor that truly appealed to Rachel. She admired Zena's quick and witty responses and her ability to disarm any possible upset.

"Speaking of things messed up!" Rachel smiled slyly. "Why don't you finish telling me about the Perils of Zena?" Rachel sipped her orange juice, and Zena took the bait.

"Thought you'd never ask!" Zena replied.

As they both settled into their respective chairs, almost as though to watch some upcoming movie on the television, Rachel waited as Zena got ready to finish her life story.

"I think we were at the Jerry Quilter part of my romantic episodes." She laughed. And again, shaking her head back and forth, she looked at Rachel and spoke. "I hope this somewhat sticky saga doesn't end up boring you to death."

Rachel laughed again and assured her friend that she'd be the judge of that. But right now, it was very interesting and perhaps, in some ways, even assisted her in understanding her own motivations and shortcomings.

"It was hot while it lasted, the relationship, that is, but, it didn't take many dates and passage of several months to understand why there wasn't a Mrs. Quilter. Jerry's whole existence revolved around his teaching and his students. His career was the love of his life. I remember being so honored when, after a movie and a great dinner, he asked me back to his condo to assist him in grading some papers. From my intellectual, egotistical side he had scored high marks. But when I could see that there wasn't going to be any intermission from this task for me, my enthusiasm began to wane."

Zena could weave a great yarn, thought Rachel, and her curiosity peaked as Zena continued.

"Initially, I blamed myself for the lackluster manner that I was perceiving his approach to his career, and then—then, it happened—again. I began to feel sorry for Jerry because I had perhaps misjudged him. What a guilt trip I put myself on, and as soon as I made myself a regular passenger on the 'trip to disenchantment and disappointment,' the relationship turned from what I believed was love and caring to intolerance, impatience, and disdain." Zena put her hand on her head, and Rachel could tell that relating this story had brought her to that spot in time. Zena was now rubbing her forehead and biting her lip. "Saying good-bye was always a kicker for me."

Rachel sat up.

"Me, too!" Rachel blurted out in amazement at hearing those words.

"We're too much alike, my friend," Zena looked up at Rachel and said softly, "and I'm afraid in the areas that are not necessarily the most complimentary." Zena stretched her long legs out from the chair and put her clasped hands over her stomach. "Nothing in the whole world is more difficult than saying adios to someone you loved or thought you loved. Except never having the chance to say good-bye." Zena stopped talking and Rachel was touched as she watched the tears begin to stream down Zena's face. Zena's bottom lip quivered as she tried to hold back a crying jag. "Darn!" exclaimed Zena, as she reached for the box of tissues on the table. "I wish I could talk about these things without going through these teary sessions." She sniffled and blew her nose.

"Please, Zena, don't feel that you have to go on, and I certainly do apologize for instigating this." Rachel could not have been more empathetic.

Zena sniffled again and after clearing her throat and sitting up in the chair, she looked at Rachel's understanding and sad expression.

"I gotta do this, Rachel. I've got to be able to talk about these things, or I will never, ever, get past them, and they will eventually consume me."

Rachel's eyes opened even wider upon hearing Zena's devastating words. "They would consume, me," rang in Rachel's head. Rachel exhaled loudly, almost in exasperation. Her head was down and she was amazed at how closely her and Zena's problems paralleled. She wiped the corner of her eye and looked at Zena, who was trying to cope with the recollection of these sad times in her life.

"Nory was only twelve when she drowned in that lake I thought I knew so well." Zena swallowed hard and almost forced herself to continue. "I really didn't have to take her with me. Mom knew she could have dealt with Nory's disappointment if I hadn't. But oh, no, not me. I was the big sister and Nory's mentor. How could I disappoint her. I couldn't. You don't know how many times I've wished I would have. At least she'd still be here, and I could tell her how sorry I was. But no, I took her with me. We had so much fun. Perhaps, too much. And when I told her we were going to rent a motorboat and take it for a little spin, she was ecstatic. I had some minor experience with small boats. Certainly, I'd been a passenger on more than one. What could be so difficult about steering one?"

Rachel knew no matter what she said at this point, it wouldn't stop Zena from finishing what appeared to be a tragic story. So she listened and cried as the story unfolded.

"I had swum in that lake a million times. Water-skied and glided over it in almost every kind of boat known to man, but on that day, that ill-fated day, that lake was to become a menacing, treacherous stranger to me." Zena finished her orange juice and proceeded. "The life jackets were on the floor of the boat. Nory and I were going to catch some rays, so we didn't want to cover up any important parts of our bodies. The sun had been shining beautifully, and so I wasn't too concerned about some clouds that looked nasty but also too far away for me to be concerned with. So far, I had two strikes against my judgment: life jackets and underestimating Mother Nature. When it became apparent that a storm was brewing, I told Nory that we would have to cut this trip a little short. Nory never did like any kind of storm, and I remember the fear that came over her face when I said the words. She said, 'I'm afraid of storms, Zena, I want to go back right now!'" Zena sighed and more tears came flowing down her face. "Don't worry, Nory,' I said. 'It will be all right. I promise.'" She sighed deeply.

"Well, it wasn't all right. The storm from hell hit, and we were like toothpicks being bounced around everywhere. I tried to hold Nory and handle the boat, too, but it was more than I could do. To be honest, I don't remember how Nory got away from me, but I remember trying desperately to hold on to that steering handle and her, as well. The next thing I remember was Nory screaming as the boat jolted and she was thrown into the churning lake. I panicked. I screamed her name and then jumped into the lake to try to find her. The lightning was fierce, but bright, and as I swam around calling and struggling to look for her, I finally saw her arm and head directly ahead of me. I yelled, 'I'm coming, Nory. Hold on . . . Nory! I'm coming.' I pushed myself like I never had before. While I wasn't an Olympic swimmer, I was a strong swimmer. I prayed for God to give me the strength to reach her and for her to stay afloat until I got there!" Suddenly, Zena stopped talking and she closed her eyes. She winced and agonized each second of that terrible tragedy.

"When I next picked up my head to make sure I was getting closer, Nory was gone. I turned and looked and swam around futilely, and then the wind and the waves pushed me around in my unsuccessful attempt to find Nory." The Kleenex was bunched up in Zena's hand, and she shook her head and sighed. "She was gone. Gone forever, my sweet Nory was gone, and it was my fault!"

There was silence again, and Rachel's tears had matched those of Zena's.

"Oh, my God, Zena. How terrible. How devastating!" Rachel sobbed.

"How unnecessary!" Zena yelled out. "None of this would have happened if I had used the good judgment the Lord gave me. My ego and my pride killed my sweet Nory, and I've prayed so hard that as punishment,

God would take my life, too. But two attempts at suicide and months of not eating and sleeping didn't snuff out this life that I don't deserve to live."

Rachel was now horrified that perhaps she had caused Zena to delve into matters that might bring her close to self-destruction again.

"Zena," cried Rachel, "let's not continue this. If I had known where my curiosity would take you, I would never have started this."

Rachel knew that Zena had told this story many times, since the therapy for learning how to accept and cope with these kinds of tragedies called for being able to talk about them. It was meant to help erase the blame and guilt so that one could get on with one's life.

"I'm okay, Rachel. I'm coping, but nobody ever guaranteed that it would be easy." She was nodding her head up and down, and Rachel stood up and walked over to comfort her.

After that conversation with Zena and learning about her unsuccessful relationships with men, Rachel began to see some of the parallels of their lives. The more they spoke, the more Rachel felt a kindred spirit with this woman who a couple of weeks ago was a complete stranger to her.

During her next sessions with Dr. October, Rachel became even more inquisitive about the possibility that she, like Zena, pitied the men with whom she fell in love. Rachel was also becoming aware that losing Donald Ramchek's love, the killing of her parents, and the subsequent divorce from Neil were losses she thought she had lived beyond. She could begin to see that they could very well have been collectively responsible for the unsuccessful parts of her love relationships afterward. Certainly, Corey was a prime example of how mixed up and confused she'd become. On the heels of that separation, came Blaise's declaration of deceit and pronouncement of love for her.

The only person that didn't fit the mold was Christian. He was the first man in her life that sparked feelings she had only imagined and sometimes even faked in her prior relationships. Even now, when she thought about Christian, she could feel the excitement building inside of her. His touch, his look, and his voice gave her chills and made goosebumps rise everywhere on her body. Being close to him was so thrilling. So captivating. She could hardly quell the passion that was forging through her. He was the only man she knew she could give herself to without reservation, without inhibition.

The questions about whether or not this was love or infatuation or just an escape from Corey and Blaise reared its ugly head more than once since they met. But Rachel could dispel any apprehensions based on her feelings.

The trust and unmistakable feelings of love for this man could only confirm that he may be her one true love. The love of her life. More and more as she examined and probed her past failed relationships, she realized that this time was different. *She* was a part of the equation, this time. *She* felt the love and passion, and there was no denying that Christian felt the same. Somehow, Rachel knew that even if she and Christian never consummated their love, he would never be apart from her. He had fused his love in her heart and soul, and no once could ever change that.

The most difficult part of her life was coming up, for she would have to tell Blaise of her decision regarding Christian. The old sympathy feelings came rushing into her thoughts, and the "what ifs" would not stop. What if Blaise can't accept her decision? What if she's putting too much emphasis on a relationship of such short duration? What if Christian doesn't feel as deeply, and, oh, my God, what if Christian felt sorry for her now that she had fallen under the weight of her apparent problems?

The possibilities were endless and frightening, but Rachel's inner core was at peace with her decision about Christian, and somehow, even though she would have to figuratively say good-bye to Blaise, she felt assured that Christian would understand and be there for her. This was consolation enough for her. Christian was older and more experienced in these kinds of things. And because he had known such a wonderful love relationship with Tia, Rachel believed that he would be more than capable of commitment and trust. Suddenly, she could feel a sense of strength and confidence. And if this *was* opportunity knocking, she wanted to be ready to answer with the same sense of confidence.

Master Randy was relentless in his questioning of Estelle. His desire to visit the cool lady was persistent. Estelle knew that he would never understand any of the reasons why Rachel ended up this way. As intelligent and well versed as he was for an eleven-year-old, he was still unfamiliar about matters like this. Both Estelle and Dr. Markham had explained every possible reason why this may have happened to his new friend, but the explanations were never enough to satisfy the endless "why" questions that spewed from this bright and concerned young boy.

He was excited about going to see Rachel on Saturday, and he knew his new friend would be as happy to see him as he was to see her. He still struggled with the awful possibility that their "date" on that ill-fated day may have somehow been too much for his cool lady. He was used to Taco Bell and McDonald's as a combined meal and popcorn and soda at a movie. But he knew this was not Rachel's usual dietary regimen and when added to the surprise visit of his Uncle Christian, it may have been too much for her. Whatever it was, Randy wanted it to be over and prayed he wasn't responsible.

Rachel fussed a bit more on this particular day because she was aware of Randy's visit and how he might magnify her every move. Being able to wear her own clothes would make it easier to put this situation in proper perspective for him. She even rehearsed what she'd say to him so that he would feel comfortable and happy to see her doing so well. Regular visits from anyone had been curtailed, and since Amber returned to New York, only Blaise came to see her on a regular basis. The only other visitors she had were other patients, like Zena.

Both Dr. Mannix and Dr. October were off this Saturday, and Rachel felt good about not having Randy come in contact with them during his visit. She would show him some of her sketches and share some of the things that she and his Uncle Christian had talked about.

Whatever medication she was taking tended to make her drowsy and listless; however, she wouldn't have to take anything until after visiting hours. She jotted down a note to make certain to ask about University Liggett's soccer team. They had been written up in the *Grosse Pointe News*, and while Randy didn't play, she knew he was a big fan. Rachel was also happy that Estelle would be with him, since she could buffer any questions that Rachel couldn't answer. It was only a couple of days away and Rachel was looking forward to seeing his young and smiling face.

The next day, Mother Nature presented the area with a God-awful thunderstorm, and Rachel stayed pretty much in her room. The flashes of lightning and the claps of thunder left her uneasy. Perhaps, if she lay down and took a nap, this turbulent storm would pass.

As she lay there and closed her eyes, she tried to block out the noises of the storm. But to no avail. The lights in her room flickered, and she sat up. "Oh no," she uttered, "please don't go out." She clasped the blanket with both hands and brought it up to her chin. The lights flickered again, and this time, they went out. Rachel let go of the blanket and reached for the buzzer on her bed. However, before she could press it, the door opened, and it was the head nurse on that floor. She was holding a flashlight and a large candle.

"Here you are, Ms. Radcliffe. I'll light this and, hopefully, the power will return soon." The little flame was enough to cast some light in her room. Rachel thanked her for the promptness of bringing the candle to her.

"Well," the nurse responded, "it's not too often that this happens, and while we do have an auxiliary power backup for the operating rooms and emergency department, we maintain a very large supply of flashlights and candles." After having asked if she could get anything else for Rachel, she left the room, assuring her that it would not be long before the power would be restored.

Although the darkness was more than a bit disconcerting, the candlelight was soft enough to add a warm glow to her room. She laid her head back on the pillow and closed her eyes once again. This time, Rachel's need for rest far exceeded both the fear of the storm and the darkness caused by the power failure. She drifted off into sleep and the mystical world of dreams. Colors of every hue danced across the horizon in front of her, and as though weightless, she moved effortlessly toward the rainbow. As she neared the bright chromatic arc in front of her, she was surprised by a shadow that suddenly loomed over her. She could feel droplets of rain on her face and in her hair. She blinked as she tried to shield herself against the spray, and when she brought up her hand to wipe away some of the moisture, she could hear her name in the far distance. "Raaaachellll," it called slowly and melodiously. "Raaachellll."

She stirred in the bed, and as though straining to hear the voice, she turned her head from side to side. Then the nightmare began—black umbrellas came from everywhere. She tried to shield herself against running into them, and when she felt them touch her arms, they would disappear as though moving through her. Rachel moaned as she struggled to get through the maze. Silhouettes of people moved around and through her.

She tried to focus on them, and when she finally felt as though she could distinguish the voice and the face, it was blank. Not a feature. They were all faceless, all transparent and all calling her name. The moisture on her face intensified, and she could feel the droplets racing down her cheeks and the sides of her face and neck. She called out, "Who are you?" But to no avail. Then the movement stopped, and one lone amorphous shaped silhouette drew near. One time taller than wide and then wider than tall. "Who are you?" she cried out.

"It's me!" the voice responded, and she squinted to see, but her focus was distorted and the rain incessant. Finally, she reached out to touch the shadow. "Who are you?" she asked again. Slowly, the mass began to take form. And again, the voice echoed "It's me." She then felt someone touch her hand, and as she looked up through the mist, the face was becoming clearer—it was, it was—"Oh," she said, as she awakened.

"Oh, my God!" she said as she wiped her face and tried to close her eyes tightly enough so she could somehow summon back the dream. But it was gone, and as she sat up, she was glad to see that the lights were back on and that the storm had passed. She got up from the bed and went into the bathroom to wash her face and comb her hair. As she looked in the mirror, she noticed how pale she had become. Reaching for some lipstick on the bathroom shelf, she spread some on her lips and rubbed a little on both cheeks. Not the best makeup job she'd ever done, but it was certainly better than before.

If only she knew why this nightmare recurred. What did it mean? Would it ever cease? She was happy that the storm had passed and the hospital activity that usually was a great disruption became a pleasant interruption. Once the floor nurses checked on all of the patients and made certain that lights and equipment were running safely, they returned to their routine of checking temperatures, pulses, and blood pressures on a regular basis.

Rachel's thoughts about Christian and Blaise plagued her. As desperately as she wanted resolution to the confusion and upset brought about by the breakdown, she was unable to focus on her eventual decision and inevitable choice between the two men. All of her old rationale came to mind. The same criteria that led her to Neil and to Corey were still ingrained in her head. Changing at this stage in her life would not be easy. The words of her friend Zena echoed in her head—"My biggest failing in relationships with the men in my life, was my confusing sympathy with love."

These words hit a responsive chord in Rachel's mind. Over and over she thought about her feelings for Neil and Corey, and the answer was always the same. Her compassion and pity for their feelings for her somehow led her to believe that she loved them. The more she deluded herself, the worse the relationship became. Her inability to surrender herself freely to either of these men always raised doubts of her inadequacies, not her lack of love. Making them happy left her somehow content but never fulfilled.

With Christian, it was different. She always felt sort of uneasy and nervous around him. Her heart would almost burst with excitement when he touched her, and surrendering herself to him became more than just fantasy, it was real. Even now as she recalled their first kiss in the underground garage of the World Trade Center, Rachel's pulse rate rose as though she were engaged in some exhilarating aerobics program. All the inhibitions ingrained in her mind and body by Mama DeRoca would disappear when she was near Christian, and she was somehow free of any past sense of guilt of immorality when they were together. It all seemed so natural. So wonderful. So right.

Suddenly, Rachel became excited about the prospect of finally meeting the one man whom she could trust and love. She felt an elation that spurred a desire to live and a passion to love. These days at Saint John were perhaps the longest and most draining of her life, but she sometimes felt as though Dr. October was unwrapping her one layer at a time. Each layer getting closer to the core of Rachel Radcliffe. Each layer getting closer to the truth.

The truth! Rachel had searched a very long time for her true love, and the journey was long and arduous. Could she be this close to finding the truth about herself and ultimately finding the key to her heart and her soul? She longed for the closeness of the one man who could make her whole. For years, she had lived with an emptiness that no other man could fill. Once she gave Christian the key, it would be forever. Nothing less would be worth all of the pain and agony.

The next days came and fled by quickly. Before she knew it, it was Saturday. Today, she would see Master Randy, and her anticipation to visit with this bright and precocious youngster was sheer pleasure. Zena was also happy today because Monty was coming to pick her up and take her home.

"Girl, you are on the right track," Zena noted astutely, "and that track will lead you straight to New York City and Christian Avian." She hugged Rachel and tears welled up in her beautiful brown eyes. "We've shared a lot of sorrow in the past few days, and I hope we've learned from one another about what things in this life really matter. We know for certain they're not material, and when the Good Lord is kind enough to put someone in our lives to love and care for us, then we better be up for the faith He's placed in us to measure up!"

Rachel, too, was filled with emotion, and tears streamed down her face as she bade her friend good-bye.

"I'll never forget you, dear Zena—dear friend." Rachel struggled to put the words together. "I will carry you in my heart wherever I go and in my prayers forever."

Zena tried hard to not make this farewell any more difficult. She uttered a couple of good wishes to Rachel and continued quietly.

"I know that my sweet Nory is with your mama and papa right now, and the peace I feel, I owe to you—my friend." They embraced once again, and Zena encouraged Rachel to go for her dream. "I have Monty, and I know once you have Christian, all will be right in this universe for you and me."

Rachel looked deeply into her friend's eyes and echoed.

"From your lips to God's ears, dear heart."

When Zena was gone, Rachel struggled to cope with the sadness in her heart. How many good-byes was she to endure before she could handle the emptiness and sorrow they left behind? Would she ever be able to overcome the fear of loss and the hesitation to commit herself in relationships that were bound to some day end? She sighed deeply and thought she might seek Dr. October's help. If anyone could help her now, it would be he.

The morning brought happier moments for Rachel on that particular Saturday, and when Master Randy peeked inside her door and spoke, she felt a sense of comfort and contentment.

"Good morning, cool lady," he almost sang. "Any time for an old friend?" he chuckled. Rachel chuckled out loud as well and held out her arms to embrace this young boy who had truly changed the course of her life.

"You bet, and particularly for such a handsome old friend." Randy rushed across the room and into the waiting arms of his cool lady. Rachel hugged him, and realizing how embarrassing such displays of affection were for eleven-year-olds, she quickly released him and offered a handshake. Randy smiled and grasped her hand in his and shook it quite heftily.

"I've missed you, Rachel, and I have so much to tell you. Do we have a time limit?" He was talking faster than usual, almost as though he were trying to say everything he had to before someone came in to cut short his time with her.

"No, Randy, no particular time constraints. I think everyone here knows how much I've been looking forward to your visit, and they wouldn't dare interrupt this special time." She smiled broadly, and Randy's eyes lit up as he stood a little taller and firmer.

"How much longer do you think you'll be here?" he asked.

Rachel could tell how uneasy the young lad was and watched as he clicked his knuckles waiting for her response.

"Well, I don't really know, but I'm feeling better every day, and Dr. October has been very encouraging about my progress. Maybe, just maybe, if I'm real good, I may be out of here by next week." Rachel looked for just a little smile on her young friend's face; however, the opposite reaction became quite apparent.

"Er, I thought you might be released by tomorrow." Randy sighed and sat down on one of the chairs closest to the windows. Rachel got the impression from the tone of Randy's voice that he knew something she didn't, so she asked him.

"Is there something you know about my release that I don't, Randy?"

Suddenly, the same look came over his face as when he slipped about his Uncle Christian's surprise visit.

"Oh, oh, I've done it again, and my mother and father will certainly kill me if they find out." He suddenly became quiet, which made Rachel more curious.

"Okay, Master Randy, since you've evidently partially let the proverbial cat out of the bag, why don't you fill me in, and I'll swear on my Captain Marvel ring that I won't tell a soul." Rachel placed her left hand over her heart as though sealing some secret vow.

Randy chuckled.

"Your Captain Marvel ring? Really, cool lady, I would have thought that you would have come up with something a little more contemporary, but that will do." He seemed relieved at Rachel's quick solution and began to relate the rest of the story.

"When my father came home yesterday, my mother asked him about you and what, if any, progress you'd made. More particularly, she asked about your eventual release. Dad said he had talked with both Dr. Mannix and Dr. October, and they thought they might release you this Sunday, providing you would agree to certain stipulations, like working only part time and continuing your sessions with Dr. October as an outside patient."

Rachel was cautiously excited by Randy's revelation. While she knew he would never willfully lie to her, she also knew that he may have overheard and misunderstood the conversation between Randall and Estelle. Even with this rationale, her penchant for wishful thinking kicked into high gear.

"Oh, Randy," she exclaimed, "I certainly hope that what you've just told me is the absolute truth."

At first, Randy appeared to be a little upset with the possibility that she would even think he'd deceive her, but when Rachel explained the reasons for her doubts and apprehensions, he was relieved. She told him that she trusted him totally, but that sometimes we tend to read things into what we hear that really haven't been said.

"I want you to be history from this place, Rachel," stated Randy. "You don't appear to be any sicker than I am, and from the economics of hospital administration, it wouldn't make sense to treat someone as healthy as you seem to be when they could be getting megabucks from other patients who are truly infirm."

Rachel tried to catch her breath as she listened to the vocabulary of this youngster.

"That was quite a mouthful, pal, and while I'll have to ruminate on it just a bit, I'd tend to agree with your observations."

"That's what I like about you," Randy continued, "you know what makes sense whether you hear it from a sixty-year-old or an eleven-year-old. You're honest with yourself and the people who are your friends!"

Master Randy smiled as broadly as he could, and Rachel noticed what a good lookin' chap he was and how very much he resembled his Uncle Christian. No wonder they were such kindred spirits, they were definitely cut from the same familial cloth.

"I guess we have created this mutual admiration society, Randy, and I've got to admit, the pleasure's been all mine." They both laughed and agreed to keep this friendship as honest and as fun-filled from that day forward.

Estelle had made a very late and much appreciated appearance in Rachel's room. She was pleased to see her son as happy and committed to this new friendship. And after a few short words about the weather and Rachel's current condition, Estelle suggested that she and Randy leave in order to allow Rachel to get some rest.

"Thank you for the wonderful visit, both of you, and I hope and pray that the next time we see one another, it won't be in this hospital." Estelle glanced at Randy, but then stood up and walked over to Rachel and embraced her.

"Get well quickly, Rachel, and I, too, share your hopes and prayers. Who knows what tomorrow will bring?"

Rachel shook hands with Randy and then hugged him.

"We'll have to see another movie real soon, okay? And, uh, I'm going to rely on you to choose it; deal?" She winked at Randy.

"Deal," he responded. "And let's hold that thought about 'real soon.' I know Uncle Christian is anxious for you to leave here, too, and when I talk to him later on, I'll find out when he plans to visit us again."

Estelle laughed and interjected.

"That will be all for now, Randall, Jr." Randy always knew he was in hot water when his mother referred to him so formally.

"Ahhh, right," he said, "take care, cool lady." With that, a nod, and a smile from Estelle, they left the room.

"Home." Rachel uttered. "Could it really be true? Am I going home?" She got up from her bed and walked over to the windows. She could see people milling about, moving about so freely. Such freedom was certainly something that she, like most everyone, took for granted. She promised herself right then and there that she'd never do that again.

Twenty-one

Blaise had been calling Rachel every day since she entered the hospital, and because he could see the toll that too many visitors took on her, he decided he would visit her only a couple of times a week. It wasn't easy to not see her every day, and now that she would soon get past some of her recent medical problems, he was leery of where all this would lead. More specifically, he was thinking about their relationship. He'd done about as much soul-searching over these past couple of weeks as Rachel had, and while he still loved her deeply, his main concern was for her happiness.

What was frightening was that that may not include him. He was, above all else, a principled and trustworthy person. The deception of his homosexuality as a ploy to get near Rachel may have been the only time in his entire life that he had ever stooped to such dishonest tactics to obtain the affection of a woman. His life, up until Rachel walked into that cocktail lounge, some eight years ago, had been uneventful and directionless. Caught up in his talent for sculpting and not really befriending another human soul, Blaise was ripe for some excitement in his life and, in particular, he was ready for a relationship. Friend or lover, he longed for the intimacy and commitment of either. To think that all of his investment of time, effort, and emotional involvement could end up without Rachel was a little more than he could handle.

What would Rachel use as the deciding factor in her choice between Christian and himself? Certainly, the longevity of their friendship would hold some weight, but quality of time as well as quantity of time would also determine the outcome. He reflected upon how happy Rachel had been when she returned from New York. He remembered, all too vividly, how her eyes shone each time she mentioned Christian's name. Much had happened since her return, too much to ever let any opportunity of winning her pass by. The scars on his head were still too obvious for him to forget that fateful fight with Corey, and he shivered as he thought about his pain and the near-death experience that ensued. He tried to dispel his feelings of fear and uncertainty and reveled in recalling how Rachel felt in his arms the day he disclosed his love for her.

Blaise had known a few women in his life, enough to be able to feel their excitement when he touched them. He recalled how Rachel became almost fluid in his embrace. Never before had a kiss caused him to feel as though his lips were bonding, almost being assimilated by hers. It felt so wonderful, so passionate, so right. He was experiencing, once again, his unwillingness to let her go. There, for a split second, he felt as though she were his, and he believed she felt it, too.

If anything was more obvious and apparent, as he thought about the entire situation, it was the timing. How many times had he heard that timing in life is everything. Well, it may be that, based on poor timing, this experience could lose the only woman he had ever loved. Blaise thought about her relationship with Corey. He felt that eventually Rachel would see this guy for the jerk he really was, and it would provide for him the perfect time to reveal the facade he'd created to eventually win her love.

However, he never imagined that a trip to New York would be the genesis of a new love. A chance meeting, a meeting so bizarre and so profound, that Rachel would fall in love so quickly and, surprisingly, so deeply. Blaise felt that if it weren't poor timing, it was certainly Murphy's Law. He felt almost helpless. Everything that he could have done up to this point had been done. Now he would have to wait, hope, and pray that something, a lot like a miracle, would lead Rachel to him. *Call it wishful thinking, call it tomfoolery, just don't call it over,* he thought.

Blaise continued his work on the newest sculpture in his growing career. He noticed that he still tired quickly since the surgery; he sat down on the sofa in his studio, laid his head back on the pillow, and closed his eyes. The image of Rachel's beautiful face, like a transparent picture in a dream, appeared before him. Her smile so beguiling and captivating almost beckoned to him. He could feel a sense of urgency to move toward her, and as he strained to do so, he awakened. He sighed and shook his head almost in disbelief. *What can I do to make her love me as much as I love her? Is it too late? What will I do if she chooses Christian? Can I accept just friendship after I've tasted her love?* Blaise struggled to suppress the passion that was raging inside him. Just thinking of her closeness caused his emotions to accelerate and his passion soar. The pounding in his chest was incredible, and every male hormone in his body was screaming for release.

Finally, he stood up and walked into the bathroom. He could see the beads of perspiration on his temples as he bent past the medicine cabinet mirror to turn on the cold water tap. He splashed water on his face and wrists and thought for a moment. He was about to take one very cold shower, but the telephone rang, and his focus and concentration were broken. He dried his hands and face and walked over to the phone and picked it up.

"Hello," he said in his usual upbeat voice.

"Hi, Blaise, this is Amber, Amber Domani."

"Yes, Amber, I recognized your voice immediately. How are you?" Blaise was curious about this phone call, particularly since he was just thinking about Rachel's trip to New York.

"Well, I'm just fine, thank you; however, the last time I spoke to Rachel, I picked up some uneasy vibes. Truth is, Blaise, I've been meaning to call you anyway because I've been thinking a lot about your involvement in this whole recent situation with Rachel, and I must admit, I'm more than just a little curious about what's happened since I returned to New York." Amber paused for a moment in order to give Blaise an opportunity to speak.

Blaise had never held back anything from Amber since his now-famous revelation, and he trusted her love for Rachel and her well-being.

"It's kind of ironic that you should call at this precise moment, Amber, since I was sitting here kind of ruminating on the events of the past several weeks. Honestly, I'm about as much in the dark as you are." Blaise swallowed and sat back in his recliner. "I talk to Rachel every day, and I try to see her twice a week. You'll recall how tired she became when you and I visited her together. We made a promise then to try not to contribute to that fatigue, and I've lived by that promise. Gotta admit, though, it's tough! I'd camp at the foot of her bed if she and the hospital administration would allow it. But no such luck." He cleared his throat and decided to ask Amber about his competition. "By the way, what's going on with Christian? I know he must be all wrapped up in his new Broadway show."

Amber tried to digest all of what Blaise had said, and she remembered the last sentence more clearly and vividly than the rest.

"He's doing a spectacular job with the show. I've had the opportunity to watch a couple of rehearsals with Carlo and Marisa, and I've got to tell you, Blaise, it's extremely exciting to watch him work."

"Great news!" Blaise responded. "An undertaking of that magnitude deserves all the acclaim it can get." Blaise was truly between a rock and a hard place where Christian was concerned. As a person, he liked him a lot. Their brief encounter during Rachel's entry into the hospital showed him how compassionate and caring a person he could be. Of course, Christian did not know or does he now, that they were both competing for Rachel's love.

"In answer to your question about Rachel and me, or anyone for that matter, I'm not the one to ask. Only she has the answer." Blaise sighed and Amber began to feel awkward about her inquiry.

"Blaise, I do apologize for seeming to be so insensitive. I realize how terrible this must be for you, and my curiosity overrode my generally good judgment." Blaise always liked Amber, and he knew that her elan sometimes did get in the way of diplomacy and tact.

"It's all right, Amber. We're all a little edgy and out of control since Rachel's medical problems began, and how can I fault you for what I'm guilty of myself? Asking about Christian wasn't so much about wondering how he's doing, but rather scoping out my competition." Amber laughed at Blaises's choice of words.

"Scoping out! I like that! It pretty much describes what we're both doing." Amber giggled. "How did Rachel look the last time you saw her, Blaise?" It didn't take him long to respond.

"She looked beautiful, always does. Only thing that might lead you to believe that she's not too well is that she's a little pale. Both Drs. Mannix and October have assured us that this is a result of extreme fatigue and that with time and proper nutrition and rest, the rosy glow on those perfect cheeks will return." Amber was elated that the doctors were in accord about Rachel's physical condition and her ability to recover completely.

"Oh, Blaise, that's terrific news. Now all we have to do is hope and pray that her recovery will be a speedy one."

"You're right on both counts, Amber. Then perhaps, when she's returned to some semblance of normalcy in her life, we can resolve this triangular dilemma. Actually, Christian is the best-positioned at this time because he doesn't even know that he's a part of this threesome." Blaise hesitated to say anything further about Christian for fear that Amber may misinterpret his motivations. He also realized early on in his acquaintance with Amber that she was much too perceptive to try to fool. "Above all," Blaise continued, "I want Rachel to be healthy and happy. She deserves some happiness, and if she chooses me to spend her life with, you can bet good money that I'll make that my number-one priority." He paused briefly. "However, if Rachel chooses Christian, he'd better have the same priority or I'll give him one excruciating headache." Amber grimaced at the tone and implications of Blaise's statement.

"Blaise, in the first place, you didn't have to tell me about your love and commitment to Rachel. You've been putting your money where your mouth is for a very long time. Secondly, I hope I don't detect any possible threat of confrontation here. God only knows, you've already paid heavily for the last altercation, and we certainly don't need another one." Amber swallowed and cleared her throat. "I guess we're all going to have to wait and see what Rachel wants to do. Right?" Blaise nodded in agreement.

"Amber?" he said rather quizzically. "Can I ask you *not* to advise Rachel one way or the other on her decision? You're her closest friend and could wield some pretty tremendous influence on her. If Christian and I are going to have a fair run here, Rachel should come to her own conclusions based solely on her evaluation of her feelings for the both of us, and, excuse the trite saying, let the best man win." Blaise took the opportunity to clear his throat and drink some of the sparkling water he had poured for himself just before Amber called.

Amber mulled over what Blaise just said and while she would have liked to reassure him of her noninterference in Rachel's decision, she also couldn't tie her hands in case Rachel really needed her input in order to make the choice.

"You know, Blaise, I'd love to say that I'll mind my own business and stay out of this entire situation. And in my heart, I believe that Rachel should come to this decision on her own; however, I don't want to short-change Rachel, either." Amber pressed her lips together and tried to be as compassionate as possible. "I'll be honest with you, Blaise. If I were to have to choose which of you would be best for her, I'd have a damned difficult time. Each of you has expressed and shown love for her. There's no question in my mind that she wouldn't be totally happy with either of you.

"However, I'm not Rachel, and her evaluation of the two of you will be on a very intimate and personal scale. She knows things about each of you that affect her physically and emotionally, and I, at best, would end up being her sounding board. So while I can't promise you that I won't somehow be a part of the decision-making process, I will tell you that because I value her friendship so deeply, I wouldn't want to jeopardize it by influencing her one way or the other. She and our friendship mean too much to me."

Blaise was sort of staring into space as he listened to Amber's response. He sighed and clenched his teeth.

"Whew, this is going to be a cliff-hanger up and until the very end. I guess, in your position, Amber, I'd be in the same predicament you've described. And as much as I'd like to sway you toward my side, the ultimate decision will be Rachel's, no matter what anyone else says or does."

"Well, I'm afraid you're right, Blaise. We are just going to have to sit back and wait." Amber sighed again. "God only knows, this will probably be the most difficult decision Rachel will ever have to make. And I think you and I have pretty much agreed that whatever it is, we will be happy for her."

"That's it, Amber," Blaise responded. "Guess we're all going to find out soon enough. In the meantime, I'm just going to keep calling and visiting her once or twice a week. Hopefully, she'll be outta there real soon."

Amber thanked Blaise for commiserating with her and assured him that she would stand by to the best of her ability until Rachel asks her for an opinion, then, and only then, will she get into the picture.

"Thank you, Amber, more particularly, thanks for caring about all of us." Amber told him to take care of himself and to give Rachel a big hug from her the next time he sees her.

"My pleasure, so long for now!" When Blaise hung up the phone, he took the glass of sparkling water and drank until it was gone. He breathed deeply and sat back in his chair.

"So much for 'what ifs?' and 'should have beens.' My only chance now rests with that beautiful lady, and I'm going to give a new meaning to the 'old college try'!" He sighed again and got up to take the glass back to the kitchen. As he stood by the sink, looking out the window of their common backyard, he brought his hand to his forehead and rubbed across it slowly. "C'est la vie," he uttered. "No use pondering my fate at this point. I've got to resist the comfort of inertia and keep a head's-up attitude. If Rachel chooses me out of some sense of pity and obligation, I will have won her on the wrong premise. I certainly can't change the past, and the future is more than a bit uncertain. But . . . I do have the present, and the rest of *my* life starts right now." Feeling like he'd done a superb job of convincing himself that this might work, Blaise headed for the bathroom and took a long shower. He languished in the hot water spray. There was something definitely therapeutic about a hot shower.

Saint John's was always such a different place on weekends. So many of the regular staff were gone, and so the patients' schedules were altered to fit the change. Drs. October and Mannix were away, as well, and with Zena now released, Rachel had to think for a few minutes about what the rest of her day was going to look like. There was always some sketching and perhaps the writing of a couple of much-overdue notes. But somehow, these didn't capture her fancy right then; she really longed to just sit and talk to someone. She looked at her watch and decided to give Blaise a call. It had been a couple of days since she had seen him, and she missed him. She sat down at the little table near the window and dialed the number she knew as well as her own. It rang only twice when she heard Blaise's distinctly pleasant voice.

"Hello." Rachel smiled upon hearing this simple greeting from her friend.

"Hello, to you," she responded.

"Ray babe! It's you! I was just sprucin' up to come over to see you. Must be true that great minds think alike." Rachel chuckled at Blaise's upbeat and reassuring attitude.

"You're an angel, you know that, Blaise? Or have I told you that lately?" she added.

"Well," he grinned, "as a matter of fact, no, you haven't, and that's why I was going to fly over to see you."

"Oh, my goodness, Blaise. That's a terrible attempt at humor." Rachel shook her head and then continued. "Being in this place for a while and being so distanced from all of the people I love and care about has shown me how terribly for granted I take them." She swallowed and sighed. "You've always been there for me, dear heart, so can you think of any reason why I wouldn't just love you?" Blaise couldn't believe his ears. But he had to make sure that what he was hearing was what she meant.

"Oh, yeah, I know, you're an old shoe, Blaise. Comfortable, available, and worn out."

"Blaise, would you stop! I'm serious." With that, she paused for a moment. "I do love you, Blaise, and I don't mean like an old shoe. The day I got sick at your house was only hours after you told me about your well-hidden charade over the past few years, and hearing you explain everything you did to stay near me because you secretly loved me . . . touched me deeply." Blaise listened intently as Rachel went on, and he remained quite silent. "Are you there?" she asked. "I don't hear you."

"Yes, I'm here, my precious. I'm just sitting on cloud nine at the moment and the altitude interfered with my hearing ability." Rachel shook her head and smiled.

"Well, sir, for your information, I shared that familiar cloud nine when you kissed me so sweetly and so passionately." Even now, as she recalled it, she could feel her emotions stir. Her heartbeat raced, and she leaned further back in the chair, almost in a reclined position. "My feelings for you are as real as yours are for me, and while my life is now truly complicated because of similar feelings for Christian, I'm not certain where this is all going to lead."

"Hmmm...," his eyebrows raised almost to his hairline. "I guess if I needed to hear anything in the world from the one person I love the most, you just said it. That you would even consider my love after the terrible deception I subjected you to is incredible." Blaise swallowed and continued quickly. "You know, Rachel, how very much I love you and that I would do anything to be your choice. However, if you do choose me, I'm proud enough to ask that pity or sympathy not have anything to do with your decision."

Rachel was startled at hearing Blaise's comments. She hadn't discussed any of her treatments or conversations with Zena about this very thing, so it had to be strictly coincidental.

"Believe me, Blaise, when I decide this time, it will be from the heart and soul. No feelings of sympathy, no delusionary thoughts about fairy-tale endings. Only true emotions based on trust and fidelity. This time, I will expect as much as I give and at least attempt to reach some mutual compromise, if necessary. It's taken me a very long time to believe that I even deserve happiness, and that it's not always up to me to make certain that everyone else is happy, as well. This time, it will be for all the right reasons—it will be for love."

There was a brief period of silence as each thought about this pretty serious conversation. Blaise discerned a kind of resolve and almost desperate tone in Rachel's voice. It sounded as though this were the last time she'd have to make a decision concerning who in her life would share her love forever. The rest of the conversation was idle chitchat.

Blaise experienced the most frustrating sense of mixed emotions he had ever felt. He was excited about Rachel's almost definite expression of love for him. Yet, he was cautious as he recalled Rachel's state of uncertainty concerning her love for both him and Christian. He was happy that he was so close to her geographically and uneasy, knowing how absence can make the heart grow fonder in some instances. "Heck!" he said to himself, almost exasperatedly, "I don't know what's going on in her mind right now, and I'm sure not going to tempt fate by pushing her into making a hasty decision before she's ready." He was dressing more quickly as his enthusiasm about visiting Rachel grew. "I love her and she said she loves me." He stopped and shook his head. "Grow up, Blaise," he uttered, "that doesn't necessarily mean that she and I will live happily ever after. But I can't chance a slipup right now. I must remain her best friend, first and foremost. She's my first priority, and her happiness means everything to me." As he listened to his soliloquy, he realized he was really trying to convince himself of it being true. "The decision will be made, and whether I'm in the winner's circle or not, I must somehow manage to come out of this triumvirate still her friend."

In New York, Christian's mind had been filled with the production and completion of "Cinema," yet not a moment passed that his thoughts didn't stray to when he was holding Rachel in his arms. He could feel her lips on his, and staying focused on his work grew more difficult each day. With the exception of a few calls from Master Randy and a duty call from Estelle, Christian sort of lost touch with the day-to-day reassurance that existed when he was in Grosse Pointe a couple of weeks ago.

Even though he talked with Rachel on a somewhat regular basis, he had noticed a change in the tone of their conversations. He tried futilely to convince himself that it was because of her illness and that the change that occurred so quickly would go away just as quickly when she felt better. He also realized that his work schedule had also caused a bit of a change in their relationship. Still, he felt very deeply about Rachel, and the excitement from his love for her made him quiver. The love he felt for her was more than therapeutic after such a long time of abject numbness. It was like being infused with life again. He could feel his adrenaline level surge, and it caused him to move more adroitly and energetically. Those who knew him well could see the difference. Sid, in particular, had mentioned it more than a couple of times to Christian.

There were times during rehearsals that he felt like he was cheating on her. This time away was necessary in his career, but her love at this time in his life had surpassed any ambition to exceed or excel in his beloved profession. It was almost as though he were consumed with the awakening of feelings he had buried so deeply after Tia died. Rachel had opened the doors to the darkest recesses of his unhappiness and brought light once again with her love and tenderness. He felt alive again.

As Christian walked to his back stage office, he thought about his brief encounter with Blaise during Rachel's untimely hospitalization. If there were anyone who would understand his deep love for Rachel, it would certainly be Rachel's neighbor and dear friend. Maybe Blaise could relieve some of his fear and apprehension about Rachel's recovery, and better yet, maybe Blaise could assure him that Rachel still cared as deeply for him.

He looked for Blaise's telephone number, then blurted out, "Here it is." He had written the number on the back of his business card. "Yes, this is it."

Christian picked up the receiver and dialed Blaise's number. The telephone rang three times before he heard Blaise's familiar voice.

Since Blaise had just hung up the phone after his conversation with Rachel, he assumed this was a call back from her with some afterthought. So he didn't bother with "hello."

"Yes, I do love you, Rachel, if that's why you're calling me back."

There was total silence, and suddenly Blaise became quite nervous. Christian was stunned at hearing Blaise's greeting, and Blaise suddenly realized that it was not Rachel on the other end of the line.

"Hello," Blaise blurted out. "Hello, who's calling, please?"

For a brief second, Christian almost hung up, but gentleman that he was, he responded.

"It's Christian Avian, Blaise. Obviously, you were expecting someone else. Rachel, to be more specific."

Blaise's heart dropped and he could feel the blood surging to his face and head. He was so embarrassed and totally surprised to hear Christian's voice. He stuttered and stammered uncontrollably.

"Uh, hello, Christian. Uh, yes, you're right. However, you're going to have to let me explain what just happened." Blaise was trying desperately to recover from this fiasco. He sighed deeply and cringed as he tried to think about what he could say to patch up his terrible faux pas.

"I'm listening," replied Christian, "In fact, I'm all ears."

Blaise cleared his throat and took a deep breath.

"You know, certainly, that Rachel and I have been friends and neighbors for many years." He hesitated as though to listen for any kind of response, but there wasn't any. He continued. "And over time, we've developed our own kind of jargon. She and I have weathered many an emotional storm vis-à-vis, Neil and Corey, and a couple of mine, as a matter of fact, so we say certain things that trigger our ability to laugh things off, and periodically, that exchange and its phrases seem to handle heavy and difficult situations."

Christian raised his eyebrows in almost total disbelief and grinned slyly.

"So what you're implying is that you and Rachel were, shall we say, fooling around?"

There it was. A question that Blaise would have to answer, being fully aware of the obvious consequences.

"Well, ahhhh, yes, sort of." Blaise was gritting his teeth by now and waiting for Christian's response.

"Sort of?" responded Christian. "Just what does that mean?"

Blaise was in a definite quandary and was struggling to figure out how he could recover from this without blowing the whole thing for himself and Rachel, as well.

"Yeah, sort of. Uh, oh." He cleared his throat. "I was playing a part at that moment. You know, . . . acting," he said, almost sheepishly.

Christian's patience was wearing thin.

"Playing a part? Now, come on, Blaise, I'm neither a dummy nor a fool. What's going on?" The decibel level of Christian's voice increased measurably and even though Blaise didn't know him very well, he could tell that he was getting very angry.

"Christian," Blaise said calmly, "listen to me. We were playing around, that's all. It was very innocent and something that was done to help Rachel get through a rather tough day. However, if we're looking for the pure, unadulterated truth here—" Blaise hesitated. "Sure, I love Rachel, always have, but that doesn't necessarily mean that we're in the middle of some torrid and illicit affair. I really think this is getting a little out of hand, and I apologize if it upset you. It certainly was pretty innocent, and it's definitely taught me a lesson about how to answer my telephone."

Christian laughed. And as he responded, he smiled.

"I guess I've been too tense these past few days, myself, Blaise, and I, too, apologize for jumping all over you the way I did." Christian's voice had softened considerably now, and he continued. "Being so far away from Rachel during this critical time has not been easy for me. And unfortunately, it's been extremely intensified by the production and completion of this new musical. Talk about being caught up in two critical aspects of my life. I hope you understand that it was this personal conflict that's made me less than courteous and more than a little irascible lately."

Blaise was suffering with his own dilemma now. If he continued to tell Christian anything further, he may destroy everything that Rachel had developed with this man. And if he lied, he could very well end up deceiving all of them. So he decided to cop out.

"No problem, Christian, and listen, I hate to run, but my doorbell is ringing and the couple of eggs I'm hard-boiling on the stove are ready to come out. Sorry about this whole mess. No damage. Right?"

Christian assured him that all was well and apologized again for his behavior. He even said he'd call him sometime to chat. Right then and there, Blaise realized that he hadn't even asked why he called in the first place.

"Jiminy crickets!" exclaimed Blaise. "How impolite I am. I didn't even ask you why you called, Christian. Is everything all right with you?"

Christian was quite gracious and said he had only wished to talk about Rachel with someone who knew about her current situation.

"It's all right, Blaise. We can have this conversation some other time. Please give my love to Rachel when you next see her and tell her I'll be phoning her real soon." Blaise was shaking his head up and down in a positive motion as though Christian could see him.

"Okay," Blaise responded. "Okay, I'll do that, Christian, and yes, by all means, call me again. Take care."

Blaise hung up the telephone and slumped down in his sofa. "Whew!" he uttered. "That was too close for comfort. Hmmm, but it's not over. I'm going to have to tell Rachel about this. His expression was one that combined sadness and fearful anticipation. "Oh, boy! This isn't going to be fun. Not at all."

Now he had to scurry, as he did not want to keep Rachel waiting. Visitors were few and far between, and he knew she was anxious for some company. A quick dash to his bedroom to splash on some of Rachel's favorite aftershave and he was out the door. The cool and changing winds of autumn were blowing, and Blaise raised the zipper on his jacket as far as it would go. Summer and fall felt like the same season the past couple of years.

The drive to Saint John's was a short one, and it wasn't too long before Blaise was pulling into the large visitors' parking lot. As he got out of the car and began to walk toward the imposing edifice directly ahead of him, he was trying to figure out how he would tell Rachel about his telephone conversation with Christian. The walk from the parking lot seemed a lot shorter, and before he knew it, he was getting onto the elevator that would take him to Rachel's floor.

When he got to her room, he peeked in the long window that ran parallel with the door. She was sitting at the table near the window and appeared to be sketching. He tapped on the window to get her attention. She smiled broadly when she turned and saw him peering at her through the glass. Rachel greeted him at the door and they embraced as though they hadn't seen one another in a long time.

"You look wonderful, Ray!" Blaise said as he drew away and looked down at Rachel. "You're even more beautiful than the last time I saw you, if that's possible. You look, ah, rested."

Rachel was happy to hear those words of praise and encouragement, and she stood on her tiptoes in order to reach Blaise's mouth. She kissed him and thanked him for coming over and for always making her feel so special.

"It's great to see you, too, Blaise, and I must admit you're looking in tiptop shape, as well." She gently ran her hand over his forehead near the healing incision. "You're a pretty darn good healer. Betcha in a couple of months, you won't be able to notice that wound at all."

It was a perfect moment for his response.

"Some wounds heal a little faster than others, and some go away forever, while some leave deep and unrelenting scars."

Rachel moved away from Blaise and looked up at him.

"Ohhh, now that's pretty profound, Mr. Kinley. Is there some hidden message in them thar words?" Blaise laughed as they walked toward the little table and sat down. He sighed deeply.

"Well, I suppose so, but it's not that ominous. Just an appropriate intro to a discussion that's not really going to make you real happy." Rachel's expression changed from her usual smile to a look of genuine concern.

"What's wrong, Blaise? Is something happening about my condition that I don't know about?"

Blaise could see the quick and almost extreme change taking place in her manner. She began to wring her hands and look about in a very nervous way. He realized, watching her, just how fragile she had become under the strain from her concern of her medical condition, and he quickly tried to allay the fear and apprehension he saw on her face.

"Hey, Ray, ahhhh, no! There's nothing that wrong, and it's just something I screwed up, that's all!"

"Oh, boy! Now, there's a don't-be-too-concerned intro if I ever heard one. You screwed up? Perhaps I should be holding on to something before you tell me this."

She looked directly into Blaise's bright and pleading eyes. She waited . . . and waited. She sighed and swallowed; it appeared as though she would have to give birth to this "pregnant moment." But Blaise finally spoke up, and Rachel listened, as she usually did, with total concentration and focus, almost hanging on every word out of Blaise's mouth.

"Well," he stuttered, "it's like this, Ray." Now he swallowed and took a deep breath. "Christian called me—"

"Oh, my God, there is something wrong or why would Christian call you?" Rachel gasped.

This was now the third time today that Blaise found himself backpedaling in a conversation over which he had no or very little control.

"Hold on, Ray, hold on. Before you start leaping to conclusions, why don't you let me finish, and then you can clean my clock." Blaise reached over and patted Rachel's hand in an attempt to reassure and comfort her.

"He called me because he was worried about you, and since I'm geographically closer to you than anyone, and since you and I are friends and neighbors, I hope . . . " he grinned as he continued, " . . . he felt I'd have a better handle on what was going on with your treatment and your progress." Blaise was trying to set the scene for Rachel so that she would understand what happened.

Rachel was both relieved and upset almost simultaneously, if that were possible. She chuckled as she envisioned Blaise when he found out that it was Christian on the telephone and not her. On the other hand, she almost panicked to think about Christian's surprise and amazement upon hearing Blaise's expression of love for her.

"Blaise" she gasped, "how did you leave things with Christian? Was he all right?" Blaise sighed and rubbed his nervous hands together. He was still back-pedaling, and Rachel could sense it. "Blaise! For goodness sake, will you answer me?" She was getting more upset by the minute, and thoughts of Christian's suspicions and eventual breakup with her flashed through her mind.

"Hold on, Ray, it's all right, I'm just trying to remember every word of his and my conversation, so I can assure you that everything is fine." He swallowed and repeated as much of that discussion as he could remember.

Rachel listened intently, her eyes never leaving his face for a single moment. When Blaise finally finished relating the entire discussion, he looked directly into Rachel's eyes and spoke very softly.

"I apologize for whatever upset my fooling around may have caused you, and I hope you know how deeply sorry I am right now for giving you any additional cause for concern. I hope you're not angry with me." That's all it took for Rachel to intercede.

"Blaise, my dear, sweet Blaise, how can I be angry with someone who has never intentionally hurt me during our entire relationship. You've been my rock during some pretty tumultuous times, and there was no way you could have ever suspected that Christian would call you directly." She held out her opened arms to him and he responded quickly. He was ready for this much needed hug. She sighed deeply as she laid her head against his chest. His heart was pounding. She moved back and looked up at him. "It's all right, dear heart, it's all right." She sighed again and laid her head back against his chest and spoke quietly.

"I'm so uneasy these days, and I'm upset with myself because of it. I've never felt as vulnerable as I have recently, and it's I who should apologize to you for somehow involving you in yet another relationship."

He loved holding her. He could tell that she had lost some weight. He could also feel her body quivering from the weakness that had developed after her collapse. There were so many days and nights over the years when he dreamed of holding her like this. But, he felt this was not the last time.

"Shhh," he whispered, "enough of this. Such a beautiful lady shouldn't have to worry about all these things. Truth of the matter is, if anyone should be worried here, it should be moi."

Once again she looked up at his handsome face. His smile and his expression, was one she had seen many times when he, and only he, was about to make her laugh and help her to forget her troubles.

"I love you, Blaise Kinley. Do you know that I love you?"

Blaise closed his eyes and held her as he felt his heart jump with joy upon hearing those words once again.

"Hmmm, Ray, you know how much I love you and that I would never ever do anything to hurt you or to make you unhappy."

Rachel raised both arms and put them around his neck. The almost foot of height differential was awkward to overcome. Particularly when she was barefoot. However, she didn't have to strain too hard, as he bent down to meet her more than halfway as their eyes met. He kissed her and held her now even more tightly. Rachel could feel a slight bit of hesitation. However, when she moved her head back slightly, he followed her mouth as though resisting the eventual separation of their lips. She opened her eyes and looked upward to meet his glance, but his eyes were still partially closed.

"Are you all right, Blaise? You seem a bit hesitant. Have I lost my kissability since I've been in this place?" Rachel swallowed and waited for his response.

Blaise was a little astonished by her comments, but he was also aware that her fragile state may have brought about the perceived careful and almost cautious manner in which he kissed her.

"I won't break, honest." She grinned.

"You're a real trooper, Ray, you know that? Here I am, trying desperately to give you enough space to get well quickly, and I thought if I played it a little cool, you'd feel better about not having to deal with someone who was making moves on you right now."

Rachel was moved by Blaise's unending concern and thoughtfulness for her.

"Well, if that's all that's going on here, I'm touched. It's true that this has been a real ordeal, being unable to move around as freely as I'm used to and to come to a level of tiredness that I never imagined would happen to me."

Blaise could not take his eyes off of her, and he did so want to get her to make up her mind one way or the other. But his gut feeling was to let it alone. He had pretty much resigned himself to accept whatever Rachel's decision would be. He smiled, and Rachel appeared relieved that there didn't seem to be anything too seriously wrong. One thing had become more and more evident to them both. There were many times when they visited and conversed that periods of profound silence would come seeping in. These were definitely awkward and gladly quite uncommon.

Rachel always felt comfortable with Blaise and was able to confide her inner thoughts and feelings with him.. However, since the terrible fight between him and Corey and the ultimate revelation about Blaise's hidden feelings for her, she felt as though she were developing a new level in their relationship. Thinking of him as a possible love partner was 180 degrees from anything they shared up until now. And she recalled quite vividly the thrill of their first kiss. Even though, by her estimation, he deceived her by leading her to believe that his lifestyle would never permit them to be anything but best friends, she was deeply touched and complimented that someone would go to such lengths out of love for her.

It had been such a long time since she had felt Christian's touch and looked into his loving eyes that she found herself almost struggling to remember. Yet their meeting and falling in love was the very answer to her prayers and could eventually be the end of any uncertainty concerning loneliness.

"Penny for your thoughts." Blaise said as he snapped his fingers, trying to get Rachel's attention. "Does that place you're at right now have any room for me?"

Rachel was a little embarrassed that she was caught daydreaming.

"I'm sorry, Blaise. Since I've been here, I'm so quickly distracted by my thoughts of the past and what's happening at the moment that I wander off. I do apologize."

In a spontaneous move, he hugged her and stroked the back of her head.

"It's all right, Ray, it's all right. I understand. But you know me, I'm perhaps overly sensitive to you and your behavior, and so I tend to watch your every move and expression and that can be annoying, I know."

Rachel swallowed and adjusted her head on Blaise's chest.

"I know you care for me, dear heart, and what you describe as an annoyance has always been anything but that for me. In fact, it has been one of the things that has endeared you to me from the beginning. I've loved your doting and humorous ways over the years. It's just that the past few weeks have caused such an upheaval in my life that it's hard to keep any sense of consistency on any given day." She then moved away and sighed. "I'm afraid, Blaise, I'm really afraid."

Blaise's expression changed from empathy to concern.

"Afraid of what, sweetie? Not of me, I hope."

Rachel couldn't believe he would ever think such a thing.

"You? Why on earth would I ever be afraid of you?"

"Perhaps I've been partly responsible for causing that upheaval, and you didn't know how to tell me because of our relationship?" Blaise was far too honest and candid with her to change, and the one thing that Rachel truly needed was honesty.

Rachel lowered her eyelids and then opened them and responded.

"No, that's not true, and that's not what I'm afraid of." She walked over to one of the chairs by the window and sat down. Blaise followed her and sat down next to her.

"Tell me, sweetie, . . . tell me what you're afraid of."

"I'm afraid of what's next in my life. I'm afraid that the one thing that has always allowed me to travel at my own speed, may be gone." There was a brief hesitation, and Blaise's curiosity was certainly piqued as he listened intently for what was coming next. "My health is in jeopardy right now, Blaise, and if both my mental and physical well-being is at risk, then my life will never allow me to follow my dream and find the love and happiness I've been searching for." Tears welled up in her eyes, and the next time she blinked, they rushed down her cheeks and onto her robe.

Blaise stood up and walked over to get her some tissues.

"Wait a minute here. I think you're letting your mind run away with you. No one here has said anything to me that remotely comes close to what you're intimating." He was determined to change Rachel's mind, and his voice lowered as he continued more emphatically. "We know what got you here. Remember? Too much work. Too much stress and the culmination of too many quick-remedy solutions. Add to that a trip to New York, meeting someone with whom you became desperately in love, and then experiencing the confrontation between me and Corey. And when I confessed my own love, my God, Rachel, no wonder you're afraid, but I believe in my heart that you will recover from all this."

She heard the words, and while they sounded encouraging and sensible, she was not totally convinced that her eventual recovery would be that total and that quick. She would always love Blaise's protective manner no matter where her life was directed. She couldn't even try to imagine life without him in it, but this time, his perceptions and hers definitely did not match.

Twenty-two

Christian had tried very hard to dispel his suspicions about Blaise and Rachel after that ridiculous phone conversation with Blaise. He'd met a lot of zany people in his career, but trying to make sense of the scenario that Blaise portrayed became more ludicrous by the moment. "He must take me for the fool of the century if he thinks I believe that fairy tale about him and Rachel."

The more he thought about it and of the way they left the discussion, the more he paced back and forth. His ire was being fueled by the wild ideas that Blaise conjured up, and he imagined all kinds of things, much worse.

What if Rachel and Blaise had been secret lovers before her trip to New York? And what if she had a string of men in her life and he was her latest? And finally, what if Blaise was telling the absolute truth? Christian sighed deeply and sat down and placed his head in his hands. "I can't let myself fall in love again only to have it taken away. I can't. And I won't!" His resolve was much too adamant, and he knew it. "Only problem is, I've already fallen. And it feels right." He got up and began to pace again.

"I don't have a whole helluva lot to hang my hat on here, but I think I still know how to love and can still determine when someone loves me." He hesitated as his thoughts flashed back to the Twin Towers and the special moments afterwards in the garage parking area. "She loves me. I know she does, and I've got to keep telling her that I love her, too." With that, he walked back to the telephone and dialed Rachel's private room at the hospital.

Rachel was still a little shaky and when the telephone rang, Blaise rushed over to answer it.

"Ms. Radcliffe's room," he answered.

Christian could not believe he was hearing Blaise's voice once again.

"Don't tell me, Blaise—you're playing checkers with Rachel, right? Some friendly tournament that's been going on for ten or twelve years."

Rachel could tell from the grimace on Blaise's face that he was surprised by whoever was on the other end of that phone line.

"Hi, Christian!" responded Blaise. "Oh, no we're not playing checkers, and rather than try to explain, why don't I just let you talk to Rachel." He handed the receiver to Rachel and shook his head sadly.

"Sorry, Ray babe, looks like I can't do anything right by you today." Rachel smiled at Blaise and took the receiver.

"Hello, Christian, how sweet of you to call." Rachel could tell that Blaise was very upset, and so she asked Christian to hold on for one minute.

With her hand on the speaker, she spoke quietly to Blaise.

"Dear heart, it's all right. Please stop thinking that you've done something irreconcilable here. Everything will be fine!"

Blaise could see her deep concern for him and quickly responded by motioning that he'd wait outside while she spoke with Christian. Rachel knew that Blaise felt dejected and concerned over the couple of instances involving Christian, but she couldn't keep Christian waiting any longer.

"I'm sorry, Christian, but the doctors and nurses never cease to check up on you at the most inopportune times. Even during visiting hours." She waited for his response, expecting him to be upset with the interruptions.

"It's all right, my darling. Although, I've got to admit that this hasn't been a very reassuring or encouraging day for me." He hesitated as though he were considering changing the subject but then continued. "There is so much I don't know about you, Rachel, that it scares me when something unexpected develops and hits me unaware and unprepared. Like calling Blaise and listening to his declaration of love for you." Christian stopped talking and sighed as he questioned even continuing with this scenario. But he also had to know, from Rachel, what her feelings were in all of this.

"I couldn't believe how easy and how quickly I fell in love with you, Rachel, and perhaps I was blinded by those sweeping emotions. I know that I absolutely threw caution to the wind when you responded that you shared those same feelings." Christian signed deeply again and then asked the question whose answer would either free him from all doubt or once again plunge him back into the dark abyss of loneliness. "Was I wrong, Rachel? Did I fall in love while you were only testing?"

Rachel clung to the receiver as she listened to the doubts that Christian imparted. The impact of the sadness in his voice and the question of trust about her love were astounding.

Oh, my God, she thought. *Oh, my God! I've placed him in the same uneasy position I was in before I left for New York.* Tears came to her eyes, and she responded quickly and concisely.

"Christian, my darling, Christian, you were not wrong about my love for you. I do love you very much." Her words now became garbled as she struggled to hold back the tears that came running down her cheeks.

"I've been on the proverbial emotional roller coaster up until the time when I met you and we fell in love. It was like waking up from an ongoing nightmare. I didn't deceive you when I said I loved you, Christian, nor did I realize that I was on the verge of an emotional collapse. All of a sudden, things started to happen to me that were confusing and unexplainable. You know what happened to Blaise when I returned home." She was trying desperately to explain things clearly to him, but she could hear herself rambling, and so, she hesitated.

"I don't know, Christian, if I can allay all your fears this instant, but I can assure you that your love for me is not misplaced and that I would never willingly hurt or deceive you. My whole life has been based on the values I learned early—trust, dependability, reliability, and I couldn't fool anyone about those things that are such a part of me."

Christian was very conciliatory and apologized for his apparent lackluster faith in their newly found love.

"It's not about you, darling," Rachel interjected, "it's about me. I'm the one who's causing the problem. I'm the one who's hospitalized."

Christian sighed deeply as he listened to Rachel blame herself for an illness she in no way could prevent.

"Wait a minute," he said quietly, "the last thing I want to do here is set up a table for serving blame. I'm probably becoming paranoid because I can't be there with you, and I guess I'm inwardly frightened that if I don't somehow keep that spark of love we ignited, you will drift away and it will die."

Rachel became quite emotional and began to openly sob.

"Please don't give up on me, Christian. I know all about the feelings of insecurity and fear. I know too, that if the love we've discovered is real, it will survive this test and any others we may eventually face." She pulled a few tissues from the box next to her and wiped her face and blew her nose. "I can't guarantee anything in life, Christian. Not in mine or in yours, but I can guarantee you that honesty and trust will get us through this time of separation and doubt. And no matter what the outcome, we, at the very least, can believe that we shared something wonderful. True love."

Christian swallowed hard, and while he felt somewhat relieved at hearing Rachel defend their relationship and its strength, he also felt a little uneasy about her implication of a possible bittersweet end to their newly found love.

"You know, Rachel, when Tia died, I almost died too. I was left behind with only fragments of myself to put together, if I could or wanted to. I cursed everyone and everything that represented anything to do with faith or any other intangible feeling. For months, I walked around almost aimlessly, going through the motions of working and pretending to live my life one day at a time."

Rachel listened intently as Christian related a part of his life she'd only guessed about.

"I quit believing in God, and ultimately, I quit believing in myself. Until I reached the stark realization that they were one and the same. It was a tremendous revelation, and after five long years of just wandering through each day, I began to feel a sense of purpose and thirst for a life I thought was lost to me forever." He hadn't intended to tell her his life story when he called, but here he was doing so, and it was too late to turn back now.

"When I could get up each day and welcome the glowing wonder of the sun and breathe in the fresh air, it was like being reborn. I had heard of other people living through that kind of grief, but I never thought it could be such hell. My mother always philosophized that when anyone hit the very depths of despair, the only direction from there was up. She also had a saying that made me both smile at its simplicity and tremble with sheer fear at its reality—'These things only happen to the living.' " He chuckled and shook his head as he recalled the many times over the last eight years that that rang in his head.

"I never thought I would fall in love again after that emotional purging. I certainly didn't want to set myself up for that kind of punishment and loss." He sighed again. "God is merciful, Rachel. He gives us our lives one day at a time. How many of those days, only He knows, but I know He knew they wouldn't all be easy.

"When I began to feel again and participate in life, I ruled out any possibility of falling in love. I declined untold numbers of invitations to go out. I disciplined myself to get involved only to a point, and then I would retreat into my safe and secure shell. The night of the Producers' Association's show, I was totally unprepared to meet what fate had in store for me."

Rachel was moved as she listened to Christian's story. He couldn't believe he had initiated this saga, but here he was, and telling it seemed to be appropriate and necessary.

"My work had become my obedient lover. I could control it—schedule it and demand its strengths and reject its failures with little or no consequence. It was a perfect partner for me. Then Randy introduced me to you, and every barrier I had erected and defended so totally came tumbling down. I couldn't believe what was happening to me. At first, I fought it, and ultimately, I just gave in." Christian sighed and chuckled. "I guess falling in love is like learning to ride a bike—once you learn how, you never forget it."

Rachel laughed. She loved his sense of humor and his ability to laugh at himself. She swallowed and breathed deeply before she responded.

"I guess my uneasiness initially was meeting you at a time when I was fleeing from any possibility of another emotional entanglement. For me, it was my first experience with falling in love, and so, I, unlike you, kept falling off the bike." She hesitated a moment and then continued.

"Forgive me, Christian, forgive me for being such an ingenue and for appearing to take so lightly your expression of love for me. I have been jostled about and tossed around in the name of love, and up until now, love to me meant sacrifice, self-denial, and the almost subservient feelings with which I could no longer cope." Now Rachel began to feel much like Christian—telling her life story wasn't what she had in mind either. But she would continue.

"When I went to New York, I was running away from a relationship that was going nowhere. I convinced myself that I was running to my lifelong friend, Amber, to seek solace and refuge from the person whom I blamed for the failure of that relationship. I'd been having the same recurring nightmare for months, with no reason why it persisted other than it was the culmination of that relationship and my mind's warning mechanism to get me out of its grasp.

"When I met you, Christian, I was caught off guard and unprepared for the swift and undeniable love I felt for you. I knew it wasn't a rebound situation because I don't believe I was ever in love with Corey. But it boggled my mind to think I could fall in love with someone so quickly and so totally. The sad part of this whole thing is that I returned home too soon, and the series of events that occurred thereafter brought me to this place, and now we've come full circle in this record-breaking telephone conversation."

There was silence as each thought about the other's story. Rachel was more inclined to leave things where they were, but Christian still felt uneasy and unassured about the continuance of this relationship in its current state.

"Forgive me, Rachel, for misjudging this entire situation. Not knowing the entire story—"

Rachel interjected as though she didn't want to hear what followed.

"Listen, Christian, this is a test. Don't you see that? True, it's a little early, but then our love is so new, so fragile. Please don't give up on it, or me. Give me—no, give us a chance to nurture this new relationship."

Christian's heart pounded in his chest, and each beat seemed to echo inside his head. A voice within him cried out, *You love her—let it be!* He pressed the phone even closer to his ear and whispered.

"I love you, Rachel. I love you so much, I couldn't stop even if I wanted to."

"Oh, my darling, you can't know how happy I am to hear you say that," she responded quickly, overwhelmed with joy. She sniffled and suddenly just kissed the phone. "Did you get that? Did you just feel that kiss I sent directly to your lips?"

Christian smiled.

"Hmmm . . . Well, I guess I will take that kiss in the absence of the real thing. However, my cool lady, when I next see you, you'll never forget our next kiss. It will be one you'll remember for eternity."

Rachel blushed and tingled at the prospect of his fulfilling that promise.

"I can hardly wait," she answered.

Blaise had long since tired of waiting outside Rachel's room. He was sitting in the visitors' waiting room at the end of the hall, when he saw Rachel emerge from her room.

"Down here," he motioned to her. "Here I am, Ray." Rachel almost ran to where Blaise had been waiting for the past half hour "Sorry, Blaise. That conversation lasted a lot longer than I thought it would."

Blaise almost knew what Rachel was about to say, but he didn't have the courage to ask.

"Oh, Blaise, can we please go back to my room? I do want to tell you about my conversation with Christian." She was almost out of breath as she scurried back to her room. Blaise was on her heels and not real anxious to hear what Rachel was about to relate. Rachel walked over to her night stand and poured herself a glass of water.

"Would you like some, Blaise?" He declined and remained silent, waiting for Rachel to speak. Rachel swallowed the last sip of water in the glass and sighed.

"No one knows better than you do, Blaise, the turmoil I've been living with these past few months." She extended her hand and placed it on Blaise's arm. In almost a reflex action, he placed his other hand on hers. "I've been confused and frustrated and truly disoriented by unsuccessful and disappointing relationships." Blaise grasped her hand a little tighter, almost preparing himself for what was to follow. "The past few days in the hospital have made me stop and take an accounting of my life. Past, present, and future. Listening to Dr. October's analysis of the basis of these ongoing problems has opened my eyes to a lot of things I never understood about myself."

Blaise's eyes were locked with hers. He was almost expressionless as Rachel continued to speak.

"Then I met Zena Porter, and I couldn't believe the similarities in our lives. It was incredible. She had struggled through a couple of relationships before she finally realized that a large portion of her problems was all about sympathy." Rachel drank more of the water and realized she might be rambling. "Oh, my goodness, Blaise, please forgive me. I'm doing it again."

Blaise didn't understand why Rachel was asking for forgiveness.

"What did you do, Ray? I'm afraid I don't know what you're talking about."

"I can't blame you for not knowing what I'm talking about, Blaise." Rachel shook her head. "I start to do something recently, and I almost end up reinventing the wheel before I get to the essence of my intent. This roller coaster I've been on is finally beginning to slow down."

Blaise didn't know if that was going to be good or bad news for him, but he had pretty well resigned himself to accept whatever Rachel decided.

"I guess, first of all, I want to make certain that what I'm about to tell you will help you to understand my decision."

Blaise's heart sank and he knew he should prepare for the worst.

"After talking with Christian just a few minutes ago, I felt a sense of comfort that's been eluding me for a very long time. I think out of this maze of bits and pieces of my somewhat scrambled life, he's put some clear definition in a couple of areas that assure me of his feelings for me, and more so, of mine for him!" Rachel was looking directly into Blaise's eyes and could see the concern and realization that her words brought. She reached for his hand and held it in hers.

"I can't deceive you or anyone, Blaise, and while I know what I'm about to say may hurt you deeply, I'm hoping and praying that you'll understand and even forgive me." She swallowed and sighed as she tried to compose herself.

"I love Christian, and I know he loves me! When we fell in love so quickly, I couldn't help but question the depth or even the truth of those feelings. Coming back to Grosse Pointe so soon after only delayed what I've known to be inevitable." She swallowed again and grasped his hand even more tightly.

"When you confessed your love for me, Blaise, I was thrown, truly, for a loop. At first, I thought you were making up the entire story, but when you kissed me, I knew you were serious. Not only that, but I, too, was moved by it. What happened to me afterwards is what always happened to me in the past."

Blaise was now listening more intently and could hardly wait to hear what was coining next.

"It's difficult to say this, my dearest, because I want you to understand that my problems of dealing with relationships have been my undoing, and it's my emotional mix-up that has caused my unhappiness, and, in truth, that of the men with whom I've been involved."

Blaise, almost out of sheer desperation and anticipation, interrupted her.

"Ray babe, please, let's cut to the chase here, all right? I think I know what you're about to tell me, but instead of greasing the skids, just tell me how you feel."

Rachel was embarrassed and upset, but she finally said what had to be said.

"I feel sorry for you, Blaise. And that sympathy I somehow confused with love. Perhaps because I am a compassionate and caring person, I let my emotions run away with me. When I finally came to that realization during my therapy sessions here, things began to fall into place. I felt sorry for Neil, and I married him. Then I felt sorry for Corey, and I almost made a second mistake. But when those same feelings started to arise with you, I knew I didn't want to hurt you as I had hurt them. Christian is the only man in my life I met on equal terms. No predispositions, no falsehoods, just honest to goodness love. It was hard for me to recognize, because I'd never been there before, but when I was made aware of my confusion between sympathy and love, it didn't take long to see where my future was leading."

Blaise's eyes never left hers. The truth, no matter how disappointing for him, was setting her free. There was a period of silence, and Rachel waited for his response.

"Blaise?" she queried. He smiled, which was not unusual, since Blaise had always been there for her in the past, and his smile was just what Rachel needed to bring her out of her feelings of almost total despair.

"You know, Ray, if I didn't know you as well as I do, I would probably be totally devastated. But I've learned some pretty hard lessons myself recently, and while you were going through your own metamorphosis, so was I going through my own."

Rachel breathed a sigh of relief as she listened to his understanding response.

"How could I have expected you to love someone who didn't give you the honesty you were searching for? I've known since the first time I met you that truth and honesty were the bases for any love relationship you wanted, and I, in my insecurity to meet you as the man I was, chose to deceive you under the guise that it was well intentioned—so who could it hurt? Well, it's a fitting conclusion to one aspect of our relationship, but I'm afraid, like it or not, I'll always be someone you can count on, someone who loves and admires you, and someone who will be content to be your friend. It's too late for me to just walk away, and I couldn't or wouldn't do that.

"If it's Christian who holds the key to your happiness, I would never stand in your way. And as tough as I thought it would be to let you go, you've enhanced my life in such a way that no one can ever change or take that away from me."

The tears came rushing down Rachel's cheeks. Blaise went to her and embraced her. He patted the back of her head as she rested it on his chest. "It's okay, Ray, everything is going to be okay."

Somehow, Rachel knew that Blaise's words were true. At last, she would be free to face her future with love, hope, and Christian. She lifted her head and looked up at Blaise's smiling face.

"I'm gonna be all right. Right?"

"You're gonna be super. But first things first. How long before you can get out of this place?" he asked.

Suddenly, the realization of where she was and what had to be done occurred to her.

"I guess the best person to ask is Dr. October, and I don't think he's here today." She hesitated, and then, as though jabbed with a pin, she stepped back away from Blaise.

"Let's call the nurse's desk and find out for certain."

Blaise could see Rachel's excitement. Even though he knew he wouldn't be the one to spend the rest of his life with her, he was content to see her this happy.

"Hello, this is Rachel Radcliffe. Is Dr. October in the hospital today?" The nurse on duty said she'd check, and after a few seconds, she returned to the phone.

"Yes, he's here, Ms. Radcliffe." Rachel smiled and asked the nurse if she would locate him and ask him to see her.

"I'll page him for you, but it will take a few minutes. Are you all right, Ms. Radcliffe? This isn't an emergency call, is it?"

Rachel responded quickly that it was not, but that she'd appreciate hearing from him before he left the hospital for the weekend.

"All right," responded the nurse, "I'll page him for you."

In the meantime, Rachel and Blaise sat and talked about all that happened, and as they recalled each event, Blaise could see that Rachel was beginning to calm down. The pressures of the past were being replaced by the excitement of the future.

"I don't really think they can keep me here much longer. Do you?"

"We'll have to wait and see, Ray babe. Although, from what I understand, their main concern was that you get enough rest to overcome the severity of your fatigue. But I've never been good at second-guessing, and I don't think my record's about to change."

"Maybe, all my prayers are going to be answered." Rachel smiled.

"Well, I'd say the Big Guy is definitely listening. You're looking better already."

Rachel's faith had always been such a large part of her life, and she was always interested in how others perceived God. Blaise was no exception. There was a period of silence, and out of nowhere Rachel spoke up.

"I wonder how Corey is doing?" Blaise's expression turned to one of absolute surprise and shock.

"Oh, boy. Where did that come from?"

"I don't know. I guess I feel somehow responsible for the upheaval in all of our lives. Corey included." Blaise shook his head in amazement.

"Only you, sweet Ray, only you! I'd bet good money that he's already cozy with some other unassuming lady, and I hope he doesn't put her through the same rigors. Hmmm, . . . Hmmm, . . . my head hurts when I think about that guy." Rachel looked at Blaise as he rubbed his head.

"Well, dear heart, if it's any consolation at all, his act of kindness in covering your hospital bill showed that he at least accepted responsibility and was sorry for his terrible act of violence. We humans are capable of all kinds of mistakes, but the ones who accept their shortcomings and try to resolve them are the ones who have a shot at healing and redemption."

Blaise agreed with her, and while Corey's show of sorrow for his misdeeds against him ended on a good note, he wasn't as positive about the lasting effects of his involvement with Rachel.

"Time is the healer," Rachel said, "and while it may not seem fast enough, at least we should try to leave all past occurrences with a good feeling. I wish him no ill, and if he managed to learn something from our relationship and your altercation with him, then perhaps we all have a shot at some happiness."

Blaise was about to respond to Rachel, when the door to her room opened. Dr. October came in and smiled at both of them.

"You rang, madam," he chuckled.

Rachel was more than just a little excited about the possibility of going home, and she blurted it out without even saying hello to him.

"I'm ready to go home, and I wanted to know if I could do so today."

Dr. October was pretty unreadable. He wasn't really too surprised at his patient's expression of joy at the prospect of leaving these surroundings.

"Well, well, I guess my first question would be, do you think, and more importantly, do you feel as though you're ready to go? And next, why so quickly?"

Rachel heard the questions, and without too much forethought responded.

"Yes to your first question. Great to your second question, and because of the answers to one and two, they should answer your third question." She chuckled as she looked at his face for some glimmer of approval.

Dr. October appeared to be processing the request, then sighed and smiled.

"All right. Now, since you obviously want my consent, I feel it's my duty to let you know my thoughts about your impromptu request. However, I'm afraid I'll have to ask your visitor to leave so I can share some of my observations and diagnoses with you in private."

Blaise stood up immediately and said he'd be happy to wait in the visitors' waiting room down the hall.

"Thank you, Blaise. I'll let you know what's going on as soon as we're through talking."

After Blaise left the room, Rachel's heart began to beat a little faster as she anticipated Dr. October's response.

"First of all, Rachel, I must tell you that I'm encouraged by your expressed feelings of well-being and your decision to leave here. I would be remiss in my service as a doctor if I did not wish that scenario for all my patients. My concerns are based on questions in my own mind relative to why this sudden request and whether or not your decision may have been influenced by someone else."

Rachel breathed deeply as she thought about this. She could understand his concern about the suddenness, but his concern about being influenced by someone else was most perceptive. Christian's reassurances were compelling, and the thought of the start of a new life was extremely exciting.

"You do your job extremely well, Dr. October, and your concern is most genuinely appreciated and right on the money. I'd be a barefaced liar if I denied that my decision was not influenced by someone else. Truth is, this particular someone has had a tremendous impact on my life, and if I hadn't collapsed so unexpectedly, I would probably be with him right now."

He sat at the table and looked down at the file he brought with him covering Rachel's case. After a few minutes, he raised his head and looked directly at her.

"While I may not know you that well, Rachel, I can tell you that during our few brief sessions, I've perceived that you do have some problems in your personal relationships. And what I'd like to prevent is the continuation of those problems in the future. Just your most recent decision to leave a relationship of fifteen years has catapulted you into a new situation miles away from your home base, and I can't help but feel that the young man who brought you in is somehow also involved in your life beyond just friendship."

Rachel was astounded by Dr. October's deductions and amazed at the accuracy of his perceptions about Blaise.

"You're batting about a thousand at this point, and, in fact, I'm getting the distinct impression that you can probably read my mind and almost predict my next move. Right?"

Dr. October detected a bit of sarcasm. in Rachel's tone, but he passed it off as part of her excitement and obvious impatience to get out of the hospital.

"I can understand how you'd come to that conclusion, Rachel, but I hope you know that my treatment of your condition is in no way meant to be divisive, nor is it intended to try to control or dissuade your decisions. Obviously, I cannot read your mind; being able to deduce from a set of circumstances one's probable direction does not make me clairvoyant." He hesitated for a moment. Then he sighed and smiled at her.

"Believe it or not, I want you to be happy and free to make your own decisions. I'd be less than professional or compassionate. if I tried to keep anyone from leading a healthy and free life."

Rachel felt almost ashamed of her brash response and she apologized for her sassy attitude.

"I don't know what's making me like this. Perhaps you're closer to the truth about my condition than I realized. Believe me, the last thing I need right now is to venture off on one more failed relationship. By nature, I'm not a dawdler, and I've always considered myself to be an optimistic and caring person. But when I act as poorly as I did just a few minutes ago, it gives me pause. Please tell me this is not uncommon in a situation like mine. I do so want to live the rest of my life on a more even keel. If you know how to help me do that, please tell me now. If this is truly love for me, it will stand the test of time."

Dr. October's smile was almost as therapeutic as his counsel. He stood up and walked over to Rachel.

"You're a very bright and vital young woman, Rachel. And it's not uncommon that you find yourself in this dilemma. You pretty much summed up your own condition when you admitted to being on an emotional roller coaster. As for an 'even keel,' I don't know if anyone ever achieves that nautical dream. At least not for any long period of time."

Rachel listened intently as he continued.

"Unfortunately, there aren't any easy solutions. Our problem here is relatively minor as compared to some of the other possibilities. I personally feel that you went off the track slightly, but I believe with some rest and some adjustment of your priorities, you can get past this bottleneck. My main concern is your well-being and your ability to get on with your life as quickly and as healthily as possible." He sat down next to Rachel and proceeded with his comments.

"The questions I'd like you to ask yourself are these: How important is it that I leave here today? What will happen if I do? And if I don't? How much of that decision is mine or someone else's? And, finally, is this what I want, or what I think someone else wants? The answers to all these questions are extremely important because they involve *your* well being. Not someone else's. If leaving here today jeopardizes your health and your future, who's going to be best served as a result of that? Would someone who truly loves you ask you to put yourself at risk just to be with you?"

Suddenly, Rachel was seeing where Dr. October was going with this scenario. Not anything different than she'd advise a friend of hers in similar circumstances. He was right, and she knew it.

"Sounds pretty sensible to me, and the bottom line here has to be what will work best for me. It's the one thing I've always pushed aside, and it's probably the main reason I'm here today. But I've got to be honest, Dr. October, I'm scared to death of the consequences of my decision. What if I lost Christian? What if I never meet anyone like him again?"

Dr. October could see the fear in her eyes, and he placed his hand on hers.

"What if you're setting yourself up for some unrealistic goals? And what if you leave now and the relationship doesn't work out? You can 'what if' yourself to death, but first of all, you must choose what's best for you, and that has to be your good health. Playing the 'if' game, let's assume what would happen if you don't get well. Nothing matters then, does it? But if you walk away from here healed and healthier, and the love you long for so desperately is still there, then its worth will be confirmed. Conversely, if it's gone, you probably didn't have it to begin with. Falling in love with love is distinctly different than falling in love with someone. Given your past history, I'm also concerned about whether or not you can see the difference."

Wow, thought Rachel, *that's pretty blatant. However, I can't be sure that he's not right.* She thought for a while and then responded.

"How does anyone really know when they're in love with someone? As far as I can remember, in talking with people who proclaimed to be in love, it was something like flying without an airplane. Hearing bells when there weren't any around. Light-headedness and blurred judgment. To be honest, Dr. October, the last time I experienced those symptoms, I had the flu."

Dr. October laughed out loud.

"Great analogy, and perhaps if we looked at those symptoms a little more closely, we'd be better off considering it to be the flu and getting proper treatment. It certainly would save a lot of heartbreak. Perhaps your saving grace, Rachel, is your humor. Many times, we tend to microscopically examine our feelings, our judgment, and our behavior. Being able to laugh at oneself, and learning not to take ourselves too seriously has helped many a person during times of stress and sheer frustration. You possess that characteristic, and so you can use it as part of the therapy required to adjust to your own lifestyle. Accepting 'what is' and working toward 'what could be' is sometimes a mile apart or a lifetime. We all have the power to change our lives. But first, we must know who we are and where we want to go. Confusion is not uncommon as we grow and mature. Then the choices and directions increase.

"I don't believe your setback is a serious one. Frankly, figuratively speaking, I think you just 'ran out of gas.' You took on more than you could handle, and you forgot two very critical items: sustenance and rest. When your mental and physical faculties were pushed beyond their limits, everything just shut down."

Rachel could not unlock her eyes from his. It was almost mesmerizing listening to him. He was so wise, so charismatic, and so credible. He continued.

"My own personal recommendation for your future good health would be that you not rush into anything at this time. You must be selfish and put yourself first here. This, from talking to you, is your first and most important hurdle. But getting proper rest and good nutrition is what I'm going to prescribe. As for any drug therapy, I'd only consider a sleeping pill if it would assist you in getting some sleep. Some exercise, a sensible eating regimen, and a reduction in your work load couldn't hurt.

"Finally, Rachel, you really don't need my approval to leave the hospital. You have the right to sign yourself out. The only way I could keep you here would be if, in my professional opinion, you might be a danger to yourself or others. Neither case is true here."

Rachel smiled and breathed a sigh of relief.

"You make it all sound so easy."

"In most cases, it is. We are the captains of our fate, and the course we chart can be simple or complicated. The number-one thing to remember is that we must first know our capabilities and our goals. If we don't set those goals too high or too far out of reach, we can achieve them. One must be truthful to oneself. You won't get anywhere if you start out by fooling yourself. You may appreciate what I do and, for some reason, believe you're qualified to do the same; however, I wouldn't sign up for a surgical procedure based on that foolish assumption."

"I love the way you make your point!" Rachel chuckled. She sighed again and asked the next obvious question.

"So, I can leave here today? Provided I follow the guidelines you've just recommended."

"Yes, you can, and you can whether or not you choose to take my advice or not. I merely am trying to help you get through this glitch."

Rachel stood up, then sat back down. She looked at Dr. October's handsome face. His eyes said so much. The knowledge in his brain and the love in his heart were a priceless combination for a doctor.

"Will I ever see you again?" she whispered.

"I hope not!" he said quite succinctly. "You mustn't misunderstand my response, Rachel. One of the many goals in my professional life is to ensure that my patients receive my very best diagnosis and treatment—and total independence of me. That means a parting of the ways eventually. It's sometimes emotional and extremely difficult to uphold those standards, but my first obligation is to the well-being of my patient, and when someone I've treated no longer needs me or my service, it's a happy day for me."

Two tears came streaming down Rachel's face as once again she was going to have to say good-bye to someone she had come to admire and care for. Dr. October was touched by her emotions, and he walked over to comfort her.

"We never truly say good-bye to those people who have made a mark in our lives. We carry them with us in our hearts and in our memories."

Rachel blew her nose and tried to compose herself.

"I'll never forget you—I won't. I don't have a clue at the moment about just where my life is headed. But for the first time in a very long time, my heart has been talking to me, and I think I'm going to listen and follow it. Maybe it's my turn to grasp the rainbow."

"A rainbow?" he queried and smiled. "I like that, Rachel. I like that a lot, and I'll pray that you get yours real soon."

He embraced Rachel and told her she should get her things together, and he would get her release papers ready. When he left the room, she felt almost weightless. A feeling that was wonderfully exhilarating, but also a little frightening. The anchor and security of the hospital were being untied and she would be leaving here soon—on her own.

"Oh, my goodness," she exclaimed. "I must hurry and tell Blaise the good news." She opened her door and met Blaise halfway down the hall. He was coming to her room after he saw Dr. October leave.

"I can go home!" she cried. "I'm going home, Blaise." He hugged her, and they walked back to her room.

"That's wonderful, Ray babe, that's truly wonderful."

Rachel looked up at her tall friend and cried once again, only this time they were tears of joy.

Twenty-three

In another part of Grosse Pointe, Master Randy had been successful in talking his mother into bringing him to visit Rachel. Estelle told him she would wait in the lobby after she accompanied him to Rachel's floor. There was a hospital rule prohibiting minors from visiting patients without an adult, but Randy was a bit more mature than most his age. He convinced himself that since Rachel's condition was not classed as "surgical" or "serious," he would win any challenge to the contrary.

When Master Randy stood at Rachel's door, he could hear voices, so he listened for a moment. Blaise asked Rachel what she was going to do first.

"I'm going to get a rainbow." She laughed.

"A rainbow?" Blaise asked. "Okay, I'll play this silly game. Does Jacobson's carry them? They have everything else!" They both laughed.

"Ohh," she sighed. "Oh, Blaise, I think I know where I can find mine!"

Blaise knew she was alluding to New York and Christian. So, since he told her he'd help her, he decided that now was the time.

"Must be a Big Apple rainbow. We don't get too many rainbows in Michigan this time of year."

Master Randy, as though pricked with a pin, bolted down the hall and rang for the elevator. Estelle was sitting in the lobby, reading a magazine, when she saw Randy come rushing at her.

"She's going home, Mother, and she's going to New York to get a rainbow."

Estelle looked at Randy as though he were losing it.

"Just a minute, Randall. What did you say? Only this time slowly, please!"

"The cool lady was talking to Mr. Kinley when I got to her room. She said she was going home, and then she was going to get a rainbow. Mr. Kinley said that the rainbow must be in the Big Apple. Ahhhh, . . . that's New York City, Mother," he grinned, "and, then I left because I didn't want to be caught eavesdropping . . . ahhh, . . . I mean standing outside her door."

Estelle smiled at her young son's blathering. She put her hands on his shoulders and looked at him.

"Well, now, that's a nice piece of news, but under the circumstances, I don't think we should pass it along until we confirm it with a more credible source." Her expression marked by her eyebrows almost touching her hairline and a look that Randy had learned to recognize from prior incidents sent a message that he had better keep this "under wraps." His father could confirm or deny this little tidbit, and in the meantime, he'd have to quell the inner urge to rush to the nearest public telephone and call his Uncle Christian.

"A rainbow, Mom. What do you think she meant? Uhhh, I know she probably didn't mean that literally, but what's the metaphoric connection here?"

Estelle was smiling even more broadly now as she observed the curious workings of her young son's inquisitive and very romantic mind.

"You know, Randy, I've never been really good at second-guessing, and my good judgment tells me that I shouldn't start now. Furthermore," she emphasized, " I don't believe it's a good idea for you either. We will know about all this in good time."

Randy was smart enough to comprehend his mother's answer but not totally convinced that this was the most interesting approach.

"Ah, all right, Mom, but if Sherlock Holmes thought like that, none of his cases would have been solved."

Estelle shook her head in amazement. She mused that young Randall did have a flair for the dramatic and an appropriate sense of humor. His sense of timing, in fact, was almost uncanny at times.

"Well, Sherlock Holmes happens to be a fictitious character, and we're dealing with very real people. I don't see the analogy. But I will give you credit for thinking so quickly. Beyond that, I'm afraid we're just going to have to wait this situation out. Is that clear, Randy?"

Randy knew his mother well enough to know that when she used this particular tone in her voice, he was much better off just dropping the subject.

"I guess that means any plans I had to call Uncle Christian are dashed!"

Estelle's rather stern expression was enough to let Randy know that her response was still the same. No! He sighed and while it appeared to Estelle that this situation had been resolved, Randy was thinking about his Uncle Christian and how pleased he'd be to hear this latest news about Rachel.

"Okay," he said, "I'll drop it for now, but, Mother, Uncle Christian should be told about the cool lady's release. Don't you think?"

Estelle was familiar with her son's persistence and was most understanding about his usual overexuberance where Rachel was concerned.

"When your father confirms what you just heard, I will permit you to call your uncle, but not until then. This is a serious situation and perhaps a very personal one to Rachel. You don't want to end up pleasing Uncle Christian, and devastating your friend, do you?"

Randy knew she was right, but logic didn't seem to be appropriate in this case.

"Yeah, uh, I mean, yes, I suppose you're right, but we're talking about affairs of the heart. No one in love uses logic. Do they?"

Estelle chuckled at her son's observations. As funny as it sounded, she had to agree.

"All right, for the sake of argument, let's say you're right. It still doesn't change that decisions of judgment should be determined by the parties who are in love."

Randy raised his eyebrows in near frustration. He knew he'd not win this time. He'd never in the past, so why should he expect to now?

"All right, Mother, you win! But, someday, I'll have the pleasure of winning one time. Let's hope that my deferring to your judgment doesn't cause undue problems for Uncle Christian and Rachel"

Estelle listened to the serious tone in Randy's voice, and while she found some truth in his assumptions, experience had taught her to never interfere in someone else's love relationship.

"I realize it's difficult for you to trust me in some of these things, and, yes, the day will come soon enough when you'll be able to override my and your father's advice. But I'm afraid that that time is not here yet, so I'm standing firm on this one."

Randy sat down next to his mother while they decided what they would do next. Estelle thought she'd call Randall to see if he knew anything about Rachel's release. She told Randy to wait a minute while she used one of the interhospital phones. As she neared the phone, she heard someone calling her name.

"Mrs. Markham. Mrs. Markham!"

Estelle turned toward the direction of the calling voice and quickly recognized Dr. Mannix as he approached her.

"Hi, Bill."

"Hello, Estelle, I thought it was you." He was a little out of breath, and after a moment or two, he continued. "Have you heard about Rachel Radcliffe's release? Dr. October is working on the paperwork right now." Estelle turned to look over at Randy, who was watching them. "Honestly, I just found out about it a few minutes ago. Did Randall call you?" he asked.

Estelle was a little nervous about telling him how she actually found out about it, so she just answered no.

Dr. Mannix did not pursue this. He expressed his pleasure about hearing that Rachel was doing well enough to go home.

"It's always a wonderful day when a patient recovers and can go home and go on with his life. This is good news, and I know you are all happy, as well."

"It's wonderful news," she replied, "and I guess we only have to wait now to see if Rachel needs us for anything."

"Well, as a matter of fact, I don't think so. Her friend, Blaise Kinley, has been with her most of the morning, and I believe he'll probably take her home. I can check that out, though, if you want me to, Estelle."

Even though Estelle knew that Blaise was there and that he and Rachel were good friends, she felt a twinge of resentment.

"Well, then, I guess Randy and I will go about our business. I'm certain with all the excitement, we can see Rachel when she's home and settled down a little."

"Are you sure?" Dr. Mannix inquired. "I can find out relatively quickly just what the situation is." He smiled at Estelle and could see that she had lost her interest to wait.

"No, thank you, I think we'll just say hi to Randall and get on with our day. I do appreciate the update and knowing that she has someone here to take her home."

"You're welcome, and I do hope it's not too long before we see each other again."

Estelle assured him that with all their common medical friends, it wouldn't be very long. She returned to where Randy was sitting and told him about her conversation with Dr. Mannix.

Randy was a little perturbed upon hearing this news.

"So, you see, now Mr. Kinley will definitely get the inside track!"

Estelle was upset at his response, and she chastised him for his insensitivity.

"Enough of this, Randy. Mr. Kinley happens to be a very good friend and neighbor of Rachel's and I think your insinuation about any competition for her affection is rude and unwarranted."

Randy wasn't having a good day at all, and it appeared that it was not going to get much better.

"I'm sorry, Mother. I didn't mean to be disrespectful or rude. And I do like Mr. Kinley. But being a friend and neighbor gives him an advantage that might upset her relationship with Uncle Christian. She's *our* cool lady, not *his!*"

Estelle chose not to add fuel to Randy's fire and she merely shrugged her shoulders and beckoned him to come with her. After calling Randall and asking him if he'd like to have dinner at the Yacht Club tonight, she and Randy left Saint John's and headed for home.

Rachel couldn't believe it; she was going home. She was totally elated to hear Dr. October say that she was fine and ready to recuperate away from there. *Going home!* What a beautiful thought.

Blaise, on the other hand, was scurrying about her room making certain that all her personal belongings were on the bed or close by.

"I'd better change my clothes," she said. "Would you mind waiting outside for a couple of minutes, Blaise?"

"Not at all, Ray, not at all! In fact, I think I'll go downstairs and bring the car around to the back door."

Rachel grinned and put up both her hands.

"Oh, well, dear heart, I think that might be just a little premature. Let's wait until Dr. October comes back with my release."

"Imagine," Blaise laughed, "you're the one getting out of here, and I'm more disoriented than you."

Rachel smiled and reached for her hairbrush and began brushing vigorously.

"I'm pretty excited, make no mistake about it. It feels so wonderful to think about getting on with my life."

Blaise walked over to her and hugged her.

"This could be the beginning of a very special time for you, sweetie. Promise me that you'll rest for a little while and take some time to get back on your feet before you blast off into the future."

Rachel hugged him and assured him that she wouldn't be so foolish as to mess up this new beginning.

"Don't worry, dear heart, I'm not going to blow this new chance. I have so many new plans, so many things to do. It takes a lot to reach a rainbow. I don't want to miss one glorious step along the way."

"Ring out the old and bring in the new," exclaimed Blaise.

Rachel suddenly turned around as though someone had pulled a switch and turned off her elation. She focused on Blaise. This was not a new beginning for him. This was an ending that would be most difficult for him.

"How selfish of me, my dear Blaise," she said sadly. "Here I am extolling my happiness, while you, on the contrary, begin some suffering over something of which you have no control. Maybe I'm still sick!" she said blatantly. "What kind of compassion is this? I must be deranged!" She sighed and shook her head in total disgust.

"Whoa! Wait a minute!" Blaise interjected. "Where does it say that the beautiful and happy Rachel has to feel sorry for her best friend? I couldn't be happier for you, you know that!" He grabbed Rachel by both shoulders and turned her around to face him. "Listen, Ray babe, this isn't the way I dreamed things would work out, and believe me, I struggled through many a time when I wanted desperately to tell you about this facade. But you know something? Things have a way of working out for the best, and we can't sit around bemoaning our fate and muttering about what could have been."

Rachel was listening as she always had to Blaise's sound and caring advice. He continued.

"There's a guy in New York, and a pretty decent one at that, who's very much in love with you. He's been suffering like the rest of us. He lost someone he loved very dearly, and he lost her totally. At least, for me, I'll get to see you achieve happiness and finally getting what you've been searching for since the day I met you. An honest to goodness faithful man who love's you as deeply as you do him. My life's not over, Rachel, and I don't want you to get on with yours believing it was at my expense. We take chances and risks. Sometimes they work out, and sometimes they don't. However, we're all survivors, and don't you forget it!"

Rachel was trying desperately not to cry, but to no avail. Two of the biggest tears came streaming down her face, and she wiped them away quickly.

"You are so special to me, my darling Blaise. You've taught me many things during our relationship. But perhaps the one thing you taught me better than anyone else was how to love. And for that, I will carry you in my heart forever."

Blaise's sense of humor was his saving grace, and right now things weren't going to be any different.

"That wasn't exactly what I had in mind, but I'll settle for that!"

The door opened and Dr. October entered with papers in his hand.

"You're free to go, Rachel," he said, looking very pleased.

"Dr. Mannix and I agree that you'll need a couple of days' rest before you jump-start back into your life. But he and I are convinced that you are well enough to leave the hospital and recuperate at home."

"That's wonderful, Dr. October, and, again, I don't know how to thank you enough for all your help. You and Dr. Mannix have given me a new perspective concerning myself and my future. I guess the rest is up to me."

Blaise walked over and extended his hand to the good doctor.

"I'd like to thank you, as well. You may have deduced that this lady is pretty special to a lot of people. Being able to take her home after her recent ordeal is a present for all of us. You're okay, doc!"

Blaise could not have been more sincere in his declaration of gratitude, and Dr. October was quite humble in accepting his kind words.

"You know, Mr. Kinley, so many times we doctors are thanked for performing incredible life-saving feats with surgery, astounding therapy sessions, and prescribing miraculously healing drugs. In many instances, the patient's will to get well is as remarkable and equally as incredible and astounding. Rachel's positive attitude and her deep and abiding faith have brought about this day just as certainly as my treatment."

Rachel and Blaise both smiled as they listened to Dr. October's words. But now, Rachel thought, she must say good-bye to this man who had, for a very brief period in time, touched her very soul with his gentleness and professional acumen.

"I couldn't possibly say good-bye to you, Dr. October. There must be another phrase that's not quite so final."

Dr. October knew this would be emotional for Rachel and he struggled for something that would make this moment easier for her.

"How about, 'so long for now'? It's a phrase I've always liked and one that promises a future encounter."

Rachel liked it, too.

"So long, then, and God bless you wherever your path may lead."

"Thank you, Rachel. Now, get your things together, and I'll have the nurse bring you a wheelchair. It's hospital policy." He smiled and nodded approvingly at her and then turned and left the room. Rachel knew she would never see him again, but she also knew she would never forget him.

Even though it had been only a month, Rachel felt a certain sadness in leaving Saint John's. She had come to learn, firsthand, why they enjoyed such a revered reputation. Walking around the room and double-checking drawers and cabinets took more time than she'd assumed, but when she had finally felt confident that she was ready to leave, she sat down on the chair next to the window. Soon she would be on her own again, back home in her own bedroom and free to walk the wonderful streets of her beautiful Grosse

Pointe. She sighed deeply and stood up and walked over to the door.

"I'm ready," she proclaimed to Blaise. "Let's go, let's go home!"

Blaise grabbed everything he could and still managed to take hold of Rachel's arm. As they opened the door, one of the nurses was coming down the hall with a wheelchair.

"Here you are, Ms. Radcliffe. Please sit down, and I'll take you downstairs to the exit." Rachel liked this particular nurse. She was one of the older ones; and her compassion and attention to her patients was a badge of honor she wore proudly.

Blaise interjected and asked if he could take Rachel from here.

"Sure can. Just make certain she goes from the chair into her vehicle and then bring the chair back into the hospital."

"I can do that," Blaise nodded, "and I promise to take good care of both Ms. Radcliffe and the chair."

They all chuckled and as Rachel sat down, with her belongings on her lap, Blaise pushed her down the hallway past the nurses' station and toward the elevator.

"Good-bye, everyone," she waved as they passed the nursing staff. They waved back and wished her luck. Blaise pushed the "down" button, and they stood there silently waiting. Suddenly, the red light lit up, and a bell rang on the elevator as the door opened. Rachel and Blaise were both stunned to see Corey Davidson standing inside the elevator.

"Corey!" Rachel blurted out, almost at the same time that he called out her name.

"Rachel, what's wrong with you? Why are you here?" Corey looked very upset.

"I'm just fine, Corey. In fact, I'm on my way home. But, what . . . what are you doing here?"

Blaise was ready to say something to him, but Corey immediately responded to Rachel's question.

"It's Bill. He had a heart attack two days ago, and he's still in ICU."

"Oh, my God," Rachel cried out, bringing her hand to her mouth. "Is he going to be all right, Corey? He's much too young to be experiencing this kind of problem." Rachel no sooner finished that sentence when she realized how foolish it must have sounded. "Oh, my, I really mean, I can't believe it. Bill always ate so nutritiously and was such a proponent of daily exercise. What happened?"

Corey was touched by her concern, but not surprised. Right now, he was really more curious about what brought Rachel here.

"It's incredible, as I think back. We were sitting in the conference room, waiting for an international call, and Bill got up from his chair to get closer to the telephone. He was up, and then he collapsed right by his chair. I cried out, and I remember having a difficult time getting out of my chair in order to get to him. Thank God, he didn't hit the credenza or anything else when he fell. I called to him and felt for a pulse on the side of his neck. I found one, but it was weak. I then dialed 911. After that, I started to perform CPR. The rescue guys said I probably saved his life. You have no idea how grateful I was that I took that CPR-First Aid course last spring. They've been evaluating him ever since he was brought in. The possibilities are angioplasty or bypass. Right now, they're still trying to get him stabilized and prepared for either. I'm telling you," he continued "I've had just about enough medical situations in the past few months. Now, I find you here, Rachel, and this is the proverbial straw for me."

Rachel and Blaise felt sorry for Corey. He was visibly shaken by the current series of events, and, once again, these three people were thrown together under dramatic circumstances. When a couple of other people walked up and stood by the elevator, the three of them realized they had been holding it up for quite some time.

"Sorry," Blaise apologized as he pulled Rachel's wheelchair away from the elevator door. Corey stepped out so that everyone waiting could get on. They went over to the visitor's lounge next to the elevator.

Corey couldn't stand it any longer.

"What's wrong with you, Rachel? Why are you here?"

Rachel could see that Corey was genuinely concerned, and she tried to explain how she got to Saint John's. Blaise wasn't as diplomatic as Rachel; he started to admonish Corey for being instrumental in her setback.

"I suppose you're right, Blaise. God only knows I've put the two of you through enough agony. And now I could lose the best friend and business partner I've ever had. If anything happens to Bill, I don't know what I'll do."

Rachel could tell that Corey was not his usual sure and cocky self. He looked almost ten years older since the last time she'd seen him. His brow was wrinkled, and his hair had grayed considerably. Not only that, but his expression was one of deep concern. His eyes reflected the fear he was experiencing.

Rachel, in a gesture of compassion, extended her hand to him and tried to console him.

"You know he's in good hands, Corey. This is a fine hospital. Their advanced cardiovascular technology is known worldwide. Just be thankful that you were with him and that you got him the assistance he needed so quickly. Believe me, this could have had a much sadder ending had you not been with him. You're a good friend to him, Corey, and Bill is a survivor. He'd have to be to work with you for so many years!"

Corey's face lit up and he laughed. His eyes suddenly were sparkling, and if Rachel didn't know better, she could have sworn she saw a tear in his eye.

"I've missed your humor and your compassion, Rachel. There's been a huge void in my life since we parted. I suppose that 'what goes around comes around' is pretty apropos, huh?"

Blaise couldn't take his eyes off Rachel, his number-one concern being to get her out of here and on her way home.

"Look, Corey," Blaise interrupted, "I'm sorry about Bill, and I certainly hope he pulls through this tough spot, but I've got to get this lady into my car and home ASAP. She's had quite an ordeal, and she needs to get home and in bed."

Rachel pulled back her hand and reached back to touch Blaise's.

"He's been my guardian now for quite some time. Couldn't have come through this without him. I'm sorry, Corey, to leave so abruptly. Tell you what, call me when you know more about Bill's condition, and I'll tell you about me. Deal?"

"Deal," Corey responded. "Are you sure, kitten—" He stopped in midsentence; the look on Rachel's face was about as descriptive as any words she might have offered. "I know," Corey said. "Guess, I'm a creature of habit. Can't stop sticking my foot in my mouth!"

Rachel smiled, and Blaise wasn't amused. At least they parted ways with two out of three of them smiling. Blaise was both concerned and pleased as he opened the door of his car and helped Rachel from the wheelchair into the front seat. Blaise quickly returned the wheelchair inside the hospital doors and rushed over to get into the car.

Driving away from the hospital was the most exhilarating feeling that Rachel had experienced during the past few weeks. She watched each car that passed them as Blaise turned down Moross and headed toward the river. It was quiet in the car except for some music playing on the radio. It was almost too quiet, but Rachel wasn't going to break this spell. It was too wonderful, and she didn't want anything to spoil the moment. She was going home!

Twenty-four

The next couple of weeks passed quickly. Getting back to some sort of normalcy was a much more difficult task than Rachel had imagined. While getting any rest in the hospital was a near impossibility, Rachel discovered that once the word was out that she was out of the hospital and back in circulation, her days of afternoon naps and sleeping in in the morning quickly became past tense. Christian called almost every day. Amber called every other day, and Blaise had put his job on the shelf in order to help Rachel get back on her feet and baby-step her way back to her career. Mrs. Longley had sent her beautiful flowers and fruit. Her neighbors, Mrs. Charboneau and Mrs. Martinez on both sides of her, sent soup and freshly baked bread almost every day. Then, of course, there was Master Randy, who made it a point of riding his bike over to see her after school.

Rachel was content to be back in the surroundings she loved among those people who loved her so dearly. Moments when no one was around and she could sit in her living room and reflect were spent thinking about her future. What was next in her life, and how long would she suppress her desire to run to Christian and begin a new dimension in their lives.

This time, fulfillment of this dream, would uproot her from her precious surroundings and propel her into a world unfamiliar, but so tempting. If anyone was aware of not being able to have it both ways, it was she. Some nice things happened, like Bill Jacoby's recovery, and even some brief exchanges with Corey had proven therapeutic. But keeping time and standing still were never areas in which Rachel stayed for too long. She thought about Zena and Dr. October. She had been given another chance, but how long would it take before she could be absolutely certain of her next move and the rest of her life. Perhaps life was never meant to be that automatic. She was ready to find out.

Amber, in recent conversations, had become almost relentless in her pleadings for Rachel to come to New York. The Domanis had offered her their home so that she could convalesce and get more acclimated to New York. It sounded wonderful, but every time she considered it, Blaise's name would come to mind, and she would think about his loneliness once she was gone. Evidently, she was not quite ready to make that move.

Christian's involvement in directing "Cinema" grew daily. Soon, he was even sleeping at the theater. Auditions and rehearsals had become his life, and the times he'd set aside to call Rachel became less frequent. His last call was spent almost entirely in begging her to come to New York. While he was as certain of their love as she, he could tell that a geographical move to New York would not be as simple for her as it was for him. Consequently, he decided not to pursue that avenue for a bit and just keep reassuring her of his love. He knew how much she loved the city of her childhood and putting himself in her shoes was not too difficult.

However, Master Randy never gave up in his pursuit to get Rachel to become his aunt, and eventually Estelle gave up trying to defuse Randy's fervor for getting his cool lady married to his Uncle Christian. Since Rachel left the hospital, Randy called his uncle regularly. The weather in New York and Grosse Pointe was fairly close in temperature, and the days were getting shorter and cooler.

The routine of working every day quickly became the main priority in Rachel's schedule. And for some strange reason, the dreams of finding her rainbow and thinking only about her new love were pushed on the back burner. The consequences of busy schedules for both Rachel and Christian brought about a sense of complacency, and the path of least resistance became most appealing as one day passed after another. With Christmas only a couple of months away, her business increased and her phone rang constantly.

As the frequency of hearing from Christian diminished, she naturally thought that his feelings for her had waned, as well. No matter how reassuring Amber tried to be when they spoke, Rachel's barometer indicated a "cooling" since her release from the hospital. Her thoughts about this romantic involvement with Christian were overridden by her real world. The bill from Saint John's was almost as much as the mortgage balance on her house, and paying it in full just about depleted her savings. So her financial health understandably became her first priority. If by some twist of fate she would ultimately end up on her own, then she would have to make darned certain that she was financially secure.

Getting back her physical and mental stability had been a real struggle, and the thought of embarking on yet another new relationship left her quite unsettled. This disquieting effect caused her to concentrate on her life just one day at a time.

No one was more aware of her complacency than Blaise. His mixed emotions about her current situation and his unchanged feelings for her bothered him immensely. Since their last conversation at Saint John's, Blaise knew that he certainly didn't have the inside track with her, but did he want to interject himself in anything that would cause her to move closer to Christian? He was almost as complacent as she, and it was almost like old times, except now he could be himself. Living next door to one another, he was aware of her comings and goings, and their occasional dining dates were always pleasant and fun.

However, Blaise knew Rachel too well to believe that this would last. His position became one of conscience. Was he content to just watch her glide through her life, unchallenged and unromantically involved, or was be to be the catalyst to get her out of the doldrums? Once again, Blaise's desires came into conflict with what was perhaps best for his friend. The one thing that made it almost impossible to decide was that Rachel was getting more beautiful every day. Her recovery had once again put the blush on her cheeks and the sparkle back in her eyes. Blaise's own dilemma brought him almost into a state of inertia. Perhaps doing nothing was the best decision—but for whom?

In Westbury, Amber's life had been raised a couple of notches. With Tony's law practice growing and Marisa and Carlo's involvement with "Cinema," she hardly had the time to do much else other than run errands and cook. The excitement of "Cinema" had kept the Domani household electrically charged. Though Carlo had made up his mind to follow in his father's steps and pursue the practice of law, he admitted that he was enjoying being a part of this Broadway extravaganza. Marisa, on the other hand, was in her element. Working and rehearsing every day gave her exposure to all the other aspects of the dramatic arts. This had certainly become the chance of a lifetime, and she intended to savor each and every delicious moment of it.

Amber surmised by Rachel's lack of communication that something had changed regarding her and Christian's relationship. With Marisa and Carlo jabbering about "Cinema" every day, Amber could tell that Christian's consuming quest for yet another hit was paramount in his life. As much as she wanted to help her friend and change the current circumstances, she knew she was powerless to do so. Amber was wise enough to know that there was a time to interject oneself into someone else's relationship and a time to leave well enough alone. She felt that this was the time to let Rachel control what was going on in her life, and that she should wait until she was asked to get involved. Although she, like Blaise, found herself in the same kind of malaise, she knew it probably wouldn't last forever. However, since she happened to be thinking about Rachel, she picked up the telephone and punched in Rachel's number. It rang only once when Rachel answered.

"Hi, doll, how goes things?" Amber asked upon hearing Rachel's voice.

"Oh, Amber, how wonderful to hear from you. I've been thinking about you."

"Really?" Amber responded almost unbelievably. "Is everything all right, sweetie? I've not heard from you in quite a while, and I'm just a little puzzled as to why."

"Yes, uh, sure, I'm fine. Just back in the routine of pursuing my career. Time sure does fly when you're having fun, right? In fact, I was just putting together some coordinates for one of my clients, and part of the ensemble is an amber pendant. Well, you know me with word association, I saw that gem and immediately thought of you."

"So, bella, what's going on?" Amber smiled but continued to inquire. There was some hesitation in Rachel's response, and Amber knew something was going on.

"Nothing much. As I said, just working and planning, back to the old grindstone. I guess."

"But how are you feeling? I don't hear any mention of that. Are you getting some rest every day and pampering yourself, too?"

Rachel smiled at her friend's choice of words. "Pampering" was not a word that Rachel ever applied to herself, but one that Amber always used regarding the people in her life.

"As a matter of fact, I'm feeling better every day, but pampering, I don't think so. You know me, dear heart, I'm always at my best looking out for someone else. I am getting back some of my strength and drive, and the status quo doesn't seem to be such a bad place."

Amber sighed and then asked the burning question.

"How's Christian? Have you heard from him recently?"

Almost instantly, at the very utterance of his name, tears welled up in Rachel's eyes. She was surprised at her uncontrollable emotional reaction and tried to contain herself before responding.

"No, no, I haven't heard from him recently, but I can't say I blame him for not calling. I've been so wrapped up in putting together the fragments of myself since my collapse, I think he's either given up on me or has been way too busy to think about it. In either ease, I think whatever we shared during those magical few weeks is over."

"Hogwash!" replied Amber. "I absolutely refuse to believe that either of those scenarios is true. People do have other things in their lives that rise and fall on their priority list. If I thought I always had to be Tony's first priority, we would have been divorced years ago, and I never would have had Carlo and Marisa. It's a life of choices and priorities, but realistically speaking, we can't even presume to be someone's number one priority one hundred percent of the time any more than we can place anyone at the top of our own list constantly. It doesn't have a flea wing's thing to do with how we feel about anyone. It has everything to do with our ability to fit into the overall lifestyle of another. And that's never easy."

Rachel listened to her friend's philosophy and nodded her head in approval as Amber continued.

"Unfortunately, bella, your mama and papa raised you as their number-one priority, which sent you the clear message that when you love someone, they must always be number one. This is not love; this bridges on the edge of obsession and possessiveness. I'm not saying this critically. God only knows how much they loved you, bella. They adored you. As their only child, they focused all their affection and love on you. How could you believe that love was any other way. Mama DeRoca, God bless her soul, never taught you how to love, sweetie! First of all, she couldn't risk losing you to anyone else, and maybe she didn't know how, herself!"

It was as though Amber flipped a switch in Rachel's mind. Suddenly, a light went on, and she knew that Amber had hit the proverbial jackpot.

"Thank you, Amber. You may have just sprung me from a past I was bound to most of my life. You may have come upon the very essence of my emotional problems."

"Well, sweetie, I know I'm good at philosophizing, but I don't think I'm that good!" Amber began to chuckle.

"No, Amber, I'm not kidding. Honestly, when I was under treatment with Dr. October, he asked me time and time again why I always felt so inadequate, so almost incapable of loving anyone. Maybe I was avoiding it because I didn't want to disappoint or betray Mama DeRoca. As I think back, Mama consented to my marriage to Neil because she knew he would never pose a threat. He was too weak, and I eventually would end the relationship and come back to her. Oh, my God, Amber, I feel so foolish and so used. And yes, so betrayed."

"Listen, bella," Amber wiped her forehead nervously, "I didn't intend to call you and open up those emotional flood gates. I just wanted to see how you were doing, and look what I've done. God forgive me, I sure don't want you ending up hating Mama DeRoca because of something I said."

"No, no, Amber, don't worry. I could never hate my mother, but maybe now I can begin to at least understand her . . . and me!"

Amber was stunned by Rachel's revelation as a result of her conversation. Now came the even more quizzical thought. *What will Rachel do now?* Having come upon this and charged with a new brand of energy to pursue this line of thinking, what might happen when she opened more doors she may be ill-prepared to handle? Amber cautioned Rachel to deal with these feelings one day at a time.

"Please, don't try to solve all of the mysteries in your life in a day, bella! God alone knows the answer, and maybe that's the way He wants it to stay. Some things are better left alone."

"I know you're right, Amber," Rachel sighed and reluctantly agreed with her friend's rationale, "and perhaps I'll never truly understand why I must remain in the dark where love is concerned, but one very positive thing that's come out of this collapse is that I haven't had my nightmare anymore. If nothing else, I've been freed from those demons."

Amber advised that perhaps it would be better to disown it forever.

"Don't even refer to it as 'my' nightmare. Maybe the power of suggestion will help you dispel those demons once and for all. Let this be a time for rainbows, bella!"

Rachel gasped; she couldn't believe what Amber just said.

"I can't believe you said that, Amber! It's pretty eerie, since that's exactly what I told Dr. October I was going after—a rainbow!"

Amber was reeling from this entire conversation now, and the only thing she felt would be close to sanity would be to just say good-bye. But she didn't want to burst Rachel's bubble, and her sense of humor came to the rescue.

"Golly, bella, if I could be as clairvoyant with Tony's law practice, we'd be millionaires."

"Well, sweetie, I guess as friends for so many years, we almost think with one mind." Rachel laughed.

"Now," chuckled Amber, "that's a real scary thought; no one we know would ever be safe again." They both enjoyed the laughter and agreed to keep in touch more often.

"That we shall do. But in the meantime, I just might open a little side business and become a psychic."

"Not bad," responded Rachel, "a psychic named 'tomorrow,' heh, you may be on the right track!"

"Yeah, right," replied Amber, "and with my luck there'd be a train on it!"

"Enough of this frivolity," Rachel gasped. "I'll call you next week, okay?"

"Okay, bella. Take care and keep me posted on your rainbow thing."

After Rachel hung up, she thought about the rainbow and what it would take to find it. Her dreams were always about black umbrellas, and not once did she ever get beyond those faceless people. *Oh well,* she thought, *maybe tonight after work, I'll jot down a few things and see what happens.*

Not too far away in another area of Grosse Pointe, Master Randy was sitting in his room trying desperately to come up with a plan for his Uncle Christian to get that rainbow for their cool lady. *This is difficult. I know it's a metaphoric rainbow, and I'm too young to be a romantic. No experience, and I can't ask Mom or Dad. How would they know anyway. They're my parents. What could they possibly know about love? Besides, they'd only tell me to forget the whole thing. I've got to talk to Uncle Christian and soon!* The more he thought about it, the more excited he became. Finally, he could wait no longer. He picked up the telephone and punched in his uncle's number.

Christian's assistant advised Randy that he was at the theater and would probably be there until the following morning. Master Randy knew his uncle's secretary and it didn't take much coaxing to have her patch him through to Christian's cellular phone.

The rehearsals had been nonstop for the past few weeks and between costume creation, makeup artists, choreographers, and musical directors, Christian could think about nothing else. However, when his secretary advised that his one and only nephew was trying to reach him, he took the call.

"Hi, Randy. Is everything all right, sport?"

Randy was happy to hear his uncle's voice.

"Yes, sir, just great!"

"Your mother all right, and your dad?" Christian inquired.

"Yeah, oh, sure!" Randy answered. "Everything's super, Uncle Christian!" Randy could hear the music in the background, and he knew that it was difficult for his uncle to hear, much less concentrate on this call.

"Then what's going on, Randy? Why the call? You're all right, aren't you?"

Now Randy was becoming uncomfortable because he was getting the feeling that he was definitely interrupting his uncle at a very important time.

"I'm fine, Uncle Christian, but, uh, I think I may have called at a bad time !" Randy swallowed and thought about how he would somehow justify this inopportune time to call.

"Well, Randy, what is it? I'm getting pretty curious here," Christian replied, almost in an exasperated tone.

"It's about the cool lady!" Randy blurted out.

Christian stood up, almost at attention.

"Rachel . . . Rachel," he gasped. "What's wrong with Rachel?" Now Randy was beginning to perspire as his uncle's upset grew and his patience diminished.

"She's fine, Uncle Christian. It's just that I overheard something she said a while back, and I thought you'd like to know about it." The music for the rehearsal number seemed to hit a crescendo as Christian strained to hear what Randy was calling about. Something to do with Rachel.

"For goodness sake, Randall, will you get to the point!" Christian was losing his patience, which is something Randy had never witnessed before. Randy was trying desperately to think of the proper words to explain the purpose of his call.

"I'm waiting, Randy, and I'm gonna lose it here if you don't tell me about Rachel!"

Randy gulped and decided to just spit it out!

"She's going after a rainbow!" When the words came out, Randy wished he could have retrieved them and put them back in his gaping mouth.

"A what?" Christian stuttered, "Did you say a rainbow?" By this time, Christian was almost hyperventilating. He raised his hand and made a cut motion across his throat; the choreographer obeyed, and the music stopped.

The sound of silence had an instant calming effect on Christian. He sighed and sat down again. He knew he must have upset Randy with his yelling and impatient manner, so he apologized and tried to find out more about Rachel and this incredible quest. When Randy was through explaining the whole situation to Christian, they both felt a sense of relief.

"Listen, Randy, I really appreciate this phone call, and you know I'll come up with something. In fact, this could be the very thing to get this situation back on cue again."

Randy smiled and wiped his brow. He was beginning to learn what it meant to be on an emotional roller coaster.

"Thanks, Uncle Christian. I knew you would want to know this." Then, almost in a tone of complete desperation, Randy said something that really got Christian's attention.

"We can't lose her, Uncle Christian. She's too special. Too cool!"

Christian stared stoically for a few seconds, just focusing on Randy's words and realizing just how precious they were.

"You're right, Randy. And we're not going to lose her!"

Christian managed to allay Randy's apparent apprehensions by telling him that he would call him as soon as he came up with a plan. Randy liked being a part of this continuing grand plan. The only downside, as far as he could determine, would be if his mother and father found out about it. Talk about mixed emotions. This was a textbook case. Anyway, for the time being, things seemed to be brightening up in Master Randy's universe.

Twenty-five

Back in Michigan, Blaise had begun to plan an evening of dining and dancing with Rachel. Although he still didn't feel it would change the way she felt about him, he thought it would be nice for her to get out and enjoy a few hours of fun and relaxation. She had been in a proverbial rut for some time now, going from home to office and back again. The Yacht Club was holding its Annual Harvest Moon Dance this coming weekend, and he recalled the last time he took Rachel there several months ago.

Much had happened in all of their lives since, and perhaps it would just be enjoyable to revisit this gorgeous place. Blaise knew that Rachel was home because her car was still in the driveway, so he went out onto their adjoining veranda in the back of the duplex and knocked on her door.

"Just a moment, Blaise!" Rachel called out as usual, and he could hear her shuffling around before the door opened. "Hi," she said and smiled. "What's up?"

"Hey, Ray, nothing much. Just checking in to see how you're doing."

"Well, not too badly," she replied. "Come on in. I'm in the middle of tidying up just before I get ready to shower and head for work."

Blaise couldn't imagine what had to be tidied up, since Rachel's place never looked cluttered or messy. But maybe that was why.

"Thanks," he responded as he walked into her kitchen. He went directly over to one of the stools at the counter and sat down. "I've been thinking about the Harvest Dance coming up at the Yacht Club this weekend, and I thought it would be a fun night out and a definite escape from both of our daily treadmills. Whattaya say? Wanna go?"

"You certainly know how to make a girl feel special, don't you?" Rachel smiled at this beautiful man. Her eyes shone, and she chuckled briefly.

Blaise laughed too, but treating her special wasn't a difficult thing for him to do. It came sort of naturally.

"Terrific! Then you'll go?"

"Why not! Although I feel compelled to refresh your memory. The last time I had a date to go to the Yacht Club, I collapsed." She laughed again, and Blaise could see the humor in her recollection.

"Oh, well, I'll take my chances, and, in fact, I'll carry my cell phone all evening just in case I have to call 911!"

Rachel sighed and placed her hand on Blaise's arm that was resting on the counter top.

"What would I ever do without you, Blaise?" He caught his breath and tried to keep his emotions in perspective.

"Probably, very well; however, from my own selfish view, let's hope you never have to!"

As much as Rachel wanted to just go up and kiss him, she didn't want to send the wrong message. Her heart still belonged to Christian, but there would always be a part of it that belonged to Blaise Kinley.

"Okay, you're on. You make all the arrangements. Tell me the time, and I'll be ready."

"Deal!" And with that, Blaise got up and planted a kiss on Rachel's forehead.

"I know we'll have a good time. You've made my day and my week, sweet lady."

When his lips touched her forehead, she felt the same kind of excitement she had experienced the first time he kissed her. It was unsettling, but wonderful!

"Mine, too, dear heart, mine, too!"

Rachel couldn't believe it was almost noon. She began to increase the speed of getting herself together in order to be on time for a 1:30 appointment on the Hill. There was a bounce in her step, and she hummed as she showered and got dressed. She thought about the dance and the Yacht Club and all the splendor that surrounded it. After she finished dressing, she spritzed a final spray over her hair and walked over to her closet. She looked at the couple of evening gowns off to one side, and oddly enough, the first dress she touched was the one she wore the night that Christian took her to the Skylight Room at the top of the World Trade Center. She thrilled as she remembered that magical night. But couldn't afford to look back right now. She pushed aside dress after dress, but nothing really caught her eye.

"I don't have anything to wear," she gasped. "Well, I guess I'm no different than any of my clients or any other woman in this world when getting ready for a special date." She felt much like the shoemaker who had a hole in the one pair of shoes he owned. "I can fix this," she said assertively. "After my meeting, I'll stop at Jake's. Haven't been there for myself in a very long time."

With a last look at shoes and purses, she closed the closet door. She grabbed for her purse and briefcase and was out the door by 1:15 P.M.

The flaming colors of leaves tickled her creative juices. The red, yellow, and orange hues danced against the greens and browns, basic colors of nature. She loved the fall and all that embraced it. The winds were getting cooler, and soon all the winter fashions would be donned by all who were waiting to take on winter and all its challenges.

The drive downtown was uneventful, and she even found a parking spot in front of the 777 Cafe. Mrs. Barrington was waiting for her, and so the lunch and the meeting could probably be over in a record two hours. Dina Barrington was a gorgeous and well-known socialite, whose husband was running for the Senate in the upcoming election. Her public exposure would do wonders for Rachel's career. As her personal fashion coordinator, Rachel would gain entry into yet another opulent area where her talents would be welcomed.

The downside of this relationship was having to listen and converse about subjects and topics not particularly to Rachel's liking. No one, as far as she knew, was aware of her political preferences, and she tried very hard to make certain that it stayed that way. The absolute worst thing for anyone serving the overall public, such as she had done for years, would be to pigeonhole herself by stating or taking a public position on any political issue. Rachel had invested a huge amount of time and spent and earned literally thousands of dollars in developing her career. She wasn't about to take risks one way or another, in defense or support of anything political.

Dina's support of her husband's platform was admirable, and it was obvious to Rachel and everyone else who knew them that they were deeply in love. Lyle Barrington appeared to be the perfect match for Dina. He was certainly more handsome than any one man had the right to be. The usual rumors about the possibility of extramarital affairs certainly didn't exist here. Their deep commitment and abiding faith in one another completely dispelled any threat to their unwavering love and respect for one another. Rachel thought how wonderful it must be to be that loved and that secure!

Dina was gracious no matter the occasion, and she would gently tease Rachel about finding Mr. Right. Since Dina and Corey Davidson went to school together, she knew him quite well and never really believed that he was right for Rachel.

"He's a social cad, my dear, and good looks and money can't fix that. You need someone whose prime focus is you and not his own image in the mirror." Rachel would smile and diplomatically change the subject. However, now, she'd be more inclined to agree if the topic came up again. Thankfully, it didn't. Rachel promised to have a draft of what items she'd suggest for Dina's next few political engagements. Dina handed her a check as a deposit to get Rachel started. This was something she had always done in the past. Usually, it was about ten percent of the approximate cost of the wardrobe plus Rachel's fee.

"There's something a little extra in there for you this time, Rachel. Maybe there's a treat you've been wanting to get. You've certainly earned it! My wardrobe is never easy, and you've never, ever complained." She reached over and hugged Rachel. "Call me when you've got something we can look at, okay, moi cher." Rachel was a little surprised and definitely excited about this unexpected bonus.

"Yes, I will call you, Dina, and thank you so much for this thoughtful gesture. As a matter of fact, I do have a special date this coming weekend, and I'll certainly put this to good use."

"Keep in touch," Dina responded. Not more than two steps away from Rachel, Dina had run into another friend and was already deep in conversation about Lyle's campaign.

My, my, Rachel thought, *I could never talk that much for such extended periods of time. But everyone did what they enjoyed in life, and supporting Lyle constituted Dina's career.*

Rachel was anxious to leave the 777 Cafe and get into her car so she could peek at the check that Dina had just handed her. She searched frantically for her car keys and upon finding them, unlocked the door. She plopped her purse and briefcase on the front seat. When she got in behind the wheel she opened up the envelope. "Oh, my," she gulped, "this is truly a generous bonus, $5,000 extra!" The check was made out for $15,000, and Rachel had estimated the wardrobe would be around $100,000. She was more than a little stunned but extremely elated. "Neat," she remarked. "This trip to Jake's is definitely going to be more fun than I had anticipated."

The next couple of weeks simply flew by. The Harvest Dance at the Yacht Club was as divine as she had anticipated. This was a place where Rachel checked reality at the door and stepped into a world of make-believe, a place where money and beauty combined to make a fantasy hallucinatory and addictive. The chandelier prisms, the Oriental rugs, and the glimmer of precious jewels adorning the necks and arms of the members were mesmerizing.

While Rachel had spent her entire life in Grosse Pointe and had achieved her fair share of success, she always seemed to be on the periphery of this magnificent club. Maybe, had she become a member, it would have become more real for her, but at this stage in her life, having this fairy-tale property as a once-in-a-while haven was just as she wanted it. Ever distant, ever tempting, and just accessible enough through her good friend, Blaise! A dream world where she could trespass occasionally while wide awake.

The winds of autumn were dancing through the falling leaves. Pushing and jettisoning them airborne everywhere. Rachel's days and nights were being consumed by work being done for Adele Longley and Dina Barrington. She had only spoken to Christian a few times, and his resolve was always the same. "Soon, beautiful cool lady, soon, you and I will be together, and then we'll never be apart or lonely again!"

"Hmmm," she mused, "a wish that would fulfill all of my dreams. A dream come true!" However, she was becoming uncertain and began to believe that that wish might be unreal, much like the world of the Yacht Club. The fervor of Christian's pursuit seemed to wane, and the routine of her everyday life saw her settling in rather than reaching out and struggling to grab that proverbial brass ring. She was guarding against becoming resolute and content that her life as it was now may very well be the way it would continue. She tried to push all negative thoughts out of her mind and just keep the faith!

When she awakened on this very bright and chilly Tuesday morning, she donned her snugly flannel Michigan robe and opened the front door to check on the mail. She was surprised to see a rather large envelope jutting out from the mailbox along with miscellaneous papers and mail. The address read: "To: Rachel," then her street address, city and state. In the upper left-hand corner was a name she knew well: "Avian Productions." She quickly gathered all the items in her arms and rushed back into her warm house. She could hardly wait to set the mail down so she could open this package from Christian. The letter opener didn't seem to work very well as she fumbled and rushed to slit the top of this very large paper envelope.

Finally, she tore off the rest of the sealed portion and took out the contents. There was a sheet of shiny, beautiful paper, folded into four sections. As she unfolded it, the shape of a magnificently hued rainbow became more and more evident. She sighed and almost gasped at the sight of the full-scale graphic. When she held it out, she smiled, and her heart began to race. There, in gold letters, right across the entire scope of the dynamic colors, it read, "I love you, Rachel!" and then, slightly below those words and just between the ends of both sides of the rainbow, it said, "Only 40 more days!"

Tears came to her eyes. She was almost transfixed as she sat down and stared at each and every aspect of this harbinger of her future. She wanted to share this excitement with someone. Blaise would be her first choice, but she reconsidered, given that it certainly would not be as exciting for him. She couldn't be that insensitive to anyone, especially not to Blaise. No, she had to share this with someone who would be as elated as she. Of course, Amber would be ecstatic. Rachel picked up the telephone, and keyed in her number.

Before Amber could say much more than hello, Rachel blurted out.

"He loves me, he really loves me!"

"Bella, is that you?" Amber questioned just barely recognizing her friend's garbled words.

"Yes, Amber, it's me. He loves me!"

Amber had learned, with Rachel, never to assume anything, and these past few months with Christian and Blaise in pursuit of her, she could virtually flip a coin on any given day.

"I know, sweetie. God loves you, and so do I and every other person in your life. Why is this so surprising at 9:00 A.M. on a Tuesday morning in the dead of autumn?"

Rachel chuckled at Amber's response.

"No, silly, I'm not talking about God! I know *He* loves me. I'm talking about Christian!"

Amber listened and then in her own monotoned voice responded.

"Yeah, and this *just dawned* on you?" Thinking about the time of day, she continued. "Sorry about the play on words, bella, but am I missing something here? Why don't we start this conversation from the beginning, okay? Hello, bella, this is Amber, how are you?" Rachel was laughing now, and she couldn't decide if it was over Amber's delightful humor or her elation over Christian's package.

"Hey, you!" Rachel replied. "You're supposed to be my best friend and my very own mind reader. You're telling me you missed the boat on this call?" Amber grinned and played along.

"Afraid so. I not only missed the boat, I obviously missed the dock, as well."

Now they were both laughing, and it took a few moments for them to compose themselves. Rachel finally caught her breath and began to tell Amber about the rainbow that was just delivered to her house this very morning.

"I think this is some sort of sign, Amber. I don't know how Christian could have known about it, but one of the last things Dr. October and I talked about was where I was going from the hospital and what my future plans included, and he asked me about it. I hesitated, but then I just said, I'm going to get a rainbow!"

Now, Amber gasped.

"No way!" she blurted out.

Rachel was having some difficulty figuring out how this could have gotten to Christian. When she could not come up with a logical answer, she shrugged her shoulders and surmised that it must have been some kind of metaphysical or divine intervention. She'd heard about those mysterious things on the psychic channel.

"Well, what do you think, Amber?"

"Wow! It's kind of eerie, but hey, maybe you two share some kind of ESP. It wouldn't be the first time something like this happened between two people who share such an intense love." Amber mulled it around in her head, and then continued.

"Don't look a gift horse in the mouth, bella. The only thing I'd be especially curious about is the forty days!"

"Yeah!" Rachel agreed. "According to my calendar, that figures out to be Saturday, December ninth. Can't think of anything significant about that date, can you?"

"Nah," replied Amber. "Maybe it's Christian's birthday, and he wants you for his birthday!" She grinned sheepishly. Rachel began to laugh again.

"If your imagination were animated, it would probably be a dodo bird, flying away at any given moment and soaring without a destination."

Amber smiled at first.

"Are you implying that I'm a bit flighty?" she asked.

"Dizzy was what I had in mind," Rachel replied. "But flighty will do."

"Wellll!" Amber countered. "Until you know for certain, it's as good a guess as any!"

"You're right, sweetie, you're absolutely right. However, I can't help but wonder what's next? It is definitely pretty thrilling."

"Have you told Blaise?" Amber queried. There was silence, and Amber felt that she may have hit a sore spot. "Sorry, bella. Did I step on touchy ground?" she added.

Rachel wasn't upset with the question, but it did bring to mind that she would have to tell Blaise, and it was going to be difficult. Especially after their wonderful evening at the Yacht Club a couple of weeks ago.

"No, Amber, I haven't told Blaise. It all happened so quickly. And I must admit, while the idea had crossed my mind, I didn't think it was such a great idea right now. The last thing I want to do is hurt Blaise any more than

I already have. If this situation plays out the way I'm hoping it will, he'll know soon enough. And I have tried to be very honest with him about my feelings for Christian."

Amber shook her head in amazement.

"I give you a lot of credit, sweetie. I don't think I would have been able to handle this situation as well. After I met Tony, he never gave me the opportunity to think about another man. And I must admit, I didn't want to."

Rachel knew that what her friend was saying was true. Amber and Tony's love story was one that most other people dreamed about and were rarely fortunate enough to achieve.

"Believe me, Amber, if I had my choice, I'd have wanted to be in a relationship like yours and Tony's. But I guess God had another plan for me, and it looks like I'm about to see just what that is!" She hesitated for a moment. She could feel the goosebumps developing all over her body, and her heart began to race. "I think this is it, Amber, I really feel like it's my turn!"

Amber was filled with happiness for her friend.

"And it's about time, bella. Ahh, listen, I've got to get moving here, but keep me posted on what happens from here. Okay? I'm going to be a basket case, waiting." She hesitated, and then as a last bit of humor, Amber chided Rachel.

"I see Christian periodically at Marisa and Carlo's rehearsals. Do you want me to ask him about the ultimate plan?"

Rachel almost yelled.

"No! Amber, I don't even want him to know that I've shared any of this with you."

"Okay, already, bella, just thought I'd offer." She grinned. "Remember, I've got a 'dizzy' imagination!"

"You're a real prize, you know that, Amber. But, there's a question in my mind as to whether it's the grand prize or the boobie." Rachel laughed, again.

"Hey, sweetie," Amber responded, "can't change at this late date. Ya gets what I got!"

"Hmmm," Rachel mused. "That's pretty funny grammar coming from you, but I'll take it!"

Suddenly, Amber almost choked, trying to blurt out her next sentence.

"I know! I know! I've figured it out. I mean I know about the forty days!"

Rachel was astounded.

"What do you mean, you know? Tell me!"

"It's the opening of 'Cinema.' It's the premiere!"

Rachel gasped.

"Oh, my God. I forgot about 'Cinema.' Isn't that strange, I never connected it."

Amber asked her to hang on while she looked for some cast notes that Marisa and Carlo had brought home within the last couple of days. She was unsuccessful in putting her hands on them and went back to explain her inability to find them.

"Well, I can't see them right now, but the forty days definitely sounds like it could be the opening night."

Now Rachel was almost reeling with the prospect that Amber could be right.

"It's so exciting, no matter how it's going to happen. But I'm going to be on the edge of lunacy until this whole thing begins to unfold."

"I really have to run, bella, but keep in touch, okay? And when I find those cast notes, I'll call you right away!"

"Thanks, Amber, and take care. Give my love to Tony and the kids."

"Will do, sweetie. Enjoy this special time in your life, dear heart! As you've said, it's your turn. Luv ya!" And with that, Rachel said good-bye and they hung up.

Rachel was so happy with all this new excitement in her life that she began to spin around in her living room, weaving in and out of the furniture. "He loves me, he really loves me!" When she stopped, she looked up and raised both arms as though reaching for the sky and yelled, "And I love him."

Blaise's work was beginning to increase with the onset of the holiday season, and he found himself wrapped up in his clients' projects. He also found himself deliberately trying to stay away from Rachel. The night at the Yacht Club was too wonderful, too perfect. But he could tell it wasn't the same for Rachel. She did enjoy herself, but he could tell that her romantic mind was elsewhere. Even though she said how much she cared for him, he knew it was not anywhere close to the love he felt for her. He assured her that he would always be a part of her life, and he meant it. The only problem was that he hadn't realized just how terribly difficult it would be to let her go. His entire focus and motivation in the last few years had been centered around the goal of ultimately ending up with her.

Well, it looked like that wasn't going to happen, so he would have to somehow quell this love that burned in his heart for only Rachel and get on with his life. Besides, he tried to convince himself, a small part of her life was eminently better than losing her totally. It crossed his mind that if you truly loved someone, you should be able to let them go. Such nobility, he thought. However, he never imagined that he would be the one to do it.

He looked at his most recent creation. An enormous wall hanging. It would hang in a very large mansion alcove with a skylight directly above it. During the day, the sun would shine brightly upon it, and so, the color scheme would have to be harmonious and dynamic. So far, it was much too neutral, and he was struggling with the one focal point that would give it the pizzazz it needed. He was standing in front of it, almost mesmerized.

"A rainbow!" he said. "A full scale rainbow would be perfect!" He thought about it for a few minutes. "I'll call Rachel and see what she thinks. She's got a sharp eye for color and contrast. She'll tell me if it's just right or too hokey!" Unfortunately, Rachel wasn't home when he called; he would have to wait until later on that evening for her advice and suggestions. Try as he may, staying away from her was darned near impossible.

Rachel left the house and found herself driving around with no particular destination in mind. She was so excited about everything since the mail arrived earlier, and a little drive sounded like a good idea. The Village was as busy as ever. As she observed the people walking up and down the street, she almost felt a sense of belonging. It was strange. It was as though she knew everyone in town. She parked the car at the first available spot, got out, and began to meander down the street among the rest of the would-be shoppers. She smiled at whoever caught her eye and was particularly pleased by those who were walking hand in hand.

It was as though she had just officially become a part of a new community —the community of those in love. She felt a sense of welcome to a place that in the past had been unknown to her. Others believed she was a member of that select community; however, in her mind and heart, she was an outsider. She liked this new exhilarating feeling. There was a fluidness in her gait, and it appeared that all the stop lights turned green as she approached them. Someone automatically opened the door for her as she neared shops of interest. This sense of belonging was long overdue, and she embraced it with open arms.

When she finally stopped to catch her breath, she was standing inside the Village drugstore, close to the greeting-card displays. The phrases rushed through her head as she looked randomly up and down the rows and columns. "Happy Birthday," "Happy Anniversary," "Thank You," "Get Well Soon," "Congratulations," "New Baby," "Deepest Sympathies," and "Welcome!" Perhaps, the most appropriate card to fit this occasion was "Happy

Birthday," for she felt as if her life was just beginning. She picked up a couple of cards and smiled. "To my darling . . . Happy Birthday!" *Imagine,* she thought, *being able to call someone "darling." And better still, having someone call you "darling," as well.* It was a word she had never used in the past, for no one ever seemed to suit it.

"My darling," she whispered. "I love you, my darling!" As she stood there smiling, she was surprised when she heard someone say, "I love you, too, darling!" She turned quickly and looked directly at the gentleman who was standing next to her. He smiled and apologized.

"Sorry, miss, but I couldn't help myself. You said that so beautifully and convincingly, I couldn't resist responding."

Rachel was more than a little embarrassed that she had actually been overheard, and she very graciously accepted the gentleman's apology and quietly walked away. If a mere stranger responded so quickly, just imagine what would happen if she had said that to Christian.

Unfortunately, that little episode brought a quick halt to her fantasy trip, and the practical matters of everyday living were waiting as Rachel exited the store.

The hubbub surrounding Halloween came and passed quickly. Before she knew it, November arrived and talk about Thanksgiving and Christmas was everywhere. Rachel had anticipated another missive from Christian long before this, but ten days had gone by, and she heard nothing. Added to that, Amber never did call her back about the cast notes and the opening of "Cinema," and once again, the old insecurities crept back into her thoughts.

Ye of little faith, she thought, *why would Christian even initiate something as wonderful as this, if he had no intention of some conclusion, some hopeful, happy ending?* In the midst of everything else, she had been looking for the right time to tell Blaise about the package from Christian and their future plans. *At this point, I'd be better off waiting until I really know what my future plans are before I lay this scenario on Blaise.*

Having time to think was not good for her right now. The uncertainty and mysterious nature of this entire situation began to bother her. She sat down at her desk and took out a yellow pad. She drew a line down the middle of the page and entitled the two columns: "Positives" and "Negatives." As she thought about all the things that had happened to her since mid-July, she was amazed.

No wonder she was in such a mental turmoil. She looked at what could be responsible for the insanity of three or four people, much less one! Yet, she thought, if she were to compare this list with anyone else's, would it be that different? Most people experience change, disappointment, illness, love, happiness, and stress in their daily lives. In general, they seemed to fare quite well. So why should she be any different? What was so unusual about her lifestyle to make it so difficult to handle?

Perhaps, she thought, *other people were stronger willed, thicker-skinned, or more tenacious. Or maybe they just lived their lives every day and dealt with whatever came down the pike.* Instead of putting everything that happened to her under a microscope, she should do as they.

Ever since her earliest recollection, everything she did had a serious consequence. Her career techniques were described as cutting edge. Her judgment was always keen. Her appearance was drop-dead gorgeous. It seemed so effortless to be considered sheer perfection, by most standards, an almost impossible level to achieve and maintain. But if you were Rachel Radcliffe, it was expected. Nothing less would do! In Rachel's evaluation, if someone were to look for the sum total of all of these superior benchmarks, one would be surprised to find that the results were: one plus zero equals one.

She sighed, "So, this perfect, outstanding, drop-dead gorgeous, cutting-edge genius had never quite had what it took to find herself a lover." Most people represent themselves as "one half looking for the other half" to make them whole. Being a "whole" within oneself equals loneliness and unfulfillment.

What's the magic formula? she thought, and why, if she was so extremely intelligent, couldn't she figure it out? *What's missing in me that apparently is in abundance in most everyone else on this planet?* Self-examination and evaluation were two things that Rachel did extremely well; however, after that stringent exercise, she would still end up unable to understand the reason for the lack of such a love life.

As she sat and continued her evaluation, she tried to remember Dr. October's caution about riding the emotional roller coaster and the ultimate frustration that would result. "Don't keep analyzing every move. Live your life and allow life to happen to you," he would say. And, worst case scenario, what was wrong with her status quo? If she compared herself to those less fortunate than she, she could be a lot worse off. He had to be right! Let life happen for a while. Maybe she'd be less anxious and able to enjoy each day. Besides, she smiled, her favorite holiday of the year was fast approaching. The season for joy and giving. A time when wishes came true and miracles were possible. Certainly, the coming of His birthday was the reason for the season, and she would have to trust in her deep and abiding faith that her love for God and His guidance up until now were not going to waver.

She took the list of "positives" and "negatves" and ran a diagonal line through it. Then in large, bold letters, she wrote: "*E n o u g h!*" She placed the pen on her desk and got up. She sighed deeply and stretched. "Enough! Enough! Enough! I'm *not* going to do this to myself one more time!" She brought her hands up to her hair and tousled it, messing up her perfectly coifed hairdo!

Today is the first day of the rest of my life, and I'm going to start living each day as though it were my last, happily and to the fullest. I certainly don't have to make any huge decisions right now. All I have to do is what I normally do. Eat, work, play, if I so desire, and get some much-needed rest. No fuss. No muss. No worries! Perhaps, if she continued to think it, it would become so.

Working on this last wardrobe would keep her busy enough for a while. The outline covering all the apparel items was complete and shopping or having them made was going to take a lot of time and effort. Fortunately, it was something that she enjoyed doing. For now, the career she loved would have to be enough. With that resolve, Rachel walked over to the stove and put the tea kettle on.

"First, a nice cup of tea, and then, time to get busy!"

Blaise had been working diligently on the wall hanging. Since he hadn't seen or talked to Rachel since the "rainbow" idea, he worked around the focal point and was pleased that everything else was falling into place so nicely.

Since Rachel hadn't visited with Blaise for quite a while, she decided that she was ready for a smiling face and an understanding ear. She sauntered over to Blaise's back door and tapped on it lightly. She was surprised at how quickly he answered. As he opened the door, he grabbed her arm as he said hello. He ushered her into his studio and positioned her directly in front of his latest creation.

"So, what do you think?" he asked rather succinctly.

Rachel had always been impressed with Blaise's talent and artistic genius.

"Well! You've certainly done it this time, my friend! This has the beginning of a great masterpiece." Blaise hugged her spontaneously.

"Thanks, Ray babe. But your compliment implies that it lacks something, right? Perhaps, a finishing touch. A pièce de résistance!" He hesitated and then added, "How about a rainbow?"

Rachel's expression was easy to read. Her eyes opened widely and her mouth opened.

"You're gaping, Ray. Why?"

"A rainbow? Did you say a rainbow?" she asked in amazement.

"Ahhh . . . yes, I did. Did I say it incorrectly or something? You appear to be in a state of shock! If you don't like the idea, sweetie, just tell me. That's why I'm asking your opinion. I did think it would give it a touch of class and distinction."

Rachel tried to compose herself and even though she was thinking about the incredible coincidence, she apologized to her friend for appearing to be criticizing his choice.

"Ahhh . . . I'm sorry, Blaise. I do love it. It's just that I didn't expect you to say 'rainbow' that's all."

Blaise was trying to assimilate all of the expressions on Rachel's face and he chuckled.

"All right, I'll play along. What did you expect me to say? Migrating Canadian geese, perhaps?"

Rachel burst out laughing.

"That's pretty funny, you know, but now that you mention it, that might be a nice touch given the whole focus on nature and its creatures. It would depend, of course, on how many and your choice of colors."

"Okay, Ray, enough frivolity. I'm serious about the rainbow. Why was that such a shock for you?"

"No, dear. It wasn't a shock! It was . . . er . . . it was a gigantic coincidence."

Blaise looked a little puzzled by this strange conversation, but he persisted, since he was now curious to hear Rachel's explanation.

"Let's hear it, Ray babe. I can hardly wait!"

Rachel took a deep breath and proceeded to relate the latest events having to do with Christian.

"I know it's not your favorite topic, but I heard from Christian a couple of weeks ago, and his message included a rainbow—"

"Oh, no! Don't tell me. He's changed his career path and is now doing pastels and oil paintings, right?"

Rachel leered at him coyly.

"Now, now, that's not what happened, and I'll be happy to tell you, if you promise to listen. Just listen!"

Blaise dutifully obeyed and sat down with his hands folded in his lap and his head bowed in a somewhat repentant position. Rachel continued, and as he listened, he could tell that she was excited about the prospect of eventually going to New York to be with Christian. He tried not to show how difficult it was for him to accept the possible finality of their relationship. But he had promised that he'd be her friend no matter what, which was where they were at this very moment.

"So what do you think, dear heart? Am I a candidate for the loony bin, or am I truly on the brink of finding out what true love is all about?"

Blaise swallowed, and as possible responses rushed through his mind, he thought about how to answer this very direct question. His first thought was his certainty that what he felt for her was definitely true love. His next thought was why she was asking him? Certainly, nothing he would say to the contrary would change her feelings for Christian or for him. He paused and began to speak sensitively.

"I think, if you feel that Christian is, in fact, the man who can give you true love, then go for it, sweetie! I can't and I wouldn't begin to play the devil's advocate here. I care way too much for you, and while your happiness means the world to me, I couldn't put myself through an exercise that would make me feel more left behind than I already do."

Rachel was watching Blaise's face intently as he spoke. She could see the love in his eyes and could hear the emotion in his voice.

"You know, Blaise, I want you to remember that this was not an easy decision for me. In fact, it may well be the most difficult decision I will make in my entire life. And if I end up losing you, I will never get over the loss." She paused for a moment. "All I know is that at this point in my life, it's a risk I'll have to take. Please don't hate me for my choice, and please, also believe that my choice had nothing to do with your lack of anything! This decision has everything to do with me and my ability to get in touch with my feelings. Hopefully, my medical problems are behind me, and I pray that this will not cause you more pain and unhappiness. God only knows, I've been responsible for a lot of it recently."

Blaise got up and walked over to where she was sitting. He extended his hands to her, and she took them and stood up. He embraced her gently and spoke to her quietly.

"You haven't caused me pain and unhappiness, Ray. And please don't worry about me. I will truly be fine. You can be assured of one thing, it's true now and it will always be true. I will be there for you if you need me. I have no intention of letting you out of my life. We do share a kind of love that is precious. One that expects nothing and is willing to give up almost everything to keep it." He hugged her again and felt her sigh as she embraced him, as well.

"You are precious to me, Blaise, and I love you. How could I not? You've been my friend and protector. My confidante and counselor. My sounding board and my buddy. And just knowing that you'll continue to be a part of my life is most reassuring and heartwarming."

"Who knows what the future holds for both of us. I won't even try to predict it. I will, like you, hope and pray that it brings you some much overdue happiness. For me, too!" Blaise kissed her on the forehead and smiled.

Rachel thought it was time to get off this subject, and so she looked at the wall hanging and told Blaise that a rainbow would be the absolute best choice as the focal point for his new creation.

"Who is it for?" she asked.

"The new heiress in town." He responded quickly.

"Hmmm that's an intriguing statement. You say that like I'm supposed to know who she is."

"Ahh, no," he replied. "I didn't mean to imply that. We were introduced at the Yacht Club, and when she found out what I did for a living, she hired me on the spot."

"Well," Rachel responded, "I know she'll be pleased with this. That's for sure! You've outdone yourself, dear heart, and you must keep me posted on her reaction when she sees it."

Blaise then asked her about her work, and Rachel told him about Dina Barrington. After about an hour of catching up, Rachel excused herself and left, and Blaise began to apply the finishing touch to his latest art work.

Rachel was not expecting to find anything in the mail when it arrived but was pleasantly surprised when she saw the same kind of envelope with the same return address. This time, as she opened the large folded paper, the rainbow was the same, but the words "Will you?" were boldly placed in the same place that "I love you" was in the prior one. Then directly under the rainbow it read: "25 days to go!"

Her heart rate quickened, and she folded the paper and pressed it to her chest.

"Will I what?" The obvious was, of course, "Will you marry me?" but she didn't want to end up with wishful thinking. However, what if it was a proposal of marriage? And what if he asked her to live in New York? And what if she had to give up her career? And . . . what if all of this were hogwash and he didn't propose after all?

Obviously, "Will I go crazy?" would be the more realistic question at this time, and the answer would definitely be "yes."

"Well," she sighed "One thing is certain. I will have to keep working until I know what's next. I don't want to starve to death in the meantime." She chuckled after she said that. Time would tell, and she was determined to live each day and let life happen.

The next few days came and went as usual. Sun came up, Rachel got up, Rachel worked, and Rachel went to bed, mostly exhausted and always a little curious about what tomorrow would bring.

She talked with Dina Barrington quite regularly as her wardrobe was coming together. Rachel couldn't remember working as diligently. It was as if this would be the last such work she'd do in Grosse Pointe for a long while. Ms. Barrington was the perfect client for Rachel's fantastic sense of color coordination and her ability to put together some pretty exciting ensembles. Dina would wear these outfits to every posh event in town for the next few weeks and was better advertising than any marketing program she could pay for herself. Although Rachel could sense that her success was imminent, and even though she may feel that it was well-deserved, it may very well be extremely ill-timed. For if Christian's ultimate goal was to ask her to marry him and stay in New York, then her newly achieved acclaim may have happened too late.

She thought about it, and if it came to a toss-up between her career and her love for Christian, there was no contest. Yes, she thought, her career was important, but her love life and the chance of ever meeting someone like Christian again was too remote. "The time for love is now!" she uttered. "I cannot sacrifice any more precious time. I've dreamed about and longed for someone to love for such a long time, and now he's here. There is no choice! It's Christian."

The mailings had become like giant pieces of a gigantic puzzle. Each time her curiosity peaked to another level. Where did she fit in the scheme of things? Three weeks was not a lot of time, but she certainly had more than enough to do to keep her busy in the meantime.

Twenty-six

In New York, Christian's involvement with "Cinema" increased with each dawning day. The rehearsals and other preparations for the premiere were almost stifling. There wasn't anything that he hadn't been through before, but for some reason, this time his spirit had been exhilarated to new heights. He enjoyed all the excitement. It were as though this was to be the musical production of his life. When he thought about it, he knew absolutely what the added ingredient was, it was his love and desire for Rachel. Since he met her, he had come alive again. His latest plan to get her to New York was conceived as he spoke to his nephew, Randy, whose inspiration and unwillingness to give up on his cool lady sparked Christian's imagination and fervor.

With the help of his very able administrative assistant, Adriana, they devised the series of communiqués that would bring Rachel to New York and into his life forever. The plot was well planned and precisely timed. It possessed enough mystery and curiosity-provoking intrigue to keep Rachel guessing and in a constant state of anticipation. Everything in Christian's life had been a production; his quest for Rachel's love would be no different. He was a master at developing just enough drama and intrigue to lead all involved to a tumultuous crescendo. The concurrent management of these two labors of love would end up being his penultimate challenge. Show business philosophy always worked for him in the past, and it was, after all, once again show time!

Of course, Master Randy could not have been more elated about all the latest developments. His own master plan was right on cue, and if all went well, this very cool lady would be his very cool aunt before too long.

Back in Grosse Pointe, Rachel was working as she never had before. Dina Barrington's wardrobe was finished and was nothing less than magnificent. Everything in Rachel's life suddenly had meaning and purpose. And even though time was flying by, Rachel was somehow managing to keep up. Her physical and mental stamina were returning to the point where she didn't even think about time constraints or pressure. The Barrington collection was a huge success and nothing pleased Rachel more than a satisfied client.

Michigan, in November, brought about turning leaves and chilly winds. Autumn's blazing colors were everywhere, and it was the time of year that Rachel adored. She had already taken out some of the holiday knickknacks and placed them around the house. The question did come to her mind, however, that she may not even be in Michigan for Christmas this year. What a different prospect that was!

The next couple of days brought two more rainbow packages from Christian. Each one adding yet another piece to this exciting and mysterious puzzle. He hadn't asked her to bring too much on her trip. One of the things he mentioned was the outfit she wore the night he took her to the Skylight Room at the top of the World Trade Center. Just recalling that enchanting night created butterflies in her stomach that she could not settle.

Christian didn't suggest anything else in regard to her wardrobe. He only asked that she be prepared for "a little stay"—and he'd take care of the rest.

Since Rachel was not that familiar with how Christian dealt with anything, she really had no idea what his definition of "a little stay" might be. A few days? A few weeks? In any case, she'd bring enough coordinates to meet any casual or formal activity.

The last missive arrived on Monday, December fourth. It was by far, the largest, and she could hardly wait to unwrap it to see what it held.

First, as she slid the bulky items out from their vessel, there was an envelope, which read:

To my darling Rachel,

These items will provide you with full passage on a journey designed specifically for you. I promise that each step will bring you to a fabulous destination!

Love always,
Christian

She put down the note and its envelope and noticed that they were only two of a similar stack. The next one was also marked to her attention. It was from Metro Limousine. The reservation instructions were for a limo to arrive at her home on Bedford at 10:00 A.M. on Saturday, December ninth. Destination: Detroit Metropolitan Airport by 11:00 A.M. At the bottom of the reservation slip were the words: "Courtesy of Mr. Christian Avian."

Rachel sighed and placed that envelope on top of the initial note. The next envelope was beautifully decorated with a rainbow spanning from the lower left-hand corner to the opposite lower right-hand corner. It contained a first-class American Airlines ticket to New York City. She looked at the time of departure: 12:00 noon from Detroit Metro, nonstop to JFK International. Estimated time of arrival: 1:15 P.M.

As she flipped to the next page, looking for a return date, she smiled broadly when she read the boldly printed words *"Open Return!"* The ticket holder was attached to yet another envelope. This one was from The Manhattan Limousine Service. Its message read: "My darling, this will bring you one step closer to us!" She shivered as she read on: "The driver will be holding a card with your name on it at the arrival gate. Please give him your baggage claim tickets. He will pick them up for you after you have been comfortably situated in your waiting limousine." She sighed deeply, trying to process this whole exciting adventure. Her heart raced as she clasped the tickets and envelopes in her hands.

"Oh, my God!" she gasped. "This is really happening!" As she put the limo reservation back in the envelope, she noticed one last folder still resting on her lap. It was smaller than the others and distinctively more recognizable as aa theater ticket envelope. She opened it quickly and took out a single ticket. She read it slowly:

Avian Productions
presents
"CINEMA"
Saturday, December 9, at 8:00 p.m.
The Imperial Theater
Broadway
New York, New York

"Front Row Center" was printed on the bottom left-hand corner. Tears welled up in her eyes. A little slip of paper was sticking out the envelope, as well. By now, she was wiping the tears from her cheeks and finding it a little difficult to read what appeared to be a final message. Again, it was in Christian's handwriting:

It's show time, my darling, and I promise you a finale you will never forget!

I love you,
Christian

She blew her nose and tried to compose herself. She had never experienced such happiness. It appeared as though all her dreams were about to come true.

When she looked away from all these marvelous items, her focus shifted directly to the calendar sitting on her kitchen counter. The date became eminently sharp; she stood up and exclaimed loudly, "Five days! I only have five days to get ready! I've got to pack! I've got to call Dina to make certain that she's all set with her wardrobe. And . . ." she uttered quietly, ". . . I've got to let Blaise know that I'll be leaving for New York on Saturday!" She began to scurry about, picking up all the items she had just received. "Can't misplace any of these!" She hurried into her bedroom and flung open the closet doors. "Oh, my dear Lord, what am I going to take with me? Christian only asked me to bring the gown I wore to the Skylight Room. What about traveling clothes?"

Suddenly, she stopped dead in her tracks. "Traveling clothes? He didn't say I should travel in that gown. If the plane arrives at 1:15 P.M. in New York and the show starts at 8:00 P.M. what am I supposed to wear in the meantime? And where? Sit in the limo?" "Now, what? Was this the last message?" she mused. "Can't believe, after all these precise instructions and plans that he'd leave out something this crucial. I'll have to call him. That's all there is to it!"

The door bell rang. "Oh, my goodness," she gasped. She looked through the peephole. There was a delivery man from Federal Express standing there. She opened the door and acknowledged him.

"Special Delivery for Ms. Rachel Radcliffe?" he inquired.

"That's me," she smiled.

"Sign here, please!" He pointed to the line right after her printed name, and she signed it. He thanked her and handed her a pretty good-sized package. She asked him to wait while she got him a tip, but he declined, stating that he had already been taken care of.

She took the package and went back into the house. Nothing unusual about this one; it was a Federal Express box all right and definitely from Christian. She opened it quickly and took out yet another box. This one was marked "Bloomingdale's," and she shrieked, "Oh, my God!" She picked up the lid and uncovered the most gorgeous red pant suit she had ever seen. It was pure silk and lined in gold satin. The matching gold lamé blouse was breathtaking. The collar and cuffs of the jacket were trimmed in gold, as well as the belt that went with the slacks.

Finally, under all these fabulous things was a matching cashmere cape. It was equally as lovely. The voluminous, rippling fabric unfolded as she stood up and held it in front of her. "What sheer elegance," she whispered. "This is certainly something I'd choose for one of my clients, but never a million years for myself!"

She twirled it around her shoulders and thrilled as she looked at herself in her full-length mirror. The reflection of herself in this heavenly garment brought tears to her eyes once again. She went back to the box from which all these magnificent pieces of apparel came and spotted an envelope inside the tissue wrapping. Again, it was Christian's handwriting: "To my darling Rachel." She opened it and took out a folder marked "Plaza Hotel" with a note accompanying it.

> Sorry about the tardiness of this package. With Christmas right around the corner, it was a little difficult to be timely. Also, I did overlook putting the hotel reservations in the last package. Forgive me.
>
> I do hope you like my choice of traveling togs. I have it on good authority that you love the color red. As for knowing the correct size, I confess that I peeked at your evening coat when you were away from the table at the Skylight Room. Everything else I leave to your exquisite taste. As for the Plaza, I thought it would provide a great dressing room for the star of my life, and I absolutely believed that you wouldn't mind being right across from Central Park.
>
> The limo driver will bring you to the hotel and return for you at 7:00 P.M. to bring you to the theater.
>
> Can't wait to see you and hold you!
>
> Love, Christian

Rachel was almost in a stupor. She could not believe all the plans that Christian had made. Not to mention finding out about her likes and dislikes in clothes. Everything felt so good—so right!

Still, she was very aware that only five days remained before she would depart for the trip of her life. One thing she knew would not be a problem; she did own both gold and red shoes with enough matching accessories to choose from. "Basics!" she uttered. "Stick to the basics and coordinates." How many times she had given this advice to her clients. Now she'd have to practice what she preached.

She took the Bloomingdale box and its contents into the bedroom. It was incredible how well everything fit, and as she stood in front of her full-length mirror, she smiled. She was pleased with the reflection. Her excitement was almost too much.

When she combined the reality of this situation with her imagined thoughts and fantasies, it left her breathless! "Okay, Rachel!" she said to herself. "Slow down, now! You must control yourself. You can't afford to mess up! This is it. This is what you've been praying for and dreaming about."

She changed back into the clothes she had been wearing and sat down at her desk. She picked up a pen and wrote "Things to Do" across the top of the page of her legal notebook.

Several items, ranging from hair appointment to stopping regular mail delivery, were the first to be listed. Then she added calling the newspaper to stop delivery, getting luggage pieces out of the closet, notifying clients, and telling Blaise. Then after a few blank spaces, she wrote, "And stay calm!" It was going to be a very busy five days. She picked up the telephone receiver and dialed her beauty salon to make an appointment for Friday afternoon. On short notice, they said they would fit her in as best they could.

By Friday night, she was a virtual basket case. Her things-to-do list had dwindled, and the only item she had not totally adhered to was "stay calm!" And of all of the items, telling Blaise was the toughest. Even though they had gotten past the emotional side of Rachel's decision to go forward with Christian, she was not insensitive to Blaise's feelings for her. Great guy that he was, he offered to be of any assistance if she needed him, but Rachel could not, in good conscience, allow Blaise to participate this time. She did promise to write to him as soon as she knew what her plans were beyond Saturday.

Blaise made certain she understood that if anything went wrong, he'd be there for her. Rachel had a special spot in her heart for Blaise, and that would never change. The last thing she wanted to think about right now was the slightest possibility of anything going wrong. The rest of her day was spent in gathering the apparel items she would take with her. She also talked with Adele Longley and Dina Barrington. They were very happy for her and wished her the very best of luck. Both said to let them know when her plans solidified.

When she finally got ready for bed, she was definitely suffering from mixed emotions. A little sad that this would be the last time she'd sleep in her bed for a while. She'd miss Blaise and was happy and excited to think about seeing Christian . . . *tomorrow!* She asked God for his guidance and to watch over her during this momentous time in her life. "Thank you, dear Lord, thank you for this wonderful opportunity. With all my heart and soul, I love you!" She rested her head on her pillow and was almost immediately asleep.

Rachel was showered and dressed when the sun came up on Saturday morning. Her luggage was sitting by the door, and she once again looked at her list to make certain that everything was done.

As she waited for the limo to arrive, she sipped on the last cup of tea she'd enjoy here for a little while. She walked through the house and looked at the photos on the walls. Each picture brought back some memories of specific times in her life. Some happy, some sad. She stopped at a picture of her and Corey in happier times, and wondered what his reaction and feelings would be when he ultimately heard of her new relationship. The picture almost directly next to that one was the photo of Mama and Papa DeRoca. Tears welled up in her eyes, and she tried to hold them back for fear of messing up her makeup.

"Oh, Mama, Papa. I wish you could have been here to share this happiness with me. When I lost you, I didn't think I'd ever know any happiness again. For years, I was numb and living my life because I had to, not because I wanted to." She sighed and smiled. "I know you're here with me, now. I love you both very much, and I sure do miss you!"

The photos of Amber, Tony, Marisa, and Carlo made her smile even more broadly. She wondered if she'd see them at the performance tonight. How ironic that she met Christian at a theater production, and now she would be attending the premiere of his new musical. She recalled his professionalism as he addressed the young, aspiring actors and actresses. His dedication and love of his work was certainly one of the things that attracted her to him.

There were times when it seemed like such a very long time ago, and then, it was as if it only happened yesterday. This walk down memory lane couldn't be over until she stood in front of Blaise's picture, his piercing blue eyes looking directly at hers. She would miss his spontaneous knocking at her door. The funny things he'd do to bring her out of a rotten mood, and his attempts just to make her smile, no matter the situation. She sighed deeply, kissed the tips of her fingers and placed them on Blaise's photo. "You're the best, dear Blaise. The very best, and I'll always keep you in my heart!"

When the limo arrived at exactly 10:00 A.M., Rachel was ready! The young driver, handsomely dressed to the nines in his tuxedo, bow tie, and cummerbund, introduced himself as Robert.

"Ms. Radcliffe, if you're ready, I'll take your luggage. and we can get on our way."

Rachel took a deep breath as she responded.

"Yes, Robert, I'm as ready as I'll ever be!" And with that, she pointed to her luggage just inside the door. As he picked them up, Rachel turned and took one last look at her home. Somehow, she knew nothing in her life would ever be the same from this moment on.

"Let's go!" she said. Once the door was locked, she walked down the stairs and got into the luxurious vehicle waiting for her.

Robert was efficient in his duties, and Rachel could tell that he also enjoyed his work. She couldn't believe the interior of the limo. Here she was sitting on what looked like a plush sofa, which started from the door and reached across the back of the limo. It continued along the other side right up to the divider that separated her from the driver.

The carpet was as close to velvet as she could determine, and a customized entertainment center replete with CD player, TV, VCR, refrigerator, and a fully stocked bar sat directly in front of her.

"Please make yourself comfortable, Ms. Radcliffe. It's about an hour's ride to the airport. There's some orange juice in the refrigerator and fresh bagels in the heated chamber next to the microwave."

She was amazed by the sound system that allowed him to talk to her with the panel that separated them in the closed position.

"Can you hear me well, Robert?" she asked.

"Yes, ma'am, I can right now. However there's a 'privacy' switch on the console to your left; if you wish to use it, please feel free to do so."

She observed the control panel he described and got a little closer to get a better idea of anything else available to her.

"It's meant to give you as much or as little privacy as possible. Also, Ms. Radcliffe, there are two separate dividers in this section between us. One panel is solid to give you ultimate privacy. The other is made of glass. And if you wish, you can view the road directly ahead. Whatever is your pleasure, Ms. Radcliffe. Whatever you wish."

"Wow," she whispered softly, "this is quite incredible."

"Yes, it is," responded Robert.

Rachel began to laugh upon hearing his response. She realized that the privacy switch was on the "off" position.

"This is quite a neat job you have, Robert. Have you been doing it long?"

"Five years," he answered, "and, yes, it is pretty neat. I've met a lot of nice people during that time, and as you can imagine, I get to be with them when they're enjoying some happy part of their lives. Can't get much better than that."

Rachel immediately saw the similarities in their respective chosen careers. She designed and coordinated wardrobes for her clients in much the same course of their lives.

As they went down roads that she had used all her life, she felt somehow different. First of all, it wasn't every day that she'd been chauffeured around in a stretch limo. Second, the windows were shaded, and it was amusing to be able to see out and not have anyone be able to see you!

She leaned back and closed her eyes for a moment. This was so exciting. She struggled to stay composed. She wanted to be able to enjoy each and every moment. Being as organized as she was, she picked up the small case next to her. It contained all of the various items that Christian had sent in conjunction with this fantasy trip. She looked for the airline ticket. She wanted to be certain to have it ready when they arrived at the airport. It was where she had put it and easily accessible.

Then she reached for her purse and took out her compact. She liked the reflection in the mirror. Her hair and makeup were to her liking. Her outfit was superb. She smiled quite contentedly. The red and gold combination was indeed regal. She felt as if she were a member of royalty. Imagine living like this every day of your life. Glamorous clothes, chauffeured limo, and the ability to travel the world whenever you wanted to. She could only guess at the possibility of the thrilling times that lay ahead of her.

She felt a bit apprehensive, though, about how she would handle walking through the airport. This outfit would not go unnoticed, and she was not used to being so apparent—so outstanding. She sighed and decided to do whatever she had to; she would act accordingly. After a while, she leaned forward and opened the small refrigerator door. It was filled with a variety of fresh fruit juices, fresh fruit, and a selection of cream cheeses and jellies. Just adjacent to the refrigerator was a shelf that held glasses, cups, plates, and cutlery. She reached for a plate and was most cautious not to drop anything on her clothing. Then she decided to ask Robert about how anyone managed to eat in a limo without making a complete mess. When she looked at the control panel, it was easier now to find what she was looking for: "Driver Panel—Up/Down." She pressed the down position, and sure enough, the panel separating them lowered.

"Yes, Ms. Radcliffe, may I help you?"

"Ahhhh, yes, you can, Robert. As a matter of fact you can. How does one manage to eat anything back here without dropping it?"

Robert smiled at her inquiry. He certainly did like her down-to-earth manner.

"To your left, under the sofa, there's a sliding table that will fold out in front of you. Do you see it?"

Rachel looked down at the area he had mentioned and could see the wooden section under the upholstered edge of the sofa. She put her hand under the ledge and felt an indentation. She pulled it forward, as he had instructed, and could see the table top. She then lifted both sides of the top, and it rose and clicked in place directly in front of her. *Amazing!* she thought. It was appropriately designed. There was a place for a dish, a hole for a glass or drinking cup, and a two-inch lip completely outlined the table top in order to prevent anything from slipping off. Another nice feature was that it moved sideways and back and forth in order to maneuver around it, if she had to.

"This is perfect, Robert! Thank you."

"My pleasure, Ms. Radcliffe. Is there anything else I can assist you with?"

"No, I don't think so—uh, oh, unless . . . would you like something, Robert? There's certainly more than enough food here for the both of us," she chuckled.

Robert laughed as well, but he was not surprised at her offer. Since people were his business, he could tell instantly what they were like. And he thought Rachel was a real gem!

"I really shouldn't but I'd love a Coke if you wouldn't mind," he responded humbly.

"One Coke coming up!" Rachel called out. "How about a bagel with some cream cheese? I can fix it up for you—no extra charge."

Robert was enjoying this trip immensely.

"Why not," he responded. "This will probably never happen to me again!"

Rachel was shocked by his response.

"Really? You mean no one ever asks you to join in on this 'movable feast'?"

"No, I'm afraid not! You're the first, and it's a rare treat for me!"

"My pleasure," Rachel responded in much the same manner and tone as Robert's.

She handed him the Coke and the bagel and cream cheese very carefully through the opened space. Fortunately, Robert, too, had a place for this snack, and they indulged themselves as the limo proceeded toward its ultimate destination.

The rest of the drive was very pleasant. The weather had cooperated, and the skies were clear and blue, with just the slightest breeze.

Rachel was very familiar with the route and the scenery as they got closer to the airport. While she hadn't traveled much in her life, she did have the frequent occasion of picking up or dropping off clients. That's why she was surprised when Robert turned before the road leading directly to the departure gates just ahead.

"Ah, . . . excuse me, Robert, but haven't you taken a wrong turn?" she asked nervously.

"No, ma'am, the executive hangar is up ahead, and that's where I'm supposed to take you, Ms. Radcliffe."

Rachel's eyes opened widely. "Executive hangar?" Her instructions didn't say anything about an "executive hangar."

"But, Robert, I'm afraid I'm a little confused here. I have a first-class airline ticket on American Airlines right here in my hands!"

Robert paused and then reiterated.

"Yes, ma'am; however, the Avian Productions' jet is waiting for you to board here very shortly. Maybe something changed before you could be notified. I'll ask the pilot when we get there. All right, Ms. Radcliffe?"

Rachel was almost in a state of shock now.

"Sure, sure, Robert, that will be just fine."

Her breathing changed as she was straining to see where Robert was taking her. She'd been down this road many times and seen the various private jets, but she'd never imagined she'd ever be going on one.

"This is it, Ms. Radcliffe," Robert stated with certitude, "and there's the jet!"

Rachel could not believe her eyes. Just beyond the corner of the hangar sat a huge twin-jet engine plane. There was no mistaking it. The name "Avian Productions" was written across the top section of the plane in bold gold letters. Not only that, but right at the end of the lettering was the most beautifully situated rainbow she'd ever seen.

"Oh!" she gasped. Tears came to her eyes. "Oh, my God!"

Robert could hear her and asked if she were all right.

"Yes," she sniffled, "I'm fine—I'm great! This is just too wonderful!"

Robert stopped just short of the tarmac. He peeked through the panel opening to ensure that Rachel was okay.

"Everything all right?" He could tell that she was a bit emotional and definitely surprised. "Obviously, this is a real surprise and a change from what you had expected."

She wiped away some of the tears and responded.

"Yes . . . yes, it is. But only in addition to everything else that's been going on."

Robert got out of the driver's side of the limo and came around to open the door for Rachel. He extended his hand to her, and she clasped it as she exited the car. She then sighed deeply.

"Thank you, Robert, for your wonderful service on my behalf. You've been terrific and I've enjoyed meeting you."

Robert made certain that she was all right before he responded.

"Believe me, Ms. Radcliffe, I've never served anyone as gracious and as beautiful as you. It's truly been my distinct pleasure." With that statement, they both laughed! It seemed like pleasurable times were the absolute topic this morning.

Everything from that moment on seemed more dreamlike to Rachel. After Robert had transferred all her luggage to the private jet, he introduced her to the pilot.

"Ms. Radcliffe, this is Captain Tom Billings."

Rachel extended her hand to him, and the captain shook her hand and welcomed her. He explained that when Mr. Avian was initially developing the plans for her trip, this jet was unavailable. However, a scheduling change brought the jet back to New York and very much in time to pick her up and bring her to New York on this brisk and bright Saturday morning.

Robert, having now fulfilled all his duties, bade Rachel a fond farewell.

"I know you're going to enjoy your flight and the rest of your trip. I'm happy to have been able to be a part of this itinerary. It's been a distinct pleasure to serve you."

Rachel shook Robert's hand and confirmed his excellent service. She said she hoped that the occasion would come again when she could avail herself of his service in the near future.

Captain Billings then escorted Rachel to the steps leading into the waiting jet. The noise from the other commercial planes landing and taking off seemed to reverberate through her with every step she took. Her cape rippled in the wind, and her hair was blown about. This was quite different than her earlier expectations and apprehensions having to do with walking through the airport. Another new experience, and one that she could only react to as it was happening. Much to her continued amazement, there was a flight attendant to greet her at the entrance door.

"Good morning, Ms. Radcliffe. Welcome aboard."

"Good morning," Rachel responded, "and thank you. This is really quite exciting for me, and I'm happy to be aboard."

The inside of the airplane was like nothing Rachel had ever seen or heard of before. There was an actual door that she walked through to get to her seat. Only there wasn't an aisle. It looked more like a living room. The seats consisted of plushly upholstered recliners, four of them positioned in a way so that the passengers could comfortably converse with one another if they wished. There were tables with lamps, and the interior walls were paneled. Luxurious drapes lined the walls, and the window treatments included the smallest miniblinds she'd ever seen.

"Take your pick," the attendant directed.

"The view from either of them is spectacular." Rachel decided to sit in the second one to her left.

"Incidentally, Ms. Radcliffe, my name is Roger Lang, and I will be at your service during the flight."

Rachel noticed the gold wings on his collar and the name tag that identified him as "Flight Attendant Roger Lang."

"First of all, since this is quite different from flying commercial, may I ask, have you ever flown on a private jet before?"

"No, this is my first time," Rachel grinned.

"All right then," he responded, "let's go over a few things before we take off." He asked her to follow him as he began the tour. "This is the compartment for your carry-on luggage." He pulled out a drawer that could accommodate Rachel's carry ons and much more.

He proceeded to go through the same instructions as mentioned on other airlines. The seat belt, the emergency exit doors, the oxygen mask, and the flotation seat if needed. He pressed a button that controlled a sliding panel in the wall directly ahead of where they were standing. It exposed a rather large screen. He explained that she could either enjoy a video movie during the flight, or she could follow the navigational routing, city by city, which they could show on that screen. He showed her the controls for a stereo system and the operational buttons for the recliners.

After he had made certain that she was familiar enough with this cabin, he directed her to the next door which led to a divided room. To her left was a full bathroom. Complete with shower stall, sink, commode, dressing table, and a full-length mirror. The other side of the room led to the galley, attendants' quarters, and the cockpit. Rachel could not believe how big the rooms were and how comfortably they were furnished.

"I can prepare you a snack if you'd like. With only one and a half hours of flight time, we're a bit limited. However, if you're hungry, I can prepare something for you."

Rachel was still a little full from the juice and bagel she had in the limo. So she thanked him and said she'd prefer to just sit and enjoy the flight.

"Okay," he responded, "I'll let the captain know that you're ready, and we should be taking off shortly. If you change your mind about having a snack or anything, just press this button."

When he left the compartment, Rachel took a quick look out her window. She really couldn't see anything too familiar. Just a lot of open space and the movements of airport ground crews and air traffic controllers. She breathed deeply and closed her eyes. This recliner was heavenly. She even thought about taking a little nap. But then she didn't wish to miss one single moment of this trip. So she sat upright again and kept looking out her window.

She then stood up and walked around on her own and noticed things she hadn't seen when they first came aboard. There was a desk behind one of the recliners directly across from her. Placed in a neat stack on one of them were what looked like manuscripts, each bound in leather. Alongside them were a selection of classics and an ample amount of magazines, all having to do with Broadway and show business. She also noticed a series of drawers alongside the wall unit in front of her. She wanted to peek inside one of them but decided against it. This was obviously Christian's personal jet, and the contents of the desk and the drawers were certain to be his.

Suddenly, she heard Captain Billings's voice over the sound system.

"Ms. Radcliffe, we're preparing for takeoff. So please be seated and fasten your seat belt. As soon as we're airborne, I'll fill you in on the flight altitude and the routing. Until then, sit back and enjoy the ride."

Rachel's heart began to race as she sat down and fastened her seat belt. The recliner was on a swivel so she turned to face the window. She took a deep breath when the plane began to move. She said a silent prayer, as she always had, that the trip would be a safe one.

She watched carefully as the large jet was starting to move in the direction of the airport hub. She was always intrigued by the markings on the field and the lettered and numbered squares along the air strips, which meant something to the pilot and control tower, but absolutely nothing to her.

They moved so slowly, she could hardly feel any movement. Then suddenly, the plane came to a dead stop. They sat in that spot for what seemed a very long time. Actually, it was only about five minutes. Once again, the plane began to move. This time, they increased the speed, and she could see the main terminals and the control tower from her window. The plane moved slowly, weaving in and out of its directed path toward the runway.

Captain Billings announced that they had been cleared for takeoff. He instructed everyone aboard to prepare for takeoff. Soon after that, the plane turned, and Rachel recognized the familiar markings on the runway.

The motors roared and revved up as the plane began to move and increase its speed. Rachel held on to the arm rests and laid her head back. The liftoff was equally exciting. She watched the geography beneath her diminish in size as this huge jet soared toward the sky. She imagined that no one could ever tire of that exhilarating feeling; however, this time she felt as if she were sitting on a cloud.

The sky was so blue, with a few fluffy clouds floating majestically by. The plane surged through them like a hot knife through butter. The ascent provided a certain sense of peace. Rachel had always felt it was the means to bring humans closer to God and his infinite kingdom. The vastness of the atmosphere was awesome; she was thrilled by the entire experience.

After twenty-five minutes or so, Captain Billings announced they had reached an altitude of 38,000 feet and that he would release the requirements for seat belts. Flight attendant Lang came by to make sure that Rachel was comfortable and to see if she wanted anything to eat or drink.

"Perhaps a nice cup of tea," she responded.

"Certainly! And how about a muffin or Danish with it?" he asked.

"Oh, all right," Rachel smiled. "Why not, a muffin would be great!"

After Captain Billings explained the routing between Detroit and New York City, Rachel enjoyed looking at the little arrow move across the large screen as the plane jetted toward its final destination.

Rachel was pretty certain that one of the fluffy masses outside her window had a sign on it that read "Cloud Nine." She had never in her life experienced this total flying privacy. It was so completely different from commercial flights. So quiet and relaxing. No other passengers getting up and down and milling about. No flight attendants rolling noisy beverage carts up and down the aisle. This was privacy beyond her wildest dreams.

She watched the little arrow icon move slowly across the massive screen. In a dialogue box just below the routing, the names of cities familiar and unfamiliar to her were displayed as the plane flew over them.

It was difficult to remain calm Her thoughts were racing through her mind as fast as the speed of the jet, and the excitement about what was ahead was almost too much to comprehend. "Breathe deeply," she whispered to herself. "breathe deeply and relax." She was trying to remember the steps she'd learned to prevent her from hyperventilating. After several deep breaths, she noticed a serene sensation creeping slowly throughout her entire body. Perhaps if she could nap for a little while, it would prepare her for the rest of the trip. When the captain announced that they were on the descent to New York City, her stomach flipped.

"Please prepare for landing, Ms. Radcliffe," Captain Billings's deep voice echoed over the PA system.

Flight Attendant Lang checked in on her to make certain she was all right.

"There it is, Ms. Radcliffe, there's New York City!"

Rachel turned to look out her window. She gasped as she saw that famous skyline. It was just as beautiful in the daytime.

"Ohhh," she said, "there's the World Trade Center!"

"Yes, ma'am," confirmed Attendant Lang. "Great restaurant up at the top of one of those towers, the Skylight Room," he exclaimed.

Rachel smiled. She wanted to scream, "Yes, I know that," but instead, she just nodded her head.

"Really?"

"Oh, well," continued Attendant Lang, "you'll probably get to see it before this trip is over. Sounds like Mr. Avian has quite an itinerary in store for you."

Rachel was surprised to hear that he might be aware of the plans.

"How do you know that?" she asked coyly.

"Well, you know . . . company grapevine," he chuckled.

Hmmm . . . company grapevine? she thought. *Just how publicized was this trip, anyway?*

Before she could imagine anything further to worry about, the jet had landed safely at JFK International Airport, and the excitement continued. The plane jockeyed around the massive runways as it approached its final destination. Rachel did not recognize the terminal, and when the plane came to a complete stop, she took a final look out her window. But she could not see anything but a huge building. Attendant Lang made certain that she had all her belongings and escorted her to the exit door. Captain Billings came out of the cockpit just as she was ready to deplane.

"Welcome to New York City, Ms. Radcliffe. I hope you enjoyed the flight."

Rachel smiled and thanked Captain Billings for a trip she'd never forget.

When the flight attendant opened the door, a chilly wind greeted Rachel. It was colder than she had expected, but she was certainly warm enough.

Attendant Lang assisted her down the metal steps and escorted her to a waiting limousine. The driver opened the door and greeted her by name.

"Good morning, Ms. Radcliffe. Welcome to New York!"

Rachel took some time to thank Attendant Lang for all his kind assistance.

"It's been my pleasure, Ms. Radcliffe. Hope you enjoy your stay in the Big Apple."

She stepped into the limo and settled into a similar setting. One much like the one in Detroit.

"My, my," she said, "I could really get used to this quickly."

Her luggage was placed in the limo trunk, and before she knew it, they were on their way. She was curious about where they were and pushed the button to talk with the driver.

"Excuse me," she said.

"Yes, ma'am," he responded.

"This is a little new to me, and I'd very much appreciate your telling me where we are." she requested quizzically.

"This is John F. Kennedy International Airport, Ms. Radcliffe. I thought you knew that," he said, surprised.

Rachel was set aback by his response, but when she thought about the way she posed the question, it justified his silly response.

"Ah, no, I didn't mean that. I'm sorry, I meant where in JFK are we?"

The limo driver apologized for misunderstanding her question and then explained that they were leaving the executive hangar, just south of the main airport terminal.

Rachel sighed and smiled as she thanked the driver. She decided to just sit back and enjoy the rest of the ride to the city. Once out of the airport, the many buildings and street signs whizzed by her shaded window. Only brief glimpses of curious onlookers caught her attention. She recalled vividly stopping and staring at limos passing by. She grinned as she remembered wondering about the passengers. She thought only the very wealthy could afford such luxury, and she got goosebumps as she was now one of those people!

The city was decorated for Christmas. Even in the daylight, sparkling multicolored bulbs and tinsel adorned the windows, street signs, and telephone poles. It truly was a holiday delight. For Rachel, Christmas always took first place on any holiday priority list, followed closely by Thanksgiving. Generally, a busy time for her because her clients were either attending huge holiday galas and charity balls. Or they might be getting ready to spend the holidays in some distant foreign land.

This year, starting with Christian's first mysterious letter, her whole focus shifted to the incredible realization of a dream come true. This, combined with Christmas, was nothing less than a miracle. Her heart began to race, and she braced herself as the limousine continued on its way to her next destination, the Plaza Hotel! So far, everything had gone like clockwork! No hitches, so why should she be worried about the Plaza Hotel. Situated right across the street from Central Park, it was only one of the most exquisite hotels in the entire world. And certainly, one she'd never be able to afford on her own!

She knew that Mama and Papa DeRoca were smiling. This was so thrilling, and yet, it felt so right. Something about all of this gave her a sense of assuredness. It could only be her love for Christian and, definitely, his expressed love for her.

"Yep, it's really happening, Mama," she said quietly. "This is the first day of the rest of my life, and Mama, I'm going to the man I finally can trust with my heart—the man I love." She no sooner uttered that final word when tears welled up in her eyes.

"Wish me well, Mama, and, you, too, Papa. I may have finally learned the one thing you never taught me, how to truly love someone. I'm not laying any fault here, because maybe that's something each of us has to learn alone. For a smart kid, it sure took me a long time." She sighed deeply.

"Anyway, I feel like it's my turn, and I know you're going to cheer for me when I finally grab that proverbial brass ring. With a whole lot of blessings from God and the two of you, it might even be a gold ring!" She sighed again. "Luv ya, both, you're always in my heart."

Rachel was grateful that one of the provisions in this luxurious vehicle was an ample supply of Kleenex. Almost forty-five minutes had passed when the limo driver lowered the window compartment separating them and announced. "There's the Plaza Hotel, Ms. Radcliffe. It's right up ahead."

Twenty-seven

Rachel leaned forward and got a clearer, sharper view of the marquee and the famous entrance.

"It's so beautiful," she exclaimed.

As the limousine pulled up in front of the main entrance, a uniformed doorman walked over to the door and opened it.

"Welcome to the Plaza Hotel, Miss."

The limo driver was already getting her luggage, and then followed her as she entered the magnificent lobby.

It was breathtaking! The chandeliers and beautifully adorned sectionals made it look extremely large. The carpeting was plush, and as she slowly placed one foot in front of the other, she grinned as she experienced a sinking sensation. The highly polished brass signs and accessories glimmered and glistened in the sunlight. The reservation counter itself was quite exquisite.

She was looking around and almost staring at the hotel activity when she heard someone talking to her.

"Good morning, Miss. May I help you?"

Rachel quickly composed herself and responded.

"Good morning, and, yes, please. My name is Rachel Radcliffe. I believe you have a reservation for me."

The hotel clerk smiled broadly as he checked the registry for her name.

"Yes, Ms. Radcliffe. You're in Suite 2000. The bellhop will assist you with your luggage."

Rachel had almost forgotten about the limo driver and her luggage. As she turned to look for him, he was standing behind her, waiting for her to check in.

"Here you are, Ms. Radcliffe. I hope you enjoy your stay in New York."

"Thank you very much. Thank you for everything!" Rachel responded. As he walked away from her, she heard another voice.

"Right this way, Miss." Rachel acknowledged the bellhop and followed him toward a rather large bank of elevators.

Everything was suddenly much more subdued. They hadn't gone far from the lobby, when there was already a change in the atmosphere. It seemed as though talking somehow wasn't allowed near the elevators. When the doors to the elevator opened up, Rachel was not surprised to find that the elevators were just as luxurious as the rest of this elegant edifice.

The bellhop rolled the brass luggage carrier into the elevator and pressed floor "20." The doors closed quietly. Rachel looked around. Velvet tapestries lined the walls and floor. Above, a mirrored ceiling enhanced the beauty and a prismatic chandelier hung over her head. *Such opulence,* she thought, *such magnificence.*

When they reached the twentieth floor, the doors opened and she walked off the elevator into a hall of continuing decorated excellence. Pristeenly painted white walls ornately highlighted with gold trim lined the hallway for as far as she could see.

Rachel followed the bellhop, who led the way down the corridor. He stopped at a set of double doors set inside a recessed area. Rachel looked up at the brass sign to the right of the door, "Suite 2000." The bellhop opened the door and motioned for Rachel to enter.

"Here you are, Ms. Radcliffe. Looks like someone is happy you're here."

As Rachel stepped into the enormous room, all she could see were flowers—everywhere. She gasped and brought her hands to cover her gaping mouth.

"Oh, my goodness," she uttered. "How absolutely beautiful!"

The bellhop was almost as awed by the sight as was she.

"I don't think I've ever seen this many flowers anywhere. Except in a floral shop," he said.

"Well, this is the second time for me." Rachel smiled as she recalled her home when she returned from New York a few short months ago.

"Enjoy your stay at the Plaza, Ms. Radcliffe, but it looks like someone has already made certain of that!" He grinned.

"Thank you," Rachel responded. She went for her purse to give him a tip, but she once again heard the same response.

"That's all right, ma'am, I've already been very well taken care of!"

"Thanks again," she said.

He handed her the keys to the suite and left the room. It was incredible. Beyond belief! She couldn't believe the interior decorations. She wasn't an expert on furniture styles, but she knew French provincial when she saw it. She walked around looking at all the floral arrangements. Each one carried the same card: "Welcome, my darling. I love you! Christian."

There were two other doors in the room, and she walked slowly toward the larger of the two. Her hand was shaking slightly as she reached for the brass knob and opened the door.

The bright sunlight shone over the most beautiful canopy bed she'd ever seen. It was sitting on a raised section of the room with two steps up. A grouping of lounging chairs and tables were arranged to the right of the bed and a gigantic dressing table and mirror to the left of the bed. Drawers and drawers lined the wall next to the table. There was yet another door. The flowers in this room were mostly poinsettias. Not plants, but more like trees, appropriately placed.

This door led to an extremely large bathroom. A sunken tub that looked more like a swimming pool than a bath tub was the focal point. It was marble, and lots of it. The commode and bidet were in a separate section of the room and across from the tub were sliding doors which led to a spacious shower area. Four brass shower heads jutted out from the marbleized wall, and a bank of lights went on as the door opened. Rachel sighed as she tried to process and absorb all the beauty. Her elation soared.

There were enough toiletries on the mirrored counter to supply a group of people for quite some time. A hair dryer, makeup mirrors, and body and bath oils and lotions of every familiar fragrance. Perfumes and shampoos galore. There were drawers alongside the mirrored area. She opened the top drawer to find the softest and prettiest towels. In yet another drawer, she found a bathrobe and shower cap and, oh yes, a pair of slippers.

Was there anything missing? Not that she could see.

She looked at herself in the mirror and realized she hadn't removed her cape. She walked back into the sitting room and placed her cape on the closest sofa. "Now," she exclaimed, "what could possibly be behind that door? Well, I guess I'm going to find out." She walked a little faster now, her curiosity at a peak.

As she opened the door, yet another light gleamed in her eyes. The room was filled with clothes: coats, dresses, suits, sweaters, furs, and shoes, and shelves of gloves, scarves, and matching hats and purses.

"Oh, my God!" she cried. "Oh, my God!" She pushed at the hangers holding gown after gown. She checked one tag: "Armani" was written across it in gold thread. A little tag under it said "Size 8." Just her size! She shook her head and tried to focus on specific items, but the tears in her eyes blurred her vision and ran down her cheeks. She brushed away the tears and turned to get her purse.

There was an envelope pinned to the coat closest to the door. "Rachel," in Christian's handwriting, stood out clearly. She looked closely at the pin. It was a rainbow! A row of emeralds, a row of rubies, and a row of sapphires and diamonds on a gold backed clasp! She held it in her hand as she opened the letter.

Welcome to New York, my darling! Hope I haven't missed anything. Can't wait to see your beautiful face and to hold you in my arms.

I love you,
Christian

She pressed the letter to her breast and closed her eyes. "I can't wait either, my darling!"

She glanced at her watch. Suddenly, she realized that it would be only a few hours until she'd be picked up and taken to the theater.

She took Christian's letter and pin and returned to the living room. The aroma of the flowers was almost therapeutic. With hardly any sleep to speak of in the past few days, she began to feel a bit sleepy. She yawned and decided to give in to it. The beautiful plush-looking sofa beckoned to her. She removed her cape and shoes and sat down. It didn't take very long for her to drift off to sleep. It was a peaceful rest, and her dreams were filled with images of pastoral valleys and limitless blue skies. She felt lifted and weightless as she moved effortlessly in this place of serene tranquility.

When she awakened, she was unsure about her whereabouts. When she finally remembered where she was, she became alarmed and checked her watch quickly. Three hours had passed! But something was different. The room was darker than it should be at this hour. She got up from the sofa and walked toward the huge windows.

The sunshine was masked by ominous black and turbulent-looking clouds. The street lights and Christmas decorations shone brightly now. Suddenly, streaks of lightning flashed across the sky, and Rachel moved quickly from the windows. "A storm?" she uttered. "A thunderstorm in December? How can this be?"

She then walked hastily around the room, turning on every light she could find. Another crack of lightning and several rolls of thunder caused her to become frightened. The room was illuminated now by the continuing flashes of lightning.

Her heart began to pound as she frantically tried to find a safe place in this very strange hotel suite. "Stay away from water and windows and anything electrical," she whispered. "Stay calm. This will be over quickly."

Then, out of nowhere, she heard a bell ringing. It took her a couple of seconds to recognize that it was the telephone, but where was it? She looked around on all the obvious tables. Nothing! She finally followed the sound of the bell to a small cabinet on the table near the entry door. She opened up the doors and there it was. She picked up the receiver and almost yelled into it.

"Hello!" she gasped.

"Rachel—is that you?" the familiar voice inquired. "Rachel, it's Christian. Are you all right?"

"Oh, Christian, I'm so frightened. This storm is terrible!" The thunder and lightning quickly intensified to a point where she could hardly hear his voice.

"Listen, Rachel, don't be frightened. You're in a safe place. Honest! I knew when this untimely storm hit that you'd be scared. But that's Mother Nature for you. Who would have expected this kind of meteorological havoc in December?"

Rachel held tightly onto the phone and smiled.

"It's just like Michigan! We never know what to expect. I thought that was a trait specifically reserved for my fair state." She hesitated and then added, "I wish right now that that were true. Where are you, Christian?" She was almost stuttering now.

"I'm at the theater, but I can come to you if you want me to!"

She could tell that he was very concerned about her, and her first thought was to scream, *Yes! Yes! Come to me!* But she tried to calm herself and assure him that she would be all right.

"No, no, that's all right. I'll be just fine. A little shaken up, but I'll survive. After all, it could have been worse. I could have been outside when this thing hit!"

"Yes, but you weren't" he replied gratefully. "Thank, God!" he added. "Really, I'm not that far away from where you are, and I could be there in twenty minutes," Christian offered one more time.

Rachel almost gave in to his convincing tone, but once again, she tried to reassure him that she would be all right.

"Honest, my darling, I will be just fine. It looks like this thing may be coming to an end anyway. It's considerably lighter in the room now than it was just a few minutes ago." She took the cordless phone and walked slowly toward the windows at the front of the suite. She sighed a huge sigh of relief. "I'm looking out the window right now, Christian, and I can actually see some blue sky between those humongous dark clouds. Whew!" she exclaimed, "And I thought Michigan storms were unpredictable."

Christian still wasn't certain that he shouldn't just get in his car and go to her. But show time was drawing closer by the second, and he didn't want to disturb any of his well-laid plans now.

"Well, all right, my darling. if you're certain that you'll be all right I'll just have to wait until I see you this evening. Tough as that is going to be."

"Believe me, the feeling is very mutual. It won't be much longer now, and I can use this time to get ready myself. I've much to do to get ready for tonight's performance."

Christian assured her that all of this would be worth it once they were together later on.

"I promise you, my love. We will both look back on this moment and recall that it was the end to a lonely chapter in both our lives and the beginning of new and exciting times." He paused for just a moment and then whispered, "I love you, Rachel, and nothing will ever change that—nothing!"

Rachel got goosebumps all over and she pressed the phone to her lips.

"I love you, too, Christian. My God, I love you so much!"

After they ended their conversation and she hung up the phone, she stood for a moment and closed her eyes. "Please God. Make it my turn . . . ahhh . . . make it *our* turn," she entreated.

As she luxuriated in the enormous Jacuzzi bath, she tried to imagine what her future would be like with Christian. The excitement of the entertainment world itself was captivating. The possibility of world travel was also awesome. The real thrill was the thought of spending each day with someone she truly loved. Talking with him. Dining with him. And, oh, yes, sleeping with him. To be able to hold him close to her and feel his arms around her. To make love with him and, once and for all, to enjoy the magical communion of body and soul.

She began to move more quickly now. As exciting as her imagination and fantasies had become, she must first get prepared for this very special evening.

It was difficult to get out of that therapeutic tub, but she did and wrapped herself in the warm blanketlike towel, and twirled around the bathroom, dancing and humming. Even though she felt silly, she was enjoying it. This had to be the closest thing to unbridled happiness she'd ever known.

When she opened the garment bag that held her gown, she gasped. It was so beautiful and so reminiscent of their first date. She removed it from its hanger and laid it on the bed. The wardrobe in the other room certainly included more expensive and lavish gowns. But none could surpass the elegance and almost magical aura of this one, for Christian had held her in this one. He had kissed her in this one. And that definitely made this gown divine.

She reveled in having the time to primp and preen. Certainly, the accoutrements available to her made a usually quick routine one of thorough experimentation. A little of this and a little of that. She'd never seen so many moisturizers, toners, lotions, and makeup combinations in her life. It was fun to dabble and experience something new.

And when, at last, Rachel had finished dressing and was ready to adorn herself with the jewelry that matched her outfit perfectly, she walked over to the full length, three-way mirror and stood there.

She sighed as she looked at herself. She was pleased with her reflection. "Now all I have to do is find a warm enough wrap and I shall be ready to fly!"

As she walked across the suite toward the wardrobe room, her gown swished and glimmered. She felt almost regal in this outfit, and she carried herself accordingly. She moved the coats and capes from one side to the next and came across a full-length white fur cape. She took it off its hanger and placed it around her shoulders. She breathed deeply and went over to the mirror closest to her. It was perfect! The ripples of fur from the top of the garment to the bottom were totally luxurious. And the empire collar framed her face perfectly. "This is it!" she exclaimed. "It's definitely it!"

When she looked at her watch, she couldn't believe it was 6:30. According to her itinerary, the limo driver would call for her at 7:00 sharp, and she would have to be ready. She thought about walking into the theater alone among all the people who would be there, presumably as couples. Her heart raced, and she became nervous at the prospect of going down the aisle alone. She sighed and said quietly. "Too late to be nervous now. I'll just smile and concentrate on following the usher who will be directing me to my seat. Once the show starts, I'll just blend in and be as lost in the crowd as everyone else."

Back at the theater, Christian was rushing around. Checking out the script, the cues, and the costumes. He had to ensure that the lighting and stage settings were not only in working condition but in proper sequence and ready to go when the curtain went up.

The performers were finishing up with makeup and doing a last-minute read of their own parts.

Carlo and Marisa knew that this was going to be the dress rehearsal to beat all dress rehearsals. The cast was somewhat confused about all the theater workers having been scheduled, as well. The doorman, ushers, and the theater manager, as well, had been summoned by Christian to make this look like opening night. It certainly added a touch of mystery to the already electrically charged evening.

Christian was on the telephone most of the day, some business, some pleasure. He was an excellent organizer, and when it came to his musicals, no one could surpass him. The concurrent arrangements for this dress rehearsal and Rachel's attendance took just about all the time and energy he could muster. "Everything must be timed perfectly!" he said to himself. "This will be the night of all nights, and a performance that Rachel and I will remember always."

When 7:00 came, Rachel's phone rang. It was the desk manager informing her that her limo driver was waiting for her in the lobby. She told him she'd be right down and quickly grabbed her wrap, purse, and gloves. She checked herself in the mirror one last time to make sure that her makeup and hair were just right. "This is it," she sighed. She shut the lights and walked out the door and down the hall to the elevator. She looked ravishing and regal as she stepped into the elevator.

Another hotel guest was already on the elevator when she got on, and he smiled at her with obvious approval.

"You look stunning, Miss," he said.

"Thank you," she replied courteously. "Thank you."

The Plaza lobby had been the meeting and gathering spot for celebrities and dignitaries from around the world. It was certainly not at all unusual to see men and women adorned in extravagant furs and jewels. But when Rachel approached the main lobby, all eyes were on her. Men and women alike smiled as she crossed their paths.

The limo driver was noticeably staring at her when the clerk advised him that this vision of loveliness was Rachel Radcliffe.

"Ms. Radcliffe?" the limo driver asked.

"Yes," she responded.

"My name is Alex, and I'm here to take you to the Imperial Theater."

"How do you do, and thank you, Alex. I believe I'm ready."

Heads turned, and admiring eyes watched as she followed the uniformed driver across the lobby, through the door, and into the limo. The doorman doffed his hat and bowed in his own gentlemanly fashion as she walked past him.

Rachel smiled as she entered yet another stretch limo, her third today! Imagine thinking that driving around in a limo had become "old hat!" She grinned, then decided to quit the nonsense and just enjoy it to the fullest.

New York City took on an almost magical aura at night. The glittering lights shining from the highest skyscrapers down to the two-story flats fused together into a chromatic scale too spectacular to describe. The headlights and brake lights streamed like ribbons up and down the streets as they sped by her.

Saturday night in New York! What an exciting time. The hustle and bustle of the theater crowd sort of set the pace. Afterwards, some of the world's most famous restaurants would be filled to capacity with performers and audience alike. Echoes of applause and snippets of criticism would meld together in a cacophony of dialogue. Some of which would make headlines in *Variety* the next day.

The aspirations of young ingenues would combine with the last hurrah of those more seasoned, and for one minuscule moment in time, their plight and their spotlight would be one and the same. For Rachel, it would be the beginning of a new life with someone who was as dedicated and famous as anyone she'd ever met.

Act one, scene one, would raise the curtain not only on "Cinema" but also on the rest of her and Christian's lives. Her heart began to race as she thought about seeing Christian again. She tried to think of something to say beyond "thanks for calling me during the storm and oh, yes, thanks for the trip of a lifetime." But words wouldn't come, and the more she thought, the more difficult the task became.

Perhaps, she thought, the best way to handle any of this was improvisational. Imagining the scenario definitely wasn't working. And spontaneity would probably achieve the best possible results.

The marquee of the Imperial Theater came into view as the limo turned onto Broadway. Rachel gasped as she read the words: "Avian Productions Presents C I N E M A."

All the promotional material she had read about the show said that this musical was a tribute to the movie personalities who made the silver screen and the Broadway stage come alive. It would review an era of some of the most entertaining and famous performers.

I wonder where Amber and Tony will be sitting. Never did talk to her before I left, and I only hope we're not too far away from one another. She thought about finding them during intermission, but this theater was quite large, and that possibility, at least right now, seemed enormously remote.

The limousine pulled up directly in front of the theater. Rachel was surprised not to see lines of cars and people milling about in front. Both the limo driver and the doorman stood by Rachel's door as she exited.

"Good evening, Miss," the doorman extended his hand to Rachel.

"Thank you," she replied, "thank you very much. I've a feeling I'm too early," and she smiled. Neither responded, and so she thanked Alex and headed for the theater doors. *Hmmmm,* she mused, *No people anywhere.* While she had never been a regular theatergoer, her recollections were that there were always lots and lots of people around whether she arrived early or a bit late.

Two ushers approached her as she entered the huge auditorium. She swallowed and looked around at the seating capacity. Private boxes and loges that appeared to be suspended from the ceiling and walls loomed overhead. On the main floor, the aisles and rows of velvet-covered seats sort of rippled down toward the orchestra pit and stage. It was not totally silent. She could hear the footsteps of other ushers and stagehands working diligently in preparation for show time. "Oh, well," she exclaimed to herself, "at least I won't have to worry about being self-conscious."

When she was seated, it became clear that no one else was going to attend. It was a strange feeling, and one that became more and more disquieting.

Suddenly, the orchestra pit lights went on and the musicians began to appear one by one. Rachel became more than a little nervous. She turned around once more to look back at the empty theater behind her. No one else was there except an usher standing at the head of every aisle.

She leafed through the program she was handed to see if she could find the dates scheduled for the run of the show. She was impressed with the many names listed in the credits section. It certainly took a great many people to put a production like this together. On the back cover there was a show schedule that read: "Premier showing—Sunday, December 10, 8:00 P.M."

Well, if that were correct, what was she attending tonight?

She didn't have much time to think about it because the theater lights began to dim. Rachel settled back in her seat. Then the familiar sound of the click of the conductor's baton, and the music began. Familiar strains of songs she could easily identify echoed throughout the very large and empty theater.

"Rain Drops Keep Falling on My Head," "Singing in the Rain," A Foggy Day in London Town," and finally, "Yesterday I Heard the Rain," were just a few of the songs in the overture. Songs from the twenties, thirties, forties, fifties, and sixties were all blended together. Hit show tunes from "Oklahoma," "Carousel," and "South Pacific" were easily identified.

The program listed the acts by song and cast member, followed by the names of those stars who made each number famous. It was to be the musical extravaganza of the century. Rachel was delighted to see as number one on the list, "Marisa and Carlo Domani impersonating Fred Astaire and Ginger Rogers doing Irving Berlin's 'Puttin' on the Ritz.'" Her anxiety was ended as the colored lights danced across the velvet, parting curtains.

Marisa and Carlo were positioned, center stage, dressed magnificently in replicas of ensembles worn by Astaire and Rogers in the late thirties. Spontaneously, Rachel began to applaud. Then, hearing only herself, she stopped. She enjoyed their performance and, as the show progressed, she eventually applauded whenever she felt like it. She thought about not totally understanding the true meaning of "command performance" until now!

Backstage, Christian had a clear view of Rachel. He stared at her beautiful face and automatically reached in his pocket and pulled out a small, black velvet box. He moved it around in his hand and then flipped open the cover. The five carat, emerald cut diamond engagement ring shone like a million stars fused together in the sky. If everything went according to plan, by the time this evening was over, it would be on Rachel's finger forever.

The show was moving along as scheduled, and there was an almost electric excitement in the air. It certainly simulated the opening-night jitters. Only this time, his dress rehearsal would be the prelude to the premiere of his career. He felt alive again. The passion he had buried so deep and so well eight years ago was now raging for release.

The finale was written especially with Rachel in mind. The blend of music and lyrics clearly expressed his love and desire for her. Rachel was totally immersed in the loveliness of the music and the thrill of Christian's production. It was as though each rendition sent a message from him directly to her. She couldn't possibly be happier. Her heart was pounding and her senses merged. She had never felt like this before. In her heart, she knew that once she saw Christian and held him in her arms she'd never let him go.

Suddenly, she heard thunder, and little flashes of lightning appeared around and over the stage. She could see rainfall and the familiar strains rang in her ears. "Yesterday I heard the rain . . . echoing your name. Asking where you've gone . . . " She wept quietly as she listened to the song that had become so much a part of her and Christian's love story. "Out of doorways, black umbrellas came to pursue me . . . faceless people. . . . " She could feel the goosebumps begin as the end of the song neared.

"Yesterday, I saw a city full of sadness, without pity, and I heard the falling rain echoing your name, echoing your name." The young man who was impersonating Tony Bennett was outstanding. His rich vocal tones and breath control evidenced long listening sessions and hard work in order to match and measure up to this singer of all time.

When the scene ended, a brightness appeared at the back of the stage and emerged mistlike creating a beautiful and encompassing rainbow. The strains and lyrics from "Finian's Rainbow" were sung on stage by the entire cast. Rachel was in complete awe. The closing familiar number brought instant tears to her eyes once again. Rudolf Friml's love song from "The Vagabond King" . . . "Someday, my happy arms will hold you, and, someday, I'll know that moment divine, when all the things you are are mine."

As the orchestra played the closing number, one by one, the cast members came center stage and bowed before Rachel. Once she started to applaud, she could not stop. And when the entire cast stood, hand in hand, across the front of the stage, Rachel rose to her feet and yelled, "Bravo! Bravo!"

Finally, Christian walked on stage and moved slowly to stand in front of his cast. He looked directly at Rachel and motioned for her to be seated. She was in a state of wonderment and amazement. *Nothing could ever surpass this joyous feeling,* she thought. *Well, almost nothing.*

"Thank you, Rachel," Christian began. "Thank you, my darling, for being the first and only person to attend and enjoy what I hope will be the quintessential musical of my career." He was composed and happy as he continued. "This production is the realization of a dream. One that was spawned in an idea, cultivated in an awakening passion in my soul, and born out of a love for you that, I promise, will grow and flourish forever." He hesitated briefly and then smiled. "You have brought a new meaning to my life, and everything I've done since meeting you has been about you!"

He then walked to the left side of the stage and came down the steps leading to the aisle directly in front of Rachel. Rachel's heart was pounding so hard, she could hardly hear anything else. The emotions erupting from the show combined with her love for Christian. She turned to face him, and when he came face to face with her, she gasped. His eyes were hypnotizing as he looked into hers. He swallowed and began to speak again.

"Rachel Radcliffe, love of my life and cool lady extraordinaire...." Rachel smiled upon hearing his description. "... will you marry me, Christian Avian, a mere man whose only mission in life from this moment forward will be to love you?"

He reached into his pocket and brought out the little black box, opened it, and took out the ring. He reached for her left hand and held it in his. Tears were streaming down her cheeks as she struggled to look at the ring and respond to the question she'd longed to hear.

"Yes," she uttered, "yes! A million times, yes!"

Christian placed the ring on her finger and then raised her face to his.

"I love you so much," he whispered. He kissed her tenderly. At that moment, all her inhibitions and fears were gone. She put her arms around him and responded to a kiss she'd remember always. This time, it was love, and a thrill to be in the arms of the only man who could make her whole and the only place she wanted to be.

Suddenly, Rachel could hear a reminiscent popping sound coming from the back of the theater. As their lips parted and Christian kissed the tip of her nose, Rachel turned to see Master Randy, Estelle, Randall, Tony, Amber, Carlo, and Marisa standing together at the back of the theater.

"Way to go, cool lady!" Master Randy yelled. He was holding his right thumb up in the approval position. "Way to go, Aunt Rachel!"

They all began to applaud Rachel and Christian, when Amber called out.

"Way to go, bella! What's next Christian? What can the world expect from you in the future that would top this night?"

Rachel and Christian smiled as he hugged her tightly and looked once again into her loving eyes.

"A baby!" he responded. "Our baby!"

The smile on her face mirrored the happiness in her heart and soul, for all Rachel's dreams and wishes became a reality at that moment. Her fervent prayers had been answered so completely. She was extremely grateful for His blessings and finally assured that the echoing name in "Yesterday I Heard the Rain" would forever be "Christian!"